Praise for Roland Merullo's *Breakfast with Buddha*

"Merullo is a pleasing writer, as affable as the Rinpoche [character] he creates. His gift is slipping gentle spiritual lessons into easy-reading narratives. . . . In the case of *Breakfast with Buddha*, you can relax and enjoy a road trip—Hershey, Pennsylvania; Youngstown, Ohio; and Duluth, Minnesota are all surprisingly endearing—even as you painlessly absorb the notion that life is really about spiritual growth."
— Marjorie Kehe, *The Christian Science Monitor*

"Merullo's skill with the pen enchants the reader with a fresh awareness of how man confronts his spiritual side in a chaotic world."
— Judy Gigstad, *Bookreporter*

"There are two journeys here, and the significant journey is not measured in miles, but in awareness; we know that it is not only the passing scenery out the window we should attend to, but to Otto's inner landscape as well . . ."
— John Dufresne, *The Boston Globe*

"Spiritual odysseys are seldom filled with baseball games, miniature golf, Mexican food and belly laughs; this one is the exception."
— Valerie Ryan, *The Seattle Times*

"Author Roland Merullo combines philosophy, spirituality, and down-to earth characters in his tale of the adventures of a nice but somewhat cynical editor and his not-quite-welcome traveling companion . . . *Breakfast with Buddha* offers an entertaining and illuminating chance to experience the world through two different lenses simultaneously and stand in the position of observer, as a single life—and then many—are changed."
— *Spirituality and Health*

"I got to liking *Breakfast with Buddha* more and more as I went along and was very sorry when it ended. . . .From Chaucer to Kerouac, the road trip in fiction has always been seen as more than a casual jaunt. At the very least, it's a way to gain access to the larger world, and at most it's a path to spiritual enlightenment. We can take for granted the latter will be happening here—with [Otto] the mildly disaffected food editor stuck in a car for about a week with Volya, reputed to be the incarnation of many a spiritual bigwig, including Buddha himself. (In fact, Volya isn't necessarily a proponent of any one religion.) As they drive from New Jersey to North Dakota, the two men give each other crash courses in different but not necessarily opposing ways to live . . . On finishing this book, I decided that Roland Merullo would be a great guy to take a road trip with."
— Carolyn See, *The Washington Post*

"Merullo is a beautifully talented writer. His books are full of great feeling, but convey that feeling humbly and respectfully. . . . His prose reflects sincere spiritual practice—there's no neediness, no unnecessary fireworks. He's sharing what he knows, instead of shouting or preaching it. . . . [*Breakfast with Buddha*] is a beautiful, moving and even necessary book . . . The simplicity of the setup, the humility of the narration, Otto's ordinariness and his understandable doubt, allows for the book's wisdom to take root—on Otto and, on the reader. . . The closing image is one of such sudden, unexpected grace that I wiped my eyes and reread the last chapter several times to figure out how it arrived there, and still can't say."
— Josh Swiller
(author of *The Unheard: A Memoir of Deafness In Africa*)

Also by Roland Merullo

Fiction

Leaving Losapas
A Russian Requiem
Revere Beach Boulevard
In Revere, In Those Days
A Little Love Story
Golfing with God
Breakfast with Buddha
American Savior
Fidel's Last Days
The Talk-Funny Girl

Non Fiction

Passion for Golf
Revere Beach Elegy
The Italian Summer: Golf, Food and Family at Lake Como
Demons of the Blank Page

Praise for Roland Merullo's Work

Leaving Losapas

"Dazzling . . . thoughtful and elegant . . . lyrical yet tough-minded . . . beautifully written, quietly brilliant."
— *Kirkus Reviews* [starred review]

A Russian Requiem

"Smoothly written and multifaceted, solidly depicting the isolation and poverty of a city far removed from Moscow and insightfully exploring the psyches of individuals caught in the conflicts between their ideals and their careers."
— *Publishers Weekly*

Revere Beach Boulevard

"Merullo invents a world that mirrors our world in all of its mystery . . . in language so happily inventive and precise and musical, and plots it so masterfully, that you are reluctant to emerge from his literary dream."
— *Washington Post Book World*

Passion for Golf: In Pursuit of the Innermost Game

"This accessible guide offers insight into the emotional stumbling blocks that get in the way of improvement and, most importantly, enjoyment of the game."
— *Publishers Weekly*

Revere Beach Elegy: A Memoir of Home and Beyond

"Merullo has a knack for rendering emotional complexities, paradoxes, or impasses in a mere turn of the phrase."
— *Chicago Tribune*

In Revere, In Those Days

"A portrait of a time and a place and a state of mind that has few equals."
— *The Boston Globe*

A Little Love Story

"There is nothing little about this love story. It is big and heroic and beautiful and tragic . . . Writing with serene passion and gentle humor, Merullo powerfully reveals both the resiliency and fragility of life and love . . . It is, quite utterly, grand."
— *Booklist*

Golfing with God

"Merullo writes such a graceful, compassionate and fluid prose that you cannot resist the characters' very real struggles and concerns . . . Do I think Merullo is a fine, perceptive writer who can make you believe just about anything? Absolutely."
— *Providence Journal*

Breakfast with Buddha

"Merullo writes with grace and intelligence and knows that even in a novel of ideas it's not the religion that matters, it's the relationship . . . It's a quiet, meditative, and ultimately joyous trip we're on."
— *Boston Globe*

Fidel's Last Days

"A fast-paced and highly satisfying spy thriller . . . Merullo takes readers on a fictional thrill ride filled with so much danger and drama that they won't want it to end."
— *Boston Globe*

American Savior

"Merullo gently satirizes the media and politics in this thoughtful commentary on the role religion plays in America. This book showcases Merullo's conviction that Jesus' real message about treating others with kindness is being warped by those who believe they alone understand the Messiah."
— *USA Today*

The Italian Summer: Golf, Food & Family at Lake Como

"This travel memoir delivers unadulterated joy . . . [Merullo's] account of those idyllic weeks recalls Calvin Trillin in its casual tone, good humor, affable interactions with family, and everyman's love of regional food and wine . . . A special travel book for a special audience."
— *Booklist*

The Talk-Funny Girl

"Merullo not only displays an inventive use of language in creating the Richards' strange dialect but also delivers a triumphant story of one lonely girl's resilience in the face of horrific treatment."
— *Booklist*

Lunch with Buddha

Roland Merullo

AJAR Contemporaries

Lunch with Buddha

AJAR Contemporaries
publisher@pfppublishing.com
OR c/o
PFP, Inc
144 Tenney Street
Georgetown, MA 01833

AJAR Contemporaries Paperback Edition, October 2012

Printed in the United States of America
ISBN-10: 0984834575
ISBN-13: 978-0-9848345-7-0
First Paperback Edition
10 9 8 7 6 5 4 3 2 1

Library of Congress Cataloging-in-Publication Data

Merullo, Roland.
  Lunch with Buddha : [a novel] / [by] Roland Merullo. -- AJAR Contemporaries paperback ed.

  p. ; cm.

Sequel to: Breakfast with Buddha.
Issued also as an ebook.
ISBN-13: 978-0-9848345-7-0
ISBN-10: 0-9848345-7-5

  1. Middle-aged men--United States--Fiction. 2. Editors--United States-
-Fiction. 3. Rinpoches--Fiction. 4. Buddhists--Fiction. 5. Voyages and
travels--United States--Fiction. 6. Self-actualization (Psychology)--
Fiction. 7. Spiritual life--Fiction. I. Title.

PS3563.E748 L86 2012b
813/.54

For Peter and Nanette Sarno

Every man takes the limits of his own field of vision for the limits of the world.
Arthur Schopenhauer, *Studies in Pessimism*

The beauty of the world has two edges, one of laughter, one of anguish, cutting the heart asunder.
Virginia Woolf, *A Room of One's Own*

Every natural fact is a symbol of some spiritual fact.
Ralph Waldo Emerson, *Nature*

I

JFK was an asylum, a processing plant, a study in chaos—snaking lines, recorded announcements, furious passengers with their taped-up baggage, clerks fielding complaints in the midst of the madness. For the better part of an hour my daughter and son and I stood there in a series of queues, mute and helpless as cattle in the pens. It wasn't the meatpacking plant that awaited us, only a flight from New York to Seattle, but with each new checkpoint I felt that another piece of our humanity was being stripped away. It was all necessary, of course; that went without saying. But set against the background of our trip, and the reason we were flying, the whole sad security dance seemed especially bothersome to me on that day. Invasive. Repulsive. Borderline obscene.

And then, at last, we were done with the processing, searched, cleared, identified, sent down a narrow walkway and a narrower aisle, seated, strapped in. The palm of fate, unreadable, pressed against the oval window. Flight attendants with their mechanical hand gestures, the pilot with his doubtless drawl—I did not want to go. When the engines roared to life and we went speeding down the runway I closed my eyes and mouthed a prayer and felt my arm being kicked by a very small foot. We were in a battle with inertia and old assumptions, the plane thrusting itself forward and up, folding in its wheels and banking west, over the city both of us had loved.

It was Delta Roulette: my children, Natasha, twenty-two, and Anthony, almost twenty, had for some reason been given seats in the row behind me. I was there in 32 C next to a Tanzanian-American black-haired beauty who held her little son, Levi, on her lap, as we angled and bumped through the cumulus. Levi had been on the planet exactly seven months. The chubby cheeks and wondrous eyes, the mood shifts from bubbly to despondent, the diaper changes, bottles, and soft toys, the crying, the ecstasy at being bounced up and down on his mother's lap—it was all right there, a catalogue of memories. For a moment I thought about turning around and saying something to Tasha and Anthony about it. I wanted to tell them how well I remembered them at that age, how much Jeannie and I had enjoyed the challenge of raising them, how exhausting it could be, how much meaning it had given our lives. But our two miracles were buried in their computer screens. A film, an e-mail that had to be sent the second we landed, a dozen YouTube clips showing favorite music groups. Anything to keep from thinking about the fourth person who should have been with us on that afternoon.

I leaned back and tried one of the meditation techniques my sister's husband, the famous spiritual master Volya Rinpoche, had taught me. Let the memories go, I told myself. Let the thoughts appear and disappear like ripples in a quiet bay. Let go of the sorrow and bitterness, release the sweet past. It worked for a while, until the plane began to bounce and shimmy, and Levi serenaded us with a patch of loud misery. His mother prepared the formula bottle. I stared down at the green buckled hills of western New Jersey. God's country.

My children and I were headed to Washington State to distribute my wife's ashes, according to her wishes, near the banks of a certain stream on the eastern slope of the Cascade range. I am not a person who has much affection for ceremonies, and we were still buried to our necks in grief, and so I'd put it off for as long as I could—as long, in fact, as my neighbor Levi had been on the planet, almost to the day. Jeannie had died in the first week of January, and here we were at the end of a steaming July, just getting around to it.

"Do you have children?" Levi's mother asked.

"These two specimens behind us," I hooked a thumb over my shoulder. "Leaving for college soon."

Levi, who'd been bouncing and bouncing between gulps from his bottle, spit up enthusiastically all down his bib.

"Empty nest," his mother said, as she cleaned him. "I can't imagine."

"Well, I'm agitating for an early pregnancy or two."

My sense of humor, I've been told, isn't for everyone. Fortunately, she was busy balancing Levi with one hand and folding the soiled bib into a plastic bag with the other. I remembered the drill. I wanted to offer to hold the boy for a moment but worried it might be taken wrong. We were flying over Pennsylvania by then.

I turned and gazed out the window, pondering the various forms loneliness can take. The loneliness of adolescence, on

3

days when it seems your friends have abandoned you and your parents inhabit another universe. The loneliness of the early, mid, and sometimes late twenties, when it seems you'll never find a mate, a career, a route through this world. The loneliness—I had known little of this—of a marriage in which you feel distant and misunderstood, mismatched, battered by regret. For so many years, surrounded every day by wife, children, and co-workers, I'd managed to keep all fear of loneliness out of my thoughts, to forget what it felt like, the grind and gnaw, the darkness. I was protected, confident, happily busy, girded with love. And then came Jeannie's diagnosis, her gradual, torturous decline, her final breath, and in what seemed like an hour the walls of the fortress had crumbled. Another few weeks now and the kids would be gone. Our house, already so big, would turn into an immense echo chamber of memories.

You wonder, at such moments, if there will be another chapter to the story, if you'll somehow survive the solitary passage across this cold land. On good days, that seems unlikely; on bad days, impossible. Still, there must have been the tiniest seed of hope turning in the dark soil of our bereavement. I spotted it, at moments, in my children: an unguarded laugh, a plan for next summer. I felt it, only rarely, in myself. Looking back, I see that this hope had something to do with my odd sister and her even odder husband, though I never would have admitted it at the time. I will go into more detail later, but for now let me say that Cecelia and Rinpoche seemed to live on the far side of some line that marked the boundary of ordinary American reality. In the bottom of my luggage I had packed a small idea: maybe, somewhere in that strange territory, the sun still shone.

2

Seattle's is the only airport I've ever been to where you have to walk eleven miles and take three escalators and a train in order to retrieve your bags. No doubt the architects wanted to make sure you were in shape before you got to the heavy lifting. But our belongings had arrived in good order, and my son and daughter seemed happy to be off the plane. They were busy with their phones, checking, asking, answering, as though an elaborate web of electronic threads reached out from their hearts into the world, and those fragile, silken links needed to be monitored every few seconds to make sure none of them snapped.

We rode a shuttle bus ten minutes to the car rental building, with Seattle's snow-topped mountains hanging in the distance above a thin fog. I let the young woman at the desk talk me into an upgrade: A black Lincoln MKX with leather interior and a dashboard you had to spend twenty minutes looking at in order to understand. Why not? We had money enough. The clerk had offered a drastic discount. And the decision brought a spark of pleasure to the eyes of my offspring, a moment of for-getfulness, a wry twist of the mouth at their father's always-entertaining lack of common sense. Instead of arguing over the front seat as they normally would have done, they both sat in back. I managed to start the vehicle and adjust the mirrors, and we headed out of the lot and north on I-5, past the stadium and the Space Needle and Seattle's silvery downtown, in the direc-tion of Whidbey Island.

"One of our famous Ringling Family Plans, huh, Dad?" An-thony said, during a pause in his texting. There was a slight edge to the remark. He'd made no secret of the fact that he thought the idea of a family ash-spreading ceremony completely absurd.

"I've left everything up to Aunt Seese."

"We're in trouble then."

"You guys are so *harsh* on her," Natasha put in.

"We love her," I said. "She makes us crazy sometimes, but we all love her."

Anthony laughed his manliest two-note laugh. "Yeah, sure, but you let her choose the *hotel*, Dad? Really?"

"It's a B and B."

"Even worse! It's gonna be *feng shui* city, man. Some kind of yurt or igloo or something. Tofu burgers for breakfast. We're up shit creek."

Beneath his not-quite-yet-a-man-but-old-enough-to-curse-in-front-of-his-father façade, Anthony's sorrow ran like the moles that savaged our garden, night creatures who traveled in deep tunnels, though you might catch a glimpse of them at noon. During the course of his mother's illness he had never once let anyone see him cry. Two days after she was gone, as I headed

6

up to bed I heard him sobbing in his room. I stood in the hall-way with the closed door between us and tried to think of something I might say. Another father, a TV or movie father, would have tapped on the door and gone in and found just the right words, but I was frozen there, a victim of my North Dakota upbringing, maybe. Of old, old rules about men and strength and shame.

Natasha was a different creature, more open to the world and its pains, a bit less anxious to separate herself from us and make her own way. During Jeannie's illness she'd spent every minute she could at her mother's side, had forfeited her next-to-the-last semester of college to be with her, and had, only when Jeannie couldn't see her, walked the rooms of the house, wet-faced and desolate. I left them alone with their mourning, and they left me alone with mine; that was our unspoken agreement.

One of the side effects of losing a spouse—at least for me—had been a peculiar inability to perform the most mundane tasks. Making plane and hotel reservations, shopping for food, setting out the trash on time—these duties, which ordinarily I would have completed with a practiced ease, now seemed as daunting as the learning of a Chinese dialect. I let things slide. For the first time in family history, bills were paid late. The dry cleaners had to call three times to remind me to pick up my shirts. My children could be harsh with me about these failings, but I took their casual criticisms like a battered old fighter takes punches. I would stand. I was determined to stand. I was determined to stay sane, and love them, and help them envision a new life after our old one had been ripped to pieces.

So I had, in fact, allowed my sister Cecelia to make the arrangements and set in place the first few pieces of our elaborate Ringling Family Plan. I should confess at this point that I consider her a peculiar soul. Warmhearted, giving, but offbeat to the point of absolute eccentricity. Before marrying Volya Rinpoche and moving back to the family farm in North Dakota, she'd made a meager living in Paterson, New Jersey, performing past-life regressions, reading palms and Tarot cards, claiming to see the future. I will say no more.

Since she, her famous husband, and their almost-six-year-old daughter, Shelsa, did not tolerate air travel well, they were taking Amtrak's Empire Builder from their home in North Dakota, across Montana's northern tier, across the top of Idaho, and southwest into Seattle. If all went well we were to meet them that evening at a bed-and-breakfast of her choosing, a place called The Inn at Chakra Creek. The inn was owned, in my sister's words, by "a very nice, very rich man who considers Rinpoche his guru." This man, whose name was Jarvis Barton-Phillips, was giving us a substantial discount, she said. More than that, as a gesture of his devotion he was donating a "beautiful" pickup truck to the North Dakota retreat center.

To complicate our travel plans further, Celia suggested that, once we'd gone through the ceremony of distributing Jeannie's ashes, she, her daughter, their dog, and my two children were going to ride back to Seattle, spend two nights there, then take the train to North Dakota for a week's vacation on the high plains. Rinpoche and I would drive the beautiful pickup across those nine hundred miles, and join them. This trip, she figured, would be a nice break for her husband, who'd been "working so hard his aura was changing." And it would be nice for me, too, in her opinion. We were friends, after all, the good monk and I.

We'd made one previous road trip together, six months before Shelsa's birth, and it had gone fairly well. "You and Rinpoche need to spend some quality time again," Celia told me over the phone as she announced these plans and made her case for them. "He misses you, misses seeing America through your eyes. You might benefit from it, too, Otto."

I didn't have the strength to resist.

And that was how, on a hot day in the last week of July, 2012, I came to be driving a Lincoln MKX along I-5 toward the Mukilteo Ferry, a ceramic jar of ashes in my bag, the two remaining loves of my life slumped on leather seats, working their fabulous machines.

3

We made the ferry crossing without incident and wound our way along Whidbey Island's two-lane roads to the town of Coupeville—which my son took great pleasure in mispronouncing as "Coupe de Ville." There, two blocks from the quaint downtown and not so very far from where my sister promised it would be, stood The Inn at Chakra Creek. It was a purple Victorian, bulging out on three sides with odd-shaped, clapboarded additions—as if the original structure had developed an illness that caused its skin to bubble. Here and there along the gravel walkway stood knee-high stacks of beach stones, arranged, it seemed to me, so that drunken late-night arrivals would be penalized for carelessness, though not too severely.

"Looks funky," Anthony said. "What's with the rocks?"

"Those are cairns," Natasha told him in her older-sister voice. "In some Native American cultures they're considered holy objects of meditation."

"They're rocks," Anthony almost spit. "Rocks piled up."

Thunp, thunp, thunp, went the Lincoln's doors. We stepped

onto the porch as a threesome. Inside, behind a counter, almost at attention, stood a young man of South Asian heritage— Indian or Nepali, perhaps—a shy way of greeting us, and nervous, wavering eyes. "Hi," he said, "I'm Abbot."

"We're the Ringling party," I told him. "Otto, Natasha, Anthony. I believe we've booked the whole place for one night."

"You're with Volya Rinpoche."

"Right. I thought he might be here by now."

"We're waiting for him," Abbot said. "And for his child, Shelsa."

As he pronounced my niece's name the young man wasn't exactly breathless, but his tone was close to that of a Manhattan clerk saying "Derek Jeter" moments before the great shortstop checked in. My sister, mostly, and Rinpoche, occasionally, would make some remark about their daughter that went beyond a parent's ordinary pride. That she'd come to earth to rescue us from a great spiritual danger, or something like that. At moments they suggested I had a support role in her work— Uncle Otto was here to help Shelsa fulfill her destiny—but that's where I drew the line. My job, as I saw it, was to be a loving uncle, nothing more or less than that.

"There's something she's been sent here to do," is the way my sister usually put it. "She has a very special purpose."

The young man at the desk seemed to have heard the same rumor.

He showed us upstairs to our three small, perfectly adequate rooms, and then, as he refused the tip I offered, he said, "Jarvis will be here any minute with the truck."

"The beautiful pickup."

Something skipped across the young man's handsome face,

some shadow, some scampering salamander of trouble. I have, for better or worse, a radar for these things. "Actually," he added, cocking his head at a rumbling sound—thunder was my first guess, a summer storm moving in—"I think that's him now."

I followed the clerk downstairs and out the front door. There, beside the Lincoln, an ancient pickup truck had been parked. Off-white with a tangerine-colored band around its middle, freckles of rust on the hood and fenders, running lights above the windshield, and a circular dent on the roof over the passenger seat, it could not, by any stretch of the imagination, be called beautiful. There was a bicycle thrown carelessly in the bed.

Walking toward us from the direction of the truck was a tall, thin man with unnaturally broad shoulders, sandy hair that was long in back and thin in front, and an earring in one lobe.

"Dude," he said, apparently to me.

He gave me one of those handshakes where the thumbs hook each other and the fingers point to the sky, then he banged his thin chest against my shoulder in the style made famous by professional athletes and patted me on the back with his free hand. "Good trip?"

"Fine," I said. "Smooth."

"This your rental?"

I said that it was.

"Cool, man. I have one at my Aspen house. You'll like it. But hey, I forgot, you're driving Uma, you and Rinpoche, aren't you?"

I thought: *My sister invited a friend named Uma to go with us. Uma will squeeze in between Rinpoche and me, peasant skirt hiked up between her knees, one leg to either side of the stick shift. She'll tune the radio to a station that plays the mating sounds of whales. She'll cringe and offer a blessing every time a moth smashes against the windshield. She'll want to give me healing massages.* I said: "Who's Uma?"

"Dude," Jarvis said, with a condescending snort, "Uma's the truck. I named her after Uma Thurman, the most beautiful woman in the universe. Her dad's a Buddhist, too."

"I get it."

Jarvis reached out a lanky arm and patted me on the shoulder so I wouldn't feel bad. "She's a classic, you know. Certified antique. Worth a small fortune these days, but it's my honor to donate her to my guru." He paused for a moment and took a breath. "My teacher."

"What year is she?" I asked, because nothing else came to mind.

"Eighty-three. And listen, in case I don't see him, tell Rinpoche I don't mind one bit if he wants to sell her and use the money for whatever purpose he envisions. I won't be offended in the least, okay? Good karma, right?"

"I'll pass that on. Is there . . . should we be aware of any mechanical issues? It's a long drive. Mountains and so on. I'd hate to get stranded in the wilds of Montana."

"Uma's all set. Tank's full. Fresh oil. Papers in the glove box, all signed. Muffler's got a little pinhole, and you might just keep an eye on the temp gauge from time to time and if you see it moving into the red just turn the heat on. Otherwise, you'll be a magnet for the babes in this thing, man." He dangled a key ring in front of me—two keys and a silvery crescent moon. "Gotta zoom. Business calls. Right livelihood, agreed?"

"Absolutely."

He lifted the bicycle out of the truck bed, hopped on, and pedaled away happily down the road. I remembered my sister saying that Jarvis had made a fortune in Silicon Valley, and that, in addition to this B and B, he owned a string of boutique hotels in Oregon and Northern California, homes in Aspen and Kaua'i. Several times a year he traveled to North Dakota to see Rinpoche and have himself a three-day retreat. And in what was, apparently, a common practice among spiritual devotees, he was making a donation of something close to his heart, simultaneously earning a tax deduction and accumulating good karma. I walked over to the truck and made an inspection. Old and battered though it was, it did have classic lines, I had to admit. In the glove box a large white envelope held a registration and an official-looking document, signing ownership of the truck over to Volya Rinpoche, "His Holiness." Everything was in order, except for two things: His Holiness, to my knowledge, could not drive. And, beneath the envelope, there was a small plastic bag of what appeared to be marijuana.

4

The plan had been for Cecelia (I call her Celia, or Seese), Rinpoche, and Shelsa to meet us at the Chakra Creek in time for all of us to go out to dinner. The whole clan would spend the night, and then we'd head up to the Cascades the next morning in a two-vehicle caravan. But the dinner hour came and went, and we still had no word from them. I pictured them somewhere in an Amtrak outback, stalled on the tracks in northern Idaho, not a timepiece or a mobile phone among them, nothing to eat but the tofu and pumpkin-seed-bread sandwiches Seese had brought along, or day-old microwaved croissants with cheese—the dining car specialty. I was hungry. We were all hungry. It was nearly eleven o'clock New York time.

We decided to leave a note at the desk and walk into town, hoping they'd arrive soon and join us. Coupe de Ville turned out to be a wonderful little village, a single commercial street set close against the Strait of Juan de Fuca, shops on both sides, all of it picture-postcard quaint. The bookstore, the ice cream parlor, a place that sold gifts, furniture, and antiques; a shop where you could buy artisanal bread and local jellies. All of it was closed at that hour, but we found one restaurant still open, and went in. We were led past a sign—a joke, probably—that read NO FIREARMS BEYOND THIS POINT and were seated at a window table with a spectacular view of the harbor and one snow-topped mountain in the distance.

The waitress bounced over and announced the specials, but we were in the mood for simpler fare that night. Anthony had the local mussels, Natasha—flirting with vegetarianism—ordered a warm spinach salad, and yours truly went the healthy route for once: pasta primavera. The simple act of looking at a menu, ordering food, sitting there in anticipation of its arrival—these things were almost a religious rite for a person like me, an opiate. I'm an editor of culinary books, picky about what I eat, in a non-snobby way, but my fascination with food is so much more than professional. I enjoy it the way other people build a pleasure palace around ballet or the NHL or the ups and downs of a presidential campaign, the way Jeannie enjoyed her flower garden. She loved the colors and textures, the miracle of bloom and the feel of dirt between her fingers. I'm fascinated by the limitless variety of ingredients, the skill of an accomplished chef or capable short-order cook, the smells, sights and tastes of the great American cornucopia.

The waitress brought warm dinner rolls and a microbrew beer and I ate and sipped and gave silent thanks—something Rinpoche always encouraged me to do. We made conversation for a while, admired the view, held to our rule of no cell phones at the table, and were more than ready to eat by the time the waitress reappeared.

"How do you rate it, Dad?" Anthony inquired after I'd taken

two bites of the primavera. Asking my opinion about a restaurant meal had become a family joke, one of many. I always played along. On that night, though, I felt we were teetering on a tightrope. I'd felt that way for months. We wanted to laugh and tease, the way we'd always done as a foursome. It had been one of the qualities—along with patience and an abundance of physical affection—that had made our family life a kind of fruit tree we could nourish ourselves from, year round. At the same time, joking in those months had come to feel wrong, improper, vaguely disloyal. I tried anyway.

"It would be fine," I said, "if the pasta hadn't been cooked to the point where it could be used as paste in a kindergarten class."

Anthony laughed, Natasha smiled.

"That good, huh?"

"The vegetables are nice and fresh, but my God, what is it with pasta? How hard is it to take it out of the pot before it turns into wet cardboard? It should have some body. It should be a worthwhile vehicle for the sauce, or, in this case, a sturdy companion to the vegetables. You should have to have a decent set of back teeth in order to eat it."

Perhaps hearing my tone of voice, the waitress swung by and asked if everything was all right. I said that it was, smiled at her, inquired as to the name of the mountain we were looking at.

"That's Mount Baker," she said proudly.

"Spectacular."

"You're kind, at least," Tasha said when we were alone again. "Kind, if picky."

Their meals were perfectly fine. Everything was more or less

all right to that point. We were running with the routine, balancing on the tightrope. We'd make it to the other side, no
problem. We'd get through tomorrow's ceremony, separate for
a while, have a quiet week together at the farm. But then Tasha
slipped, the way one of us was almost always slipping. Some
image of Jeannie, a breeze of memory, would blow across the
conversation and suddenly we'd all be falling, arms thrashing
air, faces contorted. "One of my earliest memories," she said,
stirring the salad absently with her fork, "is you blowing up at
Mom for cooking the pasta too long one night at supper."

"*Blowing up* is too strong."

"Getting mad."

"I apologized within sixty seconds. I'm sorry that's one of
your early memories. I'm sorry I'm so picky."

"It's just one of your little quirks, Dad," she said.

"Still."

"You and Mom didn't fight much," Anthony said in my defense, "compared to some of my friends' parents."

"Thank you."

"You seemed happy."

"We were," I said, a bit too stiffly. I was trying desperately to
unfreeze, to hold us up in the air above the canyon bottom. Natasha's lower lip had started to tremble. She left us—to wash
her hands, she said.

"All ready for school?" I asked my son, as a way of chasing
the dead air.

"Shipped the trunk. Suitcases packed. Room assignment all
set."

"I'll drive you up if you want."

"Thanks, Dad, but Emory's taking me . . . . And you're driving back to the farm with the Rinp anyway, and hanging out for a week, so the timing wouldn't work."

"Right. I forgot, I guess."

"You're pissed off."

"Not really."

"Sure you are. She pushes your buttons, Aunt Seese. Anybody can see that. You wanted a hotel, she got a B and B. You were on time, she's late, same as always."

"And Tash doesn't push yours?"

"Yeah, I guess. She means well, though, Aunt Seese. She just thought you wouldn't want to go straight back to the, you know, the empty house and everything."

I watched the stale old sibling resentment rise behind my thoughts, casting a shadow across their usual crooked run. I breathed. I relaxed my hand on the beer glass. I tried to smile the resentment away, or at least think about smiling it away, but it was no good. For some reason the trials of the past months had bled all the patience out of me, made a mockery of what Celia referred to as my "spiritual training." It was as if the lessons Rinpoche had taught me, the daily meditation practice, the reading of his own books and those of other masters, his friendly notes and letters, our talks—it had all built up a kind of cushion between me and the world's hard edges. The little things had stopped bothering me so much. I could get stuck in traffic en route to a Broadway show and not feel my blood pressure rising, not pound the steering wheel and mutter. I was more patient with the kids, at work, enduring a week of the flu or a back spasm on the tennis court. I worried less, laughed more. Jeannie noticed. Everyone noticed. And I gave Rinpoche the credit at every opportunity. Yes, I told one or two close friends,

it really worked, this meditation stuff. My mind was more under my control now, but it was a loose, relaxed control, like the
forehand of a good tennis player, no tension in it, just the appropriate focus and force.

But then came the routine physical that turned out to be
anything but. The tests, the doctors' somber faces and optimistic projections, the odds and percentages, the medicines, the
silent torment of radiation and chemo, the stories we heard in
person and read about on-line; then the horrible understanding
that we would not be in the fortunate majority, that Jeannie's
situation was different, much worse, and then the unutterable
misery of her suffering and of our having to stand by and observe it. Day by day, hour by hour, broken hope after broken
hope—a brief remission, word of a miracle drug, the possibility
of participating in a trial—it wore away at the cushion until, by
the time it all ended, I'd come to inhabit my old petty self again.
Jeannie had grown large in her dying, enormous there at the
last as if her spirit were swelling out from the ruined sack of
bones and flesh, the sunken eyes, thin hair, dry lips. There were
patches of anger and despair, but they were fleeting things.
Sometimes, sitting beside the bed holding her wrist very lightly
or dabbing her lips with a damp washcloth flavored with mint,
it seemed to me that my wife had turned into a dark night sky,
speckled with stars, cold and marvelous, unreachable, shining
down on me but with most of her already in some other world.

"Be large in your mind," Rinpoche had said to me years ago.
It was nothing he'd ever ventured when Jeannie was sick. He
meant it for lesser things. Be large in your mind; be big about
it.

So I tried then, with my son. "Your aunt's a nutcase, always has been. But a sweet, loving, kind, generous nutcase who surprises me sometimes in big moments."

He looked across the table at me, reached for a sip of my beer. He said, "Hard that we're leaving, too, isn't it. Me and Tash, I mean."

"You have your own lives. I want that."

"Yeah."

"What's that 'yeah?'"

He shrugged. "I just wish you could say it was hard, Dad. It would make me feel better than your wanting us to have our own life and that."

"The pretend me," I said. It was something else Rinpoche had pointed out, a tendency to behave according to some abstract *should*, instead of acknowledging the actual emotion. "It's been one of the hardest things I've ever known. Your mother and I loved having you both at home. We . . . didn't look forward to your leaving, like some parents do. We were going to enjoy ourselves, sure, but we didn't look forward. . ."

Anthony turned his eyes out the window. He wanted to see his father's vulnerability, and he didn't want to see it. "The whole thing sucks," he said. "It's a shit-show."

"Exactly."

"Come visit whenever you want, Dad. Come up for the home-game weekend stuff, it's great."

"Sure," I said. "Just what you need. Your dad there with your football buddies, beer in hand, singing the old school songs."

Natasha rejoined us. The muscles to either side of her mouth were trembling like willow leaves in the wind. Anthony pried at a mussel shell without really trying to open it. His sister spent a few seconds taking in the situation, then said, "Let it out, Dad."

"I've been letting it out. We've come to the conclusion that the whole thing sucks. We've gotten that far."

A weak smile. My mother's mouth and gray-green eyes. "We can feel you've been trying to say something ever since we got to JFK. You have that look."

"What look?"

"The I'm-about-to-make-a-fatherly-pronouncement look," Tasha said.

"All right," I said, but it took me a few seconds. "All I wanted to say was: We have to do this. Mom asked us to do it."

Nothing. They were suddenly focused on their food. Natasha pulled her chin down almost to her chest.

"Guys."

They looked reluctantly up.

"We're not going to make a big fuss. If you want to say something, that will be fine; if not, also fine. Rinpoche might say something. Aunt Seese probably will."

"It's a weird thing to do," Anthony said. "It's . . . Mom's not in that little jar you carried. That's not her."

"I know that. But she asked. Maybe she just wanted us to have a trip together before you both go back to school. A memory, that's all. She asked me to do it, and I promised her I would. Maybe something will come of this that we can't yet see. A last gift from her or something."

"Now you're sounding like Aunt Seese," Anthony said.

Natasha said nothing.

We ate the rest of the meal in a discontented silence. A TV on the wall was showing wildfires in New Mexico and advertisements for the upcoming London Olympics. For once, nothing on the dessert menu held much appeal for us. I paid, left my usual oversized tip, went out and stood on the sidewalk in the cool, salty air while my children each used the bathroom, Natasha's second time. The bad silence clung to our clothing and hair as we walked back toward the inn. I made a point, as I had done all their lives, of touching them—not for long, nothing to make them uncomfortable, just a physical signal, a token, the quick squeeze of arm or shoulder. "The medicine of touch," Jeannie had called it.

And then, from fifty yards away, we could see Rinpoche in his robe, standing in front of the purple house, a spiritual advance man. He heard our footsteps and turned. He made a study of Anthony, then Natasha, then me, and there was so much care in his face that I was cast back to the hours he'd spent at Jeannie's bedside. Between the day of her diagnosis and the moment of her death, three years, all told, they'd made probably a dozen trips east, he and my sister and their child, driven the whole way and stayed for a week each time. Prayers, baths, late-night doses of medicine, walks with the kids and Jasper into town for the distraction of a Haagen-Dazs milkshake. Just Rinpoche's presence in the house had seemed to lift a cold iron weight from my children's shoulders. I hoped he could manage that again.

Embraces all around.

"How are you?" I asked him after he'd released me from his World Wrestling Federation headlock.

Rinpoche seemed surprised at the question, as if he was always perfectly fine, and any asking about it was unnecessary. The shaved head, the gold-trimmed maroon robe that he wore in all weather, skin the color of coffee with a spoonful of cream in it and the longshoreman's face that looked carved from a stone cliff, the big smile, the ridiculously uninhibited laugh— he was a sort-of-Buddhist monk from the Russia/China border, a place called Skovorodino in the Ortyk region of South Siberia. And he was, if you believed what my sister and many thousands of others believed, an enlightened spiritual teacher from a long line of holy men.

He was, to me, mainly a brother-in-law, a friend. Kooky, maddening at times, infallibly kind, at moments direct to the point of bluntness, in possession of secret abilities—I loved him, I suppose, and trusted him at least enough to have taken meditation lessons from him over the past six years, to have read or at least perused most of the books he sent, to have allowed him and my sister to lease out most of our late parents' North Dakota farm and turn the rest of it into a "retreat center," a place of cabins and meditation rooms, wholesome cooking done by self-serious New Age types in sandals and loose clothing. I loved him, I trusted him that much, I had come to feel, after a period of doubt, that he was a good husband for my sister and an excellent father to our niece. And at the same time an ocean stood between us, a body of water too large to bridge. I was a New Yorker now, had been for the past twenty-eight years. Sophisticated, perhaps spoiled, a tad cynical, fond of strong coffee and the *Times*, witty in a big-city way, afraid of pain and death, open to the idea of a calmer mind but not yet quite to the associated antics that accompanied a serious spiritual practice. I thought of myself as a flawed, ordinary man—in my own way I tried to be good—but despite the meditation and the exotic reading, it was still an all-American way. I was, for better and worse, still me. Nothing, not even the trauma of Jeannie's passing, had changed that.

In answer to my question, Rinpoche sent me a long, piercing look and shrugged. We started down the gravel path, cairns to either side. "Train ride wery long," he said, swallowing the "v"—a new affectation—and putting a hand against his lower back as if it hurt, which I was quite sure it did not. The man was built like a sumo wrestler and was as limber as a yogi. He liked to pretend to be as weak and frail as everyone else, but he wasn't. I'd never known him to suffer from so much as a head cold, to seem tired or out of sorts, to take any medicine or vitamins at all.

"You could have been here in two hours on a plane."

He nodded, acknowledging the point. "This time, train," he said. "More safe. Shelsa saw some of the West America."

From behind, Anthony reached out and gave Rinpoche an affectionate rub of the muscles to either side of his neck. "Good to see you, Unc," he said. "Where's the rest of the gang?"

Rinpoche looped one arm around his neck and pulled him close. "Good of seeing you, too," he said.

"Where's your posse?"

"Shelsa sleeping. Wery tired. Her mother go there with her to the bed. I am waiting outside to see my two most beautiful people." He had one arm around each of their necks now and he leaned first to one side, then the other, and planted a loud kiss on their heads. I watched from a few feet behind.

"And what about my dad?" Tasha asked. "Isn't he one of the most beautiful people?"

Rinpoche turned around and looked at me, and there was something new in his face, some sorrow there that I'd never seen, a slight change, my sister would have said, in his aura. "Most best uncle and brother-and-law!" he said, much too loudly. "Shelsa cries, not seeing you so long. Tomorrow in the morning, I told her. Tomorrow you have breakfast with Uncle Ott!"

5

The Inn at Chakra Creek eschewed the decadent luxury of television, but the mattresses were firm, there was a small heated swimming pool that Rinpoche and my children splashed in happily until late, and, according to a pamphlet on the night table, ICC offered a breakfast in which nearly everything on the menu had been grown within twenty-five miles. Local eggs. Bacon, ham, and sausage from hogs raised just down the road. Biscuits from Washington State wheat, jam from an orchard in Everett. And so on. Only the coffee—and perhaps the sugar in the jam—hailed from far-off lands, and it was fair-trade coffee, the author of the pamphlet noted, "rich as molasses and with a major kick."

I clicked off the lamp and lay there in darkness, tempted to join them for a swim but too weary. The way the mind worked, Rinpoche had told me, was that it returned to inspect its bruises again and again and again. Childhood humiliation or abuse, physical trauma, argument, bereavement, loss—if you paid attention you'd notice that, when the pain was fresh, the mind would go back there every few seconds, as if checking it to make sure it was still alive. In time, the trouble burrowed deeper into the stony soil of the thoughts, but anything could awaken it and pull it back to the surface. The trick, he'd counseled me, was neither to encourage the hard memories nor push them away with too much force. The trick was to bring yourself back to the present, the air in which old hurt couldn't breathe. "Stay there with what you hear," he said, "what you see. What your hands against something feel. And if the bad thing come, just let him come, Otto. Let him run and run and bark like a dog in a big big field, until he gets tired and lays down there and goes to sleep. Okay?"

Here was the present, then: the sound of my son's happy shout and one loud splash. The smell of sea air drifting in through the open window. The feel of the cool breeze across my shoulders and cheeks, and the sheets and blanket on my legs. I let an image of my wife—she was, for some reason, standing at the stove and turning her head over one shoulder to look at me—come wandering into the field. I let it circle and trot there. More than anything on earth I wanted to hear her speak again, just once, tell me she was still intact in some other dimension, safe there, at peace. I tried not to cling too desperately to the image, and not to push it away, and in a little while the noise from the swimming pool subsided, and the pain of her absence died down, and I was able to fall asleep.

──⟨⟩ 6

It turned out that Cecelia had decided to bring along their new dog, Jasper Jr. named by Shelsa after our elderly mutt, Jasper Sr., a half-Doberman, half-Lab mix who was being minded by a kind neighbor at home. Their Jasper was a few inches shorter and a few pounds lighter but looked eerily like ours: short black coat with touches of bronze on the muzzle and breast. That same proud dignity. Karmic twins, as Cecelia put it. Jasper Jr., she told me, had been allowed onto the train only after a prolonged discussion between Rinpoche and the stationmaster. He'd make the trip up into the mountains with us, then ride back with them on Amtrak (dogs not usually allowed, but she had a letter of permission in her purse). Another Ringling Family Plan.

As the only guests that morning, we sat at two pushed-together tables in the breakfast nook, all six of us. Jasper was happily sniffing around outside. My sister's husband sat directly opposite me. He had his daughter on his knee and was feeding her sips of coffee on an empty stomach.

"You're gonna juice her all up, Uncle," Anthony said.

Rinpoche laughed his mucousy laugh and reached out and squeezed Anthony's bicep. "Strong!" he said. "After, you and me, we wessel."

"Rinpoche, I don't think that's wise," my sister cautioned. She did that sometimes, addressed her beloved by his title. 'Volya' just didn't fit him as well, for any of us, and 'Rinpoche' actually meant 'precious one', so it made sense, I suppose, between wife and husband.

"And it's 'wrestle' anyway, not 'wessle' Tasha said.

Rinpoche appeared unoffended. In all the time I'd known him, almost six years of living with my voluble sister and hosting American retreatants at the North Dakota farm, he'd made next to no progress in the language. Lately, in fact, he seemed to have lost grammatical ground. His mispronunciations were inconsistent and legendary. Sometimes he got it right, sometimes not. Wessle. Brother-in-waw. Brother-and-law. Wery. Very. He'd developed a penchant for convoluted phraseology like "Jeannie now is wery sick, couldn't she?" I'd learned, on our visits to Dakota and in New York, to let it go. But Tasha often felt obliged to correct him, and he always thanked her and tried the proper pronunciation or appropriate grammar once, then forgot it instantly. He spoke, he claimed, eleven languages, four of them fluently—his native Ortyk, Russian, Italian, and English—so this trouble with pronunciation always seemed strange to me, an act, a game. Perhaps—who could ever know with Rinpoche—he was making some statement about the mutability of language itself, the way it can stand between raw reality and the mind. A tree, after all, was not a tree; that was merely its assigned label, in one of earth's hundreds of languages.

Death was not death; it was a mystery, a passage, ineffable.

Thinking this, I realized I was angry at him on that morning, and for no good reason, no good reason at all. He'd been exceedingly kind to Jeannie and me during her illness. He'd visited, soothed her in ways I couldn't seem to, spoken privately with the kids in their worst hours. Since our previous road trip he'd taken me on as a private meditation student, a poor but fairly dutiful one, and sprayed nothing but patience and good humor in my direction . . . and that morning I was angry with him and trying to understand why. Maybe I'd expected the meditation lessons to take all the pain out of my life. Maybe I held that against him.

"Wessel," he said, looking at my daughter with his eyebrows raised, his stevedore's face, a face that never seemed to age, crinkled up in a pantomime of confusion.

"Wrestle. RRRRR. Are."

"Waaah," he said.

"Say 'Rinpoche,' Anthony suggested.

"Win—poach—hay."

"Now you're pulling my dick."

"What this *dick*?" Rinpoche asked. He looked quizzically at my sister. "Dick, dick. What this is?" He'd been ignoring me the whole morning. One hug at the top of the stairs, and then what almost felt like the cold shoulder. As if he knew in advance that I'd be angry. Or as if he were disappointed in me, thought I should be more spiritually mature by now, should have learned the advanced dance steps of the soul. I should have been able to deal with death the way he seemed to deal with it, not ignoring it, not making light, but somehow, at the same time, the farthest thing from devastated. Hadn't he been instructing me all these years—books, letters, meditation pointers, detachment, equanimity? What was my problem?

"'Dick' is a very rude word for a man's penis," my sister explained patiently, as if there were other very rude words for a *woman's* penis. "Your nephew is being uncouth and saying things he shouldn't say in front of his young cousin."

"Sorry."

The inn's daytime clerk—a dreadlocked, elaborately tattooed twenty-year-old who, after asking Rinpoche to sign the guest register that morning, had sliced the page out of his book with a Swiss Army knife and taped it to the wall beside the reception desk—interrupted this conversation with refills of the miraculous coffee. He had Bob Marley's hair and Justin Bieber's face, and a way of speaking that matched Cecelia's like a sibling. "Going up to the Cascades today?" he inquired, in a singsong, optimistic rhythm.

I nodded, attempted a smile. He filled my cup with a reverent gesture: the liquid was melted gold, a precious thing, as fine as the pamphlet promised. "Little vacation from the hectic other side?"

"Family trip," I said.

When he stood there, wanting more, Natasha filled in the blanks. "We're going out today to spread my mother's ashes."

"Cool. Your mom must have been a great lady."

Tears sprang into Natasha's eyes as if a switch had been thrown behind the gray-green circles. I ground my teeth hard enough to make free-trade porcelain. Bob Bieber didn't seem to notice. "Your dog's cool, too, dude." He seemed to be speaking to me. I was "dude" here to everyone, the mellow surfer-dad up from La Jolla for the coffee and cold waves. "He's like, what?

Lab or something?"

"Half Doberman." Be careful, I was tempted to say, or he'll bite your dick off.

"Dasper," Shelsa said.

"Cool name."

Leave us, leave us, leave us! I thought. But the gregarious fellow didn't move. Shelsa had taken to fingering her scrambled eggs and Rinpoche was holding her, watching, smiling. His style of childrearing seemed to belong to the school of affectionate lassitude. He spoke to her as if she were his equal, a fellow traveler, a full soul, and held her, tickled her, and made her laugh as if there were nothing more precious to him on this earth. What would you do, I found myself wondering, if you had to watch her die? What would happen to all the spiritual talk then, the detachment, the inner peace?

It was a terrible thought, shameful and petty, a kidney stone of distilled bitterness. Me at my worst. It pains me to confess it, but pain or no, I am going to be honest here; I promised myself that. I'm going to show myself with all my warts and sins, though I confess to a tremendous desire to tell this story with gold dust on all of it, to be the man Rinpoche kept assuring me I was, a helper to Shelsa in her important work, a seeker on the verge of a great spiritual awakening, a Bronxville saint.

The young waiter didn't appear to understand that he should leave now, that we were a family in mourning, that his presence among us was as welcome as a fluorescent bulb at 4:00 a.m. It seemed to me that he was ogling Natasha—whose nicely proportioned breasts, gift from her late mother's DNA, were pressing out against a cashmere sweater, color of sapphire. What else, what deadly poison, had been passed down in that gene pool? "We're, like, honored to have you here," the young man said, as if speaking to them.

Shelsa patted the last yellow bubbles of egg, small living ducklings, then looked up at the waiter and said "Dick" very clearly, and a great burst of laughter went up around him and he stood there, smiling, shaggy, confused, forgiven.

Freed from him at last, finished with the sumptuous, all-local repast, we gathered our things and assembled on the lawn of the Inn at Chakra Creek. This was the day I'd been dreading. The saying of grace at table, the speeches at a colleague's retirement party—any and all kinds of ritual or formality threw me back hard against the side of the North Dakota barn where my parents had stored hay and machinery. Their way of life was as orderly as the furrowed soybean fields, a formal, strict, Lutheran life ruled by ancient ritual that had ceased to have any meaning for me by the time the first hair sprouted above my upper lip. The inside of my father's Buick—and it was somehow *his* car and not my mother's—was immaculate. We sat in the same pew every week at St. John's, dressed in carefully ironed clothing. We gave thanks before meals. Cecelia and I rose at five every summer day of our young lives and went through our assigned chores with the regularity of robots. For a long stretch of years, these rites had managed to keep chaos at bay, to render the weeks predictable with their pressed Sunday trousers and polished kitchen floor. And then, one cold morning—*BAM!*—a drunk driver plowed into the Buick on a country road, and none of that mattered anymore.

This particular ceremony, the idea of finding something to say to mark the spreading of Jeannie's ashes, struck me as an impossible challenge. If you couldn't capture "table" with a word, how were you supposed to say what she had meant to us? No, it would be at once too final and not final enough; it would hurt too much to speak.

Even just standing there trying to decide seating arrangements in the vehicles—even that put me on edge.

And, of course, Rinpoche chose that moment to challenge my muscular son to a wessling match. *You bizarre man*, I thought.

But Anthony loved it. A delighted smile lit his face. He stripped off his jersey and tossed it aside in a single motion. He faced his maroon-robed opponent in a crouch. Rinpoche was laughing, circling his hands like some kind of orchestra conductor gone mad. There seemed to be no tension in his body. He was a rubber man, on the medium-short side, chunky, thick-limbed, but pliable as the stem of a dandelion. Cecelia picked up her daughter and frowned. Natasha had her hips cocked, head tilted sideways, ready for disdain, laughter, or approval, whatever seemed the appropriate posture for viewing the spectacle of feather-fluffing masculine absurdity. The dreadlocked waiter had come to the doorway and was holding my sister's forgotten sweater in his hand, watching the great spiritual master—his idol—whirl hands and laugh like a lunatic.

The combatants were standing on a patch of perfect lawn, one of them straight out of a prep school wrestling team, the other straight out of some Siberian Camp Sumo. The cairns stood at a safe distance. Rinpoche waved his hands and laughed but made no move forward, and I thought for a moment it had all been meant as a joke. But then Anthony made a charge, low, like a bull or a linebacker, muscles rippling, and somehow, in a tenth of a second, Rinpoche had him on his back on the ground and was leaning across him with all his weight, laughing and chuckling. It was Cassius Clay's phantom punch in Lewiston; no one had seen it. Sonny Liston on his back on the canvas. No one, least of all Anthony, understood what had happened. The only sign of exertion on the winner's side was that the maroon robe had ridden up the back of Rinpoche's legs. We could see his wide ass. He was wearing what were known as commando underpants, a brief-boxer hybrid I'd never cottoned to. Red in color. The muscles of his legs were like iron.

I worried Anthony would be shamed, but he was laughing, too. "All right, okay. Get off. Man, you're fat! No fair, you're a different weight class."

Rinpoche rolled back and forth across him, torso to torso, as if my son were some kind of foam cylinder in the gym. The otherwise mellow Jasper Jr. (Celia said she sometimes sang him to sleep) stood by and barked without enthusiasm, playing a role. Men wrestled. Women watched. Dogs barked. Shelsa climbed down out of her mother's arms and ran over and jumped onto her dad's backside. Anthony let out an "Oof!" and hugged her and laughed with his arms wrapped around Rinpoche, and I saw Tasha sidle over to the dreadlocked boy and accept her aunt's sweater and thank him warmly.

"Your husband's a nut," I said to Celia, trying to sail with the prevailing winds. My own words sounded sour and small in my ear.

"It's just his way of cheering them up," she said, but she was looking at the entangled bodies, not me, when she said it. She reached her hand sideways and took hold of mine, then looked. "Don't," she said, "be fooled."

"Fooled how?"

She squinted. The narrowed eyes seemed to say: why are you pretending, Otto? She started to say something else, then stopped, and went to fetch her daughter.

7

It was difficult to make the segue from that scene to the mood I thought I was supposed to be in as we headed north and east. As we left Whidbey Island—by way of Oak Harbor, route 20, then I-5 again—the road was thick with logging trucks and Winnebagos, and I was glad to see that my sister had ceded the driving responsibilities. I didn't trust Cecelia behind the wheel, either as navigator or driver. She did not like written directions. She did not know GPS from UPS. She appeared to assume that the correct route would be made known to her via some sort of celestial Morse code at the appropriate moment, and she seemed to believe that driving faster than speed-limit-minus-ten was an idea for reckless fools.

Anthony was at the wheel of the SUV. His sister, a better driver but one who didn't enjoy it as much, watched over him carefully from the passenger seat. Celia sat in back with Shelsa. I'd decided it would be best to let them lead the way, not because I worried how Anthony would handle the big machine with the jet-fighter dashboard display—he was a decent driver and I was sure his sister wouldn't be stingy with advice—but because I wanted them to set the pace, and Celia to decide when she needed to stop and let Shelsa run around or use the facilities.

And I think, too, that I wanted to be able to see my kids. It sounds strange, perhaps: I saw them every day at home, and all I could see of them in this case was indistinct shapes through the Lincoln's rear window. But I had an urge to keep them in view. Every day that summer I'd had a clearer and clearer understanding that they'd soon be leaving the house, in two months, a month, now a few weeks. That morning, when the first daylight shone through the inn curtains, I'd awakened to an acute sense of emptiness in the room, an echoing hollowness, as if my heart were beating in the massive blackness between Saturn and Jupiter. I could already feel the empty house I was going back to. I could picture myself taking the commuter train from Manhattan to the Bronxville station after a day at the office, fishing the car keys out of my pocket, making the six-minute drive home, opening the door, walking into the kitchen. Jasper would be there, at least, standing up on his creaky old legs and hobbling over to greet me. But then would come the solitary hour at the stove and table, the solitary perusal of a submitted manuscript (I still couldn't bring myself to do that work on an electronic tablet, as my colleagues did; around the office I'd gotten a reputation as a Luddite), the solitary viewing of an hour of late-night TV. The empty bed.

People said I'd eventually become accustomed to it. In my dentist's waiting room I'd read an article on grieving, and the clear message was this: time heals. People remade their lives, found a new companion, a new hobby, picked themselves up and cleaned themselves off and went on. I believed all that. But I believed it the way you believe in, say, an afterlife: hopefully, dutifully, but also haunted by the nagging possibility that it might not be so. And even if it were so, even if in a year or two years or five years the pain of Jeannie's absence would abate, that did nothing to soften the feelings of the moment, or the fact that the children, our children, would be leaving the house in a little over four weeks and I was obliged to be happy for them.

So I wanted the Lincoln in front of me, where I could see it. Rinpoche and I followed along in the certified-antique pickup, which I'd already come to love. The smooth, scalloped wheel, hard as a seashell; the torn and scratched-up leather seat; the simple speedometer display, the comforting clutch work and sound of changing gears, even the mumbling muffler—all of it brought me back to an earlier day, an earlier me bouncing along in similar vehicles on Dickinson's dusty gravel roads, splashing through new snow, revving the engine in front of a friend's trailer. It spoke to the simpler America that was either a fact or a fantasy, I was never sure. I liked it anyway. I counted on the idea of it being there, something solid beneath the modern rush and the rough tides of adulthood.

Rinpoche seemed to like his new vehicle, too. From the minute he'd set eyes on the orange-and-cream fenders, the big smile had broken open across his face. "This is what the trucks looked like when I was a young man," I told him, and he went over and slapped the rust-speckled hood with real affection. It was a gesture right out of the high plains, as American as barbecue; he was learning quickly. Inside, he ran his hands over the dashboard and seats. He worked the chrome door handle, flipped the sunshade up and down. "Pickup," he said, beaming at me. In his mouth the word sounded like "Pee-gahp," but it carried the same odd pride I felt in driving it.

With the stick in the middle, it was a bit awkward for Jasper Jr.—who wanted, that morning, to demonstrate his feelings for me. I nudged him gently away. He gave me a perplexed look, so I fondled his ears for a moment, then nudged him again. Rinpoche lifted him onto his be-robed lap, and Jasper wiggled his ass, pawed at the maroon fabric and eventually found a position that felt both comfortable and dignified, his head against Rinpoche's jaw. I saw the good monk take a sniff of one floppy ear.

The road east—we took Exit 194, Snohomish, Wenatchee, and it led us onto Route 2—was flat at first and four lanes, with marsh and grassland to either side. Soon enough it narrowed, and though it didn't rise much, you could sense it lifting its eyes to the high peaks ahead. I could, at least. I could sense it because I knew this road, remembered it the way you remember certain pieces of a long-past family vacation, an overseas trip from years before, a walk you took once, in childhood. It had etched itself into the part of my mind that seemed to keep the memories right there where you could blow one breath into them and make them stand up and walk. There were high-tension wires and hay bales, the meandering Skykomish River, and these tendrils of feeling from different days.

Jeannie and I had met in North Dakota, first made love in the Knickerbocker Hotel in Chicago, and spent most of our honeymoon in a brightly tiled *casa de huespedes* four blocks from the Palacio Nacional in Mexico City. Like a lot of optimistic young couples, we'd found a cheap walk-up in New York

City—Twenty-ninth and Eighth, in Chelsea—and set about trying to make careers in the arts. She was waiting tables and
spent her free hours taking photographs. Having abandoned
the idea of a life in architecture, I made some money correcting
standardized tests for a company with offices in Queens, and
labored away on what I hoped would be the Great American
Novel.

The novel went nowhere, but I did eventually land a job at a
small publishing house closer to home. Mindless work, for the
most part: mailing galleys, making calls to printers and design-
ers, running errands. One of Jeannie's regular customers at the
restaurant worked for a museum in Soho, and he helped her
find part-time photo work there. A happy year went by. Two
happy years. And then, by the purest of coincidences, I heard
about an editorial position—a real editorial position—at Stanley
and Byrnes, a house that specialized in food books. I applied,
managed to do well in the interview, and was told, after a week
of tense expectation, that they'd take me on—as long as I was
willing to wait the two months until one of their senior editors
retired and those beneath him moved up a rung.

A wiser couple would have spent those two months saving
up, looking far into the future toward a suburban home and a
family. But we lacked that particular kind of wisdom, Jeannie
and I, and made up for it with a sense of adventure. We knew
we wanted kids, we'd had that discussion, but, product of sensible people that we were, sensible and stultified, we knew we
wanted a little room to ramble first. For a while we thought
about going to Europe, but Jeannie had always wanted to see
the Pacific Northwest, so instead of crossing the pond we
booked a flight to Seattle, rented the cheapest vehicle available,

and set out, with backpacks and a small tent, for a two-week escapade.

Things went badly from the start. The day before we left I'd caught some kind of minor-league flu, and I was feverish, cranky, and sleep-deprived. The flight was rough, the hotel filled with a menagerie of loud misfits. We had an argument there—I don't remember what about—and then, as we headed north from Seattle there was another fight, worse this time, atypically bad for us. That one I remember. We were both well-educated young people, proud of our brains, probably especially proud because we'd come from relatively provincial folk—smart, clever, capable, well off in her case, but parents who didn't know the difference between Franco and Frankfurt, between summertime and a sommelier. Mix in a measure of twenty-something hubris and we had, in those years, I'm slightly ashamed to admit, made gods of our own mental capabilities. In this there was a measure of competitiveness, too: we not only wanted to be smart, we wanted to be smarter. On that day the competitiveness pushed its snout between us, snarling and snapping. I was at the wheel, still a bit under the weather; Jeannie had the map open across the tops of her legs, and announced that she'd found a shortcut.

"One of your famous shortcuts," I said.

She pressed her lips together, breathed through her nose, said she was trying to save us time and gas money and I should stop being so sarcastic. "It doesn't become you."

She never used that phrase. I wondered if she'd met someone at the museum, someone sophisticated and older, a savant who'd seen the great sights of Europe and who used phrases like "doesn't become you." I worried she was already dissatisfied with me and having an affair. Heading north on the bland interstate, I had a whole ridiculous fantasy going about the deterioration of our marriage. She was ashamed to tell people her husband was a North Dakota rube. There would be parties at the museum, cool Manhattan artists' parties, and she wouldn't invite me, or she'd invite me and leave me standing in a corner, Coke in hand, while she talked Eisenstein and Cartier-Bresson with older men in wrinkled linen sport coats and I looked down at the cowshit on my cheap shoes. Ridiculous, in retrospect. But this wasn't retrospect. This was the angst and trauma of untested love, as real as the pleasure we gave each other in bed, as real as the cockroaches scuttling through the kitchen drawers, and the night sirens and morning junkies on Twenty-ninth Street.

"Doesn't become you," I said bitterly. "Since when do you talk like that?"

"Since when are you such a bastard?"

The droning wheels, the big trucks passing, the sense of diverse histories girding themselves for war.

"I found a great shortcut," she said, tapping the map with two fingers. "We're having a stupid damned fight about a shortcut."

"Fine, tell me the shortcut, I'll take it. We'll save fifty cents worth of gas and you'll feel like you outsmarted the rest of the world, like you always do."

"God," she said. "You can be an ass."

A silence like the gloom of New York in February fell over us, filling the small car—a Datsun, I think it was—and pressing against our ears. We took the shortcut. It led us into a small town where we became completely lost. Neither of us could bring ourselves to stop and ask for help, so we turned left and right on the streets of Maltby for twenty minutes until I finally spotted a sign for Route 2 east and we climbed up onto that road, the same road our son was leading me along now, twenty-three years later, putting on a blinker and turning carefully left into the parking lot of a place that advertised itself with two signs: DEADLIEST SNAKES and ALBINO ALLIGATOR. In front of the main building stood a miniature red house. When Anthony pulled up and stopped beside it I saw another sign: REPTILE ZOO AND ESPRESSO.

Jasper stirred, sidled over and stood, slapping Rinpoche's face once with a wagging tail. My brother-in-law laughed and took hold of the tail and gently shook it. "What is?" he asked.

"Espresso? It's coffee. Concentrated. Very strong. Gives you energy."

"Dogs drink it?"

"No, they shouldn't."

"Kids?"

"Shelsa's too young."

"Me and you?"

"I'm up for an Italian soda, if they have them. You almost never drink even regular coffee. You'll be bouncing around like a superball."

"I'll have a trying," he said.

"Sure. Whatever you want. On me." I got out of the car and felt glad: for a moment it seemed the memories from the earlier trip had stayed behind on the torn-up leather seat.

The air in that part of the world, between the northern Pacific and Washington's mountains, was luscious and cool, touched with the scent of the sea and fir trees and moving against our skin like a lover's fingertip. The memories circled. I

45

ducked and dodged. At the little red house they offered Italian sodas in a dozen flavors. Two vanilla and two almond for the Ringlings, large, please; a chocolate milk for Shelsa, a cup of water for Jasper. For whatever reason, try as we might to convince him to go the sweet soda route, Rinpoche had his mind set on an espresso. I'd left money with the pierced young clerk behind the window, but at the moment of Rinpoche's purchase I was following Jasper Jr. a little ways into the trees at the edge of the parking lot. He was an obedient sort, but I knew from what Celia had said that if he happened to see an animal of any kind—turkey, bear, deer, hedgehog, squirrel, chipmunk, it didn't matter, as long as it breathed and moved and wasn't human—he'd be off on a chase and no amount of frantic calling or yelling could get him to return.

So, making sure Jasper didn't run off, I missed Rinpoche's maiden voyage with espresso. Anthony did not. He would tell me, months later, that the clerk had run out of small cups, and so she'd put the high-test caffeine into a larger cup, and when Rinpoche received it he assumed she hadn't filled it up all the way. He asked her, politely, if she would do that. "Oh, a double?" the girl said. Rinpoche smiled, nodded, handed over more of my money, took the cup from her a second time and glanced into it, sniffed, let a small sip pass between his lips and then, apparently pleased, downed the whole thing at once, the way vodka drinkers do at home in Russia.

Aside from the satisfied smacking of his lips and a small burp, there was no immediate reaction. By the time Jasper and I rejoined the group, the espresso had been consumed. Jasper lapped loudly at his water dish. We loitered for a while in the parking lot, linked by a morbid anticipation, peering in the window to catch a glimpse of the albino alligator. And then we were back in our vehicles and heading into the big hills.

We'd gone only a short distance—with the river still running to our right and a line of freight cars sitting there—before Rinpoche burped again and began tapping his foot. This was unlike him; he was the stillest of men, a block of bone and muscle in gold-trimmed maroon. The radio wasn't on, so the foot tapping had nothing to do with music. I heard him say "Ah," and I thought it was in reference to the scenery, so I said, "Nice, isn't it? Wait till you see what's in front of us."

"Nice, nice," he said, quickly.

There were cherries by the pound and salmon jerky for sale in roadside stands, a small white chapel to the left, closed up. We passed another sign for espresso—they were everywhere in this state; perhaps people slept so deeply in the wonderful air that they needed help waking up—and then Bubba's Road House, with a sign that read, EAT BIG FOOD.

Rinpoche had been stroking Jasper's backbone in an absentminded way, but after a while I noticed that the strokes were shorter and quicker, almost in time with the foot tapping.

"How'd you like that espresso?" I asked him.

"Good good wery good."

"How much of it did you have?"

"The cup," he said.

"Big cup or small cup?"

He brought one hand around in front of Jasper's face and put it above the other hand and I could see that the fingers were shaking. "Nice girl," he said. "Give Rinpoche little some extra."

"Little some extra, huh? That's high-test you were drinking. That's a day's worth of caffeine, and you almost never touch the stuff."

"Nice nice nice," he said, the foot going, the hand going, the head nodding back and forth as if there were a rock-and-roll song in the air, or as if he were mouthing a prayer of thanks, *muy rapido*, to the Nicaraguan bean that had so pleased him.

I let him jive. Route 2 twisted this way and that between fir-coated hills that slanted up steeply from the road's stony shoulders. There were glimpses of the taller peaks ahead, Three Fingers and Fifth of July Mountain, seven or eight thousand feet, I guessed, and then a sign for the Mount Baker-Snoqualmie National Forest.

Jasper settled down on Rinpoche's lap, and I could no longer keep the past out of the cab of the old pickup. Our silence was a happier version of the silence that had fallen over Jeannie and me, in a car of about the same vintage as Uma, on a summer day very much like this one—the mountain sunlight and crisp air, the weather-beaten wooden houses and little shops selling antiques and carved stumps, the chain-up areas and the logging trucks roaring downhill. There are all kinds of silences, but the one in which Jeannie and I moved then was a silence in which all the evil flora grew, all the poison oak and poison ivy, all the noxious weeds of the emotional world. It is a vegetation watered with anger and regret—the other people you could have married, the other places you could be. All the good news we'd gotten at home, all the fine expectation with which we'd packed and set out, all of that seemed to have mutated in the ugliest of ways. It slithered through the roots and leaves of this ugly shrubbery, venomous, mocking, looking for something to bite.

We said not a word. The plan had been to find a wilderness campground somewhere near the crest of the Northern Cascades and spend the night there under the stars or in our tiny tent. We had insect repellent and water and a small cook set and meat and vegetables. Jeannie had her contraceptive equipment, as outdated now as this old pickup and something I won't get into here. Sex for us in those days was an almost-nightly joy, as reliable as the morning coffee. And sometimes a morning joy, as well. We were well matched that way, in urge and style. Guiltless, selfless, half addicted. Outdoor lovemaking—an exotic idea for New Yorkers—sang background to the plans we'd made. Even after the small fight in the hotel it had been on my mind, and on hers, too, I'm sure of it. Now, that idea was extinguished. What we had to look forward to wasn't an hour of ecstasy under the Cascade stars but a night in the small tent with two inches of air between our bodies and separate hurricanes of bad thought swirling.

There were places we could have stopped, but we didn't. Neither of us wanted to be the first to speak. We hoped to put off the idea of making camp for as long as possible, indefinitely perhaps.

Near the summit, in a town that went by the peculiar name of Baring, there was a cluster of houses and then a sign for a general store. "I have to pee," Jeannie said. I pulled into the gravel lot and she got out and slammed the door and went into the little wooden place.

I stood outside for a time, looking up at the high slopes where patches of snow still clung in the shadier valleys. She was in there a long time. I pictured her on the pay phone, calling her older museum friend and asking if he could come and rescue her from the spoiled vacation, the erroneous marriage. I thought of other women I'd slept with. I twirled the ring on my finger. Eventually I went inside and found my wife in conversation, not by phone with a Manhattan sophisticate, but face-to-face with a tough-looking young woman behind the counter. The woman had a blurry tattoo on one bare shoulder—decades before tattoos were in style—and a face that looked like the wind gods had hacked at it with scythes. You could see from her body and the way she moved that she was young, certainly thirty or less. But stuck on top, like a mask, was the face of a middle-aged grandmother with two divorces and eight fistfights behind her. Her eyes were fixed on Jeannie in a way I will never forget, as if the two of them were soul-cousins who'd traveled very different paths and just been reunited.

"Yeah, I know," the woman was saying when I came in.

Jeannie turned her eyes to me for one second. I knew I'd interrupted something, so I raised a hand and pointed "Bathroom in back?"

A terse nod, a perusal.

Just as I was squeezing past the little post office window there and opening the narrow door I heard, "But you know, you hang in and maybe—"

The second I came back out through that door I could feel the woman's eyes on me. She knew men, knew them inside and out, their fickleness and wide-scattered lusts, their need to boss, their hard shell and pride and stubborn attitudes, and then also the something else that made you stay or return or want them in the world in spite of their boorishness. I could feel every bit of that. She was studying me as I made the short trip across the creaky old floor, appraising, ready, it seemed, to go back outside and tell Jeannie to get rid of the bum, or tell her maybe he'd turn out okay with another decade or so of seasoning. I wanted another man there for support. I wanted to give evidence, as if before some invisible court of gender dispute: *But she insists on knowing everything! It would drive you nuts. It's a competition, an Olympics of shortcuts and gas saving. It's spoiling what was supposed to be a special trip, can't you see?*

Instead, I stopped in front of her and looked at the candy offerings. I selected a Mounds bar—my comfort, in those days and now—and paid her, and she gave me change and then, with the chapped corners of her thin lips, what might have been the tiniest sign of encouragement. She was, after all, soul-cousin to my wife.

Jeannie was already in the car, facing forward. I got in and started it and opened up the candy bar and took out the first piece and held it toward her. "Other half?"

She looked down and shook her head. I opened the window as we drove and threw the other half of the Mounds out the window, from spite, because I knew she hated littering, because I didn't want to lose, because I wasn't inconsiderate or unfaithful or mean and didn't want to be put in that drawer, no matter what the woman behind the counter had been through.

There was a ski area at the summit. STEVENS PASS, the sign read. ELEVATION 4061 FEET. "Want to stop and look around? Take a picture or something?"

Another shake of the head.

It was probably four o'clock by then. I suspected that the land on the far side of the Cascade Range would be dry and unpeopled, not exactly prime camping territory. So, without asking her, when we came to a left turn a mile or so down the east slope of the mountain—SMITH BROOK TRAILHEAD said the sign—I took the car off the paved road and onto gravel, and drove along for a ways. We saw a small river there, to our left, amid stately firs. Rock slides to our right. Flat spots in the trees that looked suitable for a campsite.

"Looks like a good place," I said. Jeannie said nothing.

Naturally enough—isn't this the way the universe works?—even though we'd all made a stop only half an hour back, as we came into Baring in our Lincoln-and-pickup caravan, twenty-three years post-argument, I saw the blinker go on. Anthony pulled into the lot of the little store. It had hardly changed. Not eager to be battered by any more memories just then, I muttered something under my breath, inaudible to the world and the present day, and decided to stay in the pickup. But Rinpoche jumped out almost before we came to a stop. "Shelsa has to pee!" my sister sang out over the mountains. Julie Andrews on the Austrian slopes.

In another second, with my sister and her daughter entering the store and my children following out of curiosity, Rinpoche was beside the truck hopping up and down as if on a pogo stick. The robe flattened around him as he jumped and fluttered as he descended. Jasper looked at him, his head out the truck window. It was Skovorodian aerobics, Buddhist jumping jacks. The sound of no hands clapping.

"Nice, nice, nice," he was saying.

I stood nearby until he'd done forty or fifty jumps and tired himself out.

"Rinpoche," I said.

"Otto, my friend."

"This is caffeine."

"What is caffeine?"

"What you're feeling now. That weird energy, that high. That's what caffeine does to you. The espresso was loaded with it."

"I like what it feels."

"Sure. So do four billion other people. Wait an hour or so."

He didn't respond, but walked around the gravel in fast circles. "A good place," he said, raising his arms sideways in a gesture that seemed to encompass both the store and the tree-covered slopes. "Good energy here."

"Sure," I said. But I was remembering the tough woman's eyes on me. I was feeling like a grumpy old man. I had a run going, an interior run, bitter as coffee grounds. Here was my sister singing out happily over the mountains. Here was her husband, clowning around. They hadn't lost a spouse.

I thought I'd grown beyond that kind of pettiness. But no, I was back in my twenty-seven-year-old self, throwing Mounds bars out the window.

"Dad," Anthony called. "You have to come in. This place is incredible! They have this little post office here. It's, like, a hundred years old! You have to see it."

I didn't want to see it. The thing about self-pity is that it feeds on itself. It's akin to depression in that way and almost as painful. It hides from the world in a black-walled closet, urging you toward a masturbatory negativity.

"Dad, come on!"

I shook my head, popped the hood of the pickup, and pretended to be checking the oil or the distributor cap or the brake fluid. Rinpoche went inside. I stayed out there alone, a dog, greasy battery cables and self-sorrow for company. I had the sense—I could not know why—that the woman behind the counter had never left. She'd been there for the past twenty-three years, selling candy to young bastards and offering counsel to their wives. I didn't want to see it, to remember, to acknowledge, again, what I was missing. Jeannie and I had talked about making a return trip to this place and never done it.

But then something changed. A cool breeze of good sense blew through the mood. The woman, after all, had never said a bad word to me, and what she'd said to Jeannie, it would later turn out, was in the spirit of reconciliation not disdain. She'd probably done us a huge favor, maybe even changed our whole future, who knew? A cool breeze blew—through a door that years of meditation had opened, a door to the room that held my worst mental patterns—and I said, "Mister J., be right back," and made myself walk across the gravel and up the worn wooden treads and through the door where someone had hung a sign that read BATHROOMS FOR THE USE OF POLITE PAYING CUSTOMERS ONLY!

Our family was spread out along the two packed aisles, admiring this or that novelty. Behind the glass counter, just as I'd guessed, stood a twice-as-old version of the woman who'd been there the last time I walked through the front door of Baring's general store. The face was cut even more deeply with lines. The hair ribboned with gray. The eyes carried that same load of hardened attention. I nodded at her and she nodded back, but of course she didn't remember me. I was one of thousands in her life, and she was one of one. "You won't remember me," I wanted to say. "I was here with my wife. Twenty-three years ago. We'd been having a fight. She stopped to talk with you and I came in and went to the toilet and then bought a Mounds bar on the way out. We made up later. It had something to do with you, I think. . . ."

But of course I said no such thing. Shelsa called out "Uncle Ott" and came up and leaned against my leg, and I hugged her. Natasha and Anthony pointed out the old logging tools and the deer head, long embalmed. Celia thanked the woman for letting them use the bathroom and bought some trail mix to be polite. And Rinpoche, still buzzing, was slapping his hands gently on the fronts of his thighs and swinging his head back and forth as he took in a rack of postcards. I bought three of them, eighty cents apiece, and set them on the glass counter. The others left. I could hear Shelsa singing in the parking lot. The woman made change and at last I said, "I was here once. Long time ago. With my wife. We were on a camping trip."

She raised one eyebrow—a scar ran through it—and said, "Lot of people come back."

8

Leading the way now, making the left turn, I was almost sure I had the correct road—both Jeannie and I had remembered the name. But it didn't quite match the picture in my mind. Maybe it was only that the trees had grown taller or the road was better maintained, or that part of the hillside to our right had broken off and tumbled down in a scree of sharp-edged, charcoal-colored boulders. I went along on faith, hoping I had it right. The gravel road turned this way and that, the river, on our left side, moved in and out of view. Another moment of doubt, and then the scene finally fit my memory of it: a slight rise, a turn to the right, a place where two vehicles could pull off and park. The trees were all fir there, sixty, eighty, a hundred feet tall, with rough brown trunks and short, horizontal branches. Sunlight touched the road, but in among the firs where the river ran—Smith Brook was the official name; it would always be a river to me—there was mainly shadow. Someone, some other young couple perhaps, had made a circle of stones there, just as Jeannie and I had done decades before. They'd left a few charred sticks and ashes. Just beyond, through a mossy glade speckled with boulders, the river ran fast and cold in a series of small rapids. I felt the sound of it in my chest.

Jeannie and I had set up the tent in our furious silence, like two workers who despised their job, then we'd gone off in separate directions to gather wood. I'd started a fire, and she'd brought out the small packet of sausages in aluminum foil, two potatoes, a thermos of wine that seemed all wrong now, a celebratory note amid disaster. The bugs assaulted us. We stayed as close to the smoke and as far from each other as we could, and cooked the meat and moved the potatoes around in the coals with sticks. I drank the wine. She abstained. We ate quickly, no eye contact, and while I cleaned up she made three trips to the river for water and doused the fire.

And then there was nothing to do but crawl into the tent, kill the mosquitoes that had followed us, take off some clothes and roll them up under our heads as pillows. There was the sound of the river, and the texture of sleeping bags against our bodies, layers of papery nylon, like a colder skin. In the hour since our arrival the temperature had dropped fifteen degrees.

We hadn't been in the tent long—Jeannie still and silent, and me worrying she'd fall asleep and we'd wake up to more misery—when another small puff of good wind blew through the dark forest of my mood and I pushed the words out. "I'm sorry. I was a jerk. An ass. Sorry."

Silence. Count of six or eight or ten, and then she turned toward me and was roughly pushing the material away and holding herself tight against me. "I hate to fight like that. I hate it, Otto. I *am* a know-it-all, you're right. And you *can* be a bastard, too. We're awful."

"We're doing okay," I said, "given who our parents are."

One choked syllable of laughter. "We're too old for that now. We have to carry our own shit now."

"Heavy load, in my case," I said.

She laughed and reached down and was yanking at the rest of the clothes I had on, then unzipping the length of the bag and sliding her face down along my belly the way she loved to do. There was something different about the lovemaking that night, though. It was more than the normal release a couple feels after an argument, more than the exhilaration of the great outdoors surrounding us. There was a mysterious new tenderness, and another feeling, too: a sense that we were touching something more than each other there in that cool darkness. I hope I've made it clear by this point that I'm not a person who puts much stock in the kookier aspects of life—my sister claimed that territory from our earliest days, and I yielded it to her without hesitation. But until my last breath I will swear that there was something wonderfully eerie about that lovemaking, a vivid sense of a larger world, as if some other spirit were breathing there between us.

Another little while and I was trying to be gentle—I remember that. Her back was on the tent fabric on the hard ground. She was crying out. And we would be linked forever by that hour.

I pulled the pickup a few feet off the road and got out. Jasper jumped down from the high cab and immediately trotted over toward Shelsa for a touch, then went sniffing the air and pissing, as his nature dictated. Shelsa seemed fascinated by the dark rocks on the far side of the road. Her mother followed her there, letting her climb and wander and explore. Anthony was looking off into the middle distance. Natasha was already crying. I felt Rinpoche watching me. There was no avoiding what we'd come there to do, but I felt, suddenly, that I couldn't do it. There was a finality to it that matched the finality of death so perfectly that I didn't want to experience it again.

From the narrow storage area behind the seat of the pickup I lifted the ceramic jar I'd carried across the country. Crazed, pearly white in color, with a copper handle in the center of a circular lid, it was a beautiful piece of handiwork, a gift to Jeannie from me on the occasion of Natasha's birth. Near the very end, when we'd stopped being able to pretend there was still hope, she'd asked to be cremated—we'd had exactly one conversation about it—and asked that her ashes be spread in this place. Beyond that, she hadn't specified. No particular time, no particular form to the service. I assumed, of course, that she'd want the kids to be there, but she hadn't ever said as much. Some people we knew designed an entire memorial ceremony before they passed on: musical selections, favorite readings, hand-picked speakers. But Jeannie wasn't like that. A woman of little fuss, the last thing she would have wanted was to have a big fuss made over the spreading of her ashes. We'd had a modest service in Bronxville—friends reading and remembering, a reception to follow, all of us numb. This was more personal. Our grief had thawed and matured and we were alone with it now—no kind neighbors, cousins, or ministers. No anesthesia at all.

I removed the tape from the porcelain jar and went over and stood on the spot where we'd once set up our tent. There were two dried gardenias sitting on top of the ashes—my wife had a

great passion for her flower garden. Natasha immediately came
and stood next to me, hooking her arm inside mine, shaking.
Anthony went and sat on a boulder by the river. From the first,
as I said, he'd been against having any kind of ceremony, and
had fought with me about it several times. It was Cecelia who'd
convinced him. In private. Dad not in the room. Here came
Aunt Seese now, smiling her peaceful smile, holding her jewel
of a daughter by the fingers of one hand. Rinpoche went over
and said a word to Anthony, then joined us. When I started to
call to my son, Rinpoche very subtly shook his head, and I
stopped and let Anthony be.

"This is what Jeannie asked me—" I managed to squeeze
up past the muscles of my throat. "Anybody who wants to can
. . . speak. This is what she asked—"

We were standing in a ragged circle. A few bugs pestered
us. A few thin rays of sunlight angled down through the boughs
of the trees. We could hear the river and smell its load of fresh-
ened air. My sister said, "We love you, Jeannie. We miss you.
We know you're in a better world and that we'll join you there
and that you're watching over us. We love you."

"Love you," Shelsa echoed.

We all looked at Natasha. Tears pouring down both sides of
her face now, eyelids flickering, lips trembling. "Mom," she
said. "Mom. Good-bye. Love you." She squeezed my arm hard
and completely broke down, weeping in a way that frightened
her cousin, and pushing her face against the sleeve of my shirt
just as she'd done in childhood. Rinpoche began to hum, and
then the humming transformed itself into a quiet chant in a
voice an octave lower than his normal speaking voice, two oc-
taves lower than the sound he made when he laughed. It was in

his native language, I assumed. Ortyk. A bubbling tongue from the steppes of southern Siberia, as mellifluous as it was impenetrable, water running across rounded stones. It went on and on, a minute, two minutes. Shelsa moved over next to him and without missing a beat he lifted her into his arms and kept on with it, eyes closed now, head swinging slightly left to right, all traces of the caffeine rush and morning hilarity gone. At last, he held one long final note and was finished. There was a pause. And just as I was about to speak he yelled out, "Jeannie!" very loudly, pronouncing it *Jannie*, as he'd always done. The name echoed and rebounded against the hillsides, and I glanced over at Anthony. He looked up, then down again, scratching a stick in the dirt between his splayed legs, miserable.

I lifted the flower petals out of the jar, squeezed them tight in my hand and tossed them into the air. I hadn't prepared any words but what came to me was this: "My gift. My precious gift. I give you back." And then I felt foolish and self-conscious. It didn't help that when I went to throw the ashes into the air the breeze sent some of them back against our clothes. Tasha sobbed and sobbed. Celia had a smile frozen on her face and tears running into it. Rinpoche was bouncing his daughter in his arms, whispering something in her ear. There were ashes still in the jar. I dug my fingers in and tossed them up as best I could, and held the jar out to my daughter, who wouldn't touch them.

And then, mercifully, it was over. There was nothing left to do. Rinpoche put Shelsa up on his shoulders, one leg to either side of his neck. Tasha mumbled something angrily about her brother and let Celia wrap an arm around her. I closed the jar and walked over to where my son sat and I put a hand on his shoulder and said, "Let's go. It's okay . . ."

He stood up and looked at me, half furious that I'd forced this on him, that I'd tried to break apart the smooth manly exterior he'd built up through years of football and wrestling camaraderie, the steady girlfriends, the broken this and bruised that, the triumphant survival of high school and his first college year. He was glaring into my eyes, a cargo of tears there, willed not to fall.

"One thing," I said, though I hadn't planned on saying it. "One thing you should know."

"What?"

"This place. That spot where we were standing. That was the place we made Natasha, your mom and I."

It was another in a series of things I shouldn't have said to him, one more in a string of awkward moments. For some reason, with his departure for college the year before, with the trauma in our home since then, I'd lost the ability to speak to my son. It was nothing like the arguments we'd had in his one bad teenage year, more subtle than that, cause for great distance. I would almost have preferred the old fights.

The look he gave me then, blank but fringed with anger, seemed to say, "What am I supposed to do with that, Dad?" But instead of speaking he leaned in and gave me a hug that could snap your spine, and held on that way, neck to neck, for ten seconds, and then turned and walked fast toward the car. Grown up.

9

I think, in some way, our own grief embarrassed us. For months we'd dammed up the feelings, trying to get through the days, trying to pretend away the enormous absence in the house. And then, on that little patch of moist, buggy land, we'd been naked again, flooded with feelings, and it was almost too much. We said our good-byes quickly. There was a short discussion about Jasper: I thought it might be easier on him to travel the road with Rinpoche and me rather than go back to Seattle and—if the Amtrak authorities consented—get packed up again for the train ride east. But Natasha, speaking on her cousin's behalf, wouldn't hear of it. "No way, Dad. Just no way," she said, and none of us wanted a battle then.

So she and Anthony and Celia and Shelsa headed down the road, throwing up a cloud of dust in front of Rinpoche and me. They took a right turn onto the highway. Anthony tooted twice and accelerated, and I watched him go all the way up the long hill and over the top, watched until they were out of sight. Rinpoche and I went straight across the two climbing lanes into a sort of island cutout, turned left, and began the long descent of the Cascades' eastern slope in the company of a collection of cyclists who'd been driven to the ski area at the top of the pass and were joyfully gliding down.

At first, besides the cyclists and trees, there wasn't much of interest along the sides of this road. We were riding with the triangular windows open and the main ones partly lowered; the temperature seemed to be climbing a degree a minute, and I kept one eye on the gauge, expecting the worst. A broad, slow-moving river appeared to our right, spotted with islands of deadfall, oblong and irregular, that resembled poorly constructed beaver dams. Another mile, and the water went crashing over a long rapids and then spilled across the top of a concrete dam.

"What is?" my companion asked, pointing. I could feel a sadness radiating from him, and I wondered if leaving his daughter and wife to make a five-or-six-day trip with his bereaved brother-in-law was something he'd been coerced into doing. I hadn't been crazy about the idea myself, but at least I stood to learn something from him. What could he get from me? More weight and worry? Bits of info on the American scene? I told myself I'd at least try to be a decent friend.

I explained the way dams worked, and he seemed suddenly fascinated, as if he'd never before encountered the concept. This was the Rinpoche I knew, a man of quick enthusiasms where they were least expected. On our previous road trip, six days from New Jersey to North Dakota, he had formed a fascination with tenpin bowling, miniature golf, casino gambling and Hershey's Kisses. What would it be this time? Dams? Corn dogs? Rodeos?

"I like this idea wery much," he said, when I'd finished my

explanation. "All the water blocked up and then from it we get the power."

It was some kind of spiritual metaphor for him, I supposed, but I didn't want to go there just then. We talked for a while about windmills and solar panels, and then about the recent oil boom that had changed the North Dakotan landscape. Most of the action was to the north and west of where I'd grown up, and where Rinpoche and Cecelia now ran their retreat center. The world there had changed: jobs, oil rigs, bigger trucks; in Williston not enough housing for the newly arrived workers, traffic jams, an atmosphere of roughness in the bars and stores. The retreat center—my brother-in-law oversaw four more of them in Europe, but he'd delegated most of that work now—was as untouched by the energy boom as it was by everything else that went on in the ordinary world. Celia and Rinpoche inhabited a kind of sacred vacuum, almost entirely insulated from the life around them (though Celia said her husband had made friends with the local farmers and was learning about the growing of durum wheat and soybeans). It wasn't that he showed no interest in ordinary life; it was more that the ratio was flipped. I was immersed in commuter train schedules and peevish authors, car insurance bills (with two young drivers!) and tuition payments, the mechanic, the landscaper, the presidential race . . . and I made a little time each day for meditation and spiritual reading. Rinpoche meditated at least four hours every day, and spent time teaching, giving talks, writing books on the interior life, and rereading the sacred volumes left by other teachers in his lineage. And he made a little time each day for life's regular old activities: chatting with the farmer who leased our acreage, digging in the garden, watching two minutes of the news, taking walks with his wife. Over the years of our acquaintance I had come to see that their understanding of "real" was fundamentally different from mine and Jeannie's. It was more than a matter of emphasis. A kind of continental divide separated us: their thoughts started out close to mine—we loved our children, cared for our homes and bodies—then ran down different slopes, to other seas. Their definition of reality—of what could happen, and what could not—was, in places, as different from ours as a chocolate chip from a caper.

As I think I mentioned, because one of the effects of bereavement is a certain inability to perform mundane tasks with any efficiency, I'd allowed my sister to make the arrangements for the first two days of our trip. It was, as Anthony noted, a risk. Before leaving home I'd worried that Cecelia would put us up in a youth hostel in West Seattle someplace, that Anthony and Natasha and I would end up sleeping in bunks, making our own breakfast from a plastic bag of old granola and a carton of soy milk. But my sister, it turned out, knew me well, and she was nothing if not kind, and so she'd set us up in Jarvis's B and B, a place of cairns, good coffee, and a heated pool. A compromise, in other words. She'd even found lodging for Rinpoche and me for this, our second night. It went by the strange name Cave B Inn, just outside the central Washington town of Quincy. The "inn" part of this appealed to me, I have to say. Appealed to me as much as the "cave" part did not. I pictured myself, tired from the emotional strain and long drive and from having been bounced around in the old pickup, pulling up to the entrance of a funky motel with stone walls and no windows. It wouldn't even be Cave A, where the better-heeled adventurers slept. It was Cave *B*. Hard class. Steerage. You rode an old coal

66

car down into darkness; you went to sleep wrapped in a musty blanket.

I decided not to think about it.

Strangely enough, as we went down and down into the heat and the approaches to the town of Leavenworth, Washington, I discovered that the ceremony had skimmed a layer of sadness from my thoughts. It wasn't like I'd left Jeannie behind there on Smith Brook Road. There would be no leaving her behind. There would be no "closure"—a word I'd come to despise—no sudden relief from the awfulness of watching her die, not for me. At the same time, though, if I am to be completely honest, I have to say that the ceremony lifted part of the weight off my chest, ushered me into a new stage. It may have been the spreading of her ashes, or it may have been the presence of the man beside me, known around the world as a spiritual master but known to me as the guy who'd been nuts enough to marry my sister. Rinpoche went through his days surrounded by an eerie peacefulness, a cocoon of calm. I sometimes wondered if anything could hurt or worry him.

Leavenworth—it was Celia who suggested we stop there for lunch—turned out to be a place of amiable oddness. I began to suspect as much as we entered the town, driving past a large sign with WILKOMMEN written on it. German, as far as I knew, had not suddenly been voted the native tongue of central Washington State. Soon we pulled into the commercial district—temperature into the nineties at this point—and were surrounded by buildings in the Black Forest Chalet style, with the cutout porch railings, the colorful facades, the scores of hanging plants. Taking an open curbside spot, I noticed that the street signs said things like Park Strasse and Alpensee Strasse. I heard music from a bandstand and half expected to see Bavarians in lederhosen marching down the middle of the avenue blowing mountain flutes and singing "Edelweiss."

My sister, who has no sense of irony whatsoever, must have done a bit of research on Leavenworth, Washington. It must have seemed somehow appropriate to her that, given our German ancestry, the first post-ceremony meal I should have with her husband would be in this replica of a Bavarian village. Retired couples and vacationing families strolled past shops selling puzzles and fudge, and milled near motels with names like Der Ritterhof Motor Inn and Bavarian Ritz. In some other mood it might have sickened me. As much pleasure as they offer the traveling masses, I'm not a huge fan of Las Vegas's fake Venices or the tidy Disney towns of central Florida. I like the real, the tattered, the grit and rust of Manhattan, the docks of Bridgeport, the factories of Fall River, the hot old tobacco towns off I-95 in North Carolina with their brick courthouses and boarded-up furniture mills.

But Leavenworth had a sense of humor about itself, or it least it seemed so to me on that afternoon. I was hungry, besides, and there appeared to be an abundance of eating places. I should elaborate on something I said earlier and admit here again that I have a problem with food. The problem consists a) in my liking it too much, and b) in a certain adventurism nurtured by the white-bread-and-potato cuisine of the Dakota prairie and brought to ripeness by years as an editor of food books, in a part of the world unmatched in the variety of its culinary offerings. I was fussy, I knew that, perhaps even a bit of a snob. But most of us have our fussy spots, our territories of indulgence, don't we? Coffee, wine, an obsession with watching sports or with travel, cars, or clothing, a passion for hiking, an addiction to sex, work, cocaine, shopping, talking? Aren't we all creatures of quirk and fetish? To me, eating well had always seemed a benign addiction. I was no glutton. I exercised, tried not to overdo. That summer I'd taken to jogging with Anthony on weekend mornings. But I loved good food, loved a varied diet, and I had the notion, driving past the WILKOMMEN sign, that a tasty bratwurst and a stein of lager would go a good distance toward softening the morning's rough edges.

Rinpoche seemed not to notice that we'd stepped out of the pickup and into Kaiser Wilhelm II's back yard. He could be that way. Focused on some other dimension as he so often was, some other precinct of reality, the surfaces of the modern world could be lost on him completely. He had not yet lived long enough in America, or seen enough of our land, to be able to tell, say, that he was driving through a rich neighborhood or a poor one; he had no radar for class, almost none for race or ethnicity. As far as he was concerned, with its dirndl-wearing waitress, German beer flags, and paintings of Rhine castles on the walls, Café Christa, the second-floor restaurant to which I introduced him in Leavenworth, might as well have been a Five Guys Burgers and Fries off any interstate anywhere from Baton Rouge to Berkeley.

The hostess led us to a table. I took my place there, staring out the window at a make-believe maypole and a man on the bandstand playing the accordion and singing Johnny Cash. In my peripheral vision I could see that Rinpoche was noiselessly mouthing a prayer. The waitress approached, a happy creature named Monica with a nice smile, and an outfit of pale blue stringed bodice and flats appropriate to some fantastical Germany of another era. Bratwurst sandwich and a mug of darkish beer for me; salad and water for Rinpoche. She thanked us, gathered the menus, and did not spend one extra second eye-balling my companion's robe. Maybe she thought he was being forced to dress up for his job, too; maybe there was a Tibetan or Mongolian festival on the next block, near the corner of Parkstrasse and Playgroundstrasse, and he was taking a break for lunch.

"Celia found us a hotel for the night," I said. "An inn, actually. It's another couple hours down the road."

Rinpoche looked at me and nodded. No, that's not correct: he wasn't looking *at* me then; he was looking *through* me. I was hungry, ready for the soothing ritual of consuming food, replaying the spreading of ashes in my mind's eye, worrying, already, about the kids, trying to make a little small talk to ease the moment . . . and he was already beyond that, or below it, slicing through the niceties with his gold-flecked eyes. "A little bit maybe," he said, "Otto's sister make him angry."

"Not at all."

Another nod, two skeptical downward beats. Smile muscles flexing around the eyes, nothing more. "Little bit, maybe," he said.

"Anger's not the right word."

"Piss-ed," he said, trying out his slang.

"Not exactly, no. She pushes my buttons, that's all. Always has. The food rules—everything organic or local or good for you. The idea that everything, every decision, down to what kind of toilet paper to put in the bathroom, everything has to answer to some god of environmental guilt. The idea that we can't make the smallest mark on the earth or it will be ruined forever.

The belief that one should always be happy, smiling, upbeat, unruffled. The belief in angels and helping spirits, voices from the beyond. Hard for me, that's all. I'm a practical guy, ordinary. I take what the world gives."

Rinpoche said, "Ah," and smiled.

"All right," I admitted under his steady gaze. "A little bit pissed. Now especially. It's a hard day for me, for us. A hard time. But I love her, you know that."

Monica brought the water and salad and beer and Rinpoche thanked her. He had the habit—open to misinterpretation in these parts—of making physical contact with the serving people. Man, woman, old, young, attractive or not, Dunkin' Donuts, Ruth's Chris Steak House, it didn't matter. He thanked them, he touched a hand or shoulder, held on to a finger and squeezed. Some of them liked it and some of them did not. Monica melted, smiled, walked away.

"What is this 'buttons'?" he asked.

"It's an American expression. If you have, well, a doorbell, for example, you push the button and you get an immediate response. An elevator. A light switch. The expression refers to things people do that get a response from you, almost always a negative response. A child refuses to go to bed, for example, and he pushes your buttons. You get frustrated, upset. You might raise your voice."

"Piss-ed you on, yes?"

"*Off.* Pisses you off. Yes. Or just irritates or annoys."

"What does the buttons come from?"

"What do you mean?"

"Where is it, this buttons?"

"It's a reflex. Certain things irritate certain people, that's all.

Everyone—"*Everyone has them*, I'd started to say. But in Rinpoche's case I wasn't so sure. More than six years I'd known him, and if there were buttons, I'd never seen them pushed. Nothing about my sister seemed to particularly irritate him. It was irritating.

"What from?" he persisted.

As I was pondering this question the bratwurst sandwich arrived, accompanied by a scoop of dryish potato salad and a very nice pickle. I had a bite before answering, a swig of beer. "Who knows? From childhood, maybe. Some people like beer and some like wine, and some people don't like either. Certain kinds of behavior irritate certain people, that's all."

He nodded and crunched lettuce, absorbing this lesson in the ways of the non-monkish world. "Buttons wery important, these buttons," he said after a minute.

"Not really. One learns to live with things. A burp of disagreement now and then, that's all. A passing annoyance."

"'Life is unsatisfaction', Buddha said."

"I thought he said, 'Life is suffering'."

"No, no. That is a bad translation. In Ortyk it is *zhesta fallu nas*. *'Nas'*, it means 'unsatisfaction,' not 'suffering.'"

"*Dis*-satisfaction, we say."

"Same thing. Always in life it is. You have a dissatisfaction with your sister. You want that she should be not how she is. Should be like you want her to be."

"Not so much that, but—"

"You want life to be that way, how you want it. Small and big things. You want that Jeannie shouldn't die."

"Of course I want that she shouldn't die! Wouldn't you want that for someone you love? The mother of your kids? Your friend, your partner? What, I'm supposed to not want that?"

"Of course," he said. "Me and you, same thing."

Monica swung by with a worried look on her face. "Everything okay?"

"Perfect," I said. And then, when she was gone, to Rinpoche with a bit of an edge in my voice, "You don't have buttons?"

"Million buttons," he said.

"Then how come I've never seen them? Seese doesn't irritate you in the least. Shelsa yells and fusses, you laugh. We get caught in traffic, you breathe. You're buttonless. Perpetually satisfied."

He laughed again. "The buttons show you the linc where you stop," he said.

"I was talking about you."

"*Us.* Buttons show *us*, Otto. Patient, patient, good, good, calm, calm, and then," he chopped his hand down on the table like a karate teacher. The silverware jumped. "Button! Not what we want to be. Hah!"

"Very funny."

He shook his head. "Sometimes wery sad. But important. It's the place to work for you, for me. You feel the buttons and you work there."

"How?"

"First, you only look. You see. You see wery deep into the buttons and you maybe change a little. Cecelia has a friend who is, how you say, doesn't see?"

"Blind."

"Who is blind. Maybe you'll meet her soon. What happens to her, even the blind, she always says 'yes.'"

"I don't want to always say yes. To Jeannie's death, for onc huge example. Who would want to say yes to that? Who would want to be blind?"

"Nobody," he said, as if agreeing with me. "I don't want. You don't. Nobody."

"Exactly my point."

"Me, too, the same," he said.

I had a long drink of the beer. He was pushing my buttons, the good monk. Pushing them to the point where I had stopped really hearing what he was trying to say. Chewing bratwurst with a vengeance, sipping beer like it was a cure-all, I had a few moments of wishing I'd spent two days in Seattle—at the art deco Maxwell Hotel, for example, a favorite spot I'd recommended to Seese and the kids. Touring the islands perhaps, wading in the sea, then flying back to the comfort of my house. The sanity of the crossword puzzle, the company of my old dog.

"Beer good?" he asked.

"Not bad. Want a sip?"

He surprised me by taking the glass into one thick hand and raising it to his lips. I'd never known him to drink, or, before this trip, to use caffeine. He and Cecelia were the purest of souls in that way. He took a small taste and made a face as if he'd sampled month-old rainwater from a puddle on the porch. "Ooh."

"On the bitter side. I like it that way."

"Bubbles from metal," he said.

"You're dissatisfied. You wish it tasted differently."

He laughed approvingly and pointed at me. "Good. Otto, my friend, my brother-and-law, is working in the buttons place now."

"Thank you for the lesson."

"You're welcome. What is this music in the window?"

"Country. The late, great Johnny Cash. A famous singer. He went to prison, also, like you."

"Now died?"

"Yes, a few years ago. This is his music."

"Little bit sad," Rinpoche said.

"Yes."

"But it makes you feel happy."

"Yes, you're right."

He turned down the corners of his lips and nodded in time to the beat, as if Johnny Cash, too, had left his music as confirmation of some profound spiritual lesson. Yes, there was sadness—prison, death, heartbreak, addiction. Yes, of course. Let me make of it good music.

My brother-in-law took a piece of the rye bread and wiped the salad bowl with it, picking up the oil and vinegar and two small strips of onion and lettuce there, wasting absolutely nothing. "I think," he said, "in my next book I'll write about this buttons place. What you do there. How you work."

"You'll sell millions."

"I need a good editor now," he said, looking up at me with his head still tilted down. "Want a job?"

"I already have a job, but thanks."

"Maybe, sure," he said, without much conviction. He'd suggested, more than once, that I was in the wrong profession. Karmically out of place in this world.

"I'll help you out with it if you want, though."

"Thank you, my friend," he said, and we ordered herbal tea and coffee and sat there for a while—getting used to each other again, it seemed to me. Four or five or six days we were going to spend on the road together; there was no fixed plan. It might seem a strange way to use one's vacation time—a road trip with an eccentric monk—but I was already fingering my hidden parcel of hope then. I had long ago gingerly taken hold of the idea that my brother-in-law knew something I didn't know, about the living of life, and about dying. It was an intangible something, of course. Unlike, say, the ability to play the piano or hammer a nail, his particular skill was invisible, vaporous, the kind of thing that made itself known only subtly, periodically, in certain kinds of moments. Those moments had included, for me, his presence at my dying wife's bedside. There was something magnificent in his way of being with her, an unruffled straightforwardness combined with the deepest compassion, a facing of the situation head-on, without pity or discomfort or the smallest false note. He'd run a center for the dying somewhere in Italy. He knew life at a level I did not; I'd admitted that long ago. I wanted him to teach me.

Before we left Cafe Christa, Monica told us that Leavenworth had been a thriving town a hundred years earlier, but when the rail depot moved to Wenatchee and things changed in the lumber industry the town had fallen into the dark hole that's the resting place of so many other American communities. The world of commerce evolves so quickly, and with such little regard for the human beings involved, that whole cities—take Detroit, take Gary, take the old mill towns of New England—go into a decline from which it seems they'll never be rescued. It was like that with Leavenworth, she said, until some enterprising genius came up with the idea of making it into a replica of a Bavarian village. I could imagine the scene. People, he must have argued, would always look for a fun place to go on vacation. They wanted exotic without having to fly ten hours. So what about, say, authentic German sights, sounds, and tastes without having to board an airplane and learn the future tense of "to be blond"? I could picture the discussion around some wooden conference table in the early sixties, the mockery and disbelief, the genius's persistence, one or two men with money eventually being swayed. The genius had been right— Leavenworth not only came back to life, it blossomed and bore fruit. He'd pushed them out of their zone of assumption.

I paid for lunch, thanking the kindly Monica twice. We stopped for a moment in a small bookstore near where we'd left the pickup, then headed out, past the willows in the park and the fellow playing Johnny Cash and Die Musik Box Store. Across the Wenatchee River we went, and back into the American Northwest.

10

There, beyond the dry backside of the Cascades, the landscape
underwent a sudden change. In place of fir-coated slopes, we
were now driving our grumbling old Uma past dry hills the col-
or of a peanut shell, with well-irrigated apple and pear orchards
carpeting the valleys. There was a sign for a winery, a few poor
homes and poorer-looking trailers, an advertisement for roller
derby. Rinpoche lolled his head to one side and dozed, and I
turned on the radio, quietly, and found a sermon in progress.
Listening to such shows was another odd hobby of mine. I indulged on long drives, mostly, and only for brief stretches, but I
heard some disturbing and unforgettable things.

"God," this speaker was announcing to the prairies of eastern Washington, "has no intention of spending eternity with a
loser." I pondered this during a commercial break. I remembered reading in parts of the Bible of my youth that God rewarded the righteous with herds of oxen and barns full of grain,
with multitudes of children and servants and all good things.
We were coming back to that, it seemed to me, at least in some
circles. Wealth had become, again, a sign of being favored by

the Lord. And it didn't seem to matter one iota how the wealth had been gained. No matter if the mansions I saw now atop the dry hills just east of Monitor belonged to people who worked someone else to the bone for minimum wage or less. They were prosperous. Non-losers. Smiled upon by the Great Winner above. It was akin to the malevolent creed that equated illness with moral decay, that blamed the sick.

But the rest of the sermon was about character and doing good deeds, and it made some sense to me. "A corrupt tree cannot bring forth good fruit," the voice on the radio intoned. Okay. But very, very few of the people I knew warranted the label "corrupt." There were no thieves that we knew of among our circle of friends, relatives and co-workers, no rapists, murderers, or big-time cheats. Surely Jeannie and I and Natasha and Anthony had lived our lives according to the ancient Judeo-Christian idea of treating others the way we ourselves wished to be treated. For most of my life I'd taken a kind of refuge in that, neither a loser nor a grievous sinner. I'd been content with decency, with thoughtful parenthood and volunteering, with writing checks to charities and commiserating with disconsolate friends. I was a believer, but not a churchgoer. An upstanding, upper-middle-class man who tutored poor African-American kids once a week and went to his daughter's soccer matches and his son's football games, who didn't cheat on his wife or his taxes and put in an honest day's work.

And then I met Volya Rinpoche, Celia's boyfriend at the time, a chunky, sort-of Russian, sort-of Buddhist who looked like he hailed from Tibet or Nepal and who wrote books and ran retreat centers and meditated four hours a day. And he had tipped over the applecart of my self-satisfaction. Decency, good-

79

ness, and charity—all fine and well, he seemed to say without actually saying it. Not hurting others—wery good, Otto! But that, for him, was merely a platform. A flat place on the rocky cliffs, high above the sea in Acapulco. You couldn't stand there all day admiring your tan and quadriceps. You had to dive off into some terrifying interior world of meditation, prayer, and deep awareness. You had to step off that comfortable perch and fly and splash down into the workings of your mind, your "thought patterns" or "thought stream," as he put it in his books. I fought it, naturally. Of course I fought it. Surrounded as I was by millions of ordinary, uncorrupt peers who went to church or synagogue once a week, or eschewed belief altogether and still lived the upright life, I saw no reason to make that dive. For a long time I had seen no reason to make it.

I turned off the radio and thought about my kids, my wife, the larger questions. It seemed to me that almost all of us took the simple fact of our existence completely for granted—that is, until the expiration date appeared. We grew up, looked around to see how others were dealing with this strange predicament, and made our stand in what were mostly unoriginal ways. Our style of living was a wholesome one—safe, pleasurable, marked by duty and love. But maybe it could also be an anesthetic, and maybe it took a huge jolt of pain in order to reach through that cushion and move us.

Rinpoche stirred and burped. I guided the rumbling pickup through the edge of the busy little town of Wenatchee, where some of the signs were in Spanish and where I saw my first cowboy hat, the West's signature. There was a huge thin cross on top of one of the hills there—ten stories tall, it must have been. What did it really mean? What did the world's two billion

Christians read into it? What would Jesus have said, really, if he could see the way we spent our time now, the mansions and wars, the Super PACs, hungry kids, and hundred-million-dollar athletes? What would Buddha do about capital punishment? Before meeting Rinpoche I'd gone forty-some years without asking questions like that on anything other than the most superficial level.

Vast sweeps of ochre hillsides now, another planet. Here, too, tongues of green licked along the bases of the brown hills. Rinpoche awoke in time to catch sight of a sign for a golf course. What was the most important difference, he wanted to know, between the miniature version he so enjoyed and golf on the big course?

It's like the difference between my idea of the spiritual before I met you, I wanted to say, and my idea of it now. One is safe, one a minefield of failure and frustration, with perhaps the potential for a larger joy. But I took refuge in an ordinary explanation instead. More clubs, I told him. Bigger swings. Shoes in two colors and electric carts and cursing.

Not far beyond the golf course we passed another dam—more excitement—and a stretch of striking vistas: great humps of toasted earth everywhere. A vineyard, and then, far below us to the right, the Columbia River cutting its path like a twelve-hundred-mile, blue-gray snake.

As we drove into Quincy we saw windmills on a ridge, a hundred of them or more. There were huge fruit warehouses and, as if for the edification of curious travelers, fields with signs announcing the crops: BEANS. ALFALFA. SPEARMINT. PEPPERMINT. FIELD CORN. WHEAT. I tried to imagine my father and mother putting such things by the side of the roads that bounded their property. They would have thought it absurd, a waste of energy. People, real people, were just supposed to know.

We turned onto Baseline Road, past thirty-foot-high stacks of hay bales covered with plastic tarpaulins, the fields baking under an enormous sky with fluffy clouds on display. Another right, and there it was, a sign for Cave B, my sister's idea of fine lodging. I girded myself and said a quiet prayer for patience.

— ⁓ II

The prayer, it would turn out, wasn't needed. You reached the office of the Cave B Inn and Spa via a long entrance road with grapevines growing on either side. At the end of this promenade stood a modern-looking two-story building, all glass and stone and curved roofs. Just beyond it the land descended gradually in a scrub-brush-spotted savannah that stretched a mile or more to the river. On the opposite bank stood an intricate massif of basalt cliffs, miles of them, rising hundreds of feet from the water's edge. From our vantage point you could see past the tops of these cliffs to an enormous, parched, folded, sage-covered plain that rose and rose, gently, as far as the eye could see. "Looks," Rinpoche said after a moment of staring, "like my home."

It may have looked like southernmost Siberia, that enclave of Buddhism in communism's old frozen heart, but the building where we checked in was thoroughly American and newly made, reminiscent of a ski lodge. Beside the pretty young woman at the desk stood a bowl of cherries. I sampled, she checked her register. They were expecting us, the welcome was warm, all was well . . . until she pronounced this sentence: "We have you booked in two of our yurts for one night, Mr. Ringling."

I thought she was kidding. Cecelia must have conspired with the young woman in order to play a practical joke on her brother. "Yurts?" I said, playing along.

Smiling all the while, the woman led us across the lodge's copious main room to a set of high windows that took full advantage of the view. She gestured to her left. And there they were, white and purple round-topped tents baking in the sun. Air-conditioned, I assumed, but still baking in the sun. I did not want to stay in a yurt. I found the word to have an ugly sound, like "blog" or "pus" or "puberty." I had visions of waking with a sore back after a night of imagining wild horses neighing on the Mongolian steppe. I am not, I wanted to tell her, a yurt-type person. Not many New Yorkers are. My sister is a yurt-type person. No doubt my companion here is yurt-friendly, but my yurtish days are behind me, thank you. Can you recommend a nearby hotel?

But, not wanting to offend, I held my tongue.

"I think you'll really like them," she said.

"They look . . . cozy. But I have some spinal issues and—"

Behind us, Rinpoche was eating from the bowl, one cherry after the next, storing the pits in his left cheek, paying no attention. Even the word "yurt" hadn't roused him.

"Oh, they're quite luxurious inside, you'll see."

"I'm sure they are, but . . . are there other accommodations?"

"The cliff-houses," she said, smiling.

Those must be the caves, then. And so here was our choice: a Mongolian tent or a cave in the cliffside. Lying in the luxurious yurt fighting off dreams of Genghis Khan, or turning and tossing on bare stone. My sister would consider both options charming, authentic, in keeping with the tough-bodied original inhabitants of this sacred land.

But the clerk was pointing again, and the structures she indicated were not set into the cliff at all but perched on the crest of their land. One of them half faced us. I could see window-walls looking out on the view. I thought I spotted actual furniture inside.

"I think my brother-in-law and I would be more comfortable in the cliffs," I told her. "He comes, in fact, from a cliff-dwelling people. Are they two-bedrooms or one?"

She returned to the desk to check availability, and I changed the purpose of my prayers. Kind Lord, may I sleep in a cliffhouse tonight.

A moment. A hesitation. The nicely sculpted, uplifted face, the perfect smile that came, perhaps, from three years of orthodontia (I sympathized with her parents): a cliff house was available! And she didn't think her manager would mind her giving it to us at the same rate as the two yurts.

It didn't take me long, approximately three seconds, to close the deal. According to the pamphlet she handed us with our keys, Cave B had a spa, a wine-tasting room, and an outdoor swimming pool that looked down on the view. That news, that moment, was the beginning of something lifting up and away from me. I'm not saying the luxury of the place lessened my sorrow; this was a different weight, the weight of my feelings about my sister. In a nutshell, I had always loved Celia without admiring her worldview. The mocking interior voice I'd cultivated as a teenager had abated over the past few years, but only partly. We were different. We would always be different. Given the opportunity, she would always book me into a yurt, and given the opportunity, I would always upgrade to the luxurious cliff house.

But—and this was a momentous *but* for us—at that moment I saw that she had started to make a small change in my direction. Yes, she'd booked me into a yurt, but it was a *luxurious* yurt, and, as foolish as that may sound to someone outside our family, it was to become a landmark for me. There was hope for us to alter our relationship. I would eat her sawdust bread the next time I visited. I would try as hard as I possibly could not to mock her in my mind. I would remember her many kindnesses to my wife and my children. Remember them, really. Keep them always in view.

Carried along on this new vow, I drove the pickup the few hundred yards downhill, parked near Cliffhouse #11, and unlocked the door. Miraculous. Two big bedrooms separated by a living room with leather couch and stone fireplace, TV, gorgeous old desk. One bath with Italian tile and glass shower. Floor-to-ceiling windows facing out on a small patio and the world-class vista. It was a place where I could happily have served a life sentence.

Rinpoche, of course, did not appear to notice, or to care. Comfort seemed not to matter to him. A bed, a bathroom, a little something to eat—that was all he asked for. The size of the bed, the firmness of the mattress and pillows, thread count, color, tile or linoleum, strong shower or weak, a bowl of cherries or a five-course gourmet dinner—it was literally all the same to him, and for me it was the difference between deep relaxation and the nagging little voice of . . . dissatisfaction. I was spoiled, to use a word I dislike. I admit that. Standing at the window, smiling, soaking up the view, I wondered how that had happened. Gradually at first, and then suddenly, as Hemingway had written about a character's bankruptcy. Perhaps it had something to do with age. In our twenties, Jeannie and I had been perfectly happy to camp, perfectly satisfied with our third-floor Chelsea walkup, where the mattress sagged, the shower on full blast could barely put out a candle, and our idea of a fancy night out was dinner at the four-dollar Indian buffet on Ninth Avenue. Those years had been a kind of Garden of Eden for us. And then came the better jobs, the promotions, the house in Bronxville where our neighbors all had granite countertops and gave dinner parties with good wine. The thirties, the forties, the hard work of child rearing; our bodies changing beneath us like disloyal friends—an ache, a strain, minor surgery, expensive and unavoidable dental work, trouble digesting certain foods. It began to seem to us—to me, at least—that we were *owed* a comfortable life. After all, everyone in our circle of friends stayed in four-or five-star hotels when traveling and drove cars that were new or almost new. Having less than that was somehow wrong, the sign of a loser, someone disliked by God . . . even as we were acutely aware of the poverty and suffering that lay twenty minutes south of us on the train. How had that happened?

Rinpoche set his oversized cloth handbag on his bed. I suggested a swim. He enthusiastically agreed. We changed in our separate spaces and when he reappeared I saw that he had not yet been advised to upgrade from his too-small Speedo. Perhaps my sister never saw him in it; he saved it for road trips with Otto. Maybe she saw him in it and liked it. For my part, I hoped he'd cover up with the customary maroon robe, but the Cave B seemed to have brought out the wild man in him. There were pink flip-flops, a new wardrobe addition; the robe stayed in his room. We closed the heavy wooden door and set off along the path.

Side by side we went, brushed by grape leaves and greeted along the way by a couple with wet hair. The water, they said, was "properly refreshing." Aha! We went through the gate, Rinpoche and I, and staked out two of the metal chaises. The pool was nowhere over my head, lined with stone, inviting; our gaze was drawn down the dry slope to the river, and then out to the massifs beyond. Two young couples, one white, one black, each with a single son, lounged in the shaded area, all eyes on the wide fellow in the tiny suit and pink flip-flops. I saw glossy magazines, gold jewelry, what appeared to be a champagne bottle upside-down in an ice bucket. I splashed in and swam a lap, looked up. There was my friend doing his Skovorodian yoga, a sequence of bizarre postures—one leg and then the other held straight out in front of him for the count of thirty, both arms wrapped around his head as if he were twisting it off, a deep squat, a leap and grunt, a tiptoe stance with fists in armpits. I'd seen it before, exactly once, on a sandy beach in northern Minnesota, but it was an unforgettable display, equal parts stunning flexibility, surprising strength, and clownish theater. I swam another lap and tried to pretend he was traveling alone. It didn't work. We'd been seen together. Another lap, the children laughing now and being shushed, the men turning away, the women enchanted. At last it was over. Rinpoche made a whoop and, ignoring the NO DIVING notices, catapulted himself headfirst into the water, legs splayed, arms working in air before the splash, then swam the length of the pool and back again without taking a breath. I could do nothing but watch. When he surfaced, chest heaving, shaved head glistening in the sun, he stood triumphantly at one end of the pool, taking in the children's faces as though they'd been encouraging him the whole time, then searching out mine. "Fun, Otto, is swimming!" he yelled, rather loudly. "Fun!"

There was no disputing it.

12

After our swim, Rinpoche retired for meditation and I enjoyed a half hour of wine tasting and a stroll along the grounds.

Staked into the dry soil here and there were small signs warning of snakes, but I saw nothing more dangerous than a startled ring-necked killdeer protecting her nest. A perusal of the dining situation and the inn's Panorama Restaurant turned up news of a five-course *prix fixe* dinner for $69, more if you chose the matched wines. The view, the cliffhouse, the exercise, my new good feelings about Cecelia, the promise of a fine meal, a text from Natasha saying they were safely back in Seattle and about to take Shelsa downstairs for the Maxwell's superb pizza—it felt only proper to give thanks, so I returned to #11, sat with a pillow behind my back on the leather couch, and tried to calm my mind in the manner the good monk had shown me.

Jeannie's death—so painful and premature—had sent her spirit spinning into some other dimension of the universe, and had broken open a dam in what Rinpoche called the "thought-stream" of my mind. Six years of fairly regular practice, and I'd been able, not to stop that stream—that wasn't the point—but to slow it down, to modulate it. Exactly, it occurred to me then, the way an actual dam modulated a river. When I needed to think quickly and in complex fashion, I could. But when I needed a bit of rest, on a long flight or a sleepless hour, say, I could step into a quiet interior room for a stretch of time and find peace.

That peaceful room had been flooded now. Thoughts, all kinds of thoughts, tumbled and rushed in a tumultuous interior whitewater, and I wondered if even a spiritual master of a brother-in-law would ever be able to build another dam among the ruins.

Still, I sat there and tried. There was the usual run of thoughts—the kids, the upcoming meal, the water in my left ear, the ceremony at Smith Brook, Jeannie, Cecelia, Jeannie, the scene at the pool, Jeannie, Anthony, Natasha, work. Jeannie. Once she'd really started to suffer I seemed to lose completely the ability to put a space between those thoughts, to sink down into the edge of the world Rinpoche always inhabited. I'd been doing so well for a while. I'd even gotten to the point where meditation was invigorating, a respite from the run of mental frenzy (no wonder Rinpoche had so much energy). Now it was as if sadness and worry were the default setting. Sadness, worry, a drop of bitterness, a constant run of words and images. My friends hadn't lost their wives. Their children hadn't lost their mothers. And what to do about the huge empty house? And how would the kids make out at school with no mother to speak to? And Jeannie's face at the end. And her last word. And would there ever be lovemaking again in my life. And the guilt about even thinking that. And Jeannie again, working in her flower garden when she was well. And then, at last, one tiny stretch of quiet, the smallest glint of peace and mindfulness, a settling, a stillness. Enough.

Time to eat.

Rinpoche had told me he wouldn't be having dinner that night—a fairly common occurrence—so I made a reservation for one and changed into long pants and a dress shirt, and strolled past the grapevines and toward my evening meal. The dining room occupied half the main building and offered the same otherworldly views out over the Columbia River Gorge. It was strange: before Jeannie left this world I'd been perfectly happy to eat alone in a restaurant. When I traveled to a book show, when she and the kids were away and I went out for dinner in Bronxville, when—a rainy day tradition—I stopped at the Comfort Diner on East Forty-Fifth for their ricotta pancakes and real maple syrup before going on to the office, I was perfectly satisfied to have only a plate of food for company, and never felt awkward about holding up one finger when the hostess asked how many in the party.

Now all that had changed. Now, sitting alone in a restaurant felt like a mark of failure, a reminder of my widowerhood, a shameful act. I sensed that there were eyes on me, wondering what was the problem. Was he impossible to live with? Had he abandoned wife and family for a younger woman and been jilted and thrown out and was left now to lick his wounds and eat alone? Was he a gay man without a partner?

In any case, the anticipation of a solitary feast wasn't the pure joy it had once been. I gave the hostess—Latina, young, pleasant—my name and watched her face for signs of pity. She led me across the room. Just as we reached my chair a couple at the adjacent table looked up and smiled and the man said, "Alone? Why don't you join us?"

I don't want to, I should have said. As much as I dislike eating alone now, I really don't want the company of strangers tonight. The swim, the wine tasting, the text from my beloved daughter, this afternoon has been good to me, and I want to sit in the Jacuzzi of that good fortune and soak away the morning's pain.

But the man and woman seemed strangely eager to have me. "Please," she said. "We're on dessert and we'd just like to sit with you for a while and chat."

They were clean looking and normal seeming, well bred, well groomed, the man's dirty-blond hair combed back neatly from his forehead, the woman in gold bracelets, perhaps a bit older than her husband, with blue eyes and a straight, longish nose. He sported an off-white linen jacket; she wore a dress—beige with black trim around a high neckline—that seemed to perfectly fit the mood of the Panorama: classy but not formal. I noticed all this in a glance, of course, and the message was: These are people like me. So I thanked them and joined them, ordered the fixed-price dinner and a glass of rosé, and settled in to what I expected would be an enjoyable conversation.

For a few minutes it was. We exchanged bits of information. They were, it turned out, one of the couples I'd seen at the pool. When I asked after their young son, the husband—"Winch" he told me his name was—said, "Oh, he's back in the room watching some TV. Marty and I wanted a little alone time, and Charlie's fine on his own. What could happen?"

What could happen? At that remark a small warning bell sounded in my inner ear. The boy was all of five. What could happen was he'd choke on the snack they'd left him, or he'd decide to go for a walk and wander down to the wide river through a landscape of snakes and darkness. What could happen was he'd feel his mother and father wanted some alone time after having spent one hour with him at the pool, on vacation, and a seed of bitterness would be planted in his brain. Jeannie and I knew people who went to Europe for three weeks and left their young kids behind in the care of a semi-stranger, and it was exactly, precisely, the opposite of our parenting style. But it is an unwritten law of our society that, excepting the most egregious cases, one parent cannot wander into another's territory. We are, all of us, miniature kings and queens in our homes, the children our subjects. And the job is so difficult to do perfectly, or even well, and there are so many ways to do it. . . . I sipped my rosé—a poor choice; I should have gone with the vineyard's own Syrah, which had been rich and full of flavor—and admired the view.

Winch and Marty were from Omaha, Nebraska, they said. His family had a private investment business—of late, they'd done particularly well in gold—and she was a "completely fulfilled, stay-at-home mom." They couldn't have been more pleasant, really. They mentioned a health charity they supported—for children with birth defects. With their elegance and ease they reminded me of a latter-day Dick and Nicole from *Tender Is the Night.*

But then, after I told them I was a New Yorker on a sort-of vacation road trip, Marty said, "We saw you at the pool with . . . your friend."

I was in good appetite, as the saying goes, and partly distracted by the arrival of the first course, a crostini with four cheeses and some kind of compote on top. Huckleberry, it might have been. Everything was huckleberry in Washington State, even the ice cream. The first taste. Overture to a fine symphony. I nodded at them and chewed.

"You know," Winch put in, "there are studies now that show it can be reversed."

Distracted again. The waiter, an affable Jerry, was there at my shoulder, removing the crostini dish and replacing it with steelhead tartare. I was not exactly, as Rinpoche might have put it, in the moment. Winch sensed my dissatisfaction with the rosé, kindly called for another glass, said "Try this," and poured from his bottle of Viognier. Excellent manners!

The previous remark wandered around the walls of the room, sneaked up behind and tapped me on the shoulder. I heard the word "reversed" and tried, as I ate, to make sense of it. The steelhead had no taste; the wine was really superb. I thanked them.

Marty leaned toward me and spoke in a conspiratorial tone, "Yes. It's completely forgivable and completely changeable."

"What is?" I asked. They had my attention then. I looked up from the pink remains of the raw fish and saw two sets of eyes attaching themselves to me with such intensity that I wanted to push my chair back an inch. It reminded me of a co-worker, Andrew, who put his face one nose-length from yours when he spoke to you and maintained the healthiest of eye contact at all times. Andrew was six foot four; it had always seemed to me an insecure tall man's intimidation tactic. Shorter colleagues never tried it.

"Your choice," Marty said pleasantly.

I was confused. I thought, for a few seconds, that he was

referring to the meal I'd selected. Should I have ordered off the a la carte? Was it the rosé for which I was to be forgiven? Could it be reversed?

"We saw you at the pool."

"Yes, I saw you, too. Your son's a fine-looking boy."

With that comment some new cloud swept in over the table. Outside, the wind was making its presence known in sharp gusts, and there were one or two horizontal flashes of lightning above the far bank. I should have taken an umbrella, I thought. Jerry brought the rhubarb soup with a dollop of *crème fraiche* at the center.

Winch looked at his wife. "Homosexuality is a grievous sin," he said to me in the most somber of tones. Marty was nodding. Two men at the next table glanced over.

From time to time we would have a minor mouse infestation in our home, and Jeannie and I, having lost faith in the nonlethal versions, would reluctantly set out real traps. The choice—easy, even for us—was between killing something we did not really want to kill or living with the tiny black turds behind the toaster. Still, I always felt a twinge when I picked up the trap with the soft gray creature in it, his or her head mashed by the metal. I found myself imagining what it must feel like, that first instant when you realize the morsel of food wasn't worth it, the spring has sprung, you're caught.

"Excuse me?" I said. The soup was thick and bland. The kindest of Jeannie's kind hospice workers had been Leah, an openly gay woman from White Plains. Leah had been a saint in our home, an angel. Perhaps this seems strange, but somehow, when she was cleaning the vomit from my wife's lips, it didn't matter one bit to Jeannie or me whom Leah chose to sleep with in her off hours.

"We saw you with your friend," Marty went on, "we had to explain to Charlie what was going on. It was part of the reason we wanted to be here alone tonight, just the two of us. We hoped we'd see you and that you'd be willing to talk."

"You can't be serious," I said. The words just slipped out. Jerry came by to ask if things were going well, and I said everything was fine. The couple beside us finished and paid and walked out together. I wanted Rinpoche to be there, my "friend." I wanted to see how he would react.

"Completely serious," Winch said.

Next came a plate of gnocchi in a white sauce, the best dish so far. Cooked *al dente* and seasoned well. If my children had been there I would have passed on to the chef an exaggerated compliment. But now I had an urge to carry my plate over to the empty table, the way Jasper carried off a T-bone on a summer night, taking it away from us and settling at the edge of the bushes, holding it between his paws and looking all around for signs of trouble. I remembered Leah, remembered her holding Jeannie's fingers so gently in her own, staying long after she was scheduled to leave. . . . Another urge overtook me then. I make no excuses for it. I said, "We've been together six years, Volya and I. We're family at this point."

"But it's a grievous sin," Winch persisted. He and his wife really seemed to care for my spiritual well-being. It was, in spite of everything, an effort to dislike them. "It keeps you from the Lord."

"He's a great spiritual master. Revered around the world. I feel lucky to be in his presence, and I'm sure he's closer to God than I'll ever be."

Marty frowned. "We're Christians," she said.

"So am I."

"Well, the Bible says everything that needs to be said on the subject, we think."

"My understanding is that Jesus said nothing on the subject. Zero. Zilch."

"We'd like to help you if you'd let us."

Now came the duck course, succulent if rubbery, set on a bed of couscous that needed spice. There were clean plates and bowls stacked in a kind of sideboard that separated diners from the cooking area. As the busboy tried to remove a few of the bowls, he somehow got himself into a position where a whole stack was tilted away from him, in his hands but leaning against the back wall of the shelf. One false move and they'd come crashing to the floor. He was stuck there, frozen between embarrassment and disaster. Winch got up immediately and went to his aid, and took some of the dishes until things got straightened out. "I apologize," the busboy said.

"No need. No need, brother."

He was back. They were watching me eat. The duck was a long time going down. "I have a son," I said, when I was able to speak, "from a previous marriage. He's nineteen, college football player. He and Volya were wrestling this morning on the lawn of the B and B. He's a manly man, my Volya, despite the bathing suit and color choice and so on. Pinned my son in seconds."

I was being mean then. I couldn't seem to stop myself. I was a sinner, yes, though not in the way they thought. May God forgive me. I worked my way through the duck while Marty and Winch twirled wineglasses, and then Jerry came by with a tiny dish of lava cake. Tasty, but too small. I ordered a glass of port and offered to treat my dinner mates. They politely declined. I thought of an older friend at home who'd joked once that, when the time came, when he was in hospice and fading away, he wanted to be put on a port drip, rather than morphine. Bob Jasse was his name, a good man, a lifelong macho heterosexual who invited both straight and gay couples to dinner parties at his and his wife's New Hampshire home and came to the defense of Jamaican orchard workers being mistreated by the local cops. A true Christian, it seemed to me, though he claimed to be agnostic. I'd visited him hours before he passed on. He was gasping for breath. I couldn't bring myself to mention the port drip.

"We're really concerned," was all Marty could think to say.

From the deepest part of the big river of feeling in me, the cold, dark depths sliding toward the crash, these words came: "Your Christianity gives you solace," I said, and if Winch and Marty had been in the moment they might have heard something in my voice, sensed something.

"Yes, absolutely," she said.

"Then let other people alone, dammit!" I said, and as I said it I bumped the bottom of my fist down on the tabletop, fairly hard. Fortunately, there were only a handful of diners there as witnesses, no children. Winch and Marty leaned back away from me with identical movements. A flat, small smile cut the bottom of his face. His views had been confirmed. The sinner, firmly in Satan's grasp, had shown himself for what he truly was.

"Well, we're sorry to have upset you," Marty said after a pause. The tone hung just this side of sarcasm.

"Just let other people alone," I said, more calmly. "If they're not hurting you, not hurting someone else, let them be, would you?"

"It's not that simple," Winch said.

"I think it is."

"Well," Marty said, "one day we'll find out who's right."

"Forget the 'one day' stuff," I said. "You're obviously caring people—the charity, and so on. Just forget the sexual stuff. Just keep your minds out of other people's bedrooms, won't you? There are so many—"

"It's not about our minds," Marty said. "It's about God's word."

I thought of telling them about Leah. I thought of citing other Biblical dictums—on slavery and stoning and ritual sacrifice. But I could see very clearly that it would be like speaking to the polished metal surface of my sink.

They gave me identical looks of pity, pushed back their chairs, wished me a good evening and walked out into the rainless thunderstorm. I tucked my head down an inch, scraped absently at the last twirls of chocolate in the dish, stared at the glass of port. Jerry hovered at a safe distance, then approached and asked about coffee, and I sat there until everyone else had left, and I watched the storm flashing, wind batting the glass and pushing at the umbrellas on the patio. Christian, I kept thinking. Christian, Christian. In the news on that very day—I could not make this up—was a story about the president of the fast food chain Chick-fil-A, who'd famously said, "I think we are inviting God's judgment on our nation when we shake our fist at him and say, 'We know better than you as to what constitutes marriage'." The comment caused a sales record to be set, millions of Chick-fil-A's consumed in a righteous fury, the chicken, the Coke, the artery-choking fried potatoes. It made no sense to me. In addition to Leah and Clare, we knew a half-dozen gay couples, some of them parents. In exactly the same way as our straight friends, some were good parents; some, in my judgment, not so good. Some of the gay men and women I'd met in my life were fine human beings; some, in my judgment, not so fine. I was tired, then, of the labels, the sweeping generalizations, bigotry on the one hand, political correctness on the other. My sister was flaky, my son a jock, I was upper middle class and white and male. Marty and Winch were Christian. Natasha had gone from being a jock to an "alternative type," and now had a sneaker in each camp. How had this happened to us, this putting of souls into boxes? What purpose did it serve? In what way did it make us better, holier, more at peace with each other?

Part of me believed that eating at Chick-fil-A was the kind of thing that would invite God's judgment on our nation. And another part saw, on my side of the battle lines, how easy it was to mentally plop Winch and Marty into a sack, tie the cord tight, and drop them over the gunwale into the mid-Atlantic.

The storm had passed by the time I roused myself and walked back to the cliffhouse in the late northern dusk. What you could do, all you could really do, was try to clean the poison out of yourself in as honest a way as possible. The anger and self-pity and constant judgments, the urge to feel wiser and better, to belong to the group that was pleasing to God. You should speak the truth, yes, and stand up for the oppressed. But what you really had to do was more difficult than that, the type of thing Winch and Marty, in my judgment, would never risk. You had to look down into your own dark waters, unflinching, and trace the motivations there. First, as Rinpoche said, you had to see.

The lights were out in his half of our lodging. I sat in the dark on the leather couch, said one Our Father, then offered up a Buddhist blessing for every soul in all the universes, every soul without exception. The Leahs and Clares, the Winches and Martys, the angry Otto Ringlings, the suffering, the lonely, the confused, the different and the dead. Then I sat there in my river of thoughts for a little while, and then I went to sleep.

13

I awoke, next morning, to an absolutely pristine silence. No road noise, no hotel AC, not even the chirping birds that pulled us out of sleep on a summer day in New York. The view through the bedroom's glass door felt like a twin to that silence: still and striated gray-brown cliffs on the far side of the Columbia, and behind and beyond and above them an expanse of dry land slanting up and away. On the ridgeline there, north of the hundred windmills, ran a strip of green forest beneath an empty morning sky.

It was early for me, in the sixes. I washed quietly so as not to wake Rinpoche behind his closed bedroom door, then went out and retraced the previous day's steps. Near the pool enclosure was the start of a trail that led down to the river. Other hikers had left walking sticks there on the ground. I found one that suited me and started off. It was cool in the shade but you could feel that, once the sun climbed higher and swung around overhead, all this low area would turn into an oven. The young

woman at the desk had said the summer temperatures sometimes reached 110 in these parts. It would be dry heat, yes, so it
would be a dry oven. But an oven all the same.

At first the path went steeply downhill, rocky, tough on the
knees. But then, flattening out, it twisted through a prairie
landscape of sagebrush, small tufts of grass, and low-to-the-
ground flowers I couldn't name. Just below and ahead of me lay
the river, its surface a metal-blue sheet. I imagined that, had
Rinpoche been there, he would have made a lesson out of that
stillness, likened it to the perfected mind in meditation. That
was a sticking point for me. During the years I'd been under his
tutelage, if that is the word, I'd had moments of stillness. Just
moments—he said that was the "beginning part. Good, Otto,
good!" And there was certainly an ease and pleasure to be found
there. Sometimes that pleasure echoed later in the day in unexpected periods of calm, or . . . *reassurance* would be a better
word. I felt like I'd touched the frontier of a world beyond this
world.

At the same time, part of me kept wondering: if this is the
goal of meditation, if, ultimately, all it leads to is a quiet as pure
as this quiet, a stillness as still as a river surface on a windless
morning, then what's the point? It was like setting off on a trip
and coming to a stop sign and sitting there. Was that the ultimate goal of the spiritual life? Stopping? A cessation? The end
of thought and time? It didn't draw me, I have to say, but I had
not yet been able to admit that to Rinpoche.

And then there he was, a red-robed miniature mountain
sitting on a dry promontory that faced north toward the winding
of the water. I suppose I should have expected him to be there. I
suppose I shouldn't have been so secretly proud of myself for

rising early and making the walk instead of immediately turning on the TV to see if the Olympics had started, or opening the
computer to check e-mails, or rushing over to the main lodge
for coffee and something sweet. I walked quietly up to him and,
when he didn't stir, I sat beside him and tried to sink into meditation, too.

It was good to sit with him. It always added a dimension to
my solitary meditations, justifying them in some way, if that
makes any sense. It was like lying in the shade on a hot day.
Instead of a brain-to-brain connection there was something else
going on, heart to heart, maybe. Spirit to spirit, my sister would
have said.

After a time the monk, my goofy friend, stirred, made a
small grunt, and then stood and started in on yet another version of his bizarre stretching routine. On our first road trip together, years earlier, and during the ensuing visits we'd made to
North Dakota and he and Seese and Shelsa had made to
Bronxville, I'd come to understand that the great spiritual master was not much for talking. That was strange, because when
he gave one of his presentations he could go on glibly for two
hours or more. There were even times when it seemed he was
purposely pushing the audience toward the limits of its patience. People wanted to eat, to use the toilet, to stand up and
move around, and he'd be sitting there, cross-legged usually,
words rolling out of him like bowling balls running up the
track, one after the next after the next in a low, steady rumble.

But in more ordinary times—at dinner, on a walk, sitting
around on our couches at home with a ball game on—he
wrapped himself in a gold-trimmed silence. It wasn't an un-
friendly pose. If you spoke to him directly he always made eye

contact and replied. Once in a great while he'd initiate the conversation or toss in one of his mini-lessons on the meaning of life. Before I knew him well I thought the long stretches of silence might have something to do with his lack of fluency in English. Now I knew better. It was part and parcel of him, and so he fit into that soundless landscape like one of its own creatures—a basking lizard, a great blue heron flapping across the sky, so high up you couldn't hear its wings.

Something felt different this time, however. I'd noticed it even at the B and B, on the ride across the Cascades, at lunch in Leavenworth. His silences had—I don't know what to call it— not an edge exactly but a filigree of discomfort to them. His discomfort. And this from a man who seemed so perfectly comfortable so much of the time.

"What's wrong?" I asked him when the stretching had settled down to a slow circling of his big head, then a fluttering of his fingers, then—and I knew this was the final exercise—a rolling in and out of his lips and a flexing of the cheek muscles. He finished with a loud exhalation and looked at me from under his thin brows.

"Otto is here," he said.

"Right. Exactly. I agree completely. Here I am and stop changing the subject. Something's wrong, I can feel it."

The big smile flashed and died. My intuitive skills seemed pleasing to him. "Funny word," he said. "*Wrong*. Like the sound of a meditation bell at home. *Wronggggg. Wronggggg.*"

"What is it in Ortyk?"

"*Unhal*," he said. "For a small problem, *unhal*. For the big, *unhalHA*."

"So what's *unhal* with you?"

"What is?" he said, his voice rising up almost into a falsetto at the end, a squeak.

"Stop it. What's going on?"

"Going on is two things. One, my friend Otto, my good friend, my brother-and-law, has a sadness on him like the smell from smoke because his wife is not here."

"Right. And two?"

"Two?" There was a pause, an unnatural pause for him, an unnatural break in eye contact. He contemplated the view up-river for a moment, then the gold-flecked eyes came back. "Rinpoche is having dreams. Three times now."

"What kind of dreams?"

"Bad kind."

"Bad in what way? Tell me. Spit it out."

"Bad," he said, looking across at the striated cliffs. "I have a dream that people would come to find Shelsa now. Hurt her. Maybe kill."

Spoken by someone else, anyone else, this would have seemed to me merely the run-of-the-mill parental anxiety dream, as common as diaper rash in a baby. My friend Russ in California confessed to going into his newborn's room half a dozen times during the night in order to make sure his child was still breathing. I'd done things like that, too, as had Jeannie. The worry changed shape as they grew older—Why were they out so late? Which one of their friends was driving? What kind of people might they be sleeping with at college?—but never disappeared. Worrying was part of the job description. Wanted: person to be father or mother; must be able to work weekends and nights and to worry to the point of physical illness about a wide variety of issues.

But Rinpoche was not an ordinary father. And, if you believed him and my sister (and sometimes I did), Shelsa was not an ordinary child. What if she was the next Dalai Lama or something, and the Chinese politburo was already putting together an assassination team? In the past, I'd known Rinpoche to have prognosticatory powers, but I wouldn't admit the possibility in this case. I simply could not bear the thought of Shelsa being harmed. I didn't want to consider it, to let it wander into the field of possibility. So I said, "That's just a normal parental anxiety dream. I've had hundreds of them. I still do."

Rinpoche pursed his lips and seemed to consider that idea, but I could sense he was unconvinced.

"Why would anyone want to hurt her, anyway?"

"Why? Why they hurt Jesus? Gandhi? Martin King? All the good people like that."

Is she in that league? I wanted to ask, but I was having the bad chills then, a feeling I'd known with him before. A premonition was working its way into the molecules of air behind my ears and along the back of my neck. I did not like it one bit. In a desperate attempt to shift the subject I said, "I asked you about that years ago, and you never really gave me an answer. Why is it set up that way, the kindest people getting slaughtered? And why didn't Buddha face hatred like that?"

Rinpoche didn't take the bait. He wasn't looking at me now, but had angled his eyes down and away, and there was a dark cloud across his features—utterly unprecedented. "She knew this," he said, "from before she was born."

"But who would hurt her? Why?"

He was fingering the hem of his robe, another first, this twitchiness, this lack of physical ease. "Just a dreams, maybe," he said.

"If someone tries to hurt her, I'll forgo my oath of nonviolence," I said. "I'll buy a gun."

"Maybe, sure."

"Really?"

No response. If worry could take physical shape it would have been the shape of his square face then, the eyebrows in a straight line, the skin tugged up slightly over his cheekbones. "Hard life maybe she'll have now, pretty soon, Otto."

"Does she know that? I mean, would she be able to sense that?"

"Sure. Have to know."

"But she seems so happy."

He made a small, sad chuckle and looked up at me. "She know from before she was born. Her father is sad sometimes. Her mother sometimes wery, wery sad. She . . . not sad. She came to carry the suffering as her job now."

"But why? She's. . . I thought these people, I thought she . . . they . . . were beyond suffering in some way."

Another small, sad laugh. He reached out and clapped a hand onto my left shoulder, and he was strong again, a stone. "Do you know why you make in this life the big spiritual step."

Spirchal, was the way the word sounded on his lips.

"Not this again."

"Do you know why you finish your karma and now you are ready?"

"Tell me."

"Wery easy," he said. "Otto has many troubles, yes. Eats too much maybe, little bit. Sometimes gets mad. Has the doubt. Yes?"

"Guilty on all counts."

"But you, my friend, are a *wery*, *wery* good father! One maybe the best. Good uncle, too. A man with a *wery* big heart."

"I don't know about that," I began. I was flattered, naturally, wanting to believe him and seem humble at the same time. For whatever reason or combination of reasons, being a good father had been, to me, far far up on the top shelf of things I cared about in life, so far beyond being a good editor, making money, or seeming like a success, that it could be matched against nothing else. "I'd like to think—"

He squeezed my shoulder hard. "Lissen me," he said, and his face had taken on a fierce aspect I remembered from other moments akin to this one. "Now is the adding up of your good actions in this life. All the goodness has power with it, see?"

"No."

He threw back his head like a man laughing, but he didn't laugh. There was a small smile there, a wrinkle of a smile, almost a wince. "Walk now," he said, "with me."

In his tone, in the suggestion, I recognized the start of one of what I thought of as his "mini-lessons." And I wanted a mini-lesson then. More than anything I wanted some new word, some serving of wisdom to change the way the world seemed to me at that moment. If it really were true that Shelsa was in danger, or would be in danger down the road—and I wasn't completely convinced—then it was just more evidence of the unfairness of this life. A good woman, a mother, dying at age forty-eight. An innocent girl, hated by "bad men." Crucifixions, assassinations, bigotry in a thousand reptilian forms. Why didn't good prevail? Why, if a person did, indeed, accumulate some power from being a good father, a good soul, or a great teacher, why didn't that protect him or her from the hatred that grew everywhere on this planet like weeds in a hot lake?

We went across the sagebrush plain at the pace of an ant. The path was sandier there, wide enough for two. The air had grown warm. "This," Rinpoche said, gesturing across the river at the cliffs beyond. "I know how this is made. Rinpoche knows. What is it, the way rocks make? What word is for it?"

"Geology."

"Nice word."

"Yes."

"Rinpoche understands gee-olo-gee. Look," he said again, swinging an arm out from under the robe and encompassing the cliffs. At three or four points in the thousand-foot façade there were dark horizontal lines, almost as if we were seeing the edge of a road that had been cut there. They were, I guessed, places where the river had stayed at that level for years, perhaps centuries. Or they were horizontal outcroppings that only looked like lines from this angle, strata of denser rock that had partly resisted erosion. "The river cut down through the rock," Rinpoche said. "All in one big flood. Many years between. Then one big flood again. Like an exploding. Look how slow, Otto! Look how many years. How many you think?"

"A million, maybe. We could look it up."

"A million! For a long time the river doesn't cut, and then the explosion comes."

"I don't know. I think the river is continually cutting. Maybe a little stronger in spring when the snow melts, but I think it cuts all the time."

"No, no," he said, as if I had it all wrong. "Look at the lines and you can see. An explosion. Big cut. Then a thousand years' rest. Then another one."

I felt a prickle of irritation then: Rinpoche sounded so certain of his geological theories. *Have a little humility*, a bad voice
said. *A spiritual lesson, fine, sure. That's your area of expertise.
But do you have to sound so sure about geology?* It was a sour
run of unspoken words, probably just my wanting him to be
wrong—about the rock formations, about Shelsa.

"Same with us!" he said. "The pain cut us, cut, hurt, then
maybe we rest of a times, then an explosion and hurt, yes?"

"Sure."

"Jeannie, Shelsa. Cut us, cut."

"Okay."

"And make us beautiful inside, see?" He swung his arm at
the view, which was, in fact, more than beautiful.

"It doesn't feel that way in the slightest, Rinpoche."

He laughed in a gentle way. *He has dreams*, the bad voice
went on, *visions of his daughter being killed by evil men, and
he's laughing at the pain in the world, saying how it makes one
beautiful inside!* For the hundredth time I found myself evenly
torn between two conclusions: Either he was a fool, living in a
fool's world, not in pain himself and so constitutionally unable
to feel the pain of another. Or he was beyond pain, at least in
one dimension. It was enough to make you lose faith in him
one second and beg him to take you on as a disciple the next. I
teetered there between those extremes, watching him, wrestling
with myself.

"The hurt is real," he said. "Wery real."

I loved him for saying that . . . until he added, "On one level," and then I momentarily hated him. Or, not hated him, precisely; he was impossible to hate and, in spite of my sharp edg-

es, I am not a hating type of person. Better to say that I resented him, in a guilty way. It was the same guilty resentment the chronically ill might feel for the healthy. You don't know what this is like, they might think. Sure, you can laugh, you can philosophize, but if you had *this* pain, this hardship, if it was *your* wife who died, what would you be doing?

"The two levels of life are both of them wery real," he said.

"Buddha's 'absolute' and 'relative'."

He patted me on the back, though not in a way that made me feel like a particularly successful student. "Words," he said, dismissively. "The *real* is past words."

"Right, but words are all we have to express it."

A nod on his thick neck, but it was not a gesture of agreement. "Here in this whirl," he said, smacking himself in the middle of the chest, "we live, yes?"

"Sure."

"Wery real. The fun is real. The hurt, wery real. Being born and dying, all real."

"I sense a *but* coming."

"But," he said without irony, "but then every times in a minute—"

"Every now and then, you mean."

A distracted nod. "Something happens that shows you: Not so real, this life. Or not the only real. Or not the full real. Not the real you thought."

"But can you trust those moments? Against the mass of so-called realness you've lived in day after day, year after year? People hear voices and see the future and commune with the dead, but most of them, maybe all of them, are charlatans, fakes. I'm the Bible's doubting Thomas. I want evidence, fact.

I'm open to the idea of other lives, just not while this one is going on."

He looked around us, up, sideways, down. At last his eyes settled on a small flowering plant, a spray of yellow blossom on a pale green, spikey stem. Beside it was a stone the size of an egg. He pointed to them with both hands, the way no American would. "The flower now is real, yes?"

"Sure."

"The stone too, yes?"

"Yes."

"But in maybe one day, one week, the flower is gone, the stone is there the same."

"Okay. But in a million years the stone will be dust."

He turned his head to me and the face was painted with an expression I'd seen there countless times. A muted exasperation. He put a hand on my shoulder, as I somehow knew he would. Then, as I expected, he laughed, but the laugh had a sadness running across it like a line on the cliff. "My brother-and-law is *wery* hard to teach," he said, grinning.

"Not really. I just want to be honest. What you're saying is that there's a part of consciousness that's stable, and the world changes around that part, like planets around a sun or something, movement around stillness. And that we can go to that stable place, in meditation maybe, and maybe there the vicissitudes of life don't rock the boat so roughly."

"Wissitude, what is?"

"A big word for troubles, for what you don't want to have happen to you. In that quiet, still place the world's troubles don't bother you as much. You're beyond them. I've touched that place in meditation. But who wants to live there? It's too still for me. Too removed from feelings. I don't want to be a stone, even for a million years. I want to be alive, vibrant, feeling."

"Of course," he said. "Everybody wants."

"But a second ago you seemed to be saying the feelings are the flower and there is a stone that outlives them."

"Yes, good," he said.

I looked at him. "You," I said, "could drive a person nuts in about three minutes."

He looked back. "And you," he said, "want that the whirl, the true whirl, the wery biggest *real,* be wrapped up in words like the toy for a baby on Christmas. Words and thoughts, words and thoughts. You by now know it isn't."

"I think," I bent down, picked up the stone, and flung it toward the still river. "I think, when Jeannie first got sick, the words and thoughts became important again. I was starting, just starting, to see that maybe there was something beyond them. And then the pain of watching her suffer and die made this world the only reality. What she suffered was real. To my final breath I will refuse to let anyone tell me otherwise. I watched her. I sat by her bed for hours and hours and watched her suffer. Please don't try to tell me that wasn't real."

"Wery wery real," he admitted sadly. "But I watch, too. Many people like that I watch. Inside the real hurt, wery wery deep, something else is there. Jeannie even saw it."

"She told you that?"

"One time."

"That hurts. She never told me that."

"She and you," he said, another hand on the shoulder, "were past words. That's why. See?"

"Yes, but it hurts anyway. I feel like I have an armor that's a quarter of an inch thick and any little thing can pierce it now. I yelled at people at dinner last night. I pounded my fist on the table."

"Good, wery good," Rinpoche said, patting my shoulder again. He bent down and picked up a small stone and slid it into his robe. He'd been doing that since we arrived at Cave B, putting together a collection.

"It felt good . . . for about three seconds. And you're the one who's always counseling against anger."

"Feelings pass," he said.

"Yes, and leave a mark."

"Mark passes, too."

"Sure, everything passes. That doesn't make it all irrelevant. I don't want to be the guy sitting in meditation saying, 'It all passes, it means nothing. I might as well leave my kids alone in the room to choke on a pretzel because it doesn't matter, it isn't real.'"

"Means everything, this whirl," he said.

"There you go. You're Zenning me."

"Pushing your button," he said.

"Right. Next thing you'll be saying you're a Christian."

"Rinpoche is wery Christian," he said. "Christ, for Rinpoche, the greatest man! The best spirit!"

"Greater than Buddha?"

"Buddha-Christ are the same, Otto, don't you know it now?"

"The Christians I met last night would never say so."

"Same, same, same. Little bit different way to say the same thing. You can't see it?"

"Good. Fine, then. We'll start a new religion. Buddhianity,

we'll call it. Christianism. The Buddheo-Christian tradition. "

"Exactly, my friend!" he said, very happy now, and not out of breath in the slightest as we made the last and steepest part of the climb back toward the pool. "This is Shelsa's job on earth now. To make this new religion. You are seeing, you are seeing it now! You will help!"

I could not, of course, take this comment at all seriously. I thought only that he was twisting me around in words as he sometimes did, as the Zen masters were known for doing. Zen, he'd explained to me, was a different tradition, with a different lineage of teachers but the same basic goal, though the goal would be reached by a more austere or perhaps purer path than the one he himself practiced. Years ago he'd told me that his Ortykian school was an offshoot of a Tibetan lineage, close to something called Dzogchen, also known as The Great Perfection. He'd assured me more than once that it was very close to the Dalai Lama's brand of Buddhism; the differences were subtle. Unimportant. Ortykian Buddhism, Dzogchen, the Dalai Lama, Shelsa as some kind of special reincarnation, Rinpoche's dreams, Jesus and Gandhi being murdered—I suddenly did not like this progression, not at all.

"I couldn't help Shelsa do so much as make a fried egg," I said.

"You are her helper," he replied sternly, and I searched in vain for irony or humor in the words. The familiar cool run of molecules was making its way along the outsides of my arms and up the back of my neck. I willed myself to ignore it. "You are the uncle to help her in this life. John the Baptist was cousin with Jesus, yes? You are uncle with Shelsa."

"And look what happened to John the Baptist," I said. More

cold tickling of the skin. I was reaching desperately for a joke, for some whipsaw of cynicism with which to cut the legs out from under the conversation.

But Rinpoche was drilling his eyes into me, willing me to understand, to agree, to accept.

"What is the goal?" I asked, trying to slip away from it. "What's the whole point? Enlightenment? Eternal life? What?"

He patted me on the shoulder for the millionth time, and said, "You purify. You go and go. Life cuts you and you try and try and try and pretty soon—"

"You become beautiful."

"Yes. Good."

"But toward what are we going and going? What does the beauty look like?"

He shrugged almost helplessly, and for a moment I was gripped hard by the hand of doubt. He seemed only an ordinary man then, and I wanted more than that from him, more than cryptic answers and shrugs. A small inner voice suggested he'd been fooling us all these years, playing a role, maybe even working a scam.

"I can show you," he said. "I can't tell you."

"All right. Please show me, then. I'm having a crisis of faith. I'm a little bit lost."

He nodded sympathetically. "We find you," he said. "Don't worry too much. Shelsa will show you now the next step."

"I'll pray for her," I said. "That she stays safe."

"Good, Otto. Good." And then, instead of the usual hand on the back or shoulder, he pulled me against him and held me that way, as if we were two soldiers about to go to war.

At the top of the path, I saw that Winch, Marty, and Charlie, up at that early hour, had opened the gate to the pool enclosure and were about to step inside. I raised a hand in greeting, but they turned away.

14

Always, in my travels, I cling to the hope of finding the perfect meal. For years Jeannie and the kids teased me about it mercilessly, making fun of old Dad by pretending to complain about the coffee or the eggs at a diner, the size of the napkins, the cut of meat, the firmness or lack of firmness of the cooked ziti. I'd long ago stopped trying to defend myself against these friendly familial taunts. Jeannie had been a good cook (I did the dishes); we had similar tastes. My culinary peculiarities were rarely an issue at home (though I was sometimes known, in search of freshness, to open a new bag of pistachios before the old one was completely finished). "You should have been a food critic, Dad," Anthony said once. "Traveling the American road and trashing one place after the next. You would have had your own show on the Food Network, would have made more money, too."

But from time to time, despite my pickiness, I'd hit upon a meal that touched perfection, and I'd rave about it for years. "Remember the duck we had that one time at our friends' apartment in Paris?" I'd say. Or "I still think about the fried clams at that take-out place near Boston. On a beach. What was it called?"

It was, like the Ringling Family Plans and the frequent joking, part of our family life, one ingredient in the glue that held us.

From a patio table at Cave B that morning I texted my son and daughter to tell them that I had, once again, found a meal that was close to perfect. And it was true. Sitting there in the morning warmth and untrammeled silence, Rinpoche and I were served the continental breakfast by a fine young man named Eduardo, originally from Aguascalientes. Truly fresh, sweet, green and orange melon—a rarity in my experience: supermarket melons are so often mealy, the melon chunks of breakfast buffets hard as wood; two slices of mandarin orange; a bunch of champagne grapes smaller than peas and sweet as honey. Two slices of banana bread with chocolate chips embedded. One delectable cinnamon roll coated with the unhealthy white frosting I love. All this, plus excellent coffee and the unmatched view. Exquisite.

Eduardo had a moment to chat, and said that in the off season, moose came down from the hills and feasted on the vines after the grapes had been harvested. He was glad we were enjoying the food. It made him happy.

The patio was ours that morning. We ate slowly, done with difficult conversation for the time being, watching the windmills turn their lazy loops on the ridge, and a turkey vulture coasting overhead. *Enjoying the perfect breakfast,* I texted, but there was no answer. I pictured them still asleep in the hotel and sent a prayer toward Seattle for their well-being.

We packed up, stopped by the front desk for our checkout

and a last handful of cherries, then bade Cave B a fond good-bye and headed off. The vine-lined lane, a right turn, a left onto Baseline Road—so straight it made you wish you were a teenager with a fast car instead of a fifty-year-old in a pickup that, whenever it went above sixty, sounded like an old clothes dryer that was about to shake itself to pieces.

Uma was a comfortable enough ride, though—loud, gas-eating, but fun. The directional signals would sometimes stick, but so far we hadn't had to turn on the heat.

I had a plan in mind for that day, a little detour. Rinpoche was scheduled to give what he called a "small talking" in Spokane that evening, but we'd gotten an early start and I wanted to surprise him with something first. We took 281 to 283 north, both roads straight, flat, and free of billboards. There were irrigated fields to either side, alfalfa it looked like, and one placard advertising U-PICK APRICOTS—one of the few foods I dislike. For a little while I tuned in to an AM station, and—the country already in full campaign mode—endured a short rant about our president. The word "socialist" was used seven times in four minutes. Billions of dollars were spent on these campaigns, and millions more earned by the talk-show anger-men. It was like taking money out of the fourth-grade school lunch budget and using it to pay two kids to yell insults at each other on the playground for eight months, while their friends chose sides and wrestled.

In the small dusty city of Ephrata we stopped for a Mexican lunch. Tequila's, the place was called. The booths had high backs carved from dark wood, the food was authentic and plentiful, the waitress shy and black haired. My traveling companion revealed a new passion—chips and salsa—and this was the right place for it, I should say.

From Tequila's we kept going north then turned left onto Route 17, through the hamlet of Soap Lake, dry hills for company at first and then an amazing run of purplish-brown cliffs. Another mile and the views turned truly majestic, the cliffs rising beyond a lake to our left, and, to our right, steep-sided formations of dark rock that looked ready to break loose and crash down onto the pavement. This was a road for the ages, to go with a breakfast for the ages and a perfectly good lunch. It seemed only right that we should see a sign saying HITCH-HIKING PERMITTED, because we'd clearly entered some kind of alternate universe, everything oversized and magical and existing out beyond the boundaries of the usual tourist spots. It was beautiful, yes, but the best part was the surprise of it. No one I'd ever listened to, nothing I'd ever read in any travel magazine had advised, You *must* go to east-central Washington State on your next vacation. The scenery's amazing!

I'd learn only later that this whole area was called "scabland," a horrible moniker.

After a stretch of otherworldliness, the scabland morphed into sage prairie again, with Lenore Lake to our left, then a levee crossing a larger body of water on which a fisherman, standing in his boat, was speaking into a cell phone. Aside from a few dozen grazing cattle, an abandoned café and then an abandoned motel, this was untouched land, a moonscape, a divine stage set in which, even in the rattling Uma, sixty miles an hour felt like ten. You had the sense that this arid spectacle would stretch and stretch north, all the way to Alberta.

Probably I should have been paying less attention to the scenery and more to the speed limit signs, because just after we crossed the levee I made a left, went a mile or so, and became aware of twinkling blue lights in Uma's mirror. One feels them in one's stomach. There was that first awful jolt of recognition, the faint hope that the cruiser was after someone else and would pull out and hurry past, and then . . . surrender.

Strange though it may sound to list this as a talent (those with few abilities must pad the résumé), I have to say that I'm pretty good when it comes to being stopped by policemen. It happens every five or six years, a hazard of a lot of road time and wandering attention. I don't like it, needless to say, but my father gave me some good advice when I was a boy and I always remembered it when I saw blinking lights in the mirror. "Most policemen are decent, son," he said as he was taking the registration out of the glove box. "You treat them with respect, and they'll usually return the favor. Doesn't mean we won't get a ticket. If I deserve one here, I'll probably get it. But you can make things a lot easier by being a gentleman. Watch now."

The trick he showed me was very simple: don't argue and don't whine. You should get your documents ready. You should say something contrite like, "I was going a little quick there, officer, wasn't I?" and then take your lumps.

I turned onto the gravel shoulder and saw the cruiser pull in behind. A state trooper. I fished my license out of my wallet, calm enough until I realized that the trooper must be checking our plate against the Washington State crime database. He'd discover that the truck belonged to one Jarvis Barton-Phillips, and God knew what that dude had been up to between Silicon Valley and Kaua'i.

Just tell the truth, I reminded myself, and all shall be well.

"Rinpoche," I said, "could you reach into the glove box there and take out the white envelope?"

"What happens?" he said.

"I was going faster than the speed limit. There's a police-man behind us. I might get a ticket, that's all. No big deal."

He nodded, flipped open the glove box, and pulled out the white envelope that held the registration, title, and the letter signing the truck over to him. As he did so, a small plastic bag plopped onto the floor at his feet, an event that brought this ex-clamation from my lips: "Oh, well, shit!"

"What is?"

"Marijuana," I said, as quietly and quickly as I could. In the mirror I saw the trooper getting out of his white cruiser. "Ille-gal. Quick, put it under your robe and don't say anything."

"Mar-wanna?" He took hold of the bag and squeezed it with great curiosity, making no move to do what I'd asked. One more pinch of his strong hands and it was going to break open and spill the contents across his lap.

"Rinpoche! Hide it. Quick!"

He spent another second or two examining the greenish leaves and stems and then tucked the bag into the folds of his robe one heartbeat before the trooper's face appeared at the window.

I swallowed. I handed over the license and registration and saw that my hand was shaking slightly. It was impossible to tell if the trooper noticed. He wasn't the usual big-shouldered type, but a thin-faced, wiry, older guy with squirrel-gray eyes and a head that seemed to have been set on his neck at an uncomfort-able angle. "Going a bit quick," I said. "Sorry."

He spent a moment looking at Rinpoche, then moved his eyes across the seat to me. "Your truck?"

"No. It's a gift."

"Gift?"

"Yes, a friend gave it to my brother-in-law here, as a gift, and we're driving it back to North Dakota where he lives."

"Long trip, isn't that?"

"It is. We were in Seattle for a family gathering. We . . . Volya here lives in North Dakota. The man who gave him the truck lives in Seattle and Hawaii and so on."

It was going fairly well until I said that last part. The gray eyes locked onto me as if either the "Hawaii" or the "and" or the "so on" had struck a sour note. The officer was wearing a gray-blue Stetson and now he put his thumb under the front brim and pushed it up an inch. He was missing the top joint of his left ring finger.

"If there's any record on it, that's not me."

"Just a driver-for-hire, huh?"

"Not hire, no, but—"

There was an awful pause during which I pictured the baggie slipping out from under Rinpoche's robe. I imagined myself calling my sister from a cell in Coulee City, Washington, a small cell with two hard beds in it and a metal toilet that was lacking a seat. My spiritual teacher would be sitting calmly on the other bed, fingering his beads and studying the graffiti previous prisoners had cut into the wall, my children would be within earshot of my sister at the other end of the line, and I would be required to say something like, "Seese, sorry to bother you, but could you post bond?"

In one stroke the roles of an entire lifetime would be reversed. I'd be the screw-up, careless, inattentive, and she would be the solid citizen. It was a humbling notion, brought into sharper focus when Rinpoche, giving the trooper a direct, pleasant, sincere, thoughtful look, raised his hands off his lap in a gesture of innocence and said, "No mar-wanna, nothing. See?"

This remark was not met with a reciprocal friendliness. The trooper stared hard at Rinpoche for a few seconds, then looked back at me. "Some kind of joke?"

"Not at all. He's new to America. It's from watching *COPS*, or something. He didn't mean it in a bad way."

One blink. "What is he?"

"A monk. A spiritual teacher. I'm taking him to Spokane to give a talk tonight."

"Really."

"Yes."

"Seattle to Spokane, and you're on Route 17 in Coulee City? Little strange, isn't that?"

"I'm showing him America. He has a fascination with dams."

"Really? What's your name?"

"Otto Ringling. That's my license I just gave you. I live in New York. He's Volya, no last name, that's just how they do it where he comes from."

"And where might that be?"

"Russia."

Another evil spark in the cheek muscles. Apparently the trooper hadn't heard good things about New York, and was old enough to remember the days when Russia had missiles aimed in this direction, when a wrong word, a hasty decision, the twitch of a finger meant the end of everything we knew.

"Funny name," he said, "Ringling."

"Fairly common in Germany. My folks' parents were German."

"Circus name, wasn't it?"

"They had nothing to do with that."

There was a small "hmph," a glance at my passenger, a classic "Don't go anywhere," and then we could hear the crunch of boot heels as he returned to the cruiser. I watched him in the mirror. Once he was seated, door still open, I said, very quietly and forcefully, "Rinpoche, listen to me. Just keep the bag where it is and *do not* say anything about it. Do not say the word "marijuana" a second time. Just smile, send good thoughts. We could go to jail for what's in that bag. I mean it."

He turned down the corners of his mouth and pressed out his lips as if the idea of going to jail—going to jail *again*, in his case; he'd been imprisoned two years for political reasons back home—was of mild interest. Maybe we'd meet a fascinating person in jail. Maybe there would be chips and salsa and pamphlets on hydroelectric power. Who knew how the whole experience might deepen the meditative life?

"Rinpoche."

"What?"

"Say, 'Okay, Otto.'"

"Okay, Otto."

"And please just do what I said."

"Okay, Otto."

The trooper made us wait for a terrible few minutes, and then I saw him stand out of the cruiser and walk toward us. He handed the license and registration back and held another sheet of paper in his hand. "What's the 'His Holiness' stuff on the letter of transfer? And what's this Rin-poach? I thought you said he had no last name."

"That's his title. RIN-po-shay is how you say it. It means something like 'holy man.'"

In the gray eyes I saw just the tiniest flicker of—well, it wasn't doubt, exactly. It was more a momentary hiatus, a lacuna in what I guessed was otherwise a worldview of some consistent certainty. Maybe the officer had seen enough of life in his twenty or thirty years on the highways to know that the beast of our strange species could not be kept in a box, that humanity bubbled, mutated, and swirled in ways so unpredictable that it might just be impossible to keep everything simple and clear. This funny looking, robe-wearing Russian in front of him might just be holy—*might* being the key word—in exactly the same way that a well dressed woman in a Mercedes might be packing a pistol she was itching to use. You never knew. It was a sparkle of not-knowing that I saw in his eyes. I was grateful for it. It seemed precisely the opposite of what I'd seen in the eyes of Winch and Marty.

The trooper handed over the sheet of paper and said these beautiful words, "A warning this time, but be smart about it. Between here and Spokane there's about a hundred places you'll get stopped if you exceed the posted limits."

"Thank you," I said.

"Thank you, man!" Rinpoche echoed from beside me. This was one of those Americanisms he liked to use but didn't always get exactly right. Calling someone "man" was harmless most of the time, unless, for example, you had a bag of marijuana in your robe and you came off sounding like a stoned-out hippie from the Skovorodian steppe.

The trooper looked at him, blinked, seemed about to say, "Could you step out of the vehicle, please," then turned and went back to his car.

In the rear-view I watched him make a U-turn and head the other way. I pulled out very slowly.

"This bag, what is?"

I didn't answer for a stretch, just driving along, breathing, letting my heart rate drop back to something close to normal, thinking about mistakes, errors in judgment, "big forgets," conceit, humility, love. "Just hold on to it for a while," I said. "I'll explain the whole thing in a minute."

I drove another few miles. Somewhere just before a place called Electric City, I pulled onto the shoulder, asked Rinpoche for the bag, and walked into the rock formations as if I were heeding the call of nature. After making sure the highway was empty in both directions, I set the parcel down between two stones and left it. Those with any interest might find it there, still.

— ⟶ 15

Shortly after I finished explaining the American marijuana laws to my travel companion (he seemed less than intrigued, as if marijuana, and drugs in general, were a minor-league way of calming the mind—artificial, temporary, child's play) Rinpoche noticed a sign for the Grand Coulee Dam and looked over at me like a kid who realizes he's being taken to an amusement park as a surprise birthday present.

"A big one," I told him. "Biggest in the U.S. if I have my facts straight. A coulee is a trough in the earth, a "gulch" we call it, worn away by water."

At that moment we saw a bald eagle, soaring over the lake to our left. We passed Steamboat Rock State Park, an amusing sign that said, "Rocks Next Four Miles," and then we entered Electric City, where a complicated array of high tension wires crossed the dry hills. Not far beyond the Tee Pee Drive-In, Fast Food, we came upon the dam itself, one mile of curved concrete, thirty stories tall. When I parked in a viewing area Rinpoche fairly leapt out of the truck and hurried over to the fence. A massive white sheet of bubbling water cascaded down the dam's face. Even from a distance you could hear the muted roar of it, ceaseless as the earth's spin.

"There's a mini-museum kind of place up the road. We could stop in there for a minute if you want. I'll still get you to Spokane in plenty of time."

Yes, yes, and more yesses from the Rinpoche, though it took me a few minutes to pull him away from the fence. The Grand Coulee Dam Visitor Center was about what you'd expect: dioramas, a short film we didn't have time to watch, views out the glass walls at the spectacle, and uniformed guides behind a desk, ready to answer questions. One of them was Phillip, re-cently out of college, brimming with information, smart and helpful. While Rinpoche stared out the window, transfixed, Phillip took me over to a display and explained how the dam worked. What we were seeing, he said, was merely overflow from a particularly snowy winter; the real work took place inside the structure, where the turbines produced 21 billion kilowatt hours of electricity per year, or enough to power 2.3 million households for twelve months. "Twelve million cubic yards of concrete it took to build the Grand Coulee," he said with some pride. "It's the largest producer of hydropower in the U.S."

Since he was such a knowledgeable young man and since we were looking at a topographical map, I asked him about the Columbia River Gorge, and the cliffs we'd seen from our house at Cave B.

"Those were formed by what might be called eruptions," Phillip said. "Huge floods that occurred when ice dams broke in prehistoric Lake Missoula. They happened periodically, separat-ed by hundreds or thousands of years, and each flood—really a kind of explosion of water—cut through the basalt another hundred feet or so, which is why you see lines on those cliffs."

"I thought it happened more gradually."

"Oh, no, sir. Big bursts. Big giant bursts of water, sometimes two thousand feet deep and moving at sixty-five miles an hour. And we're talking eighteen thousand years ago now. South and east of us you have what's called the channeled scabland. You should see it from the air—amazing."

I went over and stood beside Rinpoche at the windows. "You know your geology, man."

"Power now I am thinking about," he said. He made a tight fist and held it up to me. "So much power inside the earth. It's the same inside meditation."

"I haven't sensed that, not at all. For me, if anything, there's a quietness."

"Quiet first, Otto. But quiet is not the end. You must *do* with the quiet."

"Do what?"

"Your destiny," he said. "Your purpose. The quiet lets you see it, then you do."

Destiny, I confess, was a word that had always given me trouble.

I watched the water for another few seconds and tried with some sincerity to connect its force to my interior world. Impressive as it was, the Grand Coulee had zero spiritual meaning for me. A brilliant feat of engineering; a Depression-era project that had fed families and left a lasting energy and irrigation source; a disruption of the natural order that eliminated whole towns, prevented salmon from spawning upriver, and flooded tribal hunting and fishing lands that had been used by Native Americans for millennia. Yes, to all of the above. But a metaphor for some pure, earthy energy I might somehow gain access to by sitting still? An energy that would let me pursue my destiny? No sale.

What it did make me think about, strangely enough, was my wife. We had a long aquatic history, Jeannie and I. She would go in for a swim—lake, river, ocean—at every opportunity and in weather that had other people wrapped up in flannel shirts. We liked to ski, too, all four of us. One popular Vermont mountain—Killington, it's called—has a hotel near the base lodge that sports an enormous outdoor pool, so we could combine our pleasures there. The pool is heated, and kept open year round. In cold weather you can actually get into the water indoors, a few steps from the locker rooms, and swim under a kind of curtain right into the pool without ever letting the winter air touch your torso.

Sometimes after one of the kids' Saturday sporting events, Jeannie would suggest we make a spontaneous drive up to Killington and spend Saturday night and Sunday there. This would be in the skiing off-season—September, October, April, May—and it was a crazy thing to do, really: five hours each way for less than 24 hours at the hotel. But it was her way of ensuring we had some family time, and just at the point when Natasha and Anthony were starting to leave us for the gravitational pull of friends. We had the car ride together, stops for meals. We'd take a hike and, always, spend a couple of hours in the big pool.

There, at the Coulee Dam, I was remembering a particular Sunday—late October, it must have been. No snow yet, and the foliage there, high up in the Green Mountains, had long ago

lost its color. We had the pool to ourselves. Someone—
Anthony, no doubt—suggested a one-lap race. As expected, I
came in last, victim of a ragged stroke, but I remember half-
floating at the end of the pool, head and shoulders resting on
the concrete edge, arms spread there, chest heaving, kids teas-
ing me, wife brushing back her hair with both hands. I remember looking up at the bare slopes and having a moment of the
most profound gratitude. I wanted to stop time. The kids raced
another length. Jeannie came over and kissed me on the mouth.
We all seemed to be absolutely bursting with good health and I
remember Jeannie's body against mine, the wet tops of her
beautiful breasts, and her saying, "My good husband," in a way
that had so much raw love in it that it caught and held me on a
little cloud of ecstasy. We had our arguments, Jeannie and I. We
had places that didn't mesh well. But we had moments, an
abundance of moments, of such intimacy that I felt the vibra-
tion of it—a humming oneness—running up and down between my lungs.

I don't think every couple has that.

In time I was able to prod my brother-in-law away from his
Coulee contemplation. We made a brief, desultory tour of the
southernmost edges of the Colville Indian Reservation, 1.3 million acres where the cars and pickup trucks had their own license plates and the houses were modest in the extreme. "It's
very poor there," one of the other guides had told me when I
inquired. "You can draw your own conclusion as to why."

Let's see, I thought: a billion acres of stolen land, genocide,
a brutal crushing of ancient ways in the name of civilization,
purposeful infection, the slaughter of one essential food source,

the elimination of another. How would those serve as conclusions to be drawn?

Our brief tour was depressing. An even briefer stop in the Coulee Dam Casino did nothing to cheer me up. Left completely behind on our earlier road trip was Rinpoche's fascination with places like that, with the idea of winning money for no work. He peeked in, stayed close beside me. It was a museum of hopeful indolence, a hundred slot machines whining and ringing in a windowless arena, a handful of desultory gamblers hoping to win a few hundred dollars and pass the time. There were no great destinies being pursued here, at least none that I could see. There was no stillness, no quiet, no secret energy source. If the casino was a symbol of anything, it stood for a society where stillness and quiet had all but gone extinct. We wanted action, busyness, easy riches . . . as if clanging coins and neon had the power to keep death at bay forever.

I played a dollar's worth of nickel poker, won five bucks by accident, and we walked out.

After a fill-up at Jack's Four Corners we turned toward Spokane on Route 174, crested a hill, and were suddenly in yet another new world, this one green and rolling. Farmhouses were set at great distances from one another among the huge fields of grain. It reminded me, just a bit, of home. After half an hour there was a town with abandoned tennis courts and a baseball field, a large OBAMA BIDEN sign, then one for RON PAUL. I watched the speed limits carefully and marveled at the way Washington drivers never seemed to rush. No one passed us, no one flashed lights or tooted the horn or came up too close behind. Probably people here didn't even lock their homes at night. This was not New York.

Haunted is too strong a word, so let me say I was *bothered* by our brief exchange about power and meditation and destiny. The soothing view of fields to either side could not quite wash it from my memory. As if it were a voice whispering in the depths of me, something nudged at my thoughts then, a half-formed notion. What if the future held some destiny other than what I imagined—another ten years of editing, a pleasant retirement, tossing a ball with a grandchild, traveling the world? What if pain and loss, not comfort and ease, lay hidden behind the veil of time, as it had been hidden behind my moment in the Killington pool? What if Rinpoche could see all that, and wasn't telling me?

16

Spokane was the point at which I started to make the reservations for our trip myself, rather than leaving our fate in my sister's hands. "I'll get you started," Celia had suggested in one of our phone conversations that summer. "Then you and Volya can figure out how fast you want to go and where you want to stop. Okay?"

"Fine," I'd said, because the trip was still unreal to me at that point, not something I wanted to think about or plan. "Sounds good."

"But he has a talk in Spokane, I should tell you that."

"Yes, you should, and you should tell me about any other talks or meetings, too. No surprises this time."

"I think that's the only one, Otto. I can check and get back to you, though, if you want."

She may, indeed, have checked, but she didn't get back to me. I asked about it again, in a subsequent conversation three days before we headed west, but my beautiful sister waxed evasive on me as she sometimes did, using words like "pretty sure" and "probably," and leaving the door wide open for one of what she called her "big forgets." "Oops, I had a big forget, Otto, sweetheart. The doctor called yesterday when you were out. He wanted you to bring Jeannie in this morning, if you could, for blood tests. Ten-thirty, it was supposed to be. I'm really sorry. I'm sure you can reschedule." This was on one of her visits east, and during these visits she cooked and cleaned and had long talks with Natasha on the living room sofa and helped Jeannie bathe and gave her medicine when I was at work, and generally filled the house with such selfless goodwill that even her brother, stressed to the limit as he was, and prone to criticize, found it impossible to be angry with her. I reimagined the phone call from the cell in Coulee City. I sent her good thoughts.

I had never been to Spokane, never, in fact, seen any of Washington State east of Smith Brook. Using my magical phone, I'd made reservations at the downtown Davenport Hotel, which turned out to have one of the most spectacular lobbies west of the Waldorf and bright rooms with old mahogany night tables and forceful showers. The chicken burrito had gone down well and quickly, and I was hungry again, in the mood for Italian. "There's a place you can walk to from here," the concierge told us. "It was ranked in the top twenty-five Italian restaurants nationwide."

I will, out of kindness, decline to give the name of this restaurant, and I will decline to speculate about the nationwide survey, such as it was. Suffice it to say that, after Rinpoche and I had made the walk of several blocks on that hot evening and settled ourselves at a window table in what seemed to be an authentic Italian American setting, I had a good salad followed by a criminally overcooked puttanesca. I have no Italian blood.

None. Zero. I'd be ashamed to repeat the words my parents and their friends used, so blithely, in referring to the three Neapolitan families who lived in Dickinson in the years of my youth. Had there been any places to have an Italian meal in our part of the plains, Mom and Pop would surely have found the cuisine too spicy and garlicky for their taste. "Hot" is the word my mother would have used, and it would not have been a compliment. But Jeannie and I and the kids adored it. In fact, Frank Sinatra's former hangout, a place called Patsy's, on Fifty-Sixth Street, just west of Broadway, was the site of almost all our important celebratory meals. When Shelsa was born we dined and toasted there, sending good wishes from fifteen hundred miles away. When Natasha was accepted at Brown, we immediately made reservations at Patsy's. Same with Anthony and Bowdoin. I took our most valued authors there for lunches. Stuffed squid. Escarole soup. A wine list to frame and hang on the wall. It was, to my mind, an almost perfect cuisine, on a par with Indian and Thai, and for that reason I found poorly cooked Italian food to be a sin against the delightful religion of eating.

Rinpoche, of course, paid no attention to things like overcooked pasta. He said he was in the mood for a bit of meat and asked for one meatball and the small house salad, and consumed it attentively and gratefully, as always. My dissatisfaction remained at the level of a very quiet muttering because, having waited tables for a brief spell in my late teens, I tip in the 20 percent range and try never to make the server's life more difficult than it already is. I had come, in my travels with my brother-in-law, to divide the restaurant staff into two camps: those waiters and waitresses who treated him like a human being despite his getup, his penchant for physical contact, and other odd ways; and those who shot him a nasty look or demonstrated an exaggerated trouble parsing his English, or who gave you the feeling they'd be gossiping about him, uncharitably, on the other side of the kitchen door.

Our waitress on that night fell into the former category. I told her what a nice first impression Spokane made, and that was true. Parks, a waterfall, older buildings in a low-rise grid with the stately Davenport at its center. "But what's the story with Sprague Street?" I asked. It ran past the back of the hotel, and we'd walked along it in the last of the daylight. It seemed to me that every other person we saw was either high or drunk.

"Oh, Sprague Street's a place we avoid," she said.

Which, naturally enough, made me decide to take that route again on the way back. It was the kind of thing I'd done with Anthony and Natasha in the old days, before Manhattan went sanitized and safe. Without ever risking their well-being, I'd walk with them along Ninth or Tenth Avenue and through Times Square at dusk, watching them and the people around them like a grizzly with his cubs, wanting them to see with their own eyes that the world, the real world, was more than Bronxville's sedate downtown or the shops of the Upper East Side. When they asked, Jeannie and I told them what the word 'prostitute' meant. We let them hand a dollar to subway musicians in torn jeans and bloody bare feet. At age eleven or so, Natasha inquired about an adult bookstore we drove past, and we told her the truth, in a tasteful way, and she said, "That isn't very nice, is it?" We were trying, on instinct, to suck all the bad power out of the taboo subjects, to leave the kids open-minded, sensible, unafraid, hard to shock, unprecious. I like to think it worked.

Something like the same impulse must have been in opera-
tion after our meal at the Restaurant That Shall Not Be Named.
Rinpoche understood the facts of life, of course, but I wasn't
sure he'd seen very much of America since moving to North
Dakota and settling into the retreat center. Celia told me he
rarely left the property, almost never watched TV. He insisted
that my job in this life was to guide the miraculous incarnation
we called "Shelsa," but my own feeling was that, if I had any
significant role to play in his family situation, it was to show
him my great land, warts and all. The Coulee dam, the viewing
platform at the Empire State Building, the plains, the Cascades,
the Hershey chocolate factory, Wrigley Field, casinos, suburbia
. . . and Sprague Street, Spokane.

It wasn't so bad, really. A few unsteady drunks meandering.
A shirtless, pierced twenty-year-old riding his skateboard along
and singing loudly. A ragged couple arguing at the mouth of
one alley. A woman who looked homeless and high.

Halfway up the block a small collection of souls had spilled
out the front door of a brightly lit place called Irv's. We'd passed
it on the way down and seen several muscular, six-foot-tall
women dressed in garish heels and an abundance of makeup.
I'd decided to say nothing and see if Rinpoche noticed. He did.

"What is?" he'd asked when we were safely past.

"A transvestite bar, I think."

"What that is?"

"People born in men's bodies who feel feminine," was the
best I could come up with on short notice, though I realized
after a moment that I could also have described it in reverse.
"They like to dress up as women. 'Transgendered' means people who have their bodies changed surgically, chemically, to be

more like women even though they were born men. Or vice versa."

I could sense that the subject intrigued him. There was a certain cast to his broad face when he was pondering. The mouth flattened and stretched. The eyes angled slightly down. Nothing like the excitement he'd shown at the sight of the Coulee dam, but I knew him well enough to feel his curiosity all the same, and it was part of the reason I chose Sprague Street again for our return trip. While we'd been having our meal, darkness had fallen and Irv's had grown lively. Patrons were hugging each other affectionately on the sidewalk; the tables on the other side of the front window were full, music playing. Used to being stared at themselves, no doubt, two of the taller women there, beautifully dressed and coiffed, made a frank appraisal of the two of us as we walked toward them in the night. One of them, skin the color of milk chocolate and lips painted tropical-sunset red, offered a friendly greeting. Rinpoche stopped. "How are you boys tonight?" she'd asked, so, naturally, Rinpoche said, "Good," and then put exactly the same question back to her.

I thought she might take offense, but she angled her head back and laughed. She was wearing gold eyeliner.

"What are you?"

"Monk," he said, and then, pinching the fabric of his robe and holding it toward her, "Transwestite, too."

Another uproarious laugh. The women called over a friend, more gorgeousness. While I stood by in a swirl of awkward air, the dark-skinned woman reached out and fingered Rinpoche's robe. He seemed not to mind. "Is this the best you can do?"

"This is what we dress, all the time."

"The color suits you, I have to say."

Thanks in part to the heels, she was five or six inches taller. He was smiling up at her. For a moment I thought he was actually sexually interested, or at least that her beautiful face had broken through what had always seemed a complete indifference, on his part, in the matter of good or not-so-good looks. My sister, as I might have mentioned, is a stunning woman, even in her sackcloth dresses and electrocuted hair, so perhaps I'd been mistaken about Rinpoche's tastes. Maybe he was the manly man I'd told the Christians about, a player, a lover of female pulchritude. And, I thought, if he cheated on my sister I was going to thrash him.

But of course these were my own sordid thoughts running without a leash. The famous smile lit his face. He reached out and put one hand on the woman's bare shoulder and there was nothing remotely sexual in the touch. "I go now to give a talk. Otto, where is?"

I gave the address, which I'd memorized. The woman looked me up and down and then returned her attention to the man with his hand on her shoulder.

"You are extremely cute," she said.

"Thank you."

"And if I didn't have friends coming in a little while I'd be sure to make a point of attending your talk."

"Come with your friends," Rinpoche said. "Come late. Doesn't matter."

"What do you talk about? Can we ask?" one of her companions said.

"Ask, ask," he said, "ask anything."

"She means the subject of your talk," I said.

"Subject is being your true self in this whirl," Rinpoche told her. "To go there the complete way." He was looking at all three of them now, shifting his eyes one to the next, standing there, as he always did, like some kind of stump or statue. Solid, still, exactly in his place on this earth.

The women laughed as if this were the best of all topics.

"He means it," I said. "He's a famous spiritual master. Volya Rinpoche. You should come. It's free. Starts in fifteen minutes."

"We might, we might," the first woman said. She leaned over and planted a kiss on Rinpoche's left cheek and we walked on.

"You have a smudge of lipstick there, boss," I said as we approached the building where the talk was to be held. "I can wipe it off if you want."

He'd suddenly gone deadly serious, pondering, musing. Preparing his speech, I thought. Or marveling at the variety of American street life. Or something else.

He shook his head no, and—one of us with a ruby-red imprint on his cheek—we went through the doorway of a three-story stone building and into a room that was crowded and abuzz and set up with a dozen rows of folding chairs, every seat taken.

17

On my previous road trip with Rinpoche, I had three times accompanied him to his presentations, once in a rented storefront in Youngstown, Ohio, once at a more formal conference, at Notre Dame, and a final memorable time in a yoga class in Madison. Though this setting—another vacant storefront—was similar to the one in Ohio, the crowd was much larger and, I was glad to see, not in yoga attire. His reputation seemed to have spread in the intervening years; the place was packed, electric with anticipation.

Since there were no unoccupied chairs, I stood against the back wall and examined the assembly. It was the usual motley crew, a range of humanity that went from scruffy twenty-somethings with pimply faces and worshipful looks, to neatly dressed seniors and middle-aged types like myself. Men and women, black, white, brown, yellow, red, assorted hair colors. Fat and thin, handsome and plain, tall and short. And then, just as the event's coordinator stood up to make the introduction . . . one rather spectacular transvestite came through the door. A portly middle-aged man in the back row stood up and gave her his seat.

I won't go into the whole presentation here—Rinpoche's books are widely available and the gist of his remarks can be found there, especially in one called *The Genuine Self.* But I want to give a sense of the evening. First of all, as he took his place on the slightly raised stage and sat, settling the fabric of his robe around him, Rinpoche assumed a very different air. It wasn't a matter of trying to be something he was not, of putting on a face to meet the faces that he met. It was more like a baseball player donning his uniform, a miner his steel hat, a surgeon her scrubs and sneakers. There was a job to do—that's what his body language conveyed. This is serious business, man. Listen to what I have to say. There would always be his throaty laugh, giggles, facial contortions—I'd never seen him give a presentation without those—but the underlying sense was of important information being made available. Audience members would ignore it at their peril.

A small table had been set beside him, and a glass (not a cup) of hot green tea was standing on it. Before he began, Rinpoche took his collection of small stones from a pocket in his robe. There were twenty-four in all, four neat rows of six, various colors and shapes but all of them roughly the size of a robin's egg. He set them out with great care, then ignored them. For the first half hour he spoke about authenticity and the myriad ways "the whirl," as he pronounced it, conspired to blind us to our truest self. "We have the two ways," he said, "same way and different way. When we are born we look around us to figure off how the other people are living, and then we live like that, too. Or, we look and we try to be just different from what the other people are. If our mother believed in God very much, we make a big life of believing in no God. If our father yelled at us, we make the same yelling at our little boy or girl. If the person in the house next door has a new car, we get one. Not bad, this is. None of it is bad, see? But maybe is it bad if we do these things without thinking on them ever. And maybe is it bad if we think everybody should be the same like us. And maybe, *maybe*," he said, his voice rising into a squeak that made him chuckle, "*maybe* even past the car and the yelling and the God there could be some part, wery true part of ourselves, that we don't want to work on in this life. A new part, a part that we could make in our own way inside ourselves, if we didn't always go same or different."

He paused for an uncomfortably long run of seconds and swung his eyes around the room to see if he'd been understood. Some of the younger people were reverently nodding. One or two of the older, back-row crowd sat stoically, waiting to be convinced. The woman we'd met at Irv's was holding her eyes steady on him.

"There is not one level but many levels to this true self," he went on. "Many levels! Let me show." He turned to the grid of stones and took one from the row closest to him. He held it up in the air between the second and third fingers of his right hand. "You look in yourself and you see one truth," he said. "Maybe from meditating, maybe from just from living your life on a day and day. You see: my mother used to yell at me like this, or my father used to yell. I'm now stopping yelling. You make a change inside you, a new feeling . . . Good." He put the stone into his robe and brought the empty hand out with a flourish, like a magician. "Wery simple, yes? "Could be," he said with a sly smile, "could be Rinpoche too simple for you, not so smart!" At this thought he went off into a riff of laughter, high and happy and as unselfconscious as a drunken dancer.

Then he held up the hand that had been empty and there was a different stone in it, and a few people in the crowd let out a gasp because we hadn't seen him pick it up from the table. This was a new trick. He'd been prestidigitating in Dickinson all these years, working his show. The cheeks squeezed up, the big smile lit the room as if powered by a day's worth of Coulee dam electricity. "But maybe something else is inside this new feeling, yes? What could it be?" He looked around for a suggestion. "Maybe, in the meditation one day you see something, or you feel something that you before never did. All in a sudden the world now looks little bit different. You feel like you touch God maybe. You touch the big, big intelligence that makes the stars hang in the sky and the blood go in your heart. Good, wery good! But now maybe you start to see somebody else, a transwestite maybe. Or maybe a woman with a rich car. Or maybe a gay. Or maybe a Christian on the radio, yelling. And you think in yourself: Ha! They never touched God like me!"

He chuckled briefly and happily, amused at our human foibles, then sighed and took a long drink of tea. There was, when he spoke like this, a tangible certainty about him. Not a conceited certainty, but something as simple and straightforward as a high school language teacher telling her students how to say "I saw them yesterday at the beach" in French. She'd studied for years. She'd lived in Paris on a Fulbright. She had a French husband or French parents or a Ph.D. You were there to learn the language, and she knew the language, and she was passing on her learning to you. That's how little egotism there was in Rinpoche's words, and how much confidence. His tone was contagious. The only immunity one could have to this particular contagion, it seemed to me, was the belief that one knew French better than the teacher did.

Yet that is an imperfect comparison, because he was talking not about a rule of unfamiliar grammar, but about the whole point and purpose of being alive, nothing less than that. And while all of us don't speak French, all of us have our convictions about how to live in this world and why we are here, even if we don't spend a lot of time verbalizing it. We believe that Jesus Christ was the one and only Lord, and our task is to worship him all our days. Or we believe there's no God and couldn't possibly be, that our individual existence is only another random spin of the molecular wheel without any greater meaning. Or, possibly, we believe that the point of it all is to earn as much money and grab as much pleasure as we can in our allotted stretch of years. Each of us is perfectly entitled to these opinions, that goes without saying. Underlying Rinpoche's talks—in public and private—was that humility. You could be right, he seemed to infer. Or, at least, no one else should be too sure you're wrong.

But here's what I'm getting at: the word *faith* is often used in these kinds of discussions. A person has faith or lacks it. In my brother-in-law, however, this tone, this essence I'm trying to describe, did not feel like faith; it felt, if you will forgive me, like fact. If you asked him how he knew there was a God, or a "Divine Intelligence" as he usually preferred to put it, he'd touch the ground or point to a tree or a cup or a blade of grass, as if challenging you to come up with another explanation for the simple fact of its existence. Or the simple fact of yours. If you asked him what God was like, he would always answer, "Don't know."

Simplistic, maybe. My more sophisticated friends would surely say so. They wanted elaborate philosophical arguments they could deftly counter, citing logic, history, science or psychological illusion. But that urge to argue and win, Rinpoche said, was merely the egotism of the intellect, another kind of false god, and these were people with whom he refused to engage. They took this refusal as a sign that his point of view was weak and indefensible . . . and he was perfectly at peace with that.

"Buddha," he went on, "after he taught his disciples for many many years, he held up for them one leaf from a tree." The second stone was aloft now, captured, in that odd way, between his second and third fingers. "This one leaf here, this is how much I taught you all these years," he said to them. "And the billions leaves in the forest are the other of what you could learn."

He had another sip of tea. "When you think you really know," he said, "when you touch the skin of God, maybe, then sometimes you become little bit in love with your own thinking stream. You have a good education and so you know more than everyone about how you should live. Or you are special to God and different from other people, yes? You meditate, you have speriences in meditation. Makes you special, yes?" A short laugh. "This part is not so good."

Another pause, another bit of shifting around in the audience.

"So," he inquired, "what to do with this *not so good*, all these speriences and all this special knowing?" He looked around the room for a suggestion, and when none was forthcoming he suddenly hitched up his right sleeve and swept his arm across the tabletop, knocking the other stones onto the floor in a clatter. People in the front row jumped back, or let out a yelp, or sat frowning at the disorder of it all. An almost ferocious look had come across Rinpoche's face. I suddenly remembered his wrestling match with Anthony. I remembered him talking about being in jail in Russia, and the people he'd had to deal with there. I thought: there's something else beyond the softness and kindness, another Rinpoche.

He sat back in the chair, holding an expression that said "I'm sure you understand, yes?"

But no one understood. Or at least for the time being, the youthful nodding had ceased. A curtain of perplexity had fallen over us, and I felt a swarm of small insects, the beetles of irritation, cynicism, and doubt, scampering between my ears. I couldn't keep from casting a sideways glance at the beautiful transvestite in the back row. She'd closed her eyes, making two golden gibbous moons, and it was impossible to tell what she might be thinking.

Again, Rinpoche solicited questions. This time, after a silence of half a minute, a young woman who might have been, with her reverent politeness, my sister twenty-five years earlier, raised her hand and stood and said, "From your books, Rinpoche, I thought the idea was that we should feel good about ourselves. I was raised in a tradition where we were constantly being told we were sinners, and what I liked about what you wrote was that it made me feel we should start the spiritual search from a place of self-acceptance. We should assume that we are, not perfect, exactly, but loveable. And now, tonight, it seems like you're saying when we get to a place where we feel, I don't know, *right* in the world, we should forget all about it and start over."

She sat down, not far from tears, it seemed to me. Around her the room pulsed with unspoken agreement.

Rinpoche pondered a response for a moment, gazing at her in a tender way. "When you read a book that's a good book," he said, "that you like, you read the one page, you read the one chapter. Do you stop?"

"Not usually. No."

He looked at her as if he'd given the answer and he was waiting for her to comprehend.

"I don't understand."

He tried a different angle. "The little girl or the little boy learns words," he said. "One word, next word. Pretty soon she has ten words, hundred words. She grows up, school, the college maybe. She says, 'I have enough words now. I don't know all the words, but I have enough'. Rinpoche says that sometimes, yes?"

"Okay."

"But spirchal life you don't say this "enough". You never say it. Deeper and deeper you go. You say, maybe I know something. Maybe I know many things. I understand. I am *wery* good! But you don't say, I stop now. I know God all the way. I know myself all the way. Stopping is from the ego, but God has no ego. God goes and goes, changes, plays, makes new and new, for every second, for all time! You should be like that, satisfied and not satisfied. Love yourself, yes, sure. Yourself is good. I can see in you," he pointed at her and flashed his smile, "right now, I can see the wery good inside of you. Wery wery good person I see! You should know it. And also know that new is coming for you. Love maybe, a babies, house, work, troubles, getting old or getting sick, death. Every in a little more time, if you try, there will be a new part of God, a new part of the deepness of life for you to see, and if you say always, 'I know, I know,' you can't see it, yes? You can't learn."

"Yes, okay, I think so," she said. Nobody else risked a question for a long time. Unperturbed, Rinpoche finished his tea. He looked at the stones spread around his feet as if wondering how they'd gotten there. When he tilted his head at them in a curious way, I saw the patch of lipstick on his cheek. Other people must have seen it. The silence felt to me as though it were turning a corner from puzzled to annoyed.

At last it was broken by a man who must have been in his mid-seventies, with a floppy cap of feathery white hair and a trimmed white beard to match. "I've read all your books, Rinpoche," he said, "and I have to say I think tonight you didn't really explain things very well. Excuse me, I say it with all respect. Perhaps it's just the word 'God' that's throwing me off. I've never read that word in your books, or very rarely. I'm here mainly for more peace of mind, not to become a believer, and I think your presentation has really just confused all of us."

The man had stood to speak. As he took his seat again someone in the middle of the room hissed him. He turned angrily and mouthed, "My opinion!" And the other person hissed something back at him that I couldn't hear.

We were all waiting for Rinpoche's response, but seconds passed, a minute passed, two minutes, and eventually it became apparent that he might just continue to stare down into his glass and say nothing. I couldn't tell if he was offended, angry, cooking up a good response, or what was going on. It was tremendously uncomfortable, not least for the man who'd risked the comment. At last Rinpoche looked up and around the room as if for other, better remarks, and we understood there would be no reply. Silence was the answer. Jesus with the Grand Inquisitor. Not a word. From thirty feet away you could feel the frown on the face of the white-haired man.

Silence and more silence. The shuffling and coughing that never quite breaks a difficult moment. The man who'd introduced Rinpoche was turning red, and I was silently urging him to say a closing word when twenty feet to my right I heard a sound. I turned and saw that the woman from Irv's had gotten to her feet. Her dress was very short and tight and absolutely scarlet, and it had worked its way high up toward her hips. Her legs were a runner's legs, the legs of an oarswoman. She stepped away from the chair and I expected her to turn and walk out the door, but instead she went up the aisle outside the rows of chairs, made a ninety-degree left, and walked across in front of the first row. Her heels sounded out an unignorable *tat, tat, tat, tat* on the hardwood floor, but had she glided along in silence, barefoot, everyone in the room would still have watched. She had the presence of an actor or a dancer, shoulders back, chin up, hips and muscular arms swinging. She made it about halfway from the corner to the central aisle, and then bent down, demurely, knees twisted to the side, and she picked up one of the stones, and said something quietly to the teacher. There might have been a "thank you" at the end of it, I couldn't quite hear. Then she stood and promenaded back the way she'd come and straight through the door into the night. At last there was the customary closing word from our host: that we should thank Rinpoche for taking time out of his busy schedule to make a stop in Spokane, that the local bookseller had books ready at the table and Rinpoche would be happy to sign them. There was a splash of polite applause. Five or six people approached Rinpoche and asked for his autograph on a book. One young woman simply wanted to touch him. But I sensed that most of the others walked out vaguely disappointed. I counted myself among them. It wasn't his best talk, I was telling myself. That white-headed guy was at least partly right: Rinpoche never quite closed the circle the way he might have, never quite made his point.

The crowd dispersed. Rinpoche and I walked back together along the sidewalk, the night a few degrees cooler now, the traffic thin. A sort of halo of doubt hung over me, resurrection of an older demon, and I couldn't think of anything to say. My brother-in-law went along contentedly enough, at peace with the silence. In the glorious Davenport lobby I asked if I could buy him something to drink—there was a coffee bar there off to one side. "More tea? An Italian soda?"

He shook his head and looked at me, expecting something, it seemed. Praise, understanding, a question. "What did that woman say to you?" I asked him. "At the end?"

He looked at me and grinned. "Tell you other time, man," he said, then he patted me on the shoulder and went off to his nightly prayer.

I bought a cup of tea and sat at one of the tables, running my eyes across the gold-leaf trim beneath the ceiling, the heavy chandeliers, the purposely twisted poles atop which small square lamps sat, the marble floor tiles. I liked my lessons neat. I was a fan of the clear yes or no from the depths of my logical mind. And, until half an hour earlier, I had been a fan of Volya

Rinpoche. I wanted him to succeed. I wanted him to live up to the reputation he had among my sister and some hundreds of thousands of others around the world. I was, as the saying goes, *invested* in the idea that he knew something essential I didn't know and would be able to teach me. After all these years, all these *wessons*, all the hours I'd spent in reading and meditation, if he turned out to be a kindly fraud, I think I would have taken to drink, or signed up for a lifetime of therapy, or never again in my life ventured off the safely beaten path.

Into the room came a couple in their thirties, the man about five feet six, the woman much taller. They were obviously in love, on a honeymoon perhaps. I noticed that she was wearing heels—a nice touch, I thought, as if she were saying Yes, I'm tall, isn't that fine! I liked the way he looked at her. It made me miss my wife. Jeannie had accepted my new interest in meditation and the interior life with a bemused but nevertheless respectful good humor, with her typical open-mindedness. Not for her, she said, just as beef tongue at the diner was not for her, though she was happy enough to watch me enjoy it. She had, she said, her own path, Christian in essence but not aligned with any particular group; a belief in God, in goodness, in some possibility of an afterlife. "I prefer to just deal with the moment," she told me once, but mostly we didn't speak about it. I wondered if she'd only been indulging me, the way I had, for so long, indulged my sister. I looked back and tried to see if Rinpoche's lessons, if meditation, might really have made no lasting change in my life. Maybe it was just the years of living that had changed me. Maybe I hadn't changed as much as I thought.

Again and again in his books, and in those he'd recommended, I read that it was important not to confuse the message with the messenger. Even the greatest spiritual teachers were human. If you searched for flaws, you'd find them, but outer perfection wasn't the point.

I'd never really liked that idea. I wanted, I suppose, some sort of proof, some secret way of thrusting myself up beyond the inertia and travails of this life, some kind of guarantee that the effort was worth it. I wanted to see the rules of reality stretched. I wanted love to persist and death to be a temporary inconvenience and some great secret to be hiding in the back room of the meditative life. But in the Davenport lobby on that dark night of my soul, I suspected that those rules were as unyielding as gravity, and that Jeannie, my solace, was gone from me forever.

⟶ ∽ 18

I'd like to confess here to having a map fetish, a cartographic obsession. I like the odd names (Othello, Washington, for one good example), and often build a whole imaginary world around unknown roads, cities, and towns—a great bistro, cool swimming hole, welcoming locals. On my office wall was a detailed map of North Dakota, gift from my colleagues to mark my twentieth year at Stanley and Byrnes. I spent a few minutes every day looking at it, remembering the places I'd been and wondering about those I hadn't. At home we'd always had both a world map and a map of the United States on the wall of our finished basement, and countless times Jeannie and I had sent Anthony or Natasha down there with a geography question. We'd be talking about the elections in Russia and the kids would ask where it was, and we'd take them to the map and show them the route of the Trans-Siberian, or where some of the work camps had been, in Norilsk and Sakhalin, or the farthest east the German army had pushed before being stopped at what was then called Stalingrad. When the kids were in grammar school and junior high and we'd be out for a burger and

Roland Merullo

milk shake someplace, waiting for our food to arrive, I'd sometimes quiz them. "Natasha Ringling," I'd say in a stentorian
voice, "for one hundred points, please tell me the names of the
states that border Utah." "Anthony Ringling, can you name four
countries in South America?" They loved it. It passed the time.
Jeannie and I had never wanted them to be like the many Americans unable to find Arkansas or Nevada on a map of their own
country. Nor were we priming our kids for the SATs in third
grade. We dropped bits of learning into the mix, we argued,
traveled, cleaned the house, had some fun. An ordinary, decent
family, in other words. I missed those days. I wanted them
back. But where on the map do you go in order to ask for that?

When I awoke that morning (still on East Coast time, I'd
become, in Washington state, an early riser) I sat at the table
with my Rand McNally and plotted the rest of our trip. Interstate 90 runs in a wavy line from Spokane through the thin part
of Idaho and across half of Montana and then I-94 angles off
into North Dakota and within three miles of what had once
been my parents' farm. That would have been the logical route
for Rinpoche and me to take. But I still had almost two weeks of
vacation left, and I've always believed that seeing America only
from the interstate is like Skyping with your marital partner
(something Jeannie and I had never tried). It's a substitute for
real travel, for burying yourself in the sights, smells, and stop-
light traffic, the Main Streets and boondocks of an actual nation.

Besides, I'd made arrangements for a couple of stops of my
own, and those were away from the interstate. One of our most
successful authors, Gilligan Neufaren (one does not make up a
name like that), was on a fly-fishing vacation near Ennis, and

we'd talked about getting together at a restaurant he liked. And then there was Yellowstone. If part of my job was to show the country to Rinpoche, how could I pass within a hundred miles of the greatest national park and not take him there for a visit?

Studying the map closely, going from the Montana page to the Wyoming page and back again three times, I saw that it would be perfectly feasible to leave I-90 east of Butte, dip down on Route 287 through Ennis, swing east and south through Yellowstone, and then zip back up Route 89 to the interstate at Livingston. Simple.

But, as Jeannie pointed out more than once, not only do I almost always picture a place on the map as more interesting than it actually turns out to be, I almost always assume it will take less time to get there than it actually does. In this case, to further complicate matters, I failed to recognize something she no doubt would have pointed out to me: Montana is so big that the folks at Rand McNally use a different scale for displaying it. What looks like an easy two-hour ride in Massachusetts turns out to be almost twice that in the compressed version of the map's Montana.

By the time I set the Rand McNally aside, showered, and packed up, it was still only a little after seven o'clock. Rinpoche and I had talked about getting an early start, so I went and tapped on his door. No answer. He was meditating, I assumed, or out for a sunrise constitutional. I went downstairs to the lobby and had a cup of excellent green tea and honey from the café there (which also served Red Bull at three dollars an infusion), read about the troubles in Syria , scanned an editorial calling on the Republican presidential candidate to release his tax records, admired the chandeliers, ogled a pair of attractive women rolling their luggage across the tile, checked my watch, and felt a little tap of doubt at my temples, residue of the previous night's crisis of faith.

At five to eight I climbed back upstairs and knocked more loudly on my brother-in-law's door. Nothing. I put an ear to the wood; no mooing sounds. I returned to my room and used the telephone there and by then the doubts were fully awake again, circling and buzzing like mosquitoes on an August night. Sensing that I'd finally seen through his act, the famous Volya Rinpoche had packed his things and absconded. Maybe he'd borrowed a sum of money from my sister on some pretense and had crossed the border into Canada already and was looking to find another gullible palm reader to pretend to fall in love with, a woman who'd inherited a large amount of acreage, perfect for a "retreat center," where he could hide out for another six or seven years.

I've sworn myself to full honesty here, so while I feel bound to admit all this, I do so with a measure of shame. My musings made little sense in any case. What was Rinpoche going to do, leave his wife and daughter, run away with one piece of luggage and a nice smile, and hope to make a new life in another country? True, that's what he seemed to have done in coming to America—appear out of nowhere, carrying almost nothing, find his way to a kindly, generous woman . . . and so on. But even in the depths of my loneliness and misery there in Spokane, part of me understood that I was indulging my meanest, most cynical side. He was a good man. Hundreds of thousands, perhaps millions of people counted on him for spiritual guidance. His books sold well all over the world; his monthly meditation retreats were booked half a year in advance. One mediocre talk shouldn't be enough to break the bridge of my faith in half, should it?

The thing to do, I decided, was check out of the hotel, load my meager luggage into the pickup, find myself an excellent breakfast spot, and trust that my traveling companion would make his presence known to me before too much more time passed. I left ten dollars for the cleaning woman and checked out of the room. Loaded up the truck, then set out on foot. The Spokane morning was warm and dry. Sprague Street, littered and locked up, made me think of the Sunday morning hangovers of my college years. Harmless now, touched with regret, the sidewalks smelling of stale beer, it was a place of exhausted urges and listless commerce, one convenience store advertising lottery tickets and espresso, one city bus trundling along with its handful of sleepy passengers.

I went from Sprague to Post, wandered around a bit, and was walking past a sad collection of drunks and street people in front of the Greyhound station when a flash of maroon caught my eye. Sitting on a concrete planter beside a man in greasy pants and whiskey-rouged skin was my sister's husband. The morning sun shone from his shaved head. On the sidewalk between his feet sat his battered cloth bag, a sort of oversized purse, the only piece of luggage I'd ever known him to have. Until he caught my eye, checked his left wrist as if there were a timepiece there, and wagged a scolding finger at me in a joking way, I thought my ugly suspicions had been correct: Rinpoche was leaving for Canada on the eight-thirty Greyhound, skipping out, running. I saw him pat the sagging man on the shoulder, offer a word of what sounded like encouragement, then lift his bag and come toward me.

"Hi," he said happily. "I am waiting one hour for my friend, Otto, to go."

"Funny place to wait. How'd you know I'd be walking by?"

The happy laugh, the big shoulders lifted and dropped in a helpless shrug. "I'm buying you now the breakfast you like," he said. "Close by is the place."

One block, a left turn, and Madeline's French Bakery showed itself to us like a vision of paradise. It had not quite yet opened for the day. Rinpoche and I stood at the door and waited. "You are sad last night," he said. "I could see. So I thought: What can take away the sadness from my good friend, my brother-and-law? Food can take it. This morning I asked downstairs: where is the best breakfast we can find? And the people say here."

"Is it in the top twenty French bakeries in America?"

He squinted at me. Behind him I heard the door lock snap open. My stomach made one slow somersault.

Inside, after a careful inspection of the pastry choices, Rinpoche instructed me to secure a table and wait. He was buying and he would be bringing the food. I should wait, relax, say a small prayer if I wanted to, text Natasha and Anthony.

I did all of the above. Another few minutes and he came striding over with a tray in his hands and the lighthouse beacon of a smile on his features. Caffe latte, large. Cinnamon roll the size of two clenched fists. Bowl of fresh fruit and the customary green tea for him. He set these items on the table with great care, gently, attentively, as if he were setting a newborn down in its crib, then he put the tray back and joined me.

"I wasn't sad last night," I said, "I was doubting you. I didn't like the talk you gave. I didn't think it worked. I worried you were a fake, that you'd tricked my sister and all those people into believing you had something to teach them, and that you'd tricked me, too. When I saw you at the bus station just now, with your bag all packed, I thought you were running away to Canada."

Of solid Lutheran stock, I've nevertheless always held a secret envy for the Roman Catholics and their sacrament of confession. Even without any kind of penance or intervening priest, I felt cleansed then, relieved. The worst of me, the moldy, putrid, festering worst of Otto A. Ringling, had been set out in the light of day. Already, it was drying up.

Rinpoche was busying himself with the fruit bowl, pushing the tines of his fork this way and that through the pieces of melon and pineapple to find a plump berry, which he stabbed and lifted to his mouth. Only then did he make eye contact. He nodded, smiled, reached out with fork in hand and patted me on the wrist. "Good," he said.

"Good? It didn't feel good at all. It felt like betrayal. I felt like a little boy, angry at his dad for breaking his promise about a day at the state fair."

Rinpoche shrugged, impaled a piece of melon, looked up. "Now you have now," he said, gesturing to my meal. "Coffee. Sweet. Drink the now and eat it, say a little thanks to who made."

"No talk about the talk, then?"

Another shrug, a brief flash of impatience through the eyes. "Later anytime," he said. "Now"—he gestured at the roll.

"I pictured you sneaking out of the hotel after I'd gone to sleep, sneaking down to Irv's and finding the woman who'd come to the talk and cheating on my sister with a beautiful transvestite."

A splash of amusement. A well-chewed strawberry washed down with a sip of tea.

"I wondered if the secret thing she'd said to you was, 'Come meet me,' or something along those lines."

"Sacred woman," was all he said. "Wery pure being."

"Really?"

"Wery, wery pure," he repeated. He reached over with his fork, scraped a bit of the frosting from my cinnamon roll, and sampled it.

"You're joking."

He shook his head, and the gold-flecked eyes were on me then, steady as the sun. "Last night you asked me what she say."

"Yes."

"You want to know?"

"No, I asked you because I *didn't* want to know."

He smiled sadly. "What she say to me was: 'When the trouble comes, I'll help you.'"

"When what trouble comes?"

"Eat," he said. "Drink. Look at this something." From beneath his robe he took a scrap of paper that was folded in half. He handed it across the table. I thought it would be the woman's phone number, that's where my mind resided then. She was a psychic in high heels and makeup. She looked into the future and saw trouble with Rinpoche's marriage.

I sipped the coffee, prepared myself, unfolded the piece of paper, and saw one word written there: KALISPELL.

"Her name?"

Rinpoche laughed so forcefully that a tiny piece of fruit shot out of his mouth and landed on the table between us. "Place," he said. "Mantana. We go there today, all right?"

"Why? Another talk?"

"No more talkings for me," he said. "Rinpoche is now retiring from the talkings. Near here is a good place. I think we should see it and take Otto's sadness away."

"What about *your* sadness?"

He shrugged, crinkled his eyes, but I could see it there. On top of everything else, he'd told me that Shelsa had suffered from several months of mysterious digestive troubles, serious enough for a hospitalization. He and Cecelia hadn't wanted to worry us, he said. Now, supposedly, everything was fine.

"I'll have to check," I said. "I'm supposed to have dinner with one of my authors tomorrow. I'll have to see how far away this place is, and if it's on our route."

"On, on," Rinpoche said confidently. "Check the map, pal."

This was an expression I had taught him. Where are we going? he'd ask. And I'd say, Check the map, pal. I'd been trying to tutor him in the important skill of map reading, and he was simply awful at it. Speaker of eleven languages, wrestling master, sometime mind reader and seer into the future, incarnation of one of the great teachers of the mysterious Ortyk lineage, he couldn't seem to grasp the idea of the world being laid out in colorful shapes and crooked lines on a page.

Eating and drinking, struggling to hold myself in the famous *now*, I quizzed him again about how he'd known, or guessed, that I'd be heading in this direction for breakfast, why he hadn't worried about meeting me in the hotel as we'd planned, why he'd been hanging out at the bus station talking to that man, what the woman had meant by "when the trouble comes." But it was like tapping a stone with a hammer and hoping water leaked out. An evasive shrug, a focus on his food, a suggestion that I pay attention to eating and drinking and forget the rest. Either Rinpoche was the truest of Christians, spending time with the downtrodden and outcast, the so-called sinners, the sick, the abandoned . . . or he was the most brilliant con man this side of Wall Street.

Either way, we had three or four more days on the road together. I thanked him for the meal and left him to finish his ministry of the bus station while I went back and fetched our old truck. On the way I had a text from my sister, letting me know that the train had brought them safely home to North Dakota, and asking this question: "Are you going to Kalispell?"

───── 19

U.S. Route 2 from Spokane to Kalispell carries you north through Sandpoint, Idaho, within a dozen miles of the Canadian border, then drops you down again, south into the Montana mountains. That part of the West was devoid of the scourge of bumper stickers one sees in New York, those snippets of traveling opinion, but there were plenty of road signs to compensate. On the way out of Spokane we passed Crosswind Church and a sign there, HE WHO WON'T BE COUNSELED CAN'T BE HELPED. Farther along, through a steep-hilled green landscape reminiscent of northern New Hampshire and Maine, another sign advised, ENGAGE JESUS—REJECT THE CULTS. In between were offers for Huckleberry Ice Cream and Huckleberry Lemonade and then we crossed into Priest River, Idaho, which announced itself as A PROGRESSIVE TIMBER COMMUNITY. What could this mean? I envisioned scores of liberal lumberjacks sawing away at Douglas firs and quoting the socialist senator Bernie Sanders on their coffee breaks; carpenters with *WE ARE THE 99%* tattoos; high school teachers working up lesson plans on single-payer health care and the actual dimensions of a milled four-by-eight. I tried to remember the last time Idaho had gone Democratic in a presidential election: 1582, I guessed.

Rinpoche was asleep by then, so he missed my favorite sign of the bunch: DEAR LORD, MAKE ME THE MAN MY DOG THINKS I AM.

It was a perfect day, sunny, dry, warm for those parts. The whole country was baking that summer, crops dying of thirst, newspapers running articles about the Dust Bowl days.

We arrived in the resort town of Sandpoint and found pleasant tree-lined streets with quaint houses and an Amtrak station. I'd heard somewhere that it had become an artists' refuge—a progressive painters' community, perhaps. In my thoughts, though, I couldn't completely separate it from articles I'd read and a couple of television documentaries I'd seen. Not so long ago, militia and white supremacist groups had considered the Sandpoint area their world headquarters. "Hate supremacists" Jeannie called them. They were, as we understood it, intent on ridding the world of Jews, the nation of "coloreds," and their lives of any kind of government intrusion whatsoever. Fond of murder, robbery, and hateful indoctrination, they were a bizarre man-cult of nutcases who wanted to remake the world in their own image. The Church of Jesus Christ Christian was a name that stuck in my brain from one of the articles. Perfect. That would distinguish them nicely from the Church of Jesus Christ Buddhist, Jesus Christ Hindu, and particularly from the Church of Jesus Christ Jew. I wondered what Rinpoche would make of them, but I didn't have to wonder what they would make of him. Not white, not Christian, not packing guns or hatred in his luggage, he would be, quite simply, their Anti-Christ.

But at Mick Duff's Irish Pub on the main street, there were no members of the Aryan Nation in evidence. The waitress had a sleeve of tattoo down her right arm and the friendliest of manners; on the large-screen TV the British Open was in progress, and Rinpoche was fascinated by it, asking me why they were swinging so "big," and wondering again how, exactly, it was different from "furniture golf," and when we could try it. He'd told me he'd played once or twice in Europe, years ago, but I wasn't entirely sure I believed him.

I was in the mood for All-American, and Mick Duff's Angus burger and a glass of local porter did not disappoint. Afterward, we had a brief swim in Sandpoint Lake, where Rinpoche was kind enough to forgo his yoga routine, where a flotsam of wood chips and fly larvae cluttered the lake's surface, and where a trio of big-armed brutes gave us the parking-lot evil eye. On the way out of town a blue pickup seemed to be following us. I pulled over and it sped past, and I tried as best I could to leave my paranoia there by the side of the road. No doubt the overwhelming majority of Sandpointers were honest, decent people just trying to make a good life for themselves there in the north country. Lumping them all with Randy Weaver was about as fair as lumping all New Yorkers with Son of Sam.

Still, it was a disturbing stretch for a person of my sensibilities. The radio was awash with a nationally syndicated talk-show host on an anti-Kennedy tirade. "Filthy vampires," he called that entire family. And then the ultimate epithet: "New York liberals!" Between segments—I simply had to listen for a while—came an advertisement asking, "Do you have guns in your house you don't need?"

Thousands of them.

Except for one sign advertising a Tanning-Espresso-Wi-Fi place, there wasn't much in the way of entertainment by the sides of the road until we stopped at a historical marker that told us camels had been used in those parts to pack in supplies for the gold diggers of 1864-5. I gave Rinpoche a mini-lesson on the Gold Rush, the frenzy that sent thousands of explorers out here, made a few of them wealthy, and breathed life into outposts like Spokane and Walla Walla.

"Gold in Russia, too," he said.

"Do you miss home at all?"

He shook his head and worked his Buddhist rosary. "Italy, I miss."

"Your center there?"

More headshaking. "The food. I like wery much there the way the people eat."

"Slowly," I suggested, because we'd done a book on the Slow Food movement, Italian in its origins. "Meditatively. With great appreciation."

"No," he said. "Pasta . . . with the wery small, how you say?" He placed his hands together, palm to palm, as if praying, then opened one side.

"Clams."

"Yes, *wery* much the little clam on pasta Rinpoche likes."

I considered this for a moment, tried to look behind the words to see if he was playing with me again, working some spiritual lesson, tongue-in-cheek. There were times when speaking with my friend was like playing a game of chess. Why did he put the queen's bishop over there? What's that all about? What part of my defenses does it threaten?

"Here's what I don't understand," I said. "I always had this idea that real Buddhists don't eat living creatures. 'Buddhist Delight' is an item on the menu of the Chinese restaurant where we live, and it's completely vegetarian. I've never understood that about you. A meatball the other night, a bit of bacon at the B and B. Now clams. Please explain."

"I pray for them before I eat them."

"And that's enough?"

"Buddha, he eat a little meat, Otto. First he starved himself—no food, *wery* not much food, long time. But then he said, no, not the right way, starving, and so he eats a little bit of all the food and says thank you."

"So asceticism isn't the route to salvation?"

"None of the 'isms'," he said.

"It means going hungry, giving up all pleasure. In some systems it's considered the route to enlightenment."

"Route to maybe you die," he said, and he looked over at me and grinned and I knew I'd been right to be careful. It was possible, yes, that he did actually miss the food in Italy, that he was particularly fond of *spaghetti alle vongole*, or whatever the correct term was. But it was equally possible that he'd designed the whole conversation simply to help me with my eating issues, my need for variety, comfort, and properly prepared pasta. Part of me did worry about asceticism: was that where the spiritual life would lead? And so, to protect myself from that thought . . . I ate more.

"Look at your Jasper, okay?" Rinpoche went on. "Hungry, he eat. Tired, he sleep. Gold—doesn't care about. You see?"

"Yes," I said. "I think so."

"Now you got smart, man."

We hit the Montana border in mid-afternoon and switched to Mountain Time and a seventy-mile-an-hour speed limit. A short ways into the Treasure State we passed a billboard announcing that each small white cross by the side of the road designated a highway fatality. I explained this to my curious companion and he began to hum a quiet prayer for every one we passed. I counted them: fifty-four crosses there would turn out to be, over a span of fifty-five miles, and that was a mystery. Yes, the road was steep and curved in places, the legal speed high—at least by eastern standards—but there were crosses at almost every turn, as if Route 2 to Kalispell were some kind of suicide alley, the place the distraught came to end their torment. I found myself imagining the pain and suffering each cross marked—some family broken open, some lover or father or mother lost. At one point there were eight of them bunched tight together and I pictured a school bus or a van filled with kids, the terror of the victims in their last seconds, the immense sorrow they left behind. I began to pray for them, too.

The few homes we passed were small and mostly poor, the Yaak River Valley unpeopled. I saw no road kill and wondered why: No animals here? So much available wilderness that the roadways didn't tempt them? Descending into Troy we passed a billboard asking "Is the Virgin Mary Alive?" and "Can the Dead Speak?" with a phone number one could call in order to find out. This entire day, it seemed to me, from the sad street people of Spokane to the wholesome families at Sandpoint Lake, from the lingering stink of the Haters thereabouts to the various sects and cults that paid for these kinds of billboards or listened to these kinds of radio shows—all of it said everything that needed to be said about this country. Our almost unlimited freedom was like an African plain, a vast Serengeti of possibility, capable of holding every style of opinion and belief, every kind of life. Boa constrictors, chattering monkeys, regal lionesses striding the riverbank, herds of wildebeest and zebra that wanted nothing more than to be left alone. It wasn't true, as some claimed, that with enough ambition and hard work anyone could succeed in America, climb to any height. The idea of a level playing field was at best a comforting lie, at worst a thorn under the skin of people like the kids I tutored. But it did seem to be true that we could believe anything we wanted, and say almost anything we wanted, and join these crazed herds that went racing toward the edge of the cliff looking only at each other and trampling everything in their path.

The town of Troy's United Methodist church asked "Are you a loved child of God?" which better suited my own tender notions. We stopped there, next door to a bowling alley/casino, for Italian soda and stale ice cream.

From the other trip I'd taken with Rinpoche I remembered this pattern. There would be what he called "wessons," some of them puzzling and intense, others encouraging. There were his quick enthusiasms—golf now, hydroelectric power, the workings of a stick shift—his jubilant, almost childish displays; the mysterious allusions and hints; the chess-board conversations. Somehow, once we'd made the turn at the top of Route 2 and begun heading south, away from Canada, I abandoned my foolish ideas about him making his escape, stopped worrying about my sister being hurt, my meditations invalidated. Beyond Troy he was buried in a contemplative silence, rousing himself only to ask the occasional question: Why were there so many casinos in "Mantana"? What meant that red flag with the blue X and white stars? What was this "impeach," as in the hand-lettered IMPEACH OBAMA sign flashing by to our left. What meant APACHE PAWN—GUNS, TOOLS, JEWELRY?

We were relatives on a road trip, two guys in a truck, worried about our loved ones, admiring the tree-coated slopes, feeling no great need for talk. And when, at 8:29 p.m., we pulled up to a block of buildings that included the Kalispell Grand Hotel, one of us was exceedingly hungry.

20

Speaking of crazed herds, Kalispell was, among other distinctions no doubt, the one-time residence of Lafayette Ronald Hubbard, founder of Scientology and surely one of the most eccentric characters in modern American spiritual history. With his hundreds of millions of dollars earned from the writing of sci-fi novels, L. Ron traveled the world trying to solve humanity's problems. Addiction, meaning of life, enlightenment—nothing was too big an issue for him to address. He built a fleet of his own ships, wrote millions of words, produced films, started a religion, and had followers who were convicted of breaking into government offices to alter anti-Scientology records. Three wives, seven kids, a California ranch hideout—he was larger than life. I didn't know any Scientologists personally, but there were a couple of celebrities who claimed that faith, one who'd been in the news that summer for a pricey divorce. What I knew, all I knew, was that Scientologists were vehemently anti-therapy, believed in a version of reincarnation that included lives on other planets, and that practitioners paid for their spiritual teachings in sometimes sizeable chunks. It seemed a peculiar mix, and as Rinpoche and I checked in to the small, tattered, more than satisfactory Kalispell Grand and took a creaky elevator up to our third-floor rooms, I mused about the human phenomenon that went by the title "organized religion." What, I wondered, was disorganized religion?

Dad's overactive mind, Anthony would have said.

Like its Grand Hotel, the town of Kalispell had a welcoming quaintness to it, an aroma of the true Old West. Saloons, boot-and-belt shops, the feeling that the flat street might, at any moment, be flooded with herds of cattle up from Texas for slaughter—I enjoyed the atmosphere of the place, so completely different as it was from everything I'd grown used to. If I had to find words to describe the American West, they would be: 'vast,' 'dry,' 'architecturally bland,' 'unhurried.' But it all seemed too large for words, a leave-me-alone, can-do universe where open land was plentiful, ethnic food all but unavailable, and our pickup truck—powdered with roadside dust and carrying the carcasses of a million insects—served as a kind of safe-conduct pass.

In the elevator Rinpoche had surprised me by asking to come along for dinner—that would make two nights in a row—and we ended up having a tasty Chinese meal at a Japanese restaurant called Genji. Another tattooed waitress (she told us the advent of casinos had sucked all the life out of the city's cultural scene), another glass of good local porter (with an awful name, Moose Drool), another conversation that I'd return to many times in the months that followed.

At Genji, Rinpoche ate almost nothing, a few bamboo shoots from my moo goo gai pan, two bites of rice. He was there, it seemed, mainly for the company. "I'm not a perfect man, Otto," he said with an endearing simplicity, out of the clear blue.

"I know that. I'm sorry I doubted you."

"No problem."

"It's strange, though, isn't it? Everybody who follows some kind of spiritual path, for lack of a better term, seems to need to have a perfect being at its center. Christ, Buddha, Krishna, Mohammed, Moses—they weren't ordinary guys."

"Ordinary," Rinpoche contradicted. "Wery most ordinary."

"That's not the story that's making the rounds."

He smiled, reached over without asking, and took a sip of my beer. "The bitter I like now," he said. "Getting used of."

"Used *to*. We say *getting used to* something. You're getting used to the bitter taste of beer, in this case." He looked across the table at me with an expression not of condescension, exactly, but something close to infinite patience.

"What?"

He watched me, waited, the skin of his forehead creased with three parallel lines.

"What's wrong?"

Suffering under his patient gaze, I traced my way back across the conversation. Had I missed something? "All right, okay," I said, when I'd understood. "The bitterness in beer is like the bitterness in life, right? Which the enlightened being eventually comes to appreciate. The bitterness in life is a reflection of our imperfect state here on this earth and the perfectly imperfect souls we choose to worship. Correct?"

I expected another "Wery good, Otto!" accompanied by a pat on the shoulder. Yet again the Master had taken a profound lesson from the most mundane of everyday occurrences—a sip of beer—and I'd understood it this time, solved the Ortykian koan. But he kept looking at me, grinned, said, "You should maybe teach *me* now, my friend."

"Bullshit."

"What is this *boll?*"

"You know what it is—an angry cow with horns and a penis."

"And why can't you be the teacher, give Rinpoche a rest? You are ready now for a big change in your life, my brother-and-law. Big big change."

"I've had one big change in the past year," I said. "That's all I can handle for a while."

"Two big changes then, maybe," he said, pushing me. "Maybe three."

"I can't picture that. External changes—new job, new house, kids growing up—those things I can sometimes imagine. But what does a big internal change feel like?"

"New eyes."

"The world looks different? I mean, physically looks different?"

"Sure," he said. "It goes all new, this whirl."

"Fine, bring it on. I'm ready."

"A little more help maybe, some small time, and then you are ready, yes. My father he always say that the oil is already inside the student, already there from all time. The teacher only has a match and makes it light, and then the student isn't a student anymore, just a friend, going the same way down the dark road but seeing now by himself."

"I like the image."

"You have to believe your own oil is there, though, or nobody can lights it."

"I half believe. In good moments."

He laughed and looked at me the way he'd looked at all of us outside the Inn at Chakra Creek. You couldn't ask for a more caring look than that. I understood then that on this broken earth you could never hope to have a friend who more sincerely wanted the best for you.

"What happened to the special person we were supposed to see in Kalispell?"

"Tomorrow," he said.

"Fine, good. I'm wiped. Let's pay and get back to the hotel. I'm sorry again that I doubted you. You're a good man. You're my teacher. I'll do everything I can to learn whatever it is I have to learn in this life."

He nodded and then, just as the waitress arrived with the check, he pointed one finger at me and said, "Bullshit."

21

A night of dreamless sleep, a Kalispell Grand Hotel breakfast of cheese quiche, strong coffee, huckleberries of course, and sour cream coffee cake, and we were on the road again, my spiritual teacher and I. Rand McNally puts a line of small dots next to roads it considers particularly scenic, and the route we took south on that day, Montana 93, certainly deserved that distinction. Shortly after we set out, there was a sign by the side of the road announcing a pole-dancing contest at the Outlaw Inn. I was sorry to miss it. Then a sign for a livestock auction, another piece of Americana we'd have to forgo. To our right were open pastures and clumps of pine. To our left, after we'd gone a little ways, a thirty-mile lake with a bluish mountain range stretching north-south beyond it. The peaks were snow dusted in spots, with quilts of lavender clouds gliding over them. Gray stone at the heights, green forest below, and the blue lake stretching beside us, mile upon mile. Though it wasn't radically different from the scenery of the afternoon before, it seemed, and I use the term guardedly, like sacred land. I looked over at Rinpoche.

He was his usual contented self, leaning sideways a bit on the front seat, watching me shift gears, from time to time taking a deep breath and letting the air out slowly in a long, contemplative sigh.

"Very special, isn't it?"

"Special, man!" he said.

At the bottom of the lake we passed through the town of Polson, which I read at first as *Poison*. We skipped the Polson Bay Golf Course, skipped the Miracle of America Museum. I noticed that small, fenced-in areas stood in front of many of the trailer homes. Horse corrals instead of yards. This was the Salish and Kootenai Indian Reservation now, and the signs were in English and some other amazing language—Salish, it must have been—that looked like a combination of word and mathematical formula. Some letters were raised, as in Q to the Wth power. There were apostrophes and accents all over the place, high and low. It was a linguistic work of art. I'd never seen anything remotely like it.

Farther along, in Ronan, came a sign in plain English: WE ARE ALL BROTHERS AND SISTERS. GOD LOVES YOU.

At a rest area there I decided to stop and admire the view. Rinpoche sat on the open tailgate and meditated while I fell into conversation with Sam and Johnny, two well-tanned and tremendously friendly Montana Fish and Wildlife agents who were checking the towed boats of passing motorists for evidence of the zebra mussel. A young woman colleague of theirs joined them on the way to her car. I inquired about the language. She told me her boyfriend had grown up in Arlee and had taken Salish in school, "even though he's white." She knew how to say "squirrel", and demonstrated it for us, and it was easy to see why no ordinary combination of letters could capture that sound. All *shh* and *wha* and hisses, the wind in the trees, swish of a furry tail. When she headed off, Sam and Johnny added to my knowledge of the place by telling me that "the bad grizzlies," i.e., ones who'd attacked people in Yellowstone and elsewhere, were released up in the mountains we faced. "Passed one of 'em in the road on my bike not too long ago," Johnny said. "She stood there straddlin' the line. *She* wasn't about to move, let me tell ya."

He was smiling as he said this, proudly, humbly, his partner nodding, both of them content to be something other than a member of the toughest species around. I liked them both.

I walked back toward Uma and stood for a little while, staring up at the mountains and wondering what it was that felt different here. We'd encountered so much incredible scenery on our short trip; why did this view strike me at a deeper place? A wooden tourist information sign said Native Americans had gone into that range to fast and pray and have visions, and something in their blue and green majesty made that absolutely understandable to me. Though I've had a number of peaceful moments in nature—on a Cape Cod beach at sunset, in the mountains of Maine and Vermont—only on the rarest of occasions have I felt what I felt there, just south of Ronan and north of Arlee. What could it be? I wondered. What combination of color, light, shadow and shape could evoke this sense of the presence of another dimension of life? And what, exactly, had the Indians done up there on the steep wooded slopes? What kind of big interior step had they taken, and what did the world look like when they returned?

When Rinpoche and I were on 93 again, rattling south, I asked him this question: How could the native peoples have been so unsophisticated by our standards—no lasting architectural masterpieces, no great libraries, no understanding of the history of the rest of the world—and yet so advanced spiritually, so much in harmony with the earth?

"I ask the same question to you, backwards."

"You mean, how can we be so technologically advanced and yet so immature in regard to the interior life?"

"Yes."

"Well, we're an outer-focused people, I guess. We'll have photos from Mars this summer. We'll have iPad 3 or 4, electric cars, fracking. For better and worse we can manipulate the physical universe more skillfully than any nation that's ever existed."

"Americans make so much good," he said. "Many, many inventions."

"I feel another 'but' coming."

He chuckled. "Maybe the whirl now is ready for both parts, outside part and inside. All the wery good things from the West—special phones, some medicine, nice roads and buildings, air condition—you can maybe get now in the East. And maybe the East gives something back. An inside something."

"Via teachers like you," I suggested.

"Lots of teachers now. Lots of places to learn the inside world if you want to."

"But why don't most of us want to?"

"Scary."

"Sure, I've felt that. In some odd way, sitting still and quiet makes you more aware of life, which makes you more aware of death."

"Only at the beginning, scary."

"And later on?"

185

"Later on, the scariness goes away. You learn to rest in the place that doesn't die. Then what makes you afraid is only for other people. Then you don't worry about yourself. You can live, you can die, you can be in the pain. No problem."

"And what, it's all exactly the same? Rheumatoid arthritis and a hot-oil massage, no difference?"

"Difference, sure," he said. "Just doesn't matter so much, this difference. You become small, wery, wery small, and then so your pain is small, your dying—wery small. What a nice feeling." My odd friend chuckled at the niceness of this feeling and instructed me to take the next left.

"Why?"

"Take, take, Otto."

I turned onto it, Kicking Horse Road. "It's gravel," I said.

"Your friend lives here."

"No, no, my friend is meeting us in Ennis. That's tonight. We're hundreds of miles away."

"Go," he said, "go straight now. I will show."

I went along, not pleased at myself for having turned off the road, but thinking, still, about the nice smallness he described. I was beginning to have a feeling for it, to be able to imagine it, at least. It was beginning to seem to me that the real trouble in the world came from feeling you were large. Stalin and Idi Amin had been large, in their own minds, at least. All the haters— Timothy McVeigh, Ted Kaczynski—wanted to be large, to make their mark, have their way. Maybe the Native Americans had gone up into these grizzly-infested mountains to be as small as possible, and creation had risen up around them on all sides, a multi-molecular God, a comfort.

I listened to gravel ticking up against the undercarriage and wondered what it felt like to be absolutely unafraid of death. We passed a five-acre lake with marshy banks and two men fishing from a boat. We startled a gaggle of geese and a small flock of black birds with white-tipped wings, creatures of pure elegance. There were dark clouds over the mountain in front of us now, and bad grizzlies there (the good grizzlies lived elsewhere), and I worried that, by taking this detour, we'd miss a gourmet dinner. But I went on.

The road led us past one house—there was a white teepee in the yard, used by real Indians or one of the wannabe Indians who were said to move up here, I didn't know—and then it narrowed and tilted gently upward with dense forest pinching in on either side. Two miles in, just at the point where I had promised myself I'd turn around at the next opportunity, we came upon a log cabin not much bigger than two pickups placed side by side. There was a woman sitting beside it in a lawn chair. "Your friend," Rinpoche said. My friend, whom I had never set eyes upon in this life, raised a hand in welcome.

I parked the pickup in what seemed an appropriate place— there were no other vehicles in sight—and the woman rose to greet us. I could tell at first glance that something was not quite right about her. She was dressed in old jeans and a blue T-shirt with AHS on the front, and she looked to be a year or two younger than Natasha. The body language was not exactly that of a young woman, however. Stocky, barefoot, she came across the dirt yard in a tentative way, as if afraid of approaching us too quickly, or as if there were hidden ruts or sinkholes beneath her feet and she was wary of stepping into them and disappearing forever. It wasn't until we were only about ten feet apart that I realized she was blind.

"Rinpoche?" she said. "Otto? I'm so happy you're here."

She was holding out her hand. I took it in a polite hand-shake. Rinpoche did the same. There was an awkward few seconds during which I was waiting for Rinpoche to say something, and he seemed to be waiting for me to say something, and this woman, as yet unnamed, was expecting a word, an introduction, an apology.

"I'm . . . this is Otto," I said. "I don't believe we've met, though Rinpoche here insists we're friends."

She had a laugh that tripped along quietly, almost as if it wasn't meant to be heard. This will sound strange, perhaps, but it reminded me of the small lake we'd just passed—not invisible, exactly, but hidden from the main road and the passing tourists, quiet, not quite still, beautiful in an understated way, indistinct at the edges. The essence of gentleness. "I'm Landrea. Like Andrea with an *L*, emphasis on the *ray*."

"We haven't met before, have we?"

"No, we haven't," she said, and I felt a wash of relief. I'd been sure, for a second, that she was going to say something like, "Oh, Otto, we've met many times before in the other dimension, many, many times!" I assumed, perhaps because of the "Are you going to Kalispell?" text from Cecelia, that this gentle woman was a friend of my sister's, that they'd gone to past-life-regression school together, done hundreds of aura readings in one of the places Cecelia had lived before coming to call New Jersey her home. But Landrea was half Celia's age, so that didn't make much sense. She turned, felt around in the air for a moment until she touched the top of a fence rail, and, using that for guidance, led us toward the door of her house. I looked at Rinpoche for an explanation. He smiled and nodded, as if to say, "See? I told you."

The interior of Landrea's home could not have been more simple. We could see all of it from the scratched-up wooden table at which she asked us to sit. A strip of kitchen counter with stove, refrigerator, and sink; what appeared to be a bedroom, the single bed visible through a half-open door; a bathroom the size of Anthony's closet; and a wood-floored living room that held the table, four chairs, a woodstove, and a torn leather couch, color of the inside of a potato, on which an elderly mongrel curled. The walls were plaster or Sheetrock and painted a salmon pink; nothing hung on them. There was no clock, no television, no standing lamps. Landrea's world was unrelieved darkness, but once we were inside she moved through it with a dancer's ease, taking a pitcher of iced tea from the refrigerator and pouring three glasses, carrying them to the table on a tray, setting them there in front of us. I'd had little experience with blind people, none, in fact, other than offering help once or twice on the streets of Manhattan. They seemed, in those instances, to have gotten turned around, disoriented, and were standing near a street corner with cane or dog. I'd learned to approach them gingerly, never to assume they wanted help. Sometimes they said thank you, and other times they seemed to resent the offer of assistance, to resent their own need. And who could blame them? How could you live a life among the sighted and not finger the hem of bitterness as you tapped your way along an uneven sidewalk with taxis and delivery trucks, lethal and loud, a few feet from your shoulder? I couldn't imagine how a blind person survived for more than about three days in New York City. You'd be a walking target for thieves, fondlers, teenagers looking to play a prank. How did you shop, find a toilet, get on the right bus, navigate the treacherous under-world of the subway, trust a cabdriver? And what did the light-less life look like? How was it organized? Why had they been made to carry such a burden?

Landrea sat with us. On the tray she had a bowl of sliced lemons, sugar, honey, spoons. Rinpoche clung to a stubborn, mysterious silence, the twitch of a grin at the corners of his eyes. He wouldn't look at me. Landrea slid her hand slowly along the table until it came into contact with her glass. Hers would be a world of spills and falls, unfindable toothbrushes and unkillable flies.

"How is your trip going so far?" she asked.

"Fine, it's going well. We've been on the road four days and seen some beautiful sights."

A mistake. I studied her face for signs of offense and saw none. She was eighteen or nineteen, I guessed, and though I'd assumed, for some reason, that she was Native American, she didn't look like one: hair a medium brown, clouded blue eyes. I'd had a good amount of experience dealing with young wom-en her age—Natasha, Natasha's pals, and a string of summer interns at the office. I knew a bit of their lingo and likes, what they were focused on: friends, dating, fretting a future. Landrea had a completely different way about her, as if she were middle-aged and settled, as if she'd already raised her children, made her mark in a career, lived with a husband for decades, seen the gritty middle of life. I studied her there, across the table, as she sipped from her glass. Was it only the lack of sight? Was that maturity and calm some kind of compensation for all she couldn't see and do and have?

"Excuse me," I said finally, when she went on contentedly

sipping and Rinpoche stubbornly ran his gaze over the empty walls and rough-hewn rafters and made kissing noises in the direction of the dog. "I don't mean to be rude. But we've never met, my brother-in-law here says we're friends, and I feel a little bit awkward just dropping in like this, unannounced."

"I was expecting you," she said.

I turned to Rinpoche. "Did you call?"

He pushed out his lips, raised his eyebrows, tilted his head back an inch. Me?

"Your sister called," Landrea said at last. "She said you might stop. She said I might be able to help you."

Intuition confirmed. "Help me how?"

"She said you'd lost your wife recently."

"I did."

Before I could ask Landrea a second time how she might help me, she suggested I tell her about Jeannie. I did that. Talking eased the awkwardness, for one thing, and for another, I didn't need much prompting to talk about Jeannie in those days. But I was beginning to sense the well-meaning but irritating presence of my sister in that plain room. She'd booked us at the nice B and B, yes; she'd chosen the luxurious Cave B (even though she'd expected us to stay in a yurt). But now she'd arranged for one of her associates to help me with some aura-reading fiddle-faddle, an herbal potion, an incantation for grieving men, and I felt like the blind person on Forty-Fourth Street who simply did not want help. He wanted to be left alone in his blindness, to find his own way, to escape condescension, assistance, pity of all kinds.

I told Landrea that my late wife had been born in Connecticut to a father who left the family when she was a young girl, and a mother who'd been a world-class tennis player in her youth, then married and had children, got divorced, and pursued, halfheartedly, a career in interior design before giving that up and settling into a routine of verbal abuse and an evening cocktail or four. Jeannie had wanted to get away from that life, so she'd taken the radical step of transferring to the University of North Dakota. We'd met in a Theories of Aesthetics class, senior year. I'd just given up on the idea of becoming an architect; she'd recently abandoned a major in soil chemistry—of all things—and turned to textile design. For a few months we'd hovered at the edges of each other's circle of acquaintances, and then there had been a February blizzard, a campus-wide snowball fight, men against women. She'd sneaked up behind me and put snow down the collar of my coat; I'd chased her and made a flying tackle and she stood up laughing, dripping white. We'd gone out for hot chocolate at Grand Forks' one and only all-night diner, had an excellent hour of conversation, a nice good-night kiss. We'd started dating. There was a road trip, ostensibly to see Chicago's architecture, and we'd stayed in the Knickerbocker Hotel and made love for the first time there.

Once I started I couldn't stop. Landrea seemed interested; Rinpoche watched the walls. Graduation, graduate school for me in Chicago, then the move to New York City—a place where both of us felt immediately at home. The Chelsea walk-up, the menial jobs, a wedding so informal it embarrassed her mother in front of her country club friends and at the same time forced my parents to go out and buy fancy clothes and stay in a Big City hotel. The job at Stanley and Byrnes, Jeannie's museum work, our decision to buy the house in Bronxville which we couldn't really afford but which "spoke to us," as Jeannie's sister put it. The birth of our children, the challenges and joys of parenthood, the death of her mother and my parents. I went on and on, came to the onset of her illness and suddenly stopped.

Landrea waited to be sure I'd finished, then said, "But what was she like?" and I felt again, strangely, that I was speaking with someone my own age.

"Like? She was kind, capable, giving, athletic. She hated for the house to be messy. If she had a drink at a party she'd always find a man to speak with, to fall into some deep conversation with, not exactly flirting, but it made me angry, at the beginning especially. She loved her friends, loved her flower garden, went to church only for weddings and the big holidays but professed a belief in God. She'd drive the kids all over creation and then sometimes be short with them if they skipped a chore or a homework assignment. She was physically affectionate. She would not eat scallions or lima beans or bluefish or anything malted. Every Thursday night we'd sit out on the patio in warm weather, or inside in cold, and have a glass of white wine and talk. I could go on and on. I'm sorry. I've already gone on and on. Forgive me, but how old are you, anyway?"

"Twenty."

"And you live here alone?"

"My boyfriend visits."

"And you know my sister how? From what?"

"Your sister lived for a short time with my uncle."

She lived for a short time with a lot of people, I barely kept myself from saying.

"His name was Leo. She might have mentioned him to you."

"He was killed by a delivery truck. Portland. In front of her eyes."

"Yes. I was very close with him. Celia and I were both devastated, though in different ways. I was five. We've stayed in touch since then. She's done a lot of work, as I'm sure you know, with people on the other side. My uncle started her on that path and has stayed in contact with her, and she's helped a lot of people, me included, and taught me many things. We have a deep connection, your sister and I."

There it was then. *The other side.* I was suddenly ready to leave. I shot Rinpoche an angry look. One of the things I'd always liked about him was that I never felt he was working very hard to convert me to any system of belief. He had a system, sure—something "not-really-Buddhist," as he called it—but it always seemed to me he felt so confident in it that it didn't matter very much what other people believed. It was the same with his talks. He didn't advertise, didn't self-promote, didn't keep a list of e-mail addresses. If someone asked him to, he'd agree to give a talk—sometimes for money, sometimes not—and if people showed up, that was fine, and if they didn't, also fine, and if they stomped out angrily after it was finished, or lost faith in him, all fine, too. I trusted him to be that way. It was, really, the main reason why I had let him bring me anywhere close to the world of meditation and such things in the first place.

But I didn't trust my sister in the same way, and now my lack of trust had been validated. Rather than approach me in a direct manner after Jeannie's death—she knew I'd have no tolerance for talk of contacting people *on the other side*—she'd sneakily arranged for Rinpoche to do it through this pleasant young woman. Maybe the whole idea for this trip had been a smoke screen, a ruse, a sly way of bringing me together with a twenty-year-old blind palm-reader who was going to "help" me. Sending us to Cave B, telling Rinpoche to be enthusiastic about dams, planting the Kalispell idea in his robe. I sensed a vast, far-out conspiracy. It made me furious.

"I feel," Landrea said, "that something has upset you."

For a five-count I tried to hold it in. For that short stretch I told myself I'd be kind and polite to this woman, who had such a difficult life. I made myself take a breath. Somehow, that one deliberate breath reminded me of a certain sense I had in meditation. There was no magic in this, I hasten to say. I didn't receive messages from the beyond: *Otto, this is the Lord speaking. Thou shalt be kind!* I simply touched an interior part of myself that was one degree wiser than I used to be. Not even wiser; wiser isn't even the word. More patient. I took one breath and realized I could be angry a bit later if I wanted to be angry. There would always be time for that. There was no rush. I could resist the reflex.

And so I did. I took another breath. I looked into the face of the young woman opposite me, age of my daughter, attitude of my sister, asking about my wife, and I said, "With all due respect, Landrea, I'm not really a fan of the other side. I believe in the possibility of an existence after this one. In my best moments I believe in it, I hope for it. I would very much like to think I will see my wife again in some form. But the idea of contacting her across the barrier of death—that's what you meant by 'help,' wasn't it?—that's not workable for me. Not acceptable. I don't buy it. I'm sorry."

"Why?" she asked.

"Why am I sorry, or why don't I buy it?"

"Why don't you buy it?"

"Because it's too easy, that's why. It denies the very real pain of losing someone you love. It's wishful thinking."

"To me it's very real."

"I'm sure it is. I don't mean to offend you in any way."

"I'm not offended. You couldn't offend me. I just feel, now that you've gone to all the trouble of visiting me here, you should at least let me try to make contact with Jeannie. If afterward you think it's all false, that's fine. But sit here for another little while and let me try."

"I don't know that I could bear it," I said.

She laughed. I was offended. She said, "Look what you've borne in the past few years."

"I've reached my limit," I said.

"I know a little bit about that. I can feel in myself what you've been feeling. Your sorrow has reawakened my own sorrow about my uncle, who was like a father to me. Even though all these years have passed, I can remember the pain of it. When he died, within one hour of the time he passed on, I lost my sight."

Ridiculous, I thought. I said, "But how could that be? What explanation did the doctors give you?"

"There are plenty of occurrences that defy what we think of as the unchangeable physical laws. Read Einstein. He saw it. Some people mocked him, but now he's considered a genius. I have Salish friends here and they have a very different way of looking at life, a different belief system, a different relationship to the land, different assumptions, if you will."

"But you're not Salish yourself?"

"One-sixteenth," she said. "But I'm not here because of that. This isn't the kind of thing a Salish person would do, it's not part of their spiritual tradition. It's just me, who I am. I'm here because I like the feeling of the land. It suits me. Helping people this way suits me, too. This skill that I have is just like any other skill, like being a carpenter or a cook or a ship's captain."

"I respect that," I said. "And I'll be happy to pay you. I'm awash in money now. Jeanie's insurance—"

She laughed and shook her head.

"Or not, whatever you'd like. But you have to realize how alien all this is to a person like me. I'm from a German American Midwestern farming family. There are no more practical, level-headed, unimaginative people on the face of the earth."

She touched her glass as if to be sure it was still there, but she didn't drink. "You have, with Rinpoche, the opportunity to avail yourself of another tradition of wisdom, very different from the typical American or European way. I understand you've already done that to some degree. Why would you stop there? Why pick up one stone and not the other twenty-three? Why read half the book?"

It took me a moment to get the twenty-four-stone reference. I was already into my next sentence when it registered. "Because this particular book—" I'd said, and then I remembered the little table in Spokane and the neat row of rocks, and I turned to Rinpoche and saw that the giant smile had bloomed there again. A smile the size of Siberia. Pleased as punch, as my mother used to say. He was nodding again, the whole upper part of his body moving. See, Otto?

"You are right on the edge of a momentous change," Landrea went on. She'd tilted her head sideways and upward, as if there were a bird in the rafters and she was listening to its song with her better ear. "Externally. But internally, also." A second's pause, not enough time for me to resist, and then: "I can sense Jeannie now."

And I was trapped. Caught. No walking out.

"She says she loves you very much. She sends greetings to Rinpoche. She says . . . " Landrea tilted her head another few degrees and moved her hand from the iced tea glass so that it was flat on the tabletop, fingers spread. "She says not to worry about Natasha. That something will happen with Natasha and you will be tempted to worry but that it will be fine. She's fine, she says. No pain where she is. No pain and a different kind of creativity, which she enjoys. She says—I don't understand this, but she says Jasper is not who he seems to be. She says . . . swimming, something about swimming? Did you swim with her?"

"Many times."

"That's all, then. She's fine, that's all. Sends love. Bye."

Until the last second, the very last word, I was having none of it. There were no chills running up my arms, no sense whatsoever that Landrea was actually in any kind of contact with my wife. She was a fraud, a sitcom psychic in an exotic setting. It was a waste of time and emotional energy. Most of what Landrea had said was information I'd just given her—the name of our daughter. The fact that Jeannie loved me. Even the bits about Jasper and swimming—things I hadn't mentioned—could have been something Cecelia told her in one of their conversations.

But then she said "Bye," softly, and my fortress of down-to-earth sensibility cracked. There were chills in abundance then. There was the feeling of the sensible me losing its battle, an interior unraveling. I was, for a just moment, physically afraid.

Late on Jeannie's last night on earth I'd awakened from sleep with the sense that something was wrong. We'd made a bedroom for her downstairs in what had been her study. It was more convenient that way; the hospice aide could rest on the couch. Some of her medications were refrigerated, and the kitchen was close by. There were no stairs to climb or descend. The kids could have their peace above, and I could get a good sleep. That night I woke up suddenly and listened, and then I sat up and went down the stairs—the nurse was dozing—and tiptoed into Jeannie's room, and saw her there on the bed, weak, frail, eyelids flickering, the bottles and tubes, the photos—me, Anthony, Natasha, a beautiful beach scene from a vacation in Aruba—set up where she could look at them. The second I entered the room I could hear her labored breathing, and I was just at the point of calling the hospice nurse when Jeannie turned her head an inch in my direction and fluttered the fingers of her left hand. I went and sat by the bed, took her hand as gently as if it were a paper sculpture one of the kids had brought home from second grade. "Hon?" I managed to say. "Thirsty?" The tiniest shake of the head, the smallest, smallest squeeze of the fingers with the very last ounce of her strength, the eyes held half open as if by a great exertion. I wanted to say I loved her, but I couldn't manage to get the word up out of my throat. She almost smiled. She took a breath. She said "Bye," very softly, exactly the way Landrea had said it. And she was gone.

22

Between Arlee and Ennis, a distance of close to two hundred miles, Rinpoche and I barely spoke. There was a quick stop for what turned out to be the best iced coffee on earth, at a place called Bernice's Bakery, in Missoula. There was the vast Montana landscape sliding past—mountain ranges lifting out of the horizon then sinking away, long stretches of bare brown hillside, clusters of homes and buildings that marked the occasional mining town. I didn't like to be late, for anything, especially for a meal, and I was worried about being late for my dinner with Gilligan Neufaren, but it was the hour with Landrea that held the lid of silence down over us. Although my fortress of stubbornness had cracked, it hadn't exactly crumbled. In spite of it all, in spite of the "Bye" and the chills and the reference to the twenty-four stones, I was still torn between one Otto Ringling and another. You don't cancel out fifty years of logic and assumption with a word. Even the preface of six years of meditation won't let you do that. It didn't let me do it, in any case.

But to be absolutely honest, I suspected then that Landrea

had touched if not another world, then at least another dimension of this one. The laws that had always made sense of the predicament in which I found myself—standing in a breathing body on a spinning sphere of stone—those laws had been amended, expanded, played with. Half of me, maybe a little more than half, believed that. The remaining 46 percent did not. Swooping down out of the northeastern Montana mountains, the big highway tilted and turned, its seventy-five-mile-an-hour speed limit too much for an old girl like Uma. We went along at sixty, eschewing conversation at first, Rinpoche fingering his beads and yours truly torn neatly in half between the reality of CNN and the *Daily News*, and that of a blind, twenty-year-old, one-sixteenth Salish woman in a cabin in the woods.

"So," I said to Rinpoche at last, "is that the goal of the spiritual life? Having powers to see the future and contact spirits in another world, things like that? Is that what the Native Americans did when they went into the mountains and fasted?"

He considered the question for a moment, then shook his head and looked at me. "A step maybe," he said. "A sperience. The person shouldn't get stopped there."

"But Landrea's stopped there, isn't she? I mean, she does that for a living, apparently. My sister used to."

"For other people, she does it. Cecelia, when she did it, always was doing for the other people. Helping."

"And that makes it okay? I mean, I'm sorry, but it seems somehow outside the boundary of the things you've been showing me, the path I feel like I'm supposed to be on. It was . . . impressive, I guess. Intriguing. But it seems like . . . we had a carpenter working on the house once and he could flip his hammer up in the air, end-over-end three times, and catch it by the handle. He used to do it for Tash and Anthony and they'd give him a round of applause. But it wasn't part of his work, really. It didn't help with the actual building of the sunroom. Do you know what I mean?"

"Sure," Rinpoche said.

"So what's the answer then?"

"What's the question?" he said.

"The question is: if what Landrea just did was real, if she was really able to contact Jeannie, is that the spiritual path? Is that where I'm supposed to be going?"

"You go there maybe, sure," he said. "Maybe one time, a few time. Makes you feel good. Then you knock the stones away off the table. You let go from that good feeling and you do the bigger."

"What's the bigger?"

"Bigger is one thing:" he said, going back to his beads, "you understand you're not you."

23

Gilligan Ncufaren, my author and friend, had recommended a bed-and-breakfast in the hills outside Ennis and a restaurant there called The Continental Divide. I do not, as a rule, like bed-and-breakfasts, nice as so many of them can be. It's some kind of a quirky privacy issue. I like people. I have a long list of men and women I consider friends. But there are times—and it took Jeannie a while to understand this side of me—when I need to retreat from humanity altogether for an hour or a day, have some quiet time to myself, not feel obliged to be sociable, affable, interested, or talkative.

In this way the Fisherman's Paradise Bed and Breakfast was not the perfect spot. Before my dinner with Gilligan (who refused to be called "Gill"; he said he liked the rhythm of his full name) I had hoped I'd have half an hour in my own room, meditating perhaps, or thinking of my wife, or pondering the puzzle the visit to Landrea had set before me. For all its manifold psychological levels, that puzzle was actually a very simple one; I see that now. Could a person explore the territory of the interior world, the world that lay beyond the logical thought process, and still keep one foot in the mainstream world of New York business and suburban respectability? Or would there always come a day—after years of meditation and a horrible trauma, say—when one had to make a choice? "Take hold of this," as the Tao Te Ching put it, "and let go of that." Rinpoche and my sister had clearly made their choice, not for visions and séances (Celia had, in fact, given up her regressions and palm reading when she moved to North Dakota) but for a contemplative life, an unmeasurable inner pursuit. My neighbors and office mates had clearly made another. I tried, and failed, to imagine Celia at a desk in Midtown, poring over sales numbers, or my boss, Frank Denig, sitting cross-legged on a cushion. It wasn't so black and white, of course: Celia paid her bills, and there was a chance, however remote, that Frank had a side to him that wasn't driven by power and status. But after the hour with Landrea I was torn. Since Jeannie's death my work life, my whole persona there, even my daily getup of sport jacket and shined shoes, had come to feel oddly artificial. Yet people like Celia and Landrea were too dreamy and flaky for me, wandering too far from the herd. I thought about Rinpoche's talk in Spokane—which seemed now less like a failure and more like a lesson that had been too advanced for me at the time. The point of it was: Don't make your own life in reaction to others. So maybe the whole trick of the spiritual search was "To thine own self be true." Maybe the real work was just scraping off layer upon layer of conditioning, assumption, and imitation, and finding, somewhere in the depths, your actual face. Maybe that's what Rinpoche meant by "you understand you're not you."

On the way to our B and B we passed signs showing fish

and hook, which I took to mean places where one could put a
boat into the river and cast a line. From Gilligan's descriptions
of his summer cabin in the wilds, I knew that this part of the
state was supposed to be a fly-fisherman's paradise, the rivers
bubbling with rainbows and browns, men in expensive Orvis
outfits standing in boats and flicking an artificial fly across a
brown-blue surface. And indeed, after we turned onto a gravel
road, wound this way and that up a long hill and pulled into the
driveway of the place where we'd arranged to spend the night,
we were greeted by a large wooden sign, professionally lettered:
ANGLERS WELCOME. The house was set on a hilltop and offered a view of baked hills to the north, and mountains in the
eastern distance. There were antelope grazing in the fields below.

Fisherman's Paradise was run by a couple of friendly folk
who'd retired there from Kansas City. Lena suffered from arthritis. Giorgio suffered from an inability to stop talking. Shortly after our arrival we had lemonade on the verandah, gazing
down at the view, and within twenty minutes Rinpoche and I
had gotten most of the good fellow's history: his service in Vi-
etnam, his passion for hunting elk, his parents' courageous
move from the grit of Trenton to the friendlier middle west. He
and Lena had four sons. We soon learned what each of them
did for a living, to whom they were married, and how they were
raising their children. Between these factual mile markers stood
great stretches of anecdote—everything from the neighbor
across the way, who insisted on raising lamas even though there
was no money in it, to the long, rambling tale of Giorgio's as-
cent from apprentice in an ad agency to owner of a small company that made the fibers used in 79 percent of the world's

toothbrushes.

Lena, for the most part, sat quietly by, occasionally adding a drop to this sea of words. I tried to simultaneously be polite and check my watch. At one point, as Giorgio taped this line onto the trailing edge of the toothbrush story, "And just one more little one from the time we—" Rinpoche's head lolled over to the left and he let out a snore.

"My brother-in-law's exhausted," I explained. "He gets up very early to meditate, and—"

But Rinpoche's quiet wood-sawing seemed in no way to offend our host. He didn't even seem to notice. We existed, the good monk and I, as two sets of fresh ears, our own stories unimportant, our schedules secondary.

At last I took advantage of a pause for breath and stood up. I tapped Rinpoche on the shoulder and he was immediately alert, so immediately that I wondered if it had all been an act, a wesson. We made a safe retreat to our separate accommodations—large, airy rooms with identical views and Bibles placed conspicuously on the night tables—settled in, met to review our plans for the next day, wished each other a good night, and then I headed back down the hillside into town.

The Continental Divide occupied a low, modern building a minute and a half north of tiny downtown Ennis. Gilligan Neufaren had already arrived and taken a table, and was at work on a bottle of white. He was six feet five, a former Harvard oarsman, light-skinned and light-haired and living on the proceeds from two very successful books—*Breakfast Abroad* and *Lunch Abroad*—that concerned themselves with the morning and afternoon dietary preferences in places as diverse as Zimbabwe and the Islands of Yap. His style was erudite yet conversational, his sense of humor inventive, if touched at times with an acerbic edge, and he'd made both himself and Stanley and Byrnes millions. I'd enjoyed his company on his visits to New York, and I'd been the acquiring editor of *Breakfast*, so it was a pleasure to see him there, a face from the predictable world.

He poured me a glass from his bottle, conveyed his condolences. We ordered the Caprese salad to prepare our stomachs and made small talk about fishing and road trips. The Caprese was superb, the warm rolls nothing less than spectacular. Carrying in my pants pocket a remnant of East Coast elitism, I'd begun to worry that, in crossing the actual continental divide earlier that day, we were entering a penitential desert of the culinary world. Here was an oasis.

Gilligan ordered the flank steak. I felt obliged, in those parts, to go for the trout, and in the midst of my first taste of it he said, "Word has it you're traveling with a maharishi."

"My brother-in-law. He's a sort-of Buddhist monk. How'd you know?"

Gilligan's teeth were as oversized as the rest of him. The face was rectangular, papered with a Scandinavian's pale skin and topped with a boyish shock of yellow hair. The lake-water blue eyes had a happy certainty to them: he expected the best from this world. When he smiled, his ears lifted out and away from each other. "Someone in Denig's office let it slip."

"Oh."

"And I'm not familiar with the sort-of Buddhists. What's the deal? They sort-of come back from the dead until they qualify for Nirvana? They're sort-of vegetarians?"

"In his case, yes, actually. He eats a little meat."

"And he's your brother-in-law, you said? Not celibate?"

"I don't ask. That's my sister's business, I guess."

"No offense meant."

"None taken. This trout is excellent."

"So's the steak. But what's the deal? I mean, you get what, three weeks off a year?"

"Eighteen days."

"I'd expect you to go out to the Hamptons with your kids or up to the Berkshires to golf with Denig or something. You're driving around with a monk? In Montana? Does he fish?"

"He might. We're going to Yellowstone tomorrow. I might ask around for a guide."

"Look up Danny Schoen if you're anywhere near the Little Bighorn. World class." Gilligan pondered a moment, sliced his steak neatly, chewed it thoughtfully, like the professional food-man he was. Unmarried, childless, free to travel the world with one or another in a series of marvelous women, there seemed to be a species of magic associated with him. Good things happened to him, extraordinarily good things. His Harvard crew had won at Henley. His books were fine, solid books, aimed toward the layperson's end of the food audience. Well put together, informative, funny, but, I feel obliged to say, not in any way exceptional. In someone else's hands they would have sold ten or twelve thousand copies, perhaps gone into paperback and sold another few thousand a year to a claque of ardent fans. We had dozens like that on our backlist. Somehow, though, both *Breakfast* and *Lunch* had caught on, gone mainstream, found their way into twenty languages and almost a million households. Jeannie's friends read them around the pool at the tennis club. College kids read them on the commuter trains. There had even been a pair of film options—exceedingly rare in my corner of the book business.

Gilligan seemed to expect all that, to bring it into his life the way others, more negative, brought on disaster. It wasn't conceit you detected in his bearing and tone of voice as much as a complete lack of surprise that the world should have rewarded him with a life so many people envied. He was fond of referring to his style as "the Neufaren way".

"You know," he said, "you're kind of an odd duck."

"I'm the least odd duck in the world."

He laughed, handed his empty dish to the waitress, convinced me to go for the pear tart and coffee, a glass of port. Outside the big windows the late Montana twilight moved in leisurely fashion toward night, no sense of rush here. We might have been reviving the lost art of the two-hour publisher's lunch.

"No, really," he persisted. "Denig said he went into your office and found you meditating or something."

"Once. It was lunch hour. Jeannie was dying. I was under tremendous stress."

"An awful thing. Sorry again, pal."

"Thanks."

"But, you know, meditation, the monk, the road trip out here when you don't fish. What's the real Otto Ringling story?"

Gilligan couldn't help himself. This was how he made his living, getting people to talk, working them like a massage therapist, pressing the tissue here and there until the pain, the quirkiness, the frustration, or the secret recipe leaked out into air. I felt—unusual for me—vaguely intimidated. I sipped the port and stalled.

"Out with it, man."

"You're intrigued by the way other people eat," I said. "I'm intrigued by the way other people live. By the idea that maybe we shouldn't be making some of the assumptions we make."

"Such as?"

"Such as that the main purpose of our being here is to earn money and collect things and pleasures and insulate ourselves from discomfort to the extent humanly possible before the hour of our death."

He stopped eating. "Wow!"

I tried to smile it away. I suddenly had a new appreciation for the manner in which my father and mother had used words, as if they were a collection of golden coins to be set out in plain view very very carefully, and only in front of certain trustworthy merchants.

"You some kind of socialist or something? Income redis-tributor? That's a joke. But this is unusual. I mean, I encounter this from time to time. In my travels I run into people who say things like that. But most of the others, most of the Liberians and Lithuanians and Cape Verdeans, the vast majority of them would be all too happy to make money and collect things and pleasures and have a little less discomfort."

"Sure, of course. I didn't mean that."

"Clarify, if you would."

"I suppose I just feel like I have everything I need."

"Always more women out there to get to know," he said carelessly, and then he caught himself and said, "Sorry, you know how I meant it," and offered me the last bite of his pear tart in apology.

I waved them both away, pear tart and careless remark. "I know what you mean. But don't you ever feel like there might be something else to life? If you stop for a second and look around?"

"Don't want to stop, man. Having too much fun."

"I want to say my parents' dying—they were killed in a car crash six years ago—and then Jeannie's death, I want to say those were the things that made me, I don't know, *question*. But the truth is, even before those tragedies I was looking around and asking myself, 'What's going on here?' Even as a kid."

"I had a spell of that, too," he said. "I looked around and I saw that some people had a summer home on Martha's Vineyard or a yacht in Monaco, and other people were sweltering in housing projects and I thought: Let me figure out a way to get into that former group and stay there." He signaled the waitress that he wanted the check, and no amount of protesting on my part could convince him otherwise.

"And you did it."

A nod. "And it's as much fun as it looks, believe me."

"Really?"

Just for one second then, just for one snippet of an instant, the crew shell wobbled, one or two of the oarsmen falling out of time, or stroke, or whatever the correct term might be. The big rainbow trout slipped off the hook. The sexy woman said no, she didn't really want to go with him to Kazakhstan, interesting as the name sounded. I might have imagined what I saw in that second, but I don't think so. It was similar to reading a novel and coming across a moment when you say to yourself, That's false, a false note. It doesn't ruin the whole book any more than Gilligan's flash of doubt broke apart his uber-confidence, but it was memorable nonetheless.

He seemed to be aware of it, too, seemed to feel the need to recover. "You know," he said, signing the credit card slip with a flourish and slipping his wallet into a jacket pocket. "I've seen a bit of illness and death in my travels. I don't need to tell you this, probably, but there's nothing redemptive about it, nothing fine, no lessons to be learned. I stay as far away from it as I possibly can."

But you can't, I wanted to say. Not forever. Doesn't that matter?

Gilligan was stretching his wide shoulders back, admiring the view. No more of this depressing talk, his body language seemed to say. I inquired about his next project, *Dinner Abroad*—we'd already given him a healthy advance, and we talked about that as we stepped out into the still warm air. Night now. A bloom of stars over the mountains' dark silhouette. Gilligan shook my hand in a way that made me feel almost his equal, a good editor, a good man—if older, shorter, chubbier, grumpier, and less rich.

"Where to next?" he asked.

"Yellowstone, Billings, then back to the farm."

"South Dakota, yes."

"North. Near Dickinson. Not much in the way of great fishing or food there."

He smiled. "Don't go too far into that navel-gazing stuff," he advised. "That way lies sorrow."

We parted friends. I stood in the parking lot and watched him drive off.

⟶ ⤳ 24

At breakfast—a delicious feast of peach French toast and elk sausage—Giorgio berated his wife for this and that failing, and Rinpoche, to my surprise, drank coffee again. It might have been out of desperation: people who talked constantly seemed to present the greatest challenge to his equanimity. Lena was in some pain, I could see that. I noticed, before we made our escape, that Rinpoche touched her in a certain way, two hands on one of her arms for a three-count while he pretended to thank her for the food. I'd seen him do the same thing with Jeannie on one of his visits. I had hoped—we were grasping at everything then—that she'd wake up the next morning cured, or at least with less pain. But no, there were medications for that. They worked for a time, and then stopped working, and then only the juice of the opium was left for her. God's compensation for the disease he'd created, the disease no word could ever capture.

"Dinner good last night?" Rinpoche asked as we headed south from Ennis toward the Wyoming border.

I gave him the rough outline, made one remark about the

life Gilligan led, a charmed life, it seemed to me.

"Heaven realm," Rinpoche said as we cruised down be-tween the Madison and Gravelly ranges, headed for West Yel-lowstone. I thought, for a moment, that he was referring to the three-dimensional postcard view. But then he added, "If you are hurtful to people you can be born in hell realm next time. Very bad suffering. Feels like no hope. And other time, maybe after a life of big wanting, you go to heaven realm, and you are like a god there. Everything is fine, everything almost perfect. Nice face," he circled one hand around his face. "Strong. Smart. Much money. Everything good and good."

"Sounds okay to me."

"Sure. Okay." He watched the scenery go by for a while and then, "Okay and okay and okay and then, all in a sudden, not so okay. Like this truck." He reached out and slapped the dash-board so hard that a swarm of dust motes rose into view. "Goes, goes, goes, and then one day, stops."

"No day soon, we hope."

He laughed. "The man who gave this truck for a gift is in heaven realm now, this life. Jarvis. Good man. Rinpoche tries to help him escape."

"How? Repeatedly pinning him to the ground in wrestling matches? Taking away his marijuana?"

"Three-day retreats," Rinpoche said. "No eating too much food. Nothing to do, nobody to tell you what a nice face you are having. Jarvis become *wery wery* upset. Then we talk. Then I tell him, Go home, enjoy. Eat and eat, have women, play the golf, the fish, the out in your boat. Come back, though, I say. Three months, come back."

"Little by little you'll pull him out of heaven."

"I try."

"Sometimes life does it on its own," I said. "Without any three-day retreats."

"Always times."

"So, what then? We should be suspicious of all pleasure? If we have a great life, that should worry us?"

Rinpoche shook his head. "Enjoy pleasure, Otto. Enjoy, enjoy. Only remember the people who don't have, and sometimes say a thank you."

"Thank you to whom? To what?"

"Your mother," he said, as if it were the most obvious thing on earth. "For borning you."

"And what? The father doesn't count for anything?"

"Counts. Sure it counts," he said, lightly now, enjoying my company it seemed, enjoying the ride. "But in the Bible which person from Jesus takes the lineage?"

"You mean, whose lineage was Jesus part of? I don't know. If I ever knew, I don't remember."

"The Mary," he said. "I read it last night, in the place."

25

Yellowstone is, in my opinion, an American heaven realm, Eden's back forty. We entered through the town of West Yellowstone, where it's possible to buy any kind of T-shirt, hat, bumper sticker, or sofa-sized oil painting of the old Wild West. It's a harmless enough place as tourist traps go, set in serene country south of the mountains, east of a weekly rodeo, and west of an absolutely sublime two million acres of preserved Americana.

"A lot of families come here on summer vacation," I told Rinpoche after we'd paid at the entrance and gotten pamphlets and directions. But he would have seen that soon enough on his own. The two-lane roads were a festival of SUVs and Winnebagos, with kids looking through the windows, mom and dad jumping out to take pictures of a herd of elk, retired couples motoring happily along gazing this way and that and pointing. One of the things that makes the park so special is the unmatched variety of its landscape: pristine lakes, steep mountains, hot springs surrounded by rock formations that look like something imported from the moon for a planetarium exhibit, cold rivers, hot rivers, alpine fields edged with fir trees and spotted with spouts of steam. It's a place that even hordes of tourists can't spoil. We could be boorish and stupid and petty and wasteful, and somehow, against Yellowstone's beautiful bulk, all that was just a flea nipping at a horse's ankle. From the guy showing off for his kids by chasing an eight-hundred-pound bull elk into the forest with a Nikon held out in front of him, to the Winnebago driver towing a gas-guzzling car loaded with mountain bikes, Jet Skis, two tons of suitcases, and an ultralight airplane, to the sometimes cranky Bronxville editor and his probably trustworthy Siberian friend, Yellowstone spoke to everyone. A prickle of regret came over me as we headed for Old Faithful: I wished we'd brought the kids there while Jeannie was still alive.

Rinpoche was having a bit of trouble grasping the idea of preserved land, of a national park. In the place he came from— an unimaginably vast and almost wholly unpeopled stretch of Russia twenty miles north of the Chinese border—there was little need for preservation. Preservation from what? For what? Those steppes and dry mountains were in no danger from the creeping fingers of development. A hundred years from now you'd still be able to ride the Trans-Siberian for an entire day through that part of the world without seeing a house or a human being.

I decided not to say a word about Old Faithful or the other park attraction I planned on showing him. I wanted him to experience it without preconception, free of any filters.

We found it easily enough, parked the pickup in a giant lot and followed a loose parade of other parkgoers along a path. Rinpoche liked the unexpected—thrived on it, I almost want to say. When we were driving south on 287 I told him where we were going and that I had a couple of surprises in mind for him. "Pure American fun," I said and he looked at me and smiled and patted me too hard on the shoulder as if I'd just run my personal best in the hundred-meter hurdles. For the remainder of the drive he only gazed out the window, asking once "where came from the word Yellowstone", and then holding to his customary silence. Now, he hurried along the path beside me, the disciplined man, shining with anticipation, asking nothing.

I knew the geyser spouted every hour and a half or so, but there were no signs saying when we could expect the next eruption. We came into an open area with a half circle of wooden benches facing a spout of steam on bare stone, and judging by the assembled crowd, I guessed we were fairly close. "What is?" I expected to hear from my right shoulder, but Rinpoche stayed quiet and attentive, facing the wisps of steam along with a few hundred other marvelers, studying the quick squirts of moisture that enlivened it from time to time—false starts, unfulfilled promises.

After fifteen minutes of waiting we saw these spurts grow more energetic and more frequent. It was a kid playing with an underground garden hose, lifting his thumb away from the nozzle and putting it back again. Perhaps it was only because of the spouting, but I had the same feeling I'd had on the one whale-watching expedition Jeannie and the kids and I had taken (she'd grown so seasick she swore off boat travel forever): then, it was the sense that the giant creature beneath the surface of the sea was aware of our presence and putting on a show for our benefit, appearing and disappearing unexpectedly but in a predictable place, a place humans could find when they wanted to. Here, the same. The geyser-spirit kept us waiting, teased us with these vaporous puffs, holding off until a crowd of sufficient size had gathered, and then raising the curtain.

The show began. Some larger spurts, ten, twenty, thirty feet into the air, and then the full-fledged eruption to a chorus of cheers and exclamations. The wind was blowing—from the west, I believe—and it carried the smaller drops across the safety zone and into one section of the crowd. A few adventurous teenagers ran over there to get wet, to have the full experience, and when I looked away from the spectacle for a moment I saw that Rinpoche had joined them, trotting behind the benches in sandals and robe, surrounded by a cluster of high schoolers and one tattooed dad who was showing off, face turned toward the spray, tongue out. For a moment I didn't know which show to watch.

It was soon over. Old Faithful offered a couple of last ejaculations, a hiss or two as if signaling the end of the performance, and the crowd broke up. I found Rinpoche and led him toward the adjacent lodge. There were droplets of water on his shaved scalp and a smile on his face for the viewing of which we could have charged admission. "Fun?" I asked.

He hugged me hard, radiantly happy. "Old Faceful smells," he said. He squeezed up his cheeks and went into one of his high, drawn-out chuckles.

"That's the sulfur. They call it Old Faithful because for probably half a million years it's been doing that every ninety minutes or so. People come from all over the world to see it."

"We should stay for next time, too."

"Sure, if you want to. Right now, let's go eat something."

The lodge was huge, clean, airy, with giant timbers holding

up the ceiling, and a crew of young workers—both home-grown and international—that seemed well trained. Rinpoche and I found the cafeteria and asked for bowls of chili—one meatless, one not—then went and sat at one of the long tables with families sprinkled about.

"Wery good surprise, thank you, my friend," he said.

"There's something else here, too, that I want you to see, but we'll have to change into our bathing suits."

"Not a problem, man."

"You sound like Anthony. I just sent them a text, letting them know what we're up to."

"Good father," he said between spoonfuls. "This is why you are ready now, in this life, for the spirchal teachings."

"You said that to me at Cave B, do you remember, about fatherhood?"

He shook his head. I had the sense he was fibbing.

"There are probably ten thousand good fathers—and mothers—in this park today, so I guess they're all of them ready for the spiritual teachings."

He nodded vigorously, mouth full. "All," he said confidently. "But Otto needs now not to think about other people maybe so much, okay?"

"Sure, fine."

"If you have to ride a train, like we rode to go to Seattle, then you maybe don't need so much to worry are the other people there for the train on time? Are they in the traffic? Did they left the house too late? Maybe is the baby sick and the train leaves without them? *You* need to make it on the train. You, you."

"Okay."

But he wasn't finished. "You look on the Olympets now, yes? Some of the people they can swim wery fast. Some can run wery fast. Some can jump in the air and spin upside down." He made a fluttering motion with one hand, in imitation, I suppose, of a Romanian gymnast in flight. "This is the way God, she makes everything. Some people they have spirchal lesson from meditating. Some from the sports, from the study, from loving their husband *wery* much. The man who runs, he shouldn't worry all the time about the woman who swims, see?"

"Yes, I do see. I also see that you're using the term 'God' lately, which is not something Buddhists are exactly famous for. And today God is a she."

He laughed, wiped his mouth with the paper napkin, took a long draught of water from a bubbling bottle. "Now, the next learning for you is to go past words."

"I'm a man of words, I'm afraid. Always have been."

"Sure," he said, "wery good. I like your work wery much. Cecelia gives me your books and I read them. About lunch in Africa, about growing food in clean dirt, about avocados. Wery good! But I'm now not talking about that. Now you must go past putting words on people. Who can care if I call me Buddhist or not Buddhist? If I say 'God'? What difference? Who can care if you say 'Old Faceful' or 'Blue Rabbit.' What matters is that you *see* it, that it *is*, the earth speaking up at us."

"I had that same feeling."

"Sure you do. And with people now, do that, what you did with Anthony and Tasha. With them you see beyond the names, past 'boy' and 'girl'. You see past the troubles they make for you, yes? Into your love for them. Go down deep there, Otto my friend. Go down now in your life into the deeper. You know the *om mani* prayer?"

"Of course."

"Means there is a, how you say?"

"A jewel in the lotus."

"A jewel inside you, yes. Inside *you*, inside Anthony and Tasha. You see it there, yes, in them?"

"Always."

"Always from the first minute, yes? Like I see in Shelsa. So now you must learn to see that jewel in every other person, every one! And in Old Faceful, in the mountain, in the . . . what is the animal? Big? The man yesterday shoots them."

"Elk."

"The jewel in the elk!" he almost shouted. A couple at the end of the table turned to stare. "You being the father is the perfect wesson! You see how to love the children, and you do it wery, wery well, Otto. Now you only have to move the love for the jewel in them to the other people, the animal, the tree. And for Otto himself!"

"I'll try," I said. "Not easy."

"What is that jewel? God, it is! The name for that jewel in everywhere is God. But you can use any other name you want. Jesus, you can use. Buddha-nature you can say. Anything you want, doesn't matter, man!"

"Okay. I get it. Intellectually at least."

"Do you love Anthony intellectually?"

"No."

"Natasha?"

"No."

"Then why the rest of the world?"

"Because I'm an idiot," I said.

The joke passed him by completely, or perhaps not. "Yes, wery good." He said. "Wery good, my brother-and-law. Now you have one eye little bit open like this." He squinted and put one hand to his right eye, as if pushing the lids apart an eighth of an inch.

And then the lesson was finished. As was his chili. He put his hands together and made a small bow in the direction of the Styrofoam bowl, placed his used napkin and spoon into it like a priest at the altar, with a certain reverence. Then he looked up at me, expecting me to be something I was not, hoping for a silver or bronze medal from the guy who had run in the middle of the pack all his life. He said, "Now please show me surprise the number two."

26

Surprise the number two came courtesy of a bit of travel advice from a friend I call Arlo the Arkansan. Here was his text: *If you're anywhere near Yellowstone, you have to go and take a dip in the Boiling River. It's one of my favorite places on earth!*

Had I not trusted this particular friend so completely I would have deleted the message and gone on my way. In the first place, if there's anything I've learned in years of traveling it's that one man's meat is another man's poison. Key West, for instance, held little appeal for Jeannie and me beyond the tour of Hemingway's house, yet friends of ours adore it. And in the second place, I might be alone in this opinion, but "a dip in the Boiling River," especially on a hot July day, sounded vaguely unattractive.

Still, Arlo had traveled widely, and if the Boiling River was one of his favorite places on earth, then it was worth a look. Taking a dip would be optional. From the lodge near Old Faithful (we did, in fact, stay for a second eruption, eerily similar to the first) it was roughly an hour's drive to the second surprise. The day was hot and clear, traffic not too onerous, and this little

Boiling River detour gave us a chance to see more of the park. Halfway there, after we'd passed a series of spectacular alpine fields with smaller geysers puffing away like the chimneys of underground homes, we encountered a small delay. A miniature herd of bison, half a dozen or so, had decided they had more rights to this land—including the paved roadway—than the visiting humans, and they were stubbornly blocking the flow of Winnebagos. Most of them dispersed in a couple of minutes, having discovered that eating grass was preferable to licking tar. But one of their number, a massive bull, must have liked the feeling of warm asphalt against his hooves. There he stood, head and shoulders in one lane, butt end in the other, all hairy two thousand pounds of him. I was imagining it, I'm sure, but he seemed to be giving the nearest drivers a malevolent look, daring them to try to sneak by on the horn or tail end.

Nobody sneaked by. A few brave—or foolish—souls slipped out of their vehicles and moved two steps closer with cameras raised. The rest of us waited, transfixed. While I watched—this is how the magnificent computer of the mind works—I suddenly remembered a moment on our earlier road trip when I'd wanted to tell Rinpoche about the buffalo. It was more American than the eagle, apple pie, quilting, and pro football combined, I'd wanted to say; it was the perfect symbol for everything that was right and wrong about us as a people—our great land, our strength, our murderous beginnings. I had a whole spiel all ready . . . but he'd fallen asleep, and I'd never gotten around to it.

"You know what it is?" I asked him.

"Buffalo."

"Right."

"This one, I think, is king."

"The Native Americans in these parts believed the buffalo had a particularly powerful spirit. They lived off them—meat, hide, horns—and when the U.S. government decided the Indians were a nuisance, one of the things they did, besides slaughtering them outright, was invite hunters here and pay them to kill as many buffalo as they could. General Custer was a big fan of this idea. It relieved the troops' monotony, he said, taught them to shoot better. Sometimes one man killed as many as a hundred and fifty in a day, a macho rite of passage. Seven million killed just between 1872 and 1874. Whoever came up with this brilliant idea figured that if there were no buffalo the Indians would starve, and then the land would be theirs for the taking."

"Sometimes," Rinpoche said after he'd considered that for a moment, "peoples think crooked."

After he'd kept us waiting a suitable amount of time, the bison king decided he'd take two steps forward. He was still commander of the road, still standing proudly upon the killing fields of his fellows, but at least now the slimmer vehicles could slip past his rear end. We did that, coming within a few yards of the majestic beast, so close we could almost reach out and touch the patches of mange on his coat, and then we headed on toward the Boiling River.

"What do you think the Divine Intelligence has in mind when he or she arranges for people to think crooked? On the big scale, I mean. Hitler, Stalin, Pol Pot, Idi Amin, the buffalo slaughterers and Indian killers—what spiritual purpose does that serve?"

"Don't know," Rinpoche said.

"Right, nobody knows, but if you had to hazard a guess as to why . . . I mean, it's one of the great philosophical questions. If there is a kind and loving God, why would he permit such things to happen?"

I'd asked Rinpoche this same question on our earlier trip, but now the monk had gone mute. He was looking out the window at a rock formation that resembled a mound of whipped cream that had frozen in place, gotten dirty, then been rained on.

"Care to offer a theory?"

Rinpoche swiveled his head on his thick neck and looked at me for a minute, then said, "No idea, Otto."

"Doesn't it shake your faith from time to time?"

"Means what, this *shake your faith?*"

"It means you have doubts. The doubts make you wonder if your philosophy, your spiritual position, your ideas about the world might be formed only by wishful thinking, you know: you *want* life to be a certain way, so you form a theory that's consistent with what you want but maybe not in accordance with reality."

"These doubts are thoughts, yes?" he asked.

"I suppose so."

"Rinpoche has many thoughts."

"And you've learned to ignore the ones you don't want, I know. You taught me that, and it's been very helpful. But some thoughts represent the truth, don't they? For example, if I think *I love my children*, that's not a thought I want to ignore, because it's true."

"Yes," Rinpoche said.

We were past the rock formation now, the road winding

downhill in big loops. Just where the Boiling River was supposed to be, I saw a line of cars parked along the shoulder and pulled in behind them.

"I think this is the place. I'll grab the towels and we'll walk down to the water and see what's up."

We got out and sauntered along the weedy gravel shoulder toward a ten-car parking area that was completely full. I didn't want to let the subject slip away. "So you make a decision as to which thoughts to ignore and which thoughts to embrace, correct?"

"Sometime."

"But you could be fooling yourself then, couldn't you?"

"You fooling yourself about loving Anthony and Natasha?"

"I'm acknowledging an actual feeling. I'm naming it."

"What is actual feeling? What makes?"

"I don't know. I'm just sure of it."

"Maybe wishful thinking," Rinpoche said. We'd gone past the parked cars and turned onto a narrow path that ran beside a river. A quarter mile ahead I could see people who seemed to be in the water.

"Wishful thinking that I love my kids?"

He shrugged. "Some things you know," he said. He smacked himself in the middle of his chest. "When I give you spirchal wessons, I know, that's all. Like you know you love your children. When they make you upset, do you doubt that you love them?"

"Sometimes. For an hour. In our worst moments."

"Then what?"

"Then life goes back to normal and the mood passes and I know I love them."

He took hold of my arm and held me from going forward. We waited for a father and his two teenage kids to squeeze past. Close beside us was a stone outcropping, a miniature cliff face, shoulder height. Rinpoche slapped one hand against it, then took my hand and slapped it against it the same way. "Explain," he said.

"Explain what?"

"Explain this."

"It's a stone. A rock formation. Basalt, maybe. Granite, I don't know."

"That is names. Stone, rock, granite. Names doesn't explain."

"Well, I can't then. I don't know what you mean."

"This *is*, yes?"

"Of course."

He slapped me, only a bit more gently, on the sternum. "Otto *is*, yes?"

"Yes."

"Who made?"

"I don't know."

"Something made this *is*, though, yes?"

"Science. The Big Bang."

"What made that the Big Bang *is*?"

"Even the greatest scientists don't know that yet."

"Listen me. If you understand this *is*, if you put your mind to that level and not the level where names are, where thoughts are, then you know the spirchal life. You know something bigger *is*, bigger and good, and you know it just the same way like you know you love Anthony and Natasha."

"I don't quite follow."

"When you meditate you touch the top of the *is*."

"The wordless," I suggested.

"Maybe."

"I'm still not quite there."

He let out a breath through his nose. "You pushing my buttons," he said. "When we get to the center you make a retreat." He held up three fingers. "Three days. Not eating too much. No phone. Now, no more question. We swim, you and me. Maybe in the water your mind will go a little better."

It was a funny thing to say, because there were moments after a bracing swim at the Cape Cod National Seashore when my mind did seem to change for a while. We'd be there in late afternoon, the waves pounding, the freezing ocean licking a sunbaked shore, and after a certain amount of cajoling, taunting, and daring, the kids would convince Jeannie and me that we had to go in. So we did. We'd stand for a minute, knee deep, letting our feet and ankles turn numb, and then we'd move gingerly forward, our skin splashed with particles of ice, until we reached the point where it was either dive in or be soaked anyway in the tenderest of places. In we'd go. We'd surface with a shout, take a few hard strokes to get the heart moving again. Another dive, a very short swim. Maybe we'd ride a wave toward shore or, if the water was unseasonably warm that summer, say thirty-four degrees Fahrenheit instead of thirty-three, we'd stay in and splash around with the kids for a while. It inevitably struck me as an illogical thing to do; before the swim my rational mind counseled against it. But every time, after I'd come out and toweled off and was standing in the shallows with the sun beating down on my cold skin, there would be a little stretch of—what would the words be? Inner peace? Sense of another world? Existential gratitude? A better mind.

I'd always written it off to merely a physiological reaction to the cold. Or to relief at having survived the icy plunge. But as Rinpoche and I walked farther down the path, I found myself wondering. The Native Americans had lived such a physical life, in the elements, working with their hands, hunting, giving birth, making war, living and dying in the open air. And then along came the Thinkers, the white tribes that had figured out how to make iron and write symphonies and kill seven million buffalo. I wasn't one of these people who idealized the Native American way of life. They made war, too, even before the white man came, and who knew what kinds of narrow-mindedness they might have suffered from? And who'd want to live in a world without the things the Europeans and their descendants had contributed—from Novocain to Cezanne to the internal combustion engine? You couldn't say these things in polite, educated society, of course. You'd be accused of condoning genocide on the one hand or of a soft-brained liberalism on the other. Whole libraries of subjects were off limits now, at least in my circles.

But I found myself wondering if, in gaining automobiles and radiation treatments and disinfectant and five hundred species of cheese, we might have lost something we couldn't even imagine. Maybe the development of that part of the brain—logical, scientific, discriminatory, comparative, analytical—left another part to atrophy, and that other part had something to do with this *is-ness*, this wordless appreciation for the miracle of a piece of stone or a human body. Maybe the native people, who went into the mountains to fast and pray, and Rinpoche's people, who spent large portions of the day simply *sitting* and trying to duck beneath the curtain of their thoughts, maybe they knew one or two important things we didn't know, and it was a kind of first-world hubris that made us believe otherwise. Maybe Rinpoche's whole purpose in life, his true work, was to awaken us to at least the possibility of that atrophied consciousness. And maybe we could hold on to our Novocain and Chevy Corvettes and Rachmaninoff and reach out for that wordless understanding, too.

Maybe a dip in the Boiling River would show me.

A few dozen others had taken the plunge. About ten feet of dirt slope separated us from the river and their happy faces. Below where we stood, these brave people lay in the water as if beached. It was a shallow, stony river, probably seventy-five feet wide, with a rushing current and strange puffs of steam near one shore. We left our clothes and towels on the bank and climbed carefully down to the water's edge. I put a foot in— freezing cold. Then another foot, a short distance upstream— hot-tub warm. I began to get the picture: the river was snow-melt, so frigid in most seasons it would make the National Seashore seem like a bathtub. But upstream from us on the right-hand side there must have been a hot spring pouring in. Hence the steam that made the Boiling River appear to be boiling. I crouched down and then flattened myself in the current, holding my body against the strong flow with the soles of both feet against a boulder, and I discovered that, by moving a little this way or that, I could be refreshed or scalded, depending. In certain spots, just this side of a large rock, say, you could have one cold leg and one warm. People were laughing, creeping a little ways out into the surprisingly swift current, getting cold, then moving back near shore and warming up again. Rinpoche was giggling uncontrollably. The other bathers looked at him and smiled. We stayed there for over an hour.

We got out, finally, and let the air dry us. My mind was clear; the great questions had faded; I was thinking of my kids. So I took out my phone and sent texts to both of them, telling them where we were and what we were doing, and how soon they might expect us at the farm. Rinpoche must have seen me working the magical device a hundred times already on our short trip. I was as bad as any tenth grader, compulsively checking e-mails to see if there was anything important happening at the office, watching for news from the kids, studying headlines and Olympic results, making hotel reservations. He'd always ignored me. But now, as if after our recent conversation about spiritual matters it was my turn to pay him back with some knowledge of the modern world, he asked me to show him how the phone worked, how to send a text. We stood there for probably ten minutes while I explained the system to him, and when we started back, he asked if he could hold on to the phone and try to write something that Cecelia could show Shelsa.

About halfway to the parking area I saw that a few elk had crossed the river—we'd noticed them grazing on the other side—and were now munching away close beside the path. They were huge creatures, docile it seemed, though the literature we'd been handed at the gate said it was important to keep a safe distance. Rinpoche was watching the phone, poking at the buttons. He walked up to within a few feet of the rump of a particularly large elk and I thought for a second he'd be kicked, or worse. But apparently elk have an issue with gold-trimmed maroon, because Rinpoche had his robe thrown over one shoulder and the big beast glanced back at him and sidled away.

Roland Merullo

Two seconds later a ranger came hurrying down toward us, waving an orange swatch of cloth, telling us to move away, move away. "They *will* come at you if they feel crowded," he said.

He shooed them into the water. We walked back to the car, chastened, refreshed, and set off through that brilliant Yellowstone *now*, north toward Livingston.

27

It was a beautiful drive from Wyoming back into Montana, up through the aptly-named Paradise Valley. Nine-thousand-foot mountains ran to our right in a green-gray parade, and closer by, a blue river wound through pastures that seemed made of sun-basted silk. I tried to imagine what it must have been like when the first non-natives saw this. No roads or electric wires then, no cabins with signs advertising fishing lures or float rides, no couples in rubber boats, slathered with sunscreen and drifting along. Paradise Valley. Arduous as the pioneer lives were, this scenery must have matched a vision of heaven they carried around inside themselves. The land must have whispered the promise of some Dzogchen of the American wilderness, some real-life Great Perfection.

Almost a full hour of it we had before we stopped for dinner in the small city of Livingston, Montana. This was my kind of place, a half dozen square blocks of brick buildings and colorful storefronts, a community completely lacking in the T-shirt-and-souvenir fluffery of West Yellowstone, Wyoming. We strolled around for a while, browsing in a bookstore, stretching our legs, and I realized that one of Livingston's charms was the absence of chain stores. Every shop and restaurant had the stamp of individuality on it—exactly the opposite of what you saw in so many other places now. Driving south on 95, for instance, heading for a February school vacation at Miami Beach, we'd pull off into old southern towns with block upon block of vacant storefronts. "What happened?" Jeannie would always ask. "What in God's name happened here?"

A mile or so away we'd discover what had happened—a mall with every store a chain, every employee in uniform, paychecks signed by an absentee owner or, more likely, a holding company or "Group," with headquarters in some office building a thousand miles away. There were efficiencies to this system, of course, but everything else had been sacrificed on the altar of convenience and low price. Dignity, pride of ownership, commerce on a human scale—everything.

I'd read or heard somewhere that Moses and Buddha and Jesus and Mohammed had all appeared on earth at a time and place when the spiritual traditions of the day had either mutated into poisonous forms or grown stale. Some of the religious rites that preceded Buddha, for instance, had devolved into a world of ritual sacrifice and castes. In Jesus' time there had been the absurd Pharisaical dictums—Thou shalt not heal on the Sabbath, and so on. Moses, Mohammed—those great, fresh spirits came precisely to break up and water the hard dry earth and plant some new hybrid that would bear better fruit.

Looking for a good place to eat in Livingston, I wondered if we had reached that point now in America, if Christianity and capitalism both had ossified. Enormous corporations and megachurches, each with their rules and propaganda, their need to eliminate competition, eccentricity, otherness. Wasn't it time for some brave new spirit to speak a fresh truth? Could these really be, as the radio preachers insisted, the "end times"? Maybe just the end of their times, I thought, and the beginning of better.

I was hungry again.

Hoping for something other than a burger or steak, and wanting to wash the Italian meal in Spokane from my consciousness, I led us to a humble eatery called Allegro in the middle of downtown Livingston. On the wall was a photo of the Trevi Fountain (an almost exact copy of which hung in Jeannie's study). The salad greens were fresh, the pasta *al pomodoro* properly cooked, and I couldn't keep my eyes from going to the photo. When we'd finished the meal—his treat—Rinpoche and I made a quick trip upstairs to a two-room bookstore where the owner, a young man named David, greeted us with palms pressed together and a short bow. He'd heard of Rinpoche, carried every one of his books, seemed absolutely thrilled to have the great teacher in his shop, and asked him to sign all copies. Rinpoche did so, graciously, attentively, then gave David the famous squeeze on the shoulder as a kind of blessing. In return, as we were leaving, the young man pressed upon me a copy of a book called *The Lost Years of Jesus*.

"Wery nice man," Rinpoche said when we were in the pickup again and heading for the interstate. He was turning the book over in his hands.

"What do you think of this idea that Jesus spent a lot of time in India and Tibet?"

"Not an idea," he said.

"A fact? Certifiable?"

"What else does he do all that time?"

"I don't know. No one knows. There's no mention of those years in the Bible. If I remember it right, he yells at his mother when he's twelve or thirteen; next thing you know he's coming into Jerusalem, a famous preacher, age thirty."

"He traveled," Rinpoche said.

He was in one of those moods of absolute confidence, one of those areas he seemed to have pondered and studied for years. All doubt had been banished from the right side of Uma's interior.

"Learning or teaching, or both?"

"Already inside him the learning was."

"Why would he bother traveling to the East, then? They already had their great teachers."

"Pure spirits, on this earth, want to see other pure spirits sometimes, Otto. They have a loneliness inside them, too. Like you for Jeannie now. Like me for Cecelia. The pure want to touch other pure, the good want to touch other good. The bad, same thing. The people who speak Russian, some of the times, want to find the other people who speak Russian."

"To practice."

"No," he said. "To not forget who they are. To remember the real self inside them."

"You sound so sure."

He laughed and reached out and cupped the back of my head in his spread fingers. "Rest this busy head," he said. "Let Rinpoche drive. You sit here, look, sleep, do the phone, rest the questions."

"You couldn't drive this. It's a stick shift. Four speed. Clutch. It would take you quite a while and quite a bit of practice to learn."

He laughed again and worked his right hand and left foot as if shifting. "You, too," he said, fluttering the fingers of his other hand near his temple. "Quite a while, man!"

⟋ 28

It's always a risk, arranging your lodging via the Internet. You can't trust the reviews—good or bad. You can't really be sure about the photos. You have little sense of the firmness of the mattress or the quality of the breakfast food. But we'd been lucky on that trip, able to avoid chain hotels entirely. From the Cave B to Kalispell, from the Davenport to the Inn at Chakra Creek, from Celia's selections to my own, there had been no disasters, no creaky beds or cranky clerks, nothing to complain about. Our plans weren't fixed in stone, but I figured we had only one more night on the road together and so Billings would make sense as a stopping place. Using my magical phone I found us a hotel called The Bighorn Resort, a short distance outside town and just off the interstate.

What worried me about the Bighorn was that, according to the website, it was attached to some kind of water park with slides and chutes and pools. I love swimming outdoors, a fact to which the various adventures here may testify, but indoor pools and water parks have always seemed to me nothing more than breeding grounds for the more onerous of the earth's bacteria, tepid fake ponds suitable mostly for four-year-olds to pee in and arthritic old men to soak their bones. We arrived in Billings so late, however, that I needn't have worried. The water park was long closed for the day. Even Rinpoche, who seemed in possession of an unlimited store of energy, looked tired around the eyes and told me we should sleep in the next morning, meet for breakfast at eight thirty instead of our customary seven fifteen.

This was fine with me. But what often happens when I've made a long drive into the later hours is that my body cranks itself up to stay awake, and then needs some cranking-down time. There was a bar at the Bighorn, a modest little place with sports on the raised TV and a small selection of local beers. I decided I'd have one solitary Moose Drool, watch fifteen minutes of the Olympics, and head upstairs to the room.

The bar was packed, the tables filled with what appeared to be members of a traveling theater company. Prone to wild gesticulation and loud laughter, the actors enlivened the place at least, though they left only a seat or two at the corner of the bar. I sipped my Moose Drool and watched Olympic table tennis, a game that resembles matches in the Ringling family basement about as closely as heart surgery resembles the eating of baby back ribs. I can honestly say I didn't notice the woman who sat down a stool away, on the other side of the corner, until I heard her ask, "You part of this weird crowd?" and realized she was speaking to me.

I turned to look at her. Somewhere close to forty, I guessed, with reddish brown hair hanging long and straight on both sides of her face, and eyes touched with a watery sadness. In front of her she held what looked to be a margarita, partly consumed. Her posture had a combative aspect to it, as if she expected me to take a swing at her and was more than ready to hit back.

"No," I said, "just down for a beer before bed."

"Loud, aren't they?"

I said that they were.

"Traveling with your family?"

"Brother-in-law. We're driving from Seattle to North Dakota. Every five or six years we take a road trip together. Family tradition."

"Never heard of that," she said. It occurred to me, from the way she reached for her glass, that she might have more than the one drink in her. "Your wife's brother?"

"Sister's husband. I lost my wife in January."

"Sorry."

It was a sincere "Sorry," and one spoken in the minor key of my own pain. So many things had been said to me, to us, since Jeannie died, some of them kind and others clumsy. At the service in Bronxville, for example, one of Natasha's former high school pals had come up to her and said, "I remember the time we were in the basement making a lot of noise and your mom came down and screamed at us."

It was an exaggeration, of course, if not an outright lie—Jeannie didn't scream, at kids or anyone else, ever—but the comment hurt Natasha all the same. It was offered, as I tried to explain to her, from a place of terrible discomfort. Even adults had a tough time consoling the bereaved. They said too much, or inadvertently smiled while saying it, or let slip a completely inappropriate remark—all from nervousness and, probably, a gut aversion to the hard fact of death. With our sparkling shopping malls and endlessly entertaining telephones, we pushed death into a corner and looked away for fifty or sixty or eighty-five years. It waited there patiently, though, patiently, patiently, then jumped out at us right in the middle of a table tennis game, a winter morning, a night of drugged sleep. Who could find a good thing to say about that?

"You sound like you've had a similar pain. Did you lose your husband?"

She took a drink and nodded, swallowed. "Yup," she said.

"What caused it?"

"Him being an asshole."

"Oh."

"My theory," she went on, "is that exactly ninety-two percent of men are assholes."

I worried, for a moment, that she'd be like Giorgio the B and B owner, stringing one sentence, one story, one abrasive opinion seamlessly into the next. I'd be stuck sitting there till closing time, an ear.

"They won't do a dish or change a diaper if their freakin' life depends on it, and then you see them with their buddies, fixing a water pump or a tractor axle, and they're happy as little boys. Minus the bedroom out of the equation and they'd be gone in a second." She twisted her mouth in a way that made me think she was going to spit.

"Is that what happened? He left?"

She shook her head. The flesh on either side of her mouth swung very slightly, the pendulum of age. "I booted the bastard. Four years now, and know what? Not for one second do I look back and think maybe I made a mistake."

"Kids?"

"Two girls, mostly grown. Yourself?"

"Girl and a boy, mostly grown, too. Both in college."

She made a "hmph" sound and took another drink. I had her figured for a tough divorcée living alone on a ranch outside Billings, cursing, castrating hogs. But she said, "I'm a nurse, you know. I see the worst part of life every day—sick kids, people dying, in pain, stupid people who bring all kinds of bad shit on themself with meth or booze or that. I say to my girls, Listen, you have as good a time as you can for as long as you can, and if you do decide to get married, you make damn sure you find a guy who wants more than just what's between your legs and who gives more than just what's between his."

"Good advice," I said. "I'll tell Natasha."

"Nice name. Yeah, they're not gonna end up like old mom."

"Mom's not that old," I said.

"Thanks." She twirled her drink, looked absently at the TV screen for a minute.

"A fair number of my friends wash dishes and change diapers, you know. I did."

"Yeah? Where the hell might these friends of yours be?"

"New York, mostly."

"Hah. There you go. Send one of them out west."

"Billings a nice town?"

"Nice? The people are nice, sure, the normal ones. You drive your truck off the road in winter and you'll be there about five seconds before somebody stops to help. But look at the freakin' place. You been here long?"

"Just arrived."

"We got the women's prison. We got the halfway house where every freakin' sex offender in Montana has to come before they let him out for good. Probation offices. We got the Crow Reservation down the road and those poor bastards drink and wander around. Fifty, sixty percent unemployment down there. I wouldn't call it *nice*. I'd call it *harsh*. But I tell ya, I get off work at eleven o'clock and I walk home in the decent weather and not once, not once in freakin twenty years, has anybody given me a hard time."

"You look like you can take care of yourself," I said, which probably wasn't exactly the right thing to say.

She shot me a sideways look. "I can, mister. But I don't think that's it. Good people here, excepting my stupid husband and his pals. The whoring bastard."

"Cheated on you?"

"Hah. Freakin' rooster. Anything with panties on, he'd follow it down the block like a dog after bacon. You cheat on your wife?"

"No."

"Married how long, if you don't mind me asking."

"Twenty-four years."

"And she goes and dies on ya. My husband's healthy as a horse still, even now, the stupid prick. You think the good Lord would give him the syph or something."

"You'd think so."

"Should I have another drink?" she asked.

"I'd be happy to buy you one. I'm headed out, though. We drove something like four hundred miles today."

"That's a trip to the grocery store in Montana. You going to sleep?"

"Hope so."

"Want to swing by my house on the way to bed? It's three blocks."

I was tired then, and so long removed from the world of

unexpected sexual encounters that I just sat there staring at her for a few seconds.

"You look like somebody just asked you to wipe their ass."

"Out of practice," I said. "Just . . . I don't know."

"I'd get you back *in* practice," she said, and I could see then that she was quite drunk. The tough exterior had been hiding something tender as a fingertip, and now, with one sentence, it had all been put on display. It was as though she'd lifted a sheet off a glass case with sadness relics in it. "We're talking an hour of fun. Who gets hurt?"

"No one," I said. "I'd like to. Very much. It's just, I think it's just too soon for me."

She raised and lowered her eyebrows and flexed her lips. She took a twenty- dollar bill out of her pocket and set the edge of it under her empty glass. "Well," she said, "it's not like I ask every day."

"I'm sure."

"I won't take it personal."

"You shouldn't. Not at all. Really."

She set a hand on the top of my leg and slid off the stool and I watched her walk toward the door, steadily enough, shoulders slightly hunched as if there were a big sack of troubles there and it grew especially heavy at that hour of the day.

In bed, in the few minutes before the gloved hand of sleep took hold of me, I found myself remembering lovemaking with my wife. The hunger and heat of the early years, then the familiar patterns in our Bronxville bed, a comfortable dance of give and take. In biblical parlance, when you made love with a woman you "knew" her. That seemed exactly right.

29

Next morning the monk from Skovorodino came to breakfast in his bathing suit and pink flip flops. Nothing else. I walked into the breakfast nook—a crowded place of Styrofoam and plastic knives, biscuits, waffle machines, and husky, sugar-starved Montanans—and saw him there at a corner table, bare-chested, peeling an orange and sipping tea. The looks being sent in his direction were the farthest thing from friendly, but no one seemed to have the courage to tell him to put on a shirt. I poured myself a coffee and carried it and a box of cereal over to him. "Rinpoche, most people don't wear only bathing suits to breakfast," I was about to say when I noticed a pair of teenage girls come in with their mother, the younger females in bikinis and sandals. I remembered the water park. I decided the No Shirt, No Shoes, No Service idea wasn't an important enough aspect of Americana to pass on to my friend. On the one hand I was sure he wouldn't be wandering around Dickinson, North Dakota, in a Speedo, and on the other I'd long ago resigned myself to his eccentricities: the watery high-pitched laugh that mutated into fits of giggling, the boyish enthusiasms, the wrestling matches on a B and B lawn, the running around in a crowd of teenagers anxious to get sprayed with heated sulfur water from the earth's core. They hurt no one, these spurts of bizarre behavior. My brother-in-law hurt no one, ever, was never mean or petty, rarely judgmental or selfish or curt. He simply did not care what others thought of him, and in that way, I suppose, he was the perfect match for my sister. They left the embarrassment to people like me, mainstream sorts, members of the herd, conventional to a fault.

"You miss Shelsa?" I asked him.

"Wery much."

"We're only about three hundred miles from the farm. We'll get there tonight, no problem."

"Good, good," he said, peeling away.

"Are you worried about her? I mean, what you told me earlier—people wanting to hurt her, the dreams, and so on?"

"Worried, worried, sure, yes."

"I think she'll be fine."

He nodded, refused to look up for a moment, and then met my eyes. "Maybe her father shouldn't be having the wacation now, though."

"That's the first time I've ever heard you sound even a little bit guilty."

"Maybe. Little bit."

"She's fine with Seese and the kids. They're way out in the middle of our North Dakota nowhere. Not many bad people there."

"Maybe, sure," he said, as if he wanted to talk about something else.

"It's funny, I didn't think of you as being on vacation. I don't think of what you do as work, I guess, which is pretty foolish. You write, you teach, you give talks."

"Talks finished," he said.

"Because of Shelsa?"

"Now she will give talks."

"A little young yet, isn't she?"

"Little bit."

"I've never seen you this way. What's wrong? It's something else."

"The high," he said.

"Huh?"

"In the place," he waved one arm behind him, toward the building that held the water park, "the woman say there's a slide. You have to go, she say. Wery high, wery fast, and then—pssh—in the water."

"*Have to go* is just an expression. She didn't mean it literally."

"Fun, she said."

"I'm sure. But it's mostly for kids. I've never been on a waterslide in my life, for instance. The water's—"

"Rinpoche doesn't like any high," he said. "Airplanes, slides. Wery to me scary, Otto."

"Then let's just skip it and head out. We'll get to Dickinson that much earlier."

He was shaking his head with a stubbornness I'd seen many times. Leaving without a waterpark adventure was simply not going to be an option.

"You're determined to face your fears," I said. "You're giving me some kind of lesson."

More head shaking. He put a section of orange into his mouth, chewed, swallowed, and made his eyes wide like a terrified man. An act, all of it. He should have been on stage. He should have traveled with the troupe of arm-wavers and loud-laughers who occupied the tables on the far side of the grazing ranchers. I wondered if even the fear for Shelsa's safety—something he'd mentioned exactly once—was a device, a ruse, a lever to move me where I needed to be moved. Maybe Rinpoche was light-years beyond physical fear. Maybe Shelsa was, too. "All this is for my benefit, isn't it? A metaphor."

"Me and you," he said, swooping one hand down through the air. "We go high now. Wery fast she say."

I gave up. I surrendered. Another week and I'd be back in the empty house in Bronxville, dressing in a sport jacket and neat khakis every morning, driving to the train station, buying the *Times*, riding into the city and taking the elevator to my eleventh-floor office with the map of North Dakota on the wall, photos of Jeannie and the kids on a side table, and stacks of manuscripts and contracts and meeting memos on my desk. It occurred to me that maybe I should have taken the woman up on her offer of the night before and had an hour of fun. Whom would it have hurt, indeed? And what would it matter if I splashed around in chlorine for half an hour with the brother-in-law I probably wouldn't see again until Thanksgiving? Maybe there *was* a lesson there because, in truth—could Rinpoche have known this?—I was subtly intimidated by the waterslide idea. I've gone on a roller coaster exactly once in my life—that was sufficient. I played a little football in high school, JV hockey for two years in college. I've flown a hundred times or more, in big planes and small; I've gone into the surf off Cape Cod on days when wiser men stayed onshore, and I've ventured, on my volunteer tutoring duties, into New York neighborhoods that posed some risk. But I'm not the most physically courageous person on the planet, not a daredevil, not especially afraid of heights but not a fan of amusement rides in which one gives up control over one's well-being in exchange for a few minutes of thrill.

But there I was, walking the halls of the Bighorn Resort with a few bran flakes and one cup of mediocre coffee in my belly and a bathing suit on, escorted by a brown-skinned monk with mysterious motivations and a fear, so he said, of heights.

That fear was soon tested. We paid, walked in, and found ourselves in a cement-floored wonderland of screaming kids and bored young lifeguards with flat stomachs. There was a wading pool, a hot tub, a smaller slide for the little ones, a hinged bucket that poured a hundred gallons of water down on your head from a height of forty feet . . . and two waterslides. Rinpoche and I did not speak. Moving slowly, like condemned men, we set our towels down and climbed three flights of stairs. Two ominous tubular openings greeted us there. A laconic young man said one was designed to be used with inner tubes, and one was not. The inner tubes were down below, so our only choice for that first trip was the other slide, said to be "a little faster." Rinpoche and I looked at each other. "All right. I'll go first," I said. He nodded, offered what looked to be a genuinely nervous smile. I sat on the wet plastic, leaned back, pushed off, and I was suddenly being shot through a winding cylinder, gathering speed, riding up on the turns like a man on a luge, and going almost as fast. When you were halfway down, the diabolical invention began making quick turns left and right so you were swung hard side to side, dropping, dropping, a sheet of water beneath you, your stomach left somewhere above, and then a sudden dark straightaway and you were thrown into air and a hard splashdown. Underwater. Finished. Free.

I kicked to the edge of the pool and turned so I could see Rinpoche make his exit. Long before he appeared I could hear him, an echoing "Otto! Oh! Oh!" in the tube, and then the nut-brown bulk of him came into view, face contorted, and there was a giant splash. It took him ten seconds to surface—maybe he was praying under there, giving thanks, adjusting his Speedo, retrieving a diamond ring some unlucky wife had lost. Then the face appeared, radiantly happy. He wiped one hand across his bald skull, fixed his eyes on me and shouted this command: "Again!"

We made the ride eleven more times and then switched to the slower inner-tube slide and went down twice more. The stair climbing was work, and we were certainly the oldest people in the park at that hour, but I have to admit I loved it. Once the first trip was endured it was all known territory, all thrill, all thoughtless swooping and blue, bleachy splash. By the time we finally called it quits—damp and well chlorinated—I was wondering how much it would cost to build a waterslide on the retreat center property and wishing Natasha and Anthony had been there. To share the fun. To see that their father was not yet an ancient relic.

All the way back to the room, even as we were putting our bags into the pickup and heading out of the Bighorn lot, Rinpoche kept thanking me for this particular version of American fun. "The best brother-and-law," he said at one point, and no matter how many times I told him I deserved no credit for the water park, that I'd made the reservations at Bighorn in *spite* of it, that I wouldn't even have paid the admission if it hadn't been for him, he kept telling me how brave I'd been to go first, how he might have gone only on the child's slide if I hadn't been there, how he might not have gone down a second time after seeing how fast we went on the first. And so on. He had conquered, in a small way, his supposed fear of "high." But I suspected then, and I suspect to this day, that it was all a trick. By the second run on the faster slide I realized that the proper technique involved a complete letting go, an abandoning of oneself to the fates, the skill of the waterslide engineers, and the conscientiousness of the county inspectors. A mindless, illogical trust. Was there no spirchal lesson there?

⟶⟶ 30

Billings, it seemed, was not a place you could easily get lost in. And, from our quick visit, not a place you'd want to. Filling the thirsty Uma with gas at a downtown station, I remembered the woman's comment: "You drive your truck off the road in winter and you'll be there about five seconds before somebody stops to help." But the original impression was less than favorable: the Montana Women's Prison; the Montana Department of Corrections Rehabilitation and Parole Office; a population of street people that ranged from the inebriated Native American of whom we accidentally asked restaurant recommendations to the fifty-year-old bearded drifter sitting on his duffel and bedroll in front of the Conoco station and eyeing a passing preteen girl in a way that would make any father's fists clench.

The Crow woman (I asked her as she stepped out of the supermarket, not realizing the state she was in)—stocky, pimpled, drunk or high, wandering from one corner to the next and panhandling very quietly and respectfully—didn't know any good places to eat. So after the fill-up we followed signs into the historic district—a few blocks of less-than-new buildings—and parked. Two women coming out of McCormick's Café gave it a rave review, enough of a recommendation as far as I was concerned. Inside, the good monk and I found a tin-ceilinged, brick-walled eatery suffused with natural light and crowded with close-packed tables. McCormick's had a chalkboard menu with items like Bacon Avocado Hamburger and Mesclun Salad. My kind of place, in other words. Rinpoche enjoyed a smoothie—his latest fascination—and I went for the Portobello Burger, which had a tasty patty of the succulent fungus sitting like a beret on a slightly larger piece of excellent ground beef. No relish, however. There must be something about Montana and relish, some primordial prejudice, some statewide religion that considers it sinful to chop up pickles and mix them with a bit of sugar in vinegar. But let me not complain about McCormick's Café, because it was a shrine to good food in a city where my New York prejudices had led me to expect no such thing.

Let me be forgiven for those prejudices. I am, as Celia has often pointed out over the years, a man of caustic eye and too-quick judgments. I notice the pimples on the faces of Native American women, the clouds in their eyes, the dearth of food options in a prairie city. I notice the razor wire above a prison entrance, the lust in middle-aged men's stares. I send the sharp blade of my mind knifing down into the smallest details of other lives. I like to think this comes from an interest in the human condition, a fascination with life, with America, with the infinite possibilities of how we can manage our years. But it also has roots in something less noble, a habit, born in the soil of insecurity no doubt, of seeking out flaws. The only thing I can say in my defense is that I'd become acutely aware of it on that trip, I didn't like it much, I worried I had passed it on to my kids, and I was trying to change. That kind of effort, Rinpoche had told me many times, was the mundane heart of the spiritual search. Momentous experiences on the meditation cushion were fine and good, but the real work was less glamorous. The real work was the identification of those aspects of yourself that led to what he called "the negative emotions"—anger, envy, bitterness, greed, cynicism, hatred and the like—things that poured hurt into an already overfull world. It was like an infestation of carpenter ants. First you saw them, then you traced them to their nest, and then you set about the hard work of convincing them they were not welcome. According to my wise brother-in-law, doing nothing about your flaws was a kind of spiritual laziness for which one eventually paid a heavy price. The ants were harmless little bugs, it seemed; in time, left alone, they'd eat through the walls of your house.

On that trip especially, but in my entire life, I'd encountered people who appeared so much more easygoing about these things. It didn't matter to them what they put into their mouths. Others' quirks and troubles didn't quite penetrate their daily run of thoughts. They were kind, forgiving, jovial, mellow, and I had a side that was sharper than that, critical and judgmental. Why? Did it have something to do with education? With editing—which was, after all, a constant struggle to criticize and improve? But Jeannie had been as well educated as I, certainly as sophisticated—to use a word I dislike—and she hadn't been plagued by this need to observe, compare, and comment. I couldn't blame my parents, who fought frequently with each other but were live-and-let-live people in the extreme when it came to the rest of humanity. It had something to do with an old defense system, probably: move to Manhattan from Dickinson, ND, and you're often made to feel like a rube, a hayseed, a hick; you build an armor from whatever metal is available.

Full in the belly, exhilarated from our aquatic adventure, anxious to see our kin, Rinpoche and I headed east from downtown Billings past a huge refinery and into the Montana wilds. It rained for a moment—the first precipitation since Seattle—darkening the fifty-mile views to north and south, an architecture of emptiness. On the radio the talkers were talking "Natural Rights": life, liberty, property. The government was their enemy, anger their shield. They were like children who wanted no teachers, no parents. No roads, bridges, post offices, license plates, speed limits, or taxes. They dreamed a fantasy nation of hearty individualists beholden to no one but themselves. And they were, to my mind, a twenty-first-century plague.

We hadn't been on the highway thirty minutes, vast stretches of dry, empty prairie to either side, when my phone rang on the seat. I gestured for Rinpoche to answer it, told him how to work the touch screen, watched him slash and poke and then hold it to his ear. "Yes," he said, as loudly as if he were shouting across all of east Montana. "Yes, yes, wery much!"

Holding the pickup at sixty on the nearly empty highway, I turned my eyes to him from time to time as this one-sided conversation went on. What if it was somebody calling from the office—Frank Denig, for instance—and Rinpoche was pretending to be me, playing along, agreeing to an early retirement with no compensation or benefits? And then I heard what sounded like my sister's voice, and a multitude of more painful options rushed the field of consideration.

"Sure, sure, wery good," Rinpoche was saying. I tried to get his attention. I signaled that I wanted to speak to whomever it was. But by the time he looked over at me he'd already hung up.

"Who was it?"

"I forget," he said.

"Ha, funny. My sister?"

"Who loves you wery much."

"I know that. What's the plan? I heard you agreeing to all kinds of things. Everybody okay?"

"Okay, sure. She make one nights a reservation in Medora."

"Medora?"

"Near home."

"I know where Medora is, but why aren't we just going straight to Dickinson?"

"Last part of little wacation," he said. "A barbecue. Do you eat meat?"

"You know I eat meat."

"The steak?"

"Of course."

"Fun," she says. "And some big news, too."

"There we go. I had a feeling it was something like that. The big news is the part that worries me. The rest of it is a setup, trust me. A little steak barbecue to soften up old Uncle Ott."

"News is good, she say."

And I said, "Good is relative," and drove on.

East of Forsyth in the great state of Montana one is hard-pressed to find dotted lines running next to the roads on Rand McNally, let me put it that way. We could have angled north-west to Sumatra (someone with a sense of humor named these places), but I could feel in my belly the desire to see my children. The dark stubble on Anthony's cheeks, the way Natasha had of walking—as if she were about to break into a run at any moment. I missed them.

The landscape there, on the road to Miles City, was dry as sawdust and about the same color. We passed mile upon mile of rangeland, unimaginably large swaths of uninhabited territory enlivened only by sagebrush and dry streambeds, one line of fencing along the highway, the occasional creek marked by a stripe of greenery, the occasional billboard showing an infant and a slogan like, "Take My Hand, not My Life." Here and there a few dozen head of cattle gathered close together in the heat, with a million acres of open land around them. What, I wondered, were they afraid of? What did they know of their future?

Now the radio offered sentimental Christian songs like "You Deliver Me" and "When I Feel Like I Can't Go On." Rinpoche bobbed his head to the music.

We went along for only an hour or so, then took the exit for Miles City, where the side of a barn was painted with the image of a cowboy riding a bucking bronco and the words DON'T LET METH BE YOUR LAST RIDE. An iced coffee there, a short stroll to stretch our legs. There was a fantastic western-wear shop, two floors of eight-hundred-dollar felt hats and gorgeous stitched boots, and we loaded up on gifts: pearl-button shirts, belts and belt buckles, a carved horse for Shelsa from her uncle, a nice scarf for Cecelia. I realized I'd never sent the postcards I'd bought in Baring, so I scribbled a greeting and sent off one each to Jeannie's sister, our dog-sitting neighbor, and a friend at work.

Somewhere on the road between there and Glendive, a distance of seventy-five miles, I found myself yet again replaying the conversation with the woman in the bar at Bighorn.

Strangely enough, the emptiness of the land around us made me wish I'd taken her up on her offer, walked the three blocks by her side, fallen into bed with her and tried to make the encounter into something more than mutual masturbation. It wouldn't have been easy, manufacturing an intimacy there in a bungalow on Billings' hard edges. She was pretty, though, worn and pretty and lonely, and not so drunk that she'd have invited just anyone back to her house for sex. At least that's what I wanted to believe. I wasn't superstitious enough to think Jeannie would have cared. I wouldn't have told Natasha and Anthony, any more than I'd expect them, now, to tell me. How long was I obliged to wait—a year? five years? forever?—before sleeping with another woman would no longer tarnish memories of my wife?

I didn't know. It had just felt wrong. Or perhaps I'd merely been afraid.

"What about sex?" I said aloud, without planning to. I turned off the Christian music station.

"Sex, sex, sex," Rinpoche said. "Funny word. In Ortyk we say *lahkusha*."

"That has a better sound to it. In English all the sex words are ugly: 'intercourse', 'pubic', 'fellatio', 'cunnilingus', 'orgasm.' No poetry anywhere."

Rinpoche grunted. He'd been fingering his loop of brown beads, but now he let his hands rest. "It makes life," he said.

"That and so much more. I can't think of any aspect of living that's more full of joy and trouble. You were celibate for a time, weren't you?"

"Ten year," he said. "In our tradition, ten year, then you can do."

"Must have been fun, that first time."

"Always fun," he said.

"We have a bit of a Puritan tradition still alive in this country. Between that, some of our Catholic friends and the so-called Christian conservatives there's a lot of guilt and bad feeling around the edges of the subject, seems to me. On the one hand, the TV, the Internet, the magazines—we're absolutely bombarded with sex images. On the other, there's this background refrain of guilt."

"Easy answer," he said.

"Tell me."

"Always with love."

"Always? Never just for release? For pure pleasure? For what the French call *divertissement?* Diversion, entertainment, fun?"

"Sure," he said. "But love is the main thing. If you have love in you when you do sex, maybe no trouble comes."

I thought of my children, just entering that landscape, so much delight and treachery there, as though you were traipsing barefoot across a luscious field of high grass, the day was hot but breezy . . . and there were poisonous snakes slithering near your ankles. Jeannie and I had always spoken openly to our kids on the subject, the basic facts ("We know already, Dad!"), bits of advice or caution here and there. Mainly they navigated it on their own, the way most of us do.

"For some people," Rinpoche went on, "the *lahkusha* can be a teaching."

"Everything can be a teaching in your tradition, it seems to me. Sex, sports, illness, death, birth, waterslides, prison, family life, nature. What *isn't* a spiritual lesson, I'd like to know."

"Nothing isn't, for me," he said. "For you, too, now, I think. For Otto now, everything shows the path."

"The path to what, Rinpoche?"

He sent a look of the most profound pity across Uma's front seat. He said, "Otto, my friend," in such a tender way that, wounded old sentimental fool that I was in those weeks, I felt a quick rush of water in my eyes. Two blinks took care of it; I hoped he hadn't seen. "My good friend," he repeated, "do you think, really, that all this complicated machine," he squeezed my upper arm as if by "machine" he meant my body, "and all this big," he gestured toward the windshield, beyond which the earth spread out in all directions like the Russian steppe, "is here just for the nothing?"

"No. But my question is: what's the something?"

"The something is inside," he said, tapping the top of my skull lightly with his left palm. "If you try, you can make in here a *weh-ree* quiet place. Wery quiet. And then, in that quiet place comes a new feeling."

"Describe it to me."

At that moment a man about my own age went past us on a motorcycle, plowing along in the fast lane. He had very long hair, all gray, and the wind blew it out behind him in a rippling celebration. I felt the smallest touch of envy.

When Rinpoche didn't answer immediately I glanced across the seat and saw that he'd closed his eyes, as if he were studying his own enlightenment, searching for words to make it clear.

"It feels," he said, then he opened his eyes and looked at me, "what I told you before—that you know you should die one day. You really know, you feel it. And same time you feel: this is okay."

I watched the motorcyclist growing smaller in the distance. "So then the whole point and purpose of being alive is to not be afraid of death? That's it?"

He pushed out his lips and made a small shake of his head, disappointed, it seemed, in his pupil. He tried again. "My father was the great teacher, yes? When he was dying, around him the people wery sad. 'Don't go! Don't go, Master!' everyone cry. Me, too. 'Don't go, Papa,' I say. 'Don't go now!' Know what he answer?"

"Tell me."

"He answer: Stupid people! Where do you think I could go?"

You could go to a place where nobody could see you or speak to you or touch you, I thought. But I didn't say it. The shivers were on me again, a follicle gymnastics.

"When he tell me that," Rinpoche went on, "all in a sudden, I see."

"You were enlightened."

"I *see*," he corrected. "I understand one thing, but this is the most important one. I understand in the most real way that this body doesn't belong for me."

"*To* me."

"Yes. I borrow it for a little some time, this body, just to hold my spirit. Then, little some more time, I give back."

"And you actually *feel* this?" I said. "It's not just a theory or an idea?"

"Yes. I feel. I know it in my hands and face, in my belly. Right now I feel this. All the time."

"Make me feel that, then," I said suddenly. "I mean it. I'll let go of wanting everything else—except seeing my kids. Teach me that—not just as a thought or a pretty notion. Teach me to have that understanding deep inside me and I'll let everything else go."

Rinpoche held his eyes on me for a ten-count then said quietly, eerily, as if he'd been working for six years to show me how to ride a bicycle and finally, at last, I'd gotten the balance right and was wobbling off on my own, "Otto, my friend," he said, "wery good."

With that conversation echoing inside me, we made yet another stop, in Glendive, for smoothies and a two-block stroll. A thousand miles into the trip now, I was running low on driving energy, needing to stop every hour or so and recharge. And perhaps I was procrastinating, too, wary of Celia's "news," or of what I'd just heard myself say. It was true—I'd give up almost anything to be able to feel what Rinpoche seemed to feel, to have that perspective on life, to lose all fear—but the truth had surprised me. It had spoken itself. I examined it the way an antiques dealer examines a document or a painting or a desk, for authenticity. Beyond wanting to see Natasha and Anthony and Celia and Rinpoche and Shelsa, I *was* beginning to feel that I'd exhausted or released or set aside all my other wants. Success at work, money, dinner party invitations, even good meals— somehow, on this trip most of the juice and zest had been squeezed out of those things. It was as if Jeannie's death had made me confront some central question I'd spent my life avoiding—not just the puzzle of death itself, but some larger mystery of which that was only one piece. It was as if my flaky sister had known that and had arranged this second road trip as a way of offering an answer. I told Rinpoche I wanted to walk around the block on my own. I needed a moment.

Glendive looked, to my eye, sunbaked and desolate, the kind of place where, under a Lenin or Mussolini, a radical New York City intellectual might be exiled. There was a train station. A bar. A Mexican restaurant. A row of shops. In one dusty window a placard reading THE RIGHT TO BEAR ARMS SHALL NOT BE INFRINGED! There was an electronic sign above the door of the chamber of commerce building, but its run of letters advertised community events a week or two in the past. That seemed fitting somehow, as if this part of the country lay stranded in the cattle-run days of yesteryear, or as if I had now decided to put the world's tired entertainments behind me forever. To my surprise, this wasn't a depressing idea. Intimidating, yes. Almost frightening. But not depressing at all.

The sun blasted down on Glendive's sidewalks. I wondered what it must feel like to be young there.

With the stops and procrastination, four different moments when the pickup seemed to lose its force, the engine coughing and stuttering before running strong again, it was late afternoon by the time we reached the badlands. They began, swirls of sculpted dirt, buttes, colorful rock faces, shortly after we crossed into the Peace Garden State, the place where Celia and I had come into this world. For a moment, just the tiniest moment, I tried to imagine the lovemaking that had summoned me into this life, my parents naked, in bed, young. Perhaps all children do that at some point, however reluctantly. I wondered if I'd been made in an hour of love, or just boredom or lust, or just a patch of relief from a hard week of labor. I tried to picture the embrace that had brought my spirit into this body, but it was, even for a vivid imagination like mine, a bridge too far.

 31

Shortly before six we swept down the I-94 exit ramp and into the town of Medora. A smaller and slightly less artificial Leavenworth, Medora makes a fair attempt at imitating an old western settlement. The buildings have faces of weathered wood, and there are some wooden sidewalks, too. There are horse-drawn wagon rides and cowboy shows, a cabin where Teddy Roosevelt is said to have slept, a magnificent national park named for him, a golf course, a handful of motels and restaurants, and, every summer night, something called a pitchfork fondue up on a high plateau overlooking a landscape cut by dry streambeds and marked by wandering elk.

As we glided into town, Rinpoche was kind enough to inform me that we were supposed to meet our family at the barbecue rather than at the Badlands Motel. The whole plan seemed suspect. Dickinson—where Rinpoche, Celia, and Shelsa now lived, and where I'd been born and raised—was only thirty minutes farther along the interstate. Why not just drive those last few miles and have a barbecue at what Celia and I still referred to as home? Why sign up for a meal that offered, as a main course, two things my sister never ate: steak and hot dogs? Yes, there would be salad and vegetables of various kinds, but it seemed a strange scheme, even for her. A night in a motel in Medora with all assembled? What was she thinking?

Driving up the winding road toward the pitchfork fondue parking lot, I reminded myself that Celia's thinking process was a creature that traveled along an untraceable route, off radar, a B-1 bomber of the psyche. I wondered if she'd been raising Jasper Jr. on veggie burgers and expensive supplements. I wondered if, during the long train ride and the days on the farm, she'd been indoctrinating my children with her eminently kindhearted but utterly impractical philosophies about the living of life in the U.S.A. I wondered, too—another fresh breeze—why I was so afraid of her.

And then I remembered the feeling of pushing off at the top of the waterslide. That trust, that letting go. The fact was that, impractical though she might be, my sister had managed to stay alive for forty-six years without suffering any humiliating accidents, incurring unpayable debt, or going to prison. She was happily married, a joyful mom. It was time, perhaps, for me to let her be. In the most profound way, to just let her be.

There she was, there they all were, a collection of flesh and spirit that was happy to see us. And we were exceedingly happy to see them. Shelsa, the six-year-old black-haired angel, leapt into my arms with an exclamation—"Uncle Ott! Uncle Ott!"— that warmed me to the atrial valves. Hugs all around, kisses, quick questions about our travels and theirs, the good news that Jasper Jr. was safe and well and being looked after by a worker at the retreat center.

The evening was another perfect one, hot and dry with a gentle breeze. We shared the plateau with a few hundred other hungry tourists. There was a covered area in which veggies, fruits, and bread had been set out, cafeteria style; thirty or forty picnic tables. And the main attraction: vats of hot oil into which workers dunked slabs of raw beef impaled on actual pitchforks. Carnivores and abstainers, the Ringling clan filled our plates and commandeered a table and we sat there eating and talking, so much happier than the last time we'd gathered.

"What was the best part?" Natasha wanted to know. The few days of sun had brought out the spray of freckles that crossed her nose and upper cheeks. She looked to me, at that moment, unspeakably beautiful.

I deferred to Rinpoche.

"Transwestites," he said without hesitation.

My sister was looking at him from across the table, face aglow, innocent, overflowing with love.

Anthony said, "Huh?"

Uncle Ott to the rescue. "It's a joke," I said, "a word I taught him after he heard something on the news. . . .The best part was probably the Boiling River in Yellowstone." I described our adventure there in great detail, elk and all, stretching out the story until the other subject faded away.

"And for you good people?"

"Anthony hit a guy on the train," Natasha said.

"*Hit* a guy?"

"Cweep," Shelsa said. They all laughed.

I looked at my son.

"He tried to feel up Tasha. I pushed him more than hit him,

269

the creep."

"You knocked him down."

"Defending your honor, Sis. He was drunk anyway, I think. He more or less fell over his own feet."

"And then what?"

"And then," Cecelia said, "the nice train people came and took him away and I think they made him get off at the next stop."

"All those visits to Manhattan," I said to Natasha, "and nothing. You come out here to the sensible West, and a creep makes a grab at you."

"Anthony chased the cweep away, Uncle Ott. We didn't like the cweep. He made a bad touch."

"He sure did. What did you like the most, Shels?"

"That Tasha's staying," she said, brown eyes fixed on me like a puppy's soft paws.

You could feel a shiver go across our little group, a bad wind.

"Staying with you in the motel?"

Shelsa nodded, but among the rest of the Badlands brigade there was now a terrible, post-wind stillness. A sudden, frozen, arctic silence. Just to my left a family of polar bears wandered.

I looked at my sister. "What gives?"

She cleared her throat. She glanced at Rinpoche, back at me. She smiled and lifted her face up slightly as if I were about to tilt a spoonful of chocolate syrup into her mouth for a taste.

By then we'd eaten about half the food on our plates—the steaks were perfectly cooked—but everyone except Shelsa had set down their forks.

"Oops," Anthony said.

Natasha shot him a look.

I was beginning to have a bad thought.

"Dad," my daughter said, "I've decided I'm not going back to school in September. I'm going to stay out here on the farm."

One of the benefits of meditation—and I should say at this point that there are many—is that you begin to be able to see trouble coming up from inside you before it reaches the surface. This doesn't mean you never get overly angry or say a careless word, but it does lessen the chances of those things happening. Anger, depression, resentment, what the Buddhists call craving—all those things form in your thoughts first, of course, and the practice of meditation helps you see them while they're still tropical storms, before they reach hurricane stage.

And that's what happened in this case. Part of it was that Shelsa, my darling niece, had her big eyes glued onto my face and I would have been embarrassed to say what I was thinking then, to turn to her mother and accuse her of pulling Natasha away from a promising career, convincing her to live on an isolated farm in what had always felt to me like the perfect middle of nowhere. A sarcastic college friend, visiting with us senior year from Minneapolis, had said, "It's a pretty place, Otto, but if I lived here, I'd move."

I swallowed the anger, met my daughter's eyes. "I don't understand hon."

"I'm not going back to Brown. I want to stay with Rinpoche and Aunt Seese and Shelsa. Try something different."

"But you already took a semester off," I said. "For mom."

"I know that, Dad."

"I thought you loved it there, you missed your friends."

"I do."

"What, then? You worked so hard to get in. It's such a great school. I don't see—"

"It's just something I want to do, Dad. We knew you'd be upset."

I couldn't yet risk a glance at my sister. I turned to Anthony. He twisted his mouth to one side and looked away. Rinpoche chose that moment to go back for another serving.

"I'm not upset, I'm—"

"Let's talk later, can we, Dad? It's great up here. Look, the guy's about to start his golf show. We can talk at the motel, okay?"

"Okay, sure." I swung my eyes up to my sister once. I looked down at my plate. Rinpoche sat beside me and handed me a double chocolate brownie and said, "Tell them about the Cou-nee dam, Otto."

But I was in no mood for that, and just then, a few yards to our left, the night's entertainment began. A slightly built man had set up four or five mats there, the kind you see at golf driving ranges. They were facing out into the empty pastureland a few hundred feet below us. Nearby was a golf bag and assorted other paraphernalia—a medicine ball, a unicycle, rubber tees as high as his waist. People finished their meals and gathered around. I sat in my little stew of anger, half watching. Natasha and I were somehow looking at each other with our eyes facing forward, an electric current of disagreement zapping across the table. "Throwing it away" was the phrase that kept echoing in my mind. She'd worked so hard—academically and athletically. It had meant so much to her, the envelope with the Providence postmark and the acceptance letter inside. She'd been doing so well, had such decent friends, including a boy named Steven who texted her obsessively and who'd made the trip west to attend Jeannie's memorial service. I'd been so proud of her for taking a semester off to be with her ailing mother and then, a week after Jeannie died, for having the courage to go back for spring term. But clearly, now was the time to put her own life back in order, to follow the road she'd started on: college, possibly graduate school, a career in the sciences, a life like the life we'd made for her. Comfortable home. Summer vacations, tennis camp, braces. What was wrong with that?

The others—Anthony, Tasha, Rinpoche, and Shelsa—went and sat on the grassy slope so they'd have a better view. I stayed in my seat, not sulking exactly, but wrapped up tight in my assumptions. I see that now. I didn't see it then. The fact of my sister coming over and standing behind me and giving me a shoulder massage did nothing to help me see it. "She has her own life," Celia said, as she worked. I knew that. I'd figured that out when she was thirteen. But what I'd figured out by the time *I* was thirteen was that Dickinson, North Dakota, good, solid, and decent as it would always be, was no place for a person like me. And Natasha was a person like me, wanting adventure, curious about the wider world, a lover of shopping at Forever 21 in Times Square. The nearest Forever 21, I wanted to tell her, was probably in Chicago. Chicago was eight hundred miles away. She'd be on the farm a few months, the weather would turn bitterly cold, snow up to the windowsills, Steven would stop texting, there would be no other young people within ten miles, she'd want to return to Brown and it would be too late then. She'd be stranded out here, cooking for Rinpoche's retreatants and watching the ice in the gutters drip for the one warm hour each day.

"I need time," I told my sister. "It's a shock."

She stayed there with her hands on my shoulders and said nothing.

The entertainer went by the moniker of Joey O, and even for a person like me, who played golf three times a summer and knew little about the game, he was impressive. He smashed the ball far out into the evening air, time after time, at first in the standard position, and then with both feet balanced on the medicine ball, up on the unicycle, left-handed, eyes closed, one foot raised. He made goofy jokes and received polite applause, said things like, "What you think about, you bring about," and seemed to be insisting that his incredible physical feats were brought about mostly by attitude, a set of the mind . . . plus, as he joked, "Fourteen-hour practice days."

When the show was over he sold his own books, pamphlets really, from a van emblazoned with his name and sayings. I noticed that Rinpoche bought one.

The sun was dropping behind a bank of thin clouds. The crowd dispersed. The six of us wandered into the parking lot and discussed transportation arrangements. Anthony rode with me, the rest of the gang in Celia's ancient Subaru station wagon—bought used—with 305,000 miles on the odometer.

On the short drive back to the Badlands Motel I tried to make small talk with my son about the Lincoln MKX, the train ride, the creep. But he was having none of that.

"Pop's all pissed off," he said.

"Wouldn't you be? Wait'll Tasha finds out what the winters are like here. Wait'll she wants to go shopping, or see a show with a friend, or go out for sushi, or any of the hundred other things she loves now and takes completely for granted."

Anthony was silent. I looked across at him. The long jaw and stubble, the shock of dark hair—inherited from his mother's side. The strong shoulders, neck, and forearms. The small sickle of a scar near his left eye from the time he'd fallen against a metal shelf in the grocery store, age two.

"You think I'm off base," I said, turning the pickup onto the main paved road and heading for the motel.

"Dad," he said. "Let go, man. Let us make our own mistakes. You've been a cool father in most ways, really. You have. But you brought us up with stories of you and mom living in a crappy apartment in a bad neighborhood, waiting tables with your college degrees, going where you wanted to go and letting things happen the way they happened. Personally, I think Tash is full of shit most of the time. And I think you're right: come January, Providence, Rhode Island, is gonna seem like Aruba. This place isn't for me, not at all. I love Rinp. Who couldn't love the guy? But I'm not into the meditation stuff, the guru stuff, all that alternative shit. Tasha seems happy here, though."

"She's been here three days."

"Dad, listen. We love you. The whole thing with Mom and everything was as shitty for you as it was for us. But now you should just let go. Make yourself happy and stop worrying about everything. Mom," there was just the slightest break in his voice, "would want that."

"And what about you?"

"I'm fine. Preseason starts in two weeks. Lizzie's anxious to see me. The guys. I'll be fine, really. I called and moved my flight up to day after tomorrow. If you can drive me to the airport, I'll be on my way. But now, if you want my advice, you gotta get your own stuff straight and let us do our thing."

At least, I thought, he'd called it my "stuff," not my "shit." That counted for something.

32

In the morning Rinpoche said he wanted to play golf. It so happened that there was a miniature golf course and a swimming pool on the motel grounds, but he said he wanted "Real golf, like Joey O." At breakfast my sister told me he'd read the pamphlet in one sitting the night before and was anxious to test out Joey's theory about the mind controlling the golf ball, the idea of bringing about what you think about.

I was terrible at golf, a classic hacker, and just did not have the psychic energy to accompany him that morning. Anthony was a sometime player. He kindly volunteered to take his Uncle Rinp up to the nearby course—Bully Pulpit, it was called—and treat him to eighteen holes. "You have no idea," I said, "what you're getting into," and he laughed and climbed into the pickup and told me, out the open window, "I just want to beat him in something, to make up for the wrestling match."

Natasha and I took a walk. We headed out of the motel lot and along the main drag, then veered off toward the Little Missouri, which had been dried almost to a trickle by that summer's drought.

We'd had our rough moments, Natasha and I, in the years between about fourteen and sixteen and a half. Little things, mostly. Phone use, room cleanliness, the occasional remark that Jeannie and I felt went beyond the usual adolescent rebellion and into the territory of disrespect. "You have to let them destroy you," a particularly sensitive friend had said, of teenagers and parents. And I remembered Jeannie's reply: "That seems a little extreme."

Since her senior year in high school, though, Natasha and I had gone back almost to the place we'd been when she was younger. We had a wonderful connection, the same sense of humor, similar tastes in food, a shared interest in the human condition. Like her aunt, she'd had a long string of boyfriends, each eccentric after his own fashion, and I think she appreciated the fact that I never teased her about them too roughly, that Jeannie and I allowed her to find her own way in the maze of love.

That morning, though, I felt that a small new trouble had sprouted between us.

"I want you to have a happy life," I said as we turned onto a quiet side street. "That's all I've ever wanted, and all your mother ever wanted for you."

"Too late now, Dad."

I wrapped one arm around her shoulders, gave a squeeze, let go. "Awful as it is," I tried, "horrible and unchangeable as it is, I know you can still be happy one day. I know that like I know my own name. You were wonderful to Mom. You did everything you could possibly do, and a hundred times more than anyone else your age ever thought of doing."

"Yeah, you, too. You were great. I just feel like I haven't

laughed in a whole year and I'll never be able to again."

"Rinpoche makes me laugh."

"Yeah," she said, and I could feel her then, drifting along on a river. She could either paddle hard and pull herself away from the pain, or turn the rudder two degrees and end up going back over a waterfall of sorrow that she'd crashed through a hundred times since her mother died. She and Jeannie had been extraordinarily close for a mother and daughter—more like friends than anything else. The pain filled her, still; I could see it in her eyes, hear it in her voice.

"What do you think . . . What they say about Shelsa, any truth to that?"

"To what, Dad?" she said, distracted, drifting.

"She's supposed to be, I don't know the right word . . . something other than an ordinary six-year-old girl, I guess."

It brought her partly back. "I've been watching her. She's really not a normal kid, if you look closely. There really *is* something special."

"Like what? Tell me what you see."

"I wake up early and come downstairs and she's in the living room, praying. Most kids would be watching *Sesame Street* or something. She's praying."

"Just imitating her father, maybe. You used to pretend to edit books when you were about that age. Do you remember?"

"No."

"That's natural."

"Is it natural to sit so still out in the yard that birds come and land on your shoulders?"

"That happened?"

"A bunch of times. Another time I woke up and she was

next to the bed staring at me in this weird way, nothing like a little kid would look at you. I had the feeling she was, like, praying for my soul or something."

"Creepy?"

"No. It made me feel good. Other times she's just a little kid, fussing, laughing, throwing things."

I made a humming sound, noncommittal, nonconfrontational.

"Want to hear what Aunt Seese says about you?"

"Only if it's good."

"That your real work in this life is different than what you're doing now. That you were born to help Shelsa fulfill her destiny."

"Which is what, exactly?"

"The harmony of all religions or making a new religion, or something."

I'll be the L. Ron Hubbard of my generation, I thought. But it was just a defense reflex, a little sarcasm-armor I'd been throwing up around myself for as long as I could remember. The truth was, I had a feeling then that I'd had two or three times before, though always in the company of Rinpoche. To describe it as chills running up my arms or spine would be easy but inaccurate; it was more as though the temperature around me had changed a few degrees and I was being physically shaken, but only once. One shake. It was the dependable world going unstable on me for a second or two. I didn't ignore it, exactly. It was about as easy to ignore as an irregular heartbeat, a tooth breaking, a toenail falling off. I rationalized it. Just a reflex, I told myself. Like making a small jump sideways if a kid yells "Boo!" in the bushes on Halloween night. For all his wisdom about the spiritual path, my favorite monk had this part of it wrong. I loved Shelsa, loved being with her as an uncle, loved the warmth and the joy and the sense that she loved me. All of that was perfectly natural, ordinary, and good. But I remained noncommittal about her special spiritual purpose, and I knew, like I knew it was morning in North Dakota, that if she did have some special role to play in this life, her uncle had absolutely nothing to do with it.

But I didn't want to get into an argument with Natasha on the subject, not then. We looped around behind the buildings, a dry cliff rising to our left, then the miniature golf, the pool, the motel and parking lot to our right.

"Anthony and Rinpoche were out here till really late last night, playing mini-golf. I watched for a while."

"I thought the place closed at nine."

"Rinpoche charmed the woman at the desk—they're all volunteers—and she said she'd stay and watch as long as he had energy to play. He's good!"

"I wondered why Anthony didn't come into the room until late. I thought maybe he had a girlfriend here or something."

"He's with Lizzie."

"I know he's with Lizzie. I thought he might be just . . . out someplace having a drink."

"You think he'd *cheat* on Lizzie?"

"Not at all, not for a second."

"You don't have somebody, do you, Dad? Already?"

"Absolutely not," I said. And then, "Let's make another loop. I wanted to talk to you about your decision."

"There's nothing to talk about. I'm staying at the farm. There's plenty of room. The people who go there on retreat, most of them, pay, so Aunt Seese says she can pay me, too, and I'll have two days off every week if I want to go someplace."

To that point I'd been diplomatic, restrained, wise. And then this slipped out: "You're throwing everything away."

"Like what, Dad? I finish college and maybe go to grad school and cost you, like, another two hundred thousand bucks? And then I get a job and get a promotion and get married and move out to the suburbs with my husband and we have kids. And we love them, and love each other, and raise them, and then they go away, and then he dies, or I die?" With each phrase of this recitation her voice had become frailer and frailer. By the time she said, "What good is that, tell me?" it was all broken up into shards.

"Mom loved her life, Tash. If there's one thing I know it's that she loved it, loved me, loved bringing up you and your brother, loved our house and her garden and being able to take a train into the city. She spent her whole life helping people, me, raising you guys, helping her friends, nursing Grandma at the end."

"Right. Exactly. And look where she ended up. Look what happened to her."

"You think she'd want you to leave school?"

"Don't play that card, Dad. Please!"

"All right. I'm sorry. And it's your decision, of course. At this point in your life it's all your decision. Anthony said I should leave you alone, but—"

"He did?"

"In the strongest terms. . . . But I can't let you make a big decision like this without at least telling you what I think. It's my job. I'd be shirking my duty. And what I think is: I admire you. I love you more than you can possibly imagine. It's been the great privilege and joy of my life to raise you and your brother, not even to raise you, just to be on earth with you. Mom felt exactly the same way. Some people say having kids puts a strain on the marriage but it was just the reverse with us. There were some strains beforehand, and once you arrived they got smaller, much smaller, not bigger. . . . But I don't see why you can't finish college and *then* come and work here. What's wrong with that idea?"

"Because inertia will take me away from this, that's what. I see what happens to the people who come here. I hear what they say about their lives. I see the effect Rinpoche has on them."

"But you've been here three days, hon!"

"I've seen it when we visited other times. A week every summer, on holidays. I was paying attention, Dad. Maybe nobody else in the family was, but I saw what he did for them. I even talked to some of them. But it's not even just that. It's not like he gave them *therapy* or something. It's deeper than that. He made their lives make sense in a new way, and I want to figure out that new way. I want to have that, *first*. And maybe then I'll feel comfortable getting a job and getting married and having the house and kids and all that. Maybe then I'll feel, I don't know, *comfortable* with what happened to Mom."

At that point she started sobbing quietly, a sound that had always ripped me in half. I put an arm around her and kept it there and we stood with our backs to the motel and the happy noises from the pool and looked at the sandy cliff. There were small holes in it here and there, tiny caves where who knew what kinds of vipers waited.

"Isn't that why you got into the meditation and stuff?" Tasha asked through her tears. "Isn't that why you took this trip with him?"

"Yes," I said.

"Well then why not let me do it? Because I'm not old enough? I could live only another hour, Dad. Another day, another month, another five years. And what? I should wait until I raise my kids and I'm old and *then* pay attention to this stuff?"

"No," I said. "You shouldn't wait. I just don't want you to be poor and trying to get a job without a degree. I've worked with the poor. I've been volunteering in the Bronx since you were two years old. I've seen poverty close up. Some of those people, many of them, are wonderful, sweet, generous, even happy in spite of everything. But I don't think that kind of a hard life is any fun at all, or even any prescription, necessarily, for spiritual solace. It's a terrible strain, a constant pressure, a giant force pressing against them telling them they're less. Their kids cool off in a fire hydrant instead of going to the Cape for two weeks. They drive old, shitty cars, or no car at all. They live in hot apartments, with roaches and rats."

"That would never be me. You know that. Mom left us money, for one thing."

"Not enough to make a life on."

She turned toward me and I let my arm drop back to my side. Her face was wet, but she made no move to brush the tears away. A strand of hair went across one eye; she was looking slightly up at me. "Dad," she said, and she was all unprotected then, heartbreakingly unprotected and real, the way I remembered her when she was two and three and four. Now, for all her adult strength, she could barely get the words out. "Right now I don't want to learn about oceanography or Spanish or study climate change. I . . . want . . . to . . . figure out what happened . . . to my mother, why, where she went, what's the point of everything. They don't teach that at Brown. I want you to say you understand. That's all. I want to hear you say you understand."

For a second then, two seconds, I felt myself tempted to retreat from our raw intimacy and take up position in my fatherly fortress. My father would have done that, I'm sure of it. Older, wiser, the one who knew, the one who paid for everything, made sacrifices, the Boss. Three or four words and I could have taken refuge there, hurt her and protected myself, my position, my status. I watched that possibility, that option, rise up inside my thoughts like a man lifting a sword over the head of a prone captive. I watched it. And I let it go. It was hard for me to speak then, but I managed to say, "I do."

And I did.

—⟶ᨀ 33

After that conversation I went back to the room and changed into my bathing suit. I needed a fifty-lap swim, or a twenty-mile hike, or to run a half-marathon—some rigorous physical exertion that would clear away the storm clouds that seemed suddenly to have gathered in my interior world. Tasha's decision, her argument about the fragility of bourgeois life, had hit me like an eighth-round punch. I was cloudy headed, wobbly legged. This is what happens, I told myself as I walked across the parking lot toward the Badlands pool: you let go of your fatherly authority, your position as the older, wiser one, the life-veteran, the Dad Who Knows, you let that guard down for one second and BOOM! the fist of doubt catches you mid-jaw. Bathing suit and bare chest and all, I had the bizarre urge to walk into town and try to find a copy of the *Daily News*. There would be no articles on meditation and retreat centers (unless some married congressman had been discovered having sex with a West Village yoga teacher). All the assumptions we lived by would be safely in their place: the world was a dangerous zoo filled with crooks and schemers; the goal, the only response to our predicament, was to make money, have things, get your kid into a

good college, so she could marry well, have a career that provided a new car and a big house in a neighborhood that made no
bad headlines, so she could join a beach club or have a summer
cottage, write tuition checks . . . so her child could go to a good
college, and have a career that provided a new car and a big
house in a neighborhood that made no bad headlines . . .

I knew this about myself: the best thing to do in such a mood
was to jump into water, the colder the better, and swim until my
arms and legs turned to rubber. I did that, scaring a bevy of
teenage girls off to one side of the pool while the old guy swam
his laps. It was therapy for me. It was a strange form of revenge,
too—not on the teenage girls, but on my own shame, because I
hadn't learned to swim until I was twenty-two years old.

There, it's out in the open. One of Otto Ringling's great se-
crets. Afraid of the water into early adulthood.

My excuse is this: while there were two municipal pools in
the Dickinson of my youth, Mom and Pop weren't exactly keen
on driving us in there for lessons. Swimming was not a skill
that mattered on a farm in the dry plains; it wasn't on my parents' radar any more than teaching their children mah-jongg
had been. All this wouldn't have caused any trouble for me—
lots of people go through life without learning how much fun
can be had in the water—except that Jeannie's family made a
kind of religion out of water sports. They swam, they sailed,
they were expert at cracking ice cubes out of the tray and watching them melt in a glass of Maker's Mark.

Her mother owned a modest, four-bedroom "cottage" in
Falmouth, on Cape Cod, two blocks from the beach, and even
before we were married I went there as an invited guest (sepa-

rate bedrooms, of course!). Before she started drinking for the day, Jeannie's mother—Ethel, by name, Rubbsie by nickname (don't ask!)—would go out and swim what she called her 'morning mile.' I can picture her still, slapping in through the screen door while we late risers were at breakfast, the salty, tanned skin, the flapping flip-flops, the look of triumph on her bony face as she went to the sink for water. I can hear the acid-tipped remarks for which she was famous. "J" she called her daughter. As in, "What's the matter with your beau, J, worried about sharks?" Later, after lunch, she and Jeannie and Jeannie's sister and a cousin or two would all be cavorting in the surf, far out over their heads, and yours truly would take a jog along the beach, then wade in chest deep and splash around. Sometimes, just to make her mother crazy I think, J would swim over and wrap her legs around me, and we'd bob there, crotch to crotch, faces a few inches apart, and that would more than compensate for the eighty-proof barbs that would fly across the table at dinner.

For Rubbsie, the issue wasn't just the swimming or the Midwestern roots or my relative sobriety or the fact that she knew I was living with her daughter in a state of sin. It was more the idea that I was to blame for taking her from a 4.0 average to a grimy walk-up on Ninth Avenue, a waitressing job, a life in which, outside the bedroom, our greatest pleasure was a bag of roasted chestnuts and a walk in Central Park. I, we, had not yet bought into the system. We hadn't yet traded freedom for comfort. We had not yet abandoned the idea that we could make a life according to a pattern of our own original design, and to hell with what others might think.

On my fifth or sixth or seventh visit to Falmouth we shared

the cottage with a visiting uncle named Eugene, Jeannie's god-
father (Jean and Gene—source of an endless supply of family
jokes). Diminutive, stocky, a former fighter pilot in the Korean
War, his pleasant face topped by what looked to be about five
pounds of silky, pure white hair, Uncle Gene saw me splashing
in the shallows one afternoon and immediately sensed my dis-
tress. That evening he took me back to the beach, just the two of
us, and with an otherworldly patience taught me to swim. He
was, it seemed to me as I churned through my laps in Medora,
a sort of Rinpoche of the watery world, someone sent to push
me past my fears and self-imposed limitations and into a happier dimension.

Back and forth I swam, thinking of Uncle Gene, thanking
him, trying to let go of my concern for my daughter's future.
Wasn't it true that she was just doing what Jeannie and I had
done? Did I really want to burden her with the cargo of parental
disappointment we'd had to carry in those early years? Was I
really better off, having first traded my dreams of being a radical
architect, and later a renowned novelist, for a paycheck every
two weeks and the humble satisfactions of editing?

Yes. No. But around me I could feel—as if they were actual
creatures nipping at my skin—the voices of friends, neighbors,
and co-workers, the very people we'd told, with so much pride
and pleasure, about Natasha's acceptance to Brown. I imagined
their faces and words when I informed them she'd decided to
leave school and live on the family farm in North Dakota, cooking, digging in the dirt, watching the snow fall. She was just
taking a year off, I'd say. The shock of her mother's death, and
so on. Brown would let her return.

Brown might very well let her return, but the rest of it

would be a lie, and I was trying to swim the lie away as if it were filth on my arms and hands. I swam and swam with my clumsy stroke, kicking, breathing hard, trying to crawl my way back to the walk-up on Ninth Avenue, the arduous thrill of those days, the living in the moment, the sure sense that all would be well.

When I finally stopped, chest heaving, and stood at the shallow end of the pool, I saw my sister coming through the chain-link gate, holding her reluctant daughter by the hand.

"Uncle Ott can show you," she was saying. "Don't be afraid, honey. Look at Uncle Ott."

Shelsa's pretty face was painted in Cezanne-esque blocks of terror. I swam over to the side nearest them and hoisted myself up onto the edge. "Sit here with me, Shels," I said.

She leaned back and shook her head. I patted the concrete. "Sit with your Uncle Ott."

The headshaking grew smaller. I patted the concrete another few times. "Come on. I saved you a special place."

It took a minute or two, but we convinced her to come and sit beside me. I kicked my feet, making a big splash, and got her to do the same. We were side by side, splashing away, her mother in a lawn chair, watching. "How's Jasper?" I asked Shelsa, to distract her.

"He's a bad boy. He catches birds (*boohds* was how she said it) in his mouth."

"When we get home tonight I'll punish him."

"No, no!"

I told her I was kidding, and I dropped into the pool in front of her. I stood there for a little while and rubbed her wet feet, tickling, making her laugh. I took handfuls of water and splashed them down over my head, making her laugh again and again. Then I took a very small handful and dropped it on her head, too. She spluttered at first, blinked hard, and then smiled and asked for a repeat. I saw her eyes go to three kids who were horsing around happily in the shallow end. "Want to learn to swim?" I asked.

She shook her head, no.

"You sure?"

No again.

"Not sure? Want to try?"

A brave nod.

We spent the next hour in the pool. Very, very gradually, holding her in my arms most of the time, I got Shelsa accustomed to being in water, then to holding her breath, and then—the hard part—putting her face under the surface. I held her arms and let her kick, nose and mouth in air. Held her midsection and let her swing her arms. It was a younger-child version of the way Uncle Gene had done it for me—step by step, finding the edge of my comfort zone, pushing me past it, taking on the fear in small bites. By checkout time she wasn't swimming, but I'd gotten her through the baptism, at least. Kicking, breathing out underwater. One good dead man's float.

"Was it fun?" her mother asked when we were out and wrapping ourselves in towels.

"Lot of fun, Mami."

Cecelia hugged the girl tight against her and winked at me over her head. "Look what a nice Uncle Ott you have, honey. Look at how brave you are!"

34

My parents had owned two thousand acres of prime Stark County farmland—sloping, windswept fields where they grew durum wheat and soybeans mostly, and a smaller amount of corn, barley, canola and sunflowers, depending on the market. They cultivated a kitchen garden, too, fifty square feet of seed and sweat, that helped feed us for much of the year. When they were killed by a drunk driver on a nearby highway, the house, barns, and land came down to Celia and me, and after some difficult discussions between the two of us, we agreed that we'd continue to lease eighteen hundred acres and use the rest as a retreat center for Rinpoche. This meant paying for the main barn to be converted into a dormitory-like setup with small rooms on the second floor and a large, open meditation space on the first. Rinpoche, Cecelia, and Shelsa—just born then— settled into the white clapboard farmhouse, and after a couple of years they had a local carpenter build three cabins in one corner of their acreage. These were for solitary retreats, and each one of them had a woodstove, electric hotplate and small refrigerator, a shower and toilet, a bedroom and a small open room used for "sitting," yoga, and reading.

There was a fair amount of expense involved in all this—especially getting water to the cabins and figuring out what to do with the waste—but the land was valuable, and the lease payments covered some of it. Rinpoche earned a surprisingly good sum from his talks and books. And a few of the retreatants, like Jarvis, were wealthy, and paid handsome "tributes" for the privilege of living alone for a week under Rinpoche's tutelage or sleeping in the dormitory and meditating six times a day with him and their fellow seekers. Jeannie and I had decided not to take any of the proceeds from the lease and not to make use of the mineral rights. Perhaps in compensation for the years of barbs and ridicule, her mother had left her a healthy inheritance; I was a senior editor with twenty-plus years of service at a profitable publishing house, and I made more than enough to support us; she'd worked, too, once the kids were in high school, taking photos for the local art museum and socking the money away. Twice a year we'd fly to Fargo on a family pilgrimage; and twice a year Seese, Shelsa, and Rinpoche would drive or take the train east and return the favor. These visits were a joy, not a chore. There was plenty of room in both houses, plenty of food and laughter. We always took them into Manhattan in cold weather, out to the Cape in warm. They worked hard to find things for us to do in North Dakota—tenpin bowling at the local lanes, drives along the Missouri River or to a reservation festival, snow forts and snowball fights and sledding.

And then Jeannie was diagnosed and went into her long, slow, brutal decline, and all that ended.

I was thinking of her, of course, as we drove east from

Medora on that day, turned off the highway and onto a gravel road, and pulled up the long drive toward the house where I'd been raised. I saw Jasper Jr. come out across the porch, black tail wagging. The sight of him made me think of our Jasper, curled up at Jeannie's feet in her last weeks, and it raised another small tide of sorrow in my throat. Something like eighty-five per cent of women with Jeannie's diagnosis survived the disease. I'd wondered, a million times, why she couldn't have been in that group.

We settled in. Though the day was fine and warm, I could feel an old claustrophobia pressing against me, the same sense of airlessness that had chased me east in the first place. I surfed the Internet for a while, read the campaign coverage, answered e-mails, but I could hear the armies of boredom marching toward the house the way they'd marched thirty-five years earlier. I wondered how Tasha would defend herself against them.

Rinpoche suggested a two-hour welcome-home meditation, but I pled tiredness and lay in the same upstairs bed I'd lain in as a boy and took a nap. The others went off on a walk to inspect the newest cabin or to look for birds—Shelsa's passion, apparently. There would be pheasant, partridge, ruffed grouse, a dozen smaller songbirds.

That afternoon, after a nice lunch that consisted mainly of grilled vegetables that had been grown a hundred feet from where we sat, Anthony made his good-byes and carried his knapsack and computer bag to the pickup. He and I set off for the airport in Fargo. The landscape changed as we drove eastward, from the dry prairies of midstate to the flat fertile fields of the Red River Valley. It's a different North Dakota there, touched less by the Wild West than the Midwest, closer to Min-

nesota than Montana—geographically, politically, and cultural-
ly. My son had his BlackBerry against one raised knee and was
reading and typing and letting out the occasional laugh. Between us hung some kind of curtain, I could feel it. Love, of
course, certainly. But a thick fabric of years and difference, too.

Not lost on me was the fact that my own father—whom Anthony adored—had taken me on a similar drive the day I left
home for New York. I'd like to say it made for a sweet sym-
metry, but the memory wasn't particularly sweet. If there was a
curtain of generational difference between Anthony and me, the
space between my father and me sported a wire-topped Berlin
wall. He and my mother had wanted me to go to college,
pushed me to go, in fact. And the study of architecture made
some sense to them. What didn't make sense was the aban-
donment of that career path and the decision to leave the heart-
land and live in Manhattan. New York, to them, represented
everything that was repugnant about the non-Dakota world.
Crime, people who didn't speak English, exotic food that would
poison your digestion, heinous traffic, dirty streets, a life of
money and rush that made eye contact and slow conversation
obsolete. The murder rate in New York City—just that statistic
alone—was confirmation that they lived a good life, they'd made
the right choices, they'd never leave.

What had they expected? That I'd settle on the farm with
them, marry Cindy Meerschum from third grade and ease
Pop's load by driving the tractor in planting season?

Something like that. Their imaginations stretched only a
short distance beyond the boundaries of their own lives. Even
this drive had been a risk for my dad; in Fargo and on the surrounding roads, anything might happen. He'd changed out of

his overalls for the occasion and was wearing a dress shirt and chinos—church clothes. He gripped the wheel with his two powerful hands, watched the road, worked his crooked teeth against the inside of his cheek. I looked at the passing farms and thought about making love with Jeannie.

Somewhere near Valley City he said, without turning his head, "You ain't comin' back, then."

I said no, Pop, probably not, but assured him I'd get home to visit whenever I could.

He pondered that for a dozen miles, the tires of the pickup whirring. If someone had asked me, "Does your father love you?" I would have answered, "Yes, of course," reflexively, but I would not have been able to go down into that love and speak its essence. Neither could he or my mother. We were a practical, capable, decent people, but emotionally illiterate; not one of us was schooled in the calculus of affection. It was my wife who would teach me that.

"Well," my dad said, as we drew into the outskirts of Fargo and turned north on I-29, "take good care of yourself back there, won't you?"

I said that I would. Another few minutes and we pulled up in front of the terminal building. He coughed, lowered his window, and spat. He seemed old to me then, grizzled, going gray, forty-eight years on the earth. I saw him swallow. I had an urge to say or do something, but I had no model for that. Our best moments had consisted of standing next to each other at the end of an exhausting day of baling hay, the sweet smell of it in the air, sweat drying on our shirts, the sun sinking low, my mother ringing the porch bell that meant supper was almost ready. Fine moments, really, a manly, high-plains code of mutual affection and respect, but empty of word or touch. In front of the terminal then, all I knew how to do was reach over and shake his hand and look into his eyes. I thanked him for the ride, promised to write, and then I was out of the truck and moving toward my freedom. I remember that he waited there, watching, until I'd gone through the glass doors. And I remember that I didn't turn around.

When Anthony looked up from his phone for a moment I asked about his courses. He was not much like his sister, a happier child, strong, confident, immune to doubt. Sophomore year, and he already had his future drawn up: business school, then working his way up to Director or Chief Fundraiser of a medical charity. He wanted to have a hand in curing cancer, he said. "Payback, Dad, big-time." Eventually, he wanted to settle someplace with Lizzie—who was a junior and pre-med—and start his own consulting firm for charitable fundraising, have a house and family, maybe a country club or beach club membership so the kids could swim on hot summer days and he and Lizzie could play golf or tennis on the weekends. He'd taken the money his mother had left him and with two other well-off Bowdoin friends, had made a down payment on a duplex in Brunswick, which they rented out. At his age I'd been drinking beer and trying marijuana and faking my way through trigonometry. He knew a bit about the tax code, investments, long-term strategies.

Over those last twenty miles I struggled to find something to say to him. *We have a new line of books coming out on organic produce. Rinpoche says I'm on the verge of a breakthrough. Your sister is a lot like her aunt. I hope you'll bring Lizzie home for a visit once in a while; I like her.* But all those things were too safe and predictable, modern-day versions of "Take good care of yourself back there, won't you?" Still paying bills with paper checks and struggling to understand my new phone, I must have seemed to him like a troglodyte, a relic, a sexless old father who needed to get his stuff together and move on.

We turned onto I-29. Anthony put his phone in his pocket and looked out at the landscape as if he might miss it. He said, "Rinpoche's a nightmare on the golf course."

"I bet."

"He had a wicked case of the shanks. He kept going into the deep grass near the river to look for his ball. I kept telling him there were snakes in there, bad snakes, maybe. He called them 'nakes'. He kept saying, 'Nakes never bite Rinpoche. Bad luck for them. Bad karma.'"

"Sounds like him. And I bet he'd never get bitten, either."

"Yeah." Anthony was silent for a while. "He made four holes-in-one in a row in mini-golf, though, did I tell you that?"

"No. You played late."

"Yeah, he convinced the woman to keep it open, don't ask me how. Slipped her twenty bucks or something, maybe. Four holes-in-one in a row, Dad! You know how hard it is to do that? And then he missed the next two by about an inch. And then he seemed to kind of stop caring and just fooled around."

"Maybe he has a practice area in the barn someplace," I said.

Anthony looked over at me and smiled. He had his mother's mouth. My eyes. "He says he wants to come east and see a game. I said I'd take you and him to a party afterward. 'I'll give you the whole experience, Rinp,' I said. 'You can flirt with some girls, have a few brews, help us clean up the puke the next morning.'"

"Sounds like fun. Count me in. He's a good uncle, isn't he?"

Anthony nodded, waited, said, "And you're a good dad."

Another quick wash in the eyes. I took a breath and let a few automatic responses pass across my brain without finding the route to my mouth, and then, as we turned into the airport, the fog cleared for a moment, blessedly, and I said, "And as a son, you've been a major pain in the ass."

The right note for once. Anthony laughed uproariously, unaffectedly, the way he might laugh with a friend.

Not long after I dropped him off (a hug and a handshake both) I did something I almost never do, and something, probably, that I shouldn't have done: I picked up a hitchhiker. A thin-built, slightly hunched man with a red-brown beard and a knapsack, he looked like a lonely soul, not particularly threatening. The sky above him did look threatening, however. There was a bubbling purple cloudbank creeping in, and he was standing a bit furtively at the bottom of the ramp, no shelter anywhere within hundreds of yards. I had second thoughts almost as soon as I'd put on the brakes, but he was already hurrying toward Uma's right rear fender by then, looking vulnerable, grateful, the last thing from trouble.

There was a whiff of whiskey and smoke when he sat in the cab. He thanked me immediately, one eye on the sky. I asked him to put on his seatbelt and he said, "Oh, sure, no problem," in an obliging way.

Once we were on the highway I asked him where he was headed.

"Williston," he said. "Workin' an oil job. But if you can git me as far as Bismarck, that'd work. Friends there."

"I'm going to Dickinson."

"Bismarck's fine, then. I'm grateful."

We went along without speaking for a little while, moving toward the clouds as they moved toward us. "Sky showing evil," my mother would have said, but it was no surprise in that part of the world in summer: without any mountains to slow it down for five hundred miles to the west of us, evil weather had a way of hatching without warning from what seemed the most benign of afternoons.

"Mind if I smoke?" my passenger asked. "Rundy, by the way." He held a calloused hand across the shift.

"Otto. I'd rather you didn't."

"No problem. You a Dickinson guy?"

"Used to be. I was born and raised there. New York now."

"Never been."

I could feel him appraising me across the seat, not in an unpleasant way, really, just in the way of a person trying to figure you out, size you up, understand who he was riding with. I had friends at home who confessed to being ill at ease in the company of working folk, touched by a sliver of shame when they walked past the carpentry crew in their suit and tie. But I'd worked hard as a kid, and even now never suffered from that particular form of discomfort. The best idea, it seemed to me, was just to be yourself and let people—richer or poorer, less or better educated—think what they wanted.

Just as I was musing on that theme, I heard this:

"You're not associated with them nutfucks out there, are ya?"

"Not that I know of." I had no idea what Rundy meant. I heard the slight hard turn in his voice but it didn't worry me. We passed a sign: BISMARCK 177.

"Them Muslim nutfucks."

The first hard drops slapped the glass. I rolled up my window and put on the wipers for a few swipes. I was watching the road, the sky.

"They have some kinda mosque or something out there," Rundy went on.

"Near Dickinson? I've never seen it. I—"

"They do," he said, with certainty, and it was that certainty more than anything else that sounded a small alarm.

"I've been there a lot. There are probably some Moslems, but I can't say I've ever seen a mosque. Dickinson? You sure?"

He was surer than sure about the Muslims, but "Maybe it's some kind of prayer center or something, a camp. I thought somebody said mosque but that part could be off."

It began to rain in earnest. The wipers slapped. We passed through the spray of a string of eighteen-wheelers.

I had a bad thought then, and was not quite able to keep it to myself. "You're not talking about Volya Rinpoche's retreat center by any chance, are you?"

"That's it."

"They're Buddhists," I said. "They meditate there. Don't bother a soul."

"Not what I heard."

"What did you hear?"

"Some kind of training place or something. Terrorists or

301

something, could be. Who knows what. Muslim nutfucks."

It wasn't easy, hearing that and trying to concentrate on the road with the trucks throwing up sheets of water and the tar slick and now the wind gusting from the southwest and pushing against the front left side of the truck. "Listen," I said. "Listen to me." I couldn't turn my eyes to look at him. "I know those people. I know the whole family. They're Buddhists, not Moslem, and even if they were Moslem, so what? They're good, kind people who don't cause anybody any trouble. They're not nutfucks. They're not even nuts. And there's no mosque or militia or terrorist training or any of that."

"Yeah?"

"Yeah. I've been there. You haven't been. You should stop spreading rumors like that."

"Sure," he said. "No problem." And then, two seconds later. "Pull over, would ya?"

"For what?"

"Just pull over. There's a rest area up ahead. You can leave me there."

"It's absolutely pouring rain. You'll get soaked, number one, and the state troopers will pick you up for hitching there, number two."

"Number three, pull over," he said. He'd been holding the knapsack on his lap but now he turned it so the opening was facing his right hand. He reached in and began rummaging around. I pulled in behind one of the tractor trailers and then saw the rest area, turned in, and stopped. From the knapsack Rundy drew a slicker. He wriggled into it. His head popped through, red in the beard, red lines in the whites of his eyes.

"You'll get soaked" was all I could think to say.

"Appreciate the lift, nutfuck," he said, and he got out, slammed the door so hard the glass rattled, and walked along past a parked school bus, in the direction we'd come.

The rain pounded down, the wipers were on high. I caught sight of his back in the mirror for a few steps, then I merged carefully onto the highway and headed home.

35

It was late by the time I got back to the farm. The clan was in bed, only the kitchen light on. I had started to rummage through the fridge, looking for something I might eat, when I heard the scratch of slippers in the downstairs hallway and saw my sister there, wearing a blue cotton bathrobe Jeannie had given her for Christmas the year she was pregnant. Her eyes were foggy, hair all over the place; it was clear I'd pulled her out of sleep. Against my vehement objections, Seese made me sit at the kitchen table and she prepared a late-night breakfast. German biscuit and ham, with a poached egg set on top. She asked if I wanted coffee and I said no, I would like a beer, though, and she'd gone to the trouble of stocking up on that, too, though neither she nor Rinpoche drank. She made herself a cup of herbal tea and sat at the table with me while I ate.

"You're too good," I said. "Best sister I've ever had."

She missed the joke, thanked me, watched me eat.

"No one could have gotten Shelsie into the water like you

did," she said when I was mostly finished.

"Somebody did the same thing for me."

"It was amazing. The kids you and Jeannie raised are amazing, also. They have the auras of a spiritual prince and princess."

"I lose sight of that sometimes, but they love you and Rinpoche and Shelsa." I was thinking about what Rinpoche had said—his dreams, his worries. As I had been for the past three hours, I was trying to understand if the hitchhiker and the people he listened to posed any real danger to my family, or if they were just part of that crowd of American haters, searching always for a new target. Black, gay, Mexican, Moslem—the targets moved this way or that every generation or so, but the hatred surged on. I thought, again, of Hitler and Stalin and Mussolini and Pol Pot, the Hutus, the Tutsis, the Serbs and Croats and Bosnians, the Catholics and Protestants in Northern Ireland, the Jews and Palestinians. I thought of the 92 percent of men who were said to be certified assholes, and the things I'd heard about women over the course of my long life. Where, I wondered, was the first spark of it? Before any violence was done, before any bad history, where did the hatred begin? In the thought-stream, Rinpoche would say. But how did it get into the thought-stream, and why did it thrive and fester in some and seem almost completely absent in others?

Maybe human beings weren't designed to tolerate differences. And if that was so, then surely it was a miracle, really, truly a miracle that a place as diverse as America had managed to survive for so long.

"You know, Otto, I didn't suggest to Tasha that she stay here. I never would do something like that."

"Okay. I believe you."

"You don't sound like you do."

"I do. It's hard. I had other ideas for her. She had other ideas for herself."

"She'll live a long life," my sister said, as if she knew that from a study of the creases on Natasha's palm, as if there would be a multitude of opportunities to get a college degree, many, many chances for my daughter to be twenty-two years old. Celia toyed with the string on her tea bag and looked up. "Would you ever think of staying?"

"Here?" It came out too harsh. I tried to think of a way to soften it. Too late.

"What do you have now, in New York?"

"What do I have in New York? My life, Sis. Friends, work, the house, Jasper."

She was looking at me with something akin to pity. "You could edit Rinpoche's next book," she said. "You could counsel some of the retreat visitors."

"I can't even counsel my own self, my own kids. Counsel them how?"

"I'm so far out," she said, smiling. "And Volya is . . . well, Rinpoche. They feel he's a million miles beyond them. You're more like they are. You could talk to them about real life in a way we can't. The spiritual lessons can be really esoteric sometimes. People get to a certain point, and they have experiences and it starts to seem crazy to them, like pretend magic, like something that could never be applied to the real world. You could help us with that part."

"Thanks, but I have a job," I said. "And it's about the one place left on earth where I feel qualified to counsel anybody."

She looked at me as if there were so many things I still didn't know. I was glad, at least, that she hadn't mentioned anything about helping Shelsa with the great work she'd come to earth in order to complete. I counted that as progress.

"Have you had—" I started to say, and then I felt the way I'd felt on the interstate ramp, just after I'd put on the brakes to pick up Rundy. Celia was watching me, and the muscles to either side of her mouth tightened just slightly, as they so often did, ready to smile at a good word. "Rinpoche told me he worries sometimes about, you know, safety issues."

She kept looking at me, the green eyes, the quarter of a smile. I should have kept quiet then, but I was going to be leaving my daughter in this place, a place where at least some of the people thought of her as a terrorist-in-training. "Have there been any threats or anything? Stupid stuff like that?"

The muscles unflexed; that was the only change. Celia's eyes were steady, and what I saw there surprised me. Bravery, it looked like. Physical courage. I wasn't used to thinking of her that way.

"We went through a stretch where somebody was calling," she said.

"And saying what?"

"Unkind things. We changed the phone number and it's mostly stopped."

"Did you notify anyone, the police, the FBI?"

She shook her head.

"Rinpoche seemed to think it would be . . . people from other countries, but this sounds local."

She shrugged, already tired of the subject. "They persecuted Volya and his father back home. He expects it. He's used to it."

"Imagining it, then?"

"Not really. He's had dreams. He's told me about them. I think, probably, all this is a little ways in the future, but when . . . but all through history if there's been someone like Shelsa, there have been hateful people who wanted to hurt her."

"You know, phrases like *I think, probably* aren't exactly what I want to hear. And *a little ways in the future* means what, exactly?"

She looked at me with a maddening patience. "I understand why you'd be worried, Otto, but can we talk about this in a few days? Would you mind?"

"All right, fine. But I won't let it drop."

I was tired then, more than ready for bed. The plans we'd made had me staying for the rest of that week and then flying back with Natasha, but now her ticket would have to be changed, and I didn't know, until my sister spoke again, what we'd do to pass the hours.

Cecelia stood up and put a hand lovingly on my right shoulder. I thanked her for the meal. "I'm glad you liked it," she said, "and that you filled up. Because Rinpoche wants you to do a three-day solitary, and there's some partial fasting involved. He's going to wake you up at six tomorrow morning and tell you the rules and all, take you to one of the cabins. That's why I didn't want to keep talking. You should probably go to bed."

"I don't believe I've signed on to this plan," I told her, but she'd gone behind me and was doing the shoulder-massage thing again, ignoring me. I took a breath. "Seese." I took another breath. "I agreed to sit with him. But I never said anything about a retreat. And fasting is absolutely out of the question. Crazy, for a person like me."

"I know," she said. I felt her kiss the top of my head, and then she shuffled back down the hall and I heard a door close quietly there.

36

I suppose I could have objected more strongly. There would be moments in the succeeding days when I felt that I should have. Many moments. But several factors were at work. First, I'd seen so clearly of late how badly I wanted my son and daughter to be friends, and also how different they were, and I wondered if they'd learned, in some way, from my example with my sister. So I thought I might humor her for once instead of criticizing her in my thoughts. I thought that might be a step toward the kind of relationship I still hoped to someday have with her, a relationship of mutual respect that would serve as a good example for my children.

Second, while I did not for a nanosecond believe Rinpoche when he told me I was on the cusp of some important interior realization, I couldn't deny, except in my most cynical moments, that I'd benefitted from his company, his books, and from the regular practice of meditation to which he'd introduced me. At that point in my life I wouldn't have characterized it, necessarily, as a *spiritual* benefit. It was more like substitute therapy, only much less expensive. Still, I'd noticed a change and, while the benefits had eroded with the stress of Jeannie's illness, I was fairly sure the meditation practice had enabled me to witness the torture she'd gone through without going out into the back yard and shooting myself.

Third, and this may be the hardest to explain, there was a way in which being around Anthony and Natasha—two wonderful athletes—made me realize that my life was almost completely lacking in physical challenge. When did I ever push myself these days? Over the summer I'd jogged a mile or a mile and a half with my son every Saturday and Sunday morning. In the winter I worked out three times a week at a health club—mostly so I could keep eating all the foods I liked without turning into one of those guys I saw on the train, middle-aged office-workers who lugged around a sagging stomach as if they were soon to give birth to a litter of walruses.

But what I'm talking about here goes beyond vanity. I remembered, however vaguely, the feeling I'd had as a high school football player. Number 39 on the jersey, a skinny-legged tailback with a total career playing time of fourteen minutes, I nevertheless went to all the practices, ran myself to exhaustion on hot August days, and endured the contact and the scrapes, bruises, strains, and one broken little finger with a degree of stoicism. Since then, however, with the exception of my brief JV hockey career at UND, I'd opted for comfort whenever possible. Aside from the rare cold Atlantic swim and maybe one or two sets of singles tennis in the heat of July, I hadn't really pushed my body in something like thirty years. Maybe watching bits of the London Olympics had had some effect on me, but I wanted to get back in shape, and I decided that a little fasting wouldn't be a bad place to start.

So that was my mind-set the next morning when Rinpoche tapped on my door. I wanted, facing him, to be tough again. Or at least tougher.

My brother-in-law was in a jolly mood. Possibly that came from seeing his family, or from being liberated from my tiresome company, or from hearing that Shelsa had almost learned to swim, or from not having any idea what some of the people in Williston were saying about him. Whatever the reason, he hugged me warmly and said, "Otto will make a good retreat. I can see."

"All suited up," I said, which, of course, meant nothing to him. "What should I bring along?"

"Three days clothes and toothbrush," he said, as if he'd said it to hundreds of penitents before me. He held out one of Seese's all-natural grocery sacks.

When I'd packed my small bag (sneaking in, I'm embarrassed to admit, three Mounds bars and my phone), Rinpoche and I headed out. From the front porch of our house, the morning sun in your face, you descend three old steps and find yourself in the gravel area where we park our cars and pickups. There are two barns behind the house and three galvanized-steel grain storage bins on stilts there. Close by to your left is a smaller storage building that was used for feed, fertilizer, rakes, shovels, and so on. Beyond that is a rutted farm road that led, in the old days, to what Pop and Mom always referred to as Blake's Field. Who this Blake character was, no one seemed to know. Some early settler who'd put his name on the acreage, no doubt. In any case, Blake's field, all hundred-some acres of it, had been allowed to go to grass, and there, among the fescue and locusts, the meadowlarks and pocket gophers and pesky moles,

Rinpoche, my sister, and a local carpentry crew had constructed a string of three wooden cabins, well spaced.

I followed my brother-in-law along the dirt road, carrying my luggage, studying the sway of his robe, and wondering if I was about to make another foolish mistake. It would be worse than the nearly crippling yoga class in Madison on our previous road trip. It would be a kind of violence done to my already half-ravaged soul. Fasting. Solitude. Empty hours. What had I been thinking?

But we trudged along. The final cabin was only about a quarter mile from the house and the road led right past its door. The building was probably twenty feet by twenty, with a shiny metal roof, unpainted cedar siding, a window, a stovepipe running outside one wall. Standing there in the newborn sun Rinpoche turned to face me. "Now," he said, "listen me."

"Listening."

"Today is Friday. You stay until Sunday just as the darkness is there."

"Sunday at sundown."

He ignored me.

"For the breakfast, there's food to make. Oatmeal. Some kind of the tea with no caffeine. Bread, yelli, some of the fruit. Plenty. For the lunch, somebody come here and bring you, okay?"

"So far, okay. I'm waiting to hear about dinner."

He smiled. "Dinner." He held up one finger and shook his head.

"No dinner?"

More shaking. The smile grew wider. In Ortyk, apparently, missing dinner was cause for amusement.

"Can I snack on the breakfast food before bed?"

"Tea, you can have. But wery important. You must go hungry to sleep and then you can have, in the morning, the Big!"

"All I want."

"Sure," he said.

"And what do I do when I'm not eating or thinking about eating?"

"You have books. Four. Read wery good these books. You have the yoga mat. If you want you can take the chair outside and sit and look. When the person comes with the lunch you can talk a little while."

"I suspect there's a TV with very limited reception."

He patted my arm. "Good you can make a joke, my friend. Wery good. But these three days are the wery most important time for you! Most important time for Otto, my friend! At the end, I will come get you. Okay?"

"Anything special I should do?"

"Sure. Meditate in the morning before you eat, then later after you eat, then before you eat the lunch, then after, then before you go to bed. Maybe four, five hours all together. Can you do it?"

"I'll try."

"Good. Try, only try, and when you try, go outside yourself and meet Jeannie in the place she goes outside herself, understand?"

"No."

"The overlap," he said, pronouncing the word carefully and correctly, as if he'd practiced it.

"I don't know how to go outside myself."

"Retreat is for that. Meditate, try, then we talk, and then," he made a shoveling motion with one hand toward his mouth, "eat and eat." He made his eyes wide, "TV and TV." He pantomimed a person sleeping and couldn't keep from laughing. "Rest and rest."

He put both hands on my shoulders, closed his eyes, and began a quiet murmuring/singing chant, something very much like what I'd once seen him do in a bowling alley in Indiana, with a rough character I thought might take a swing at him. It went on for perhaps a minute, then he hugged me again, released me and stood there looking.

"What?"

He made a motion like one makes when one puts a phone to one's ear and talks, then he held out his right hand, palm up. I smiled guiltily, half surprised. Nothing magical here, I told myself. A lucky guess, that's all. Seese must have told him I'd want to have my phone. I fished around in the bag in a way that kept the Mounds bars from being seen, and handed it over. "If my boss calls," I said, "tell him I'm fasting and can't be reached."

"Friday," he said. "Summer. Boss not there, right?"

The New York publishing world in early August. No one was ever righter.

My brother-in-law the spiritual master put the phone deep into the folds of his robe, looked at me without smiling, with a tremendous intensity, in something like the way Coach Michalson had looked at us on the gridiron before a particularly hard workout or a game against the notorious Bismarck High Demons, then he gave one short nod and sauntered off in the direction of the house where my sister and I, ordinary Americans in the extreme, had been raised.

——⟋ 37

For the first little while it wasn't so bad. Rinpoche had said nothing about sleeping, so I lay down on the small, fairly comfortable bed and snoozed for an hour and a half. Jeannie appeared in a dream, fleetingly, just a quick snapshot of her face. It had happened a hundred times since her death and always left me feeling as though I were reaching for her, wanting to hear her voice, touch her one more time, but that some invisible limitation had been placed on me. There was always a particular kind of emptiness after those dreams, and I woke to that again and lay looking up at the rafters, blinking the truth away.

I got up and made an inspection of the kitchen. The small refrigerator held milk and jam and a selection of fresh fruit. Bottled water by the gallon. One stick of butter. I put my candy bars in there because I like them crisp. There was oatmeal and a loaf of Seese's homemade bread, crackers, herbal teas, peanut butter, canned cashews, one box of Cheerios. Nothing else. The Spartan bathroom. The sort-of closet in which I was to sleep. A chair. A yoga mat. A meditation cushion and an old and somewhat ratty couch. A bookshelf that held, as Rinpoche had promised, exactly four volumes. I made inventory:

The Inner Life, by Hazrat Inayat Khan, apparently a Sufi mystic and teacher.

I and Thou, by Martin Buber, a Hebrew scholar, translator, and teacher.

Intimacy with God, by a Catholic monk named Thomas Keating.

Leaves of Grass, by Walt Whitman, radical Protestant.

Nothing Buddhist. Nothing by Volya Rinpoche. Not one single copy of *US, People, Vanity Fair, Sports Illustrated, The New Yorker*, or *Westchester Magazine*.

I began to retreat in earnest. From everything. From the memories of my late wife, the prospect of an empty house, the idea of Tasha living here instead of going back to school, the worry about her safety, the thought that three days of this lay in front of me, as pleasing to anticipate as oral surgery and the subsequent bill. It made sense, I decided during a patch of interior muttering, to try a little yoga. After my first road trip with Rinpoche, I'd started taking lessons—private lessons; I didn't want any more group humiliations—and I'd enjoyed it, lost a few pounds, felt stronger, maybe a bit calmer. Once Jeannie fell ill, though, yoga had been one of the things that had gradually gone by the wayside. Lately, I'd been starting up again on my own, half an hour here and there.

It seemed like a good way to fill the time, but just as I was unrolling the yoga mat I decided it would be wise to have the first candy bar, or at least half of it. Possibly I should have waited, but the little voice inside my skull, a most convincing little voice, said: Why not fortify yourself for the ordeal ahead, step off on a good foot, build up the sugar level, lift the mood? I ate one half of the Mounds, then took one more tiny bite and wrapped up the rest and set it back on the shelf in the nearly empty mini-fridge. "I've been in hotel rooms with more food than this," I said aloud. I laughed. I went into the main room, stripped to my underwear, and did twenty minutes of down-ward-facing dog and upward-facing lazy man. No headstands, no extreme backbends. There was still some kind of a workout involved, a bit of sweat and pumping blood, a wash of yogic ex-hilaration. But no risks were taken.

I had a longish shower.

I stepped out the only exterior door and felt the warmth of the day, took in the sweet smell of cut alfalfa from the leased acreage, heard the sound of a truck passing somewhere in the distance and then the cry of a freight train. Went back inside. Got ready to sit down to meditate, then decided it would be wis-er to start, as I sometimes did, with a short reading. I was famil-iar with Whitman, and decided to save him for later and take a quick look at *I and Thou*. Somewhere or other I'd heard of the book, or at least heard that phrase "an I-and-Thou relationship." God knew what it actually meant.

At home, what I liked to do before meditating was to take one of the books Rinpoche had given me at random, open to a page at random, and read a paragraph or two. I would then set the book aside and "sit," as he'd taught me. He'd made a point of saying that this premeditation reading was not in order to have something to think about. The point was not to contem-plate what one had just read. "Meditation is the opposite of that," he'd said. The point of the reading was only to place myself in the grasp of a different perspective. When I read the *Times* or, even more so, the *Daily News*, I felt the world and all its assumptions surging into me, pure emotion in an IV line. I'd get upset at national politics or feel a wave of compassion for some poor soul who'd been raped, molested, or killed. I'd worry about the war in Syria, the deadlock in Congress, the Iranian nuclear program, the Palestinian-Israeli conflict, the drug cartels in Mexico, the Midwestern drought, the erosion of democracy in Russia, the U.S. poverty statistics, the stock market, a Yankees slump (not so far this year, thankfully). I'd have a sudden urge to see a play or a new TV show that had gotten a rave review. I'd marvel at some trio of mathematicians who'd spent their careers trying to solve a single problem that no one else on earth could even begin to understand.

The meditative reading often sent me in another direction, into a different world. Often, the passage I chose had some bearing on a particular difficulty I was having, and that's close to what happened with *I and Thou*. I sat on the couch with a pillow behind my back, picked up the paperback copy, opened by chance to page 154, and came upon this: "When a man loves a woman so that her life is present in his own, the You of her eyes allows him to gaze into a ray of the eternal You."

I did not understand this, not fully. But it did ring some faint bell, and so I read on for a while, hoping Martin Buber had the answer to a question I couldn't quite formulate.

I read two or three pages, skipped ahead, tried another page—dense, complex, obtuse, but ringing that same faint bell in places—then set the book aside and tried to meditate as I'd been taught. I sat in a comfortable position. I folded my hands. Closed my eyes. Drew a long breath, taking on the pain of the world and sending out strength, peace, harmony, love. Again. Again.

But my mind was a circus on that morning. A surge of self-pity, odd bits of memory—Jeannie frowning at me over the tennis net; little flickers of triviality—Frank Denig's habit of sticking his head around the doorjamb and flashing a thumbs-up for no good reason at all; it was something he'd learned, along with publishing-speak, in a management seminar; there was an itch above my right ankle—was it chiggers? A tick? Did Anthony have everything he needed for football? Wasn't Jasper due for a shot at the vet's? Guilt over the candy I'd brought along. It was a lie, really, wasn't it? A fib. Don't be so harsh on yourself. I remembered I was meditating and tried to breathe. How was I going to go without dinner? What was the point? Buddha ate everything, didn't he? I started to think of meals I'd have once I got back to New York. The ricotta pancakes at Comfort Diner. I'd do that first. I owed myself that much. The fine beef kabob at that Afghani place on Ninth Avenue. What was it called? I'd pamper myself. I'd been through a lot. Look what Jeannie went through. If she had meditated, would it have been easier for her? Impossible to believe that. She handled it with great courage. Would I be that brave? Would I have to be one day? I was meditating. Breathe, relax the body. What was Rinpoche pointing me toward? Why did so many people admire him? Would Natasha progress faster than I did? Reach enlightenment? What was that, enlightenment? Was Seese enlightened? If so, what was the point? Breathe. I thought of Rundy preferring a drenching rain to a softheaded New York liberal like me.

Finally, I gave up. Opened my eyes, stretched, stood, decided once and for all that the retreat idea had been a mistake. But it wouldn't look good, especially in front of Tasha, to walk out now, go back to the house, and tell them it wasn't for me. Even if it meant sleeping and reading away the three days, I'd stick it out.

I stepped outside and watched the clouds for a while, then went through the kitchen cabinets again, wondering if I'd missed something—some fresh-baked croissants, eggs, bacon, real maple syrup and whole-grain pancake mix, a slice of peach cobbler that the previous retreatant had accidentally left behind. No. Nothing had been missed. I walked around the cabin ten times to get a little exercise. Came back inside, picked up *I and Thou,* set it down again.

I lay on the bed with my hands behind my neck and thought about work, about Gilligan Neufaren and his happy way. Maybe he'd been sent into my life just now in order to show me another route to salvation, something that suited me better than Rinpoche's maddening riddles, periods of fasting, and faith in meditation as the healer of all things. Maybe the Neufaren way was the better route for me now—a healthy, well-off, single man in his earliest fifties. There were still so many pleasures to take hold of, so much life to live, so many meals, books, trips, fine conversations, all of it lying there before me.

After an hour or more of this I heard the door crack open and a tentative voice say, "Uncle Ott?"

I hustled out of bed and tried to look as though I'd been doing something other than what I had been doing. Too late. My niece was in the main room, staring at me, carrying an old-fashioned picnic basket and ready to report on her lazy, duplicitous uncle.

"Shels, give me a big hug."

She set down the basket and came over and jumped into my arms. I twirled her around once and set her on the couch. She looked up at me with the intense, serious, curious, older-than-her-years gaze for which she was already famous in our family. She seemed, for just a moment, to shimmer.

"What?" I said.

"Yunch!" She jumped to her feet.

"Already? The time's gone by so fast. Your mom and dad sent you with food for Uncle Ott?"

For an instant she seemed to see right through me, the way her father so often did. I half expected her to say, "Yes, Uncle Ott. A little yunch to go with your Mounds bar."

But of course she didn't.

We sat together at the table and she insisted on showing me, one item at a time, what was in the basket. I was hungry, but not ravenous. I was able to hope that some of the food, at least, would not be green, that my sister had sent the girl here with two portions, not one, or that Shelsa had already eaten.

With great attentiveness she lifted away the two hinged wooden covers. Beneath them, someone—Celia, probably—had set a folded, blue-checked cloth. Shelsa lifted this off and put it aside like some kind of surgeon preparing for incision. She took out a single Bartlett pear, said, "Pear," showed it to me, and waited for a reaction.

"Uncle Ott *loves* pears," I said.

She reached in and took out a square plastic container, two inches high, and said, "Um-us."

"Hummus. Good. My favorite."

"Cwakers."

"Perfect."

"Sell ree."

"Crunchy."

Each time she reached in I tried to get a sense of how far down she was digging, how many more layers there might be. This was, after all, my nourishment for the next eighteen hours.

She took the checkered cloth and put it back into the basket.

"That's it?"

She nodded somberly.

"Are you hungry?"

"Wery."

"Well, let's eat, then."

I found two mismatched glasses and filled them with cold water. Shelsa was busy arranging the food, spacing everything evenly, keeping the hummus and crackers exactly halfway between us. I was very glad for the company. She stopped me as I was about to eat. "Pray first, Uncle."

We bowed our heads and were silent for a moment. I was thinking about dinner. We began to eat.

"Has Jasper Junior been bad today?"

She shook her head.

"What are Mom and Dad doing?"

"Mami's cooking. Papi's doing a walk."

"Where?"

She made a big circle with one hand. "Around the fawm."

"Are they worried about Uncle Ott?"

She shook her head. "Mami says you're having a big weewization. Are you?"

"Not yet. Soon, though. Anytime now."

I sliced the pear in half and cut out the pit, and we shared the juicy flesh for dessert. I like to have something sweet at the end of a meal, and the pear flesh was not quite the ticket. I was an inch away from saying, "Hey, I have a candy bar in the fridge. Don't tell anybody, okay. We'll share it." But some interior Congress voted that notion down.

She helped me tidy up, and when that small task was finished I didn't want her to leave. "Do you do this for all the other people who come to stay? Is this your job?"

"Only Uncle Ott," she said, and then she leaned against the side of my leg and hugged, and said, "Going now," and closed the door quietly behind her as though someone were sleeping. I went over and opened it and watched her go along the road until it dipped and turned behind a patch of fescue and she was no longer visible.

— ☙ 38

As the afternoon wore on, as the first real hunger appeared and began to gnaw away at my entrails like some small animal determined to grow big, I decided the books had been put there not to be skimmed, but to be read in their entirety. Maybe Martin Buber had something to say about hunger, I thought. Maybe there would be a sentence claiming it was perfectly fine to eat on solitary retreats. As much as one wanted. Anytime. I began *I and Thou* at the introduction and went forward. "Buber taught me," the writer of the preface said on page 23, "that mysticism need not lead outside the world. Or if mysticism does, by definition, so much the worse for it."

Good. I agreed. Walter Kaufmann was his name. I fully agreed.

Though the actual text proved to be slow going, every once in a while there would be a sentence or a passage that stopped me. That familiar bell rang. I felt that some marvelous new emerald of wisdom might be lying ahead, there on the next page, that I might, as Rinpoche suggested, be ready for a realization, a big step, that everything would then be solved. I would laugh and joke my way through the last thirty years of my life and pass on quietly into a new dimension. See my wife. Guide our kids from above. Eat whatever I wanted without gaining weight.

I stopped and did a short meditation. I managed another ten minutes of yoga. I read on.

There were many difficult passages in *I and Thou*, actual sentences like this one, commas correctly included, on p. 102: "That I discovered the deed that intends me, that, this movement of my freedom, reveals the mystery to me."

Who, I thought, would make any money from publishing this? What kind of mind went this deep? How far could a guy like me follow?

The afternoon light faded, and, setting the book aside, I was for once not sorry to see the day go. I brewed myself a cup of tea and I have to say I took more time doing this, paid more attention, carried the cup out the door with a considerably greater gratitude than I used to carry a bottle of fifty-dollar Santa Margherita onto the patio at home. I stood sipping, studying the western sky. The hunger gnawed away. I missed my wife and tried to make sense of the last bit of instruction Rinpoche had given me. Overlap yourself with herself. Go outside yourself, Otto. What did that mean? Buber's "two basic words" were I and Thou, or I and You. He seemed to be saying that everything in life is a relationship between one person and another, or one person and a tree, a cloud, a rushing river, a bug, a snake, a cup of tea. Maybe somewhere deep in the heart of that I-Thou connection lay what Rinpoche would call the God-spirit. The Divine Intelligence. Is that where a good wife went when she died? To the mysterious center of God's mind? To the hyphen in the I-Thou? If so, how did a living husband follow?

⟶ 39

That night, freed from the exertion of digestion, I slept the sleep of the ancient Egyptians in their tombs. I woke up wondering if I should get out of bed and make breakfast or simply devour the pillow, blanket, and mattress and then eat the metal frame.

I got up. I badly wanted coffee. Very badly. For me, coffee is not an addiction, it's a necessity. One, perhaps two cups on waking. And then, later in the morning, one or two more. Either black or with a little cream, no sugar, strong as you can make it. In the tiny kitchen I went through the boxes of tea, seeing my sister's fingerprints on each one. Mint Mindfulness. Joyful Morning. Restful Evening. Hibiscus Blend. Cactus Orange Cinnamon Nut Good Mood. After a small period of indecision, I went with Joyful Morning—three cups—and remembering Rinpoche's remark that I could eat as much as I wanted for breakfast, I made myself seven pieces of sawdusty toast with butter and jam. Added a bowl of grapes. And then, for dessert, one small serving of oatmeal with local honey. The entire feast lasted almost an hour.

Too much. There was a distended feeling, not pleasant. I knew that if I tried yoga with a full belly like that I'd end up with some kind of rupture, so I paced the living room to work it off. My watch read 6:20, which seemed impossibly early. By reflex I went to check it against my phone, but the phone wasn't there. Confiscated. I'd not had anything confiscated since my Bic spitball shooter in fourth grade. I tried to meditate, but the overdose of grain seemed to have an adverse effect on my ability to focus, so I made twenty loops around the outside of the house, watched the rain clouds approach, then went in and sat on the couch and listened to the first drops tap the metal roof, and then a deluge against the window.

From the shelf, needing lighter fare, I took *The Inner Life.* I read fifty pages and clung to two things: On page 18, something very much like what Rinpoche had told me on the road in Montana: "Once man has experienced the inner life the fear of death has expired, for he knows death comes to the body, not to his inner being."

I read that over four times and set it, in my mind's eye, beside the *Daily News* headlines. They'd go out of business if people lost their fear of death. They and the rest of the news organizations stoked the fear of death like Inuits around a winter campfire a thousand years ago. Let it expire and all was lost.

And this, on page 31: "Very often therefore it becomes difficult for an intellectual person, who through life has learned things and understood them by the power of intellect, to attain to the inner life, for these two paths are different. The one goes to the north and the other goes to the south."

With that, the universities would go out of business. Everyone's daughter would move to a farm.

I set the book down and decided I'd meditate for one hour, cross-legged, on the cushion that had been provided. I lasted fifteen minutes. Leg pain. I moved to the couch, but there it was the same story as in the previous session: worry about the kids, the Haters, thoughts of food, scraps of distraction about the trivialities of life—who, for instance, had named the different kinds of teas? How much was he or she paid? What was her official title? Leaf logician? Sales associate for the cataloguing of consumable leaf beverages? When he went on a date, what did he tell the person across the table about his daily regimen?

My mind was, in other words, whitewater.

At some point in the last third of the hour I did enjoy a stretch of peace for a minute or so. Not thoughtlessness so much as a slowing down of the whole process, an awareness, an unwillingness to follow my foolish notions as they veered off this way and that. I'd known this feeling, the great pleasure of this peace, before. I recognized it the way one recognizes the familiar gait of a friend from a distance of several blocks. When I at last opened my eyes I asked a blessing on Jeannie's soul, went to the refrigerator and took the half-eaten candy bar and gobbled it. I opened another one and gobbled it, too. Both pieces. I felt proud of myself, in spite of that, on the road to some weewization I could not imagine. I did another half hour of yoga, had a shower, read another few chapters of Inayat Khan, did another, shorter meditation, and was thrilled, again, to hear footsteps on the path and see Shelsa tentatively opening the door and looking in. It was noon. It felt like 4:00 p.m. the next day.

There was the picnic basket—she could barely lift it onto the table—and the rite of naming each piece of food and setting it out for my reaction. An avocado this time. A container of sun-flower seeds. Carrots. A salad with an oil-and-vinegar dressing. And the main course, one large baked potato onto which we dropped a large chunk of butter and into which, with some de-light, we dipped our spoons. There was something so adult in my niece's manner—in the way she carried herself, in the utter sincerity with which she spoke her amusing dialect of Eng-lish—that I found myself wanting to say, "Tell me about your mission here on earth," or "Do you believe what people say about why you were born?" Something certifiably absurd like that. Watching her remove a white crumb of potato from her lower lip with a delicate dab of napkin, I had the thought that even the Dalai Lama probably hadn't been aware of his role when he was five and three quarters. Not consciously aware, at least; not able to verbalize it. Tibetan legend had it, of course, that the time of his birth had been known to certain great living masters, that news of it had been sent to them, like the news of Christ's birth, in a dream or vision. They were the Wise Men from the East, these great teachers. They were told where he was to be born, and approximately when, and a committee of them then traveled to that Himalayan Bethlehem with objects from a previous lama's life and interviewed these young boys. One of the boys picked the correct cup and eyeglasses out of a lineup, and they had their man.

I was musing along these lines, watching Shelsa sip water and wondering where I might teach her to really swim—Cape Cod, next summer, perhaps—when I was hit broadside by a new idea. On our earlier road trip, just before the famous Wis-consin yoga debacle, I'd eaten in a Nepali restaurant with the good Rinpoche. After the meal he'd pointed to a religious paint-

ing on the wall and told me—hinted, was more like it—that Cecelia would bear a daughter, that this daughter would be a special creature with an important mission, and that I would have
some essential role to play in her life. What if by "special creature" he'd meant something like the next Dalai Lama? Why
should it be a boy? Why should he be born in Tibet? Why
shouldn't the great spiritual masters of our era—Rinpoche and
his ilk—have an inkling of her birth before it actually occurred?
And what if it were true, and I was watching the next Dalai Lama wipe her mouth?

On the heels of this run of thought came another, more disturbing notion: what if the Chinese heard about her and her
mission? Wouldn't there be a chance, at least, that they'd do
what they could to prevent the succession? Hadn't they proven
themselves willing to do more vicious things to suppress the
Buddhist faith? A million Tibetans slaughtered, for instance?
Couldn't that mean sending some sort of team of assassins here
to Dickinson with Shelsa as the target, guided by the likes of
Rundy and his friends, those Muslim-haters?

No doubt I was beginning, thanks to the food and coffee
deprivation, to sink into the swamp of insanity. But the thought
persisted, and, really, to call it a thought is not quite accurate. It
felt like more than that; it had more weight. Not quite a premonition, it nevertheless felt somehow as though, in separating
myself, however briefly, from the usual distractions—phone,
food, TV and newspaper, other adults—I'd allowed a kind of
interior smog to disperse. As the sky cleared, this new possibility was revealed: Shelsa was the next great spiritual leader, a
Jesus for our time, or a John the Baptist, a Mahatma Gandhi, a
Martin Luther King. And look what had happened to those good

souls.

In order to protect myself from this line of thinking, I decided to make conversation. Shelsa was sipping from her water glass now, eyeing me, expecting a word.

"You were sick a little while ago, your Papi told me."

"Yes," she said.

"Was it bad? Did it hurt?"

"A little." She laughed the way he did, a big river of a laugh that turned to a trickle of chuckling and then dripped and dripped for another little while. "I saw the hospital!"

"Were you scared?"

"No, no, Uncle," she said. "The nurses were wery nice. But the pool scared me."

"You were almost swimming there, you know. When you come visit us in New York, I'll take you again and you'll really swim. You'll never be scared after that."

"Aunt Jeannie won't be there."

Another quick rush of tears, more lumps in the breathing apparatus. There was no end to it. "No," I said. "Aunt Jeannie passed on. She died. You won't see her."

"I hear her," she said.

"No, honey, you won't hear her, either. She's gone. She loved you, though."

She looked at me as if I were making a joke, another foolish adult misinterpreting the world's signals, coming to all the wrong conclusions. We thought people died. We thought the world was round. We thought children lacked understanding. "I hear her, Uncle Ott," she repeated.

I couldn't argue. I smiled in a strained way, nodded like a fool. Shelsa and I packed up the basket and hugged, a new ritual for us, a retreat rite, and then she was gone again, trotting through the light rain, and I was watching her. This time, though, the premonition hung there like a scent. I went back and did a meditation, the less hurried run of thoughts interrupted now and again by my wondering how difficult it would be for the Chinese team, those murderous heathens, to find Dickinson, North Dakota.

⎯⎯⎯ ⁀ 40

The second afternoon and evening were the worst of it for me, a kind of dark night of the soul—though I'd bet that an actual dark night of the soul is a bit more trying. Time, it seemed, had completely stopped. Hunger was an issue, yes, but worse than that was a major-league boredom, an emptiness I couldn't seem to fill. I read the rest of *The Inner Life*, which I found to be a wonderfully open-minded treatise on our common humanity, clearly the work of a special soul. I did three more meditation sessions, an hour of yoga. Then there was a nothingness as vast as the prairies of eastern Montana. I wasn't tired enough to sleep. I'd had my fill of reading. I slowly made a cup of tea, slowly drank it, but even then it was only a quarter to nine and there was no TV, no going into town with Jeannie for a late glass of wine at Sammy's, no newspaper, crossword puzzle, game of chess, or walk with the dog.

Though it was almost physically painful to do so, I made myself sit on the couch for one more meditation session. I would try, I told myself, for half an hour. Beforehand I took one last peek at the pages of *The Inner Life*, where I read this: "Many people make a profession of clairvoyance and spirit communication; these are a degeneration of real mysticism."

Maybe that was why Seese had given it up.

I tried to do what Rinpoche had encouraged me to do: step out of myself into some mysterious territory where my spirit and Jeannie's spirit overlapped. There was the usual circus, and then a settling, a peace, and then, for a little while, it seemed to me that all the "I want" had been confined to a certain space. I felt this space—oddly—as a pickle barrel. The urge for television, companionship, food, and busyness was all there in the barrel, so many pickles floating or, better, so many fish swimming this way and that, bumping the sides, frantic to get out. And then there was something else. For a little while there was this something else. I don't know exactly how to describe it. The sense that I was not limited to my body, perhaps. The notion that Natasha and Anthony and Shelsa and Cecelia and Rinpoche and the other seven billion of us were not limited to our bodies either. We breathed the same air. It linked us. We shared, all of us, the marvelous surprise of being.

An old mocking voice appeared. The notion fled.

41

I woke on the third day feeling like a runner who had lost faith in his ability to finish the marathon and then realizes he's in the twenty-fifth mile and, really, there isn't that much farther to go; it looks like he'll make it. I had a shower, cleaned things up a bit, sang to myself while preparing breakfast. I'd cut down to only four pieces of toast, fruit, tea, some leftover sunflower seeds. The last Mounds bar tempted me but I decided to wait.

I'd saved *Intimacy with God* for that last day. It turned out to be the easiest read of the three spiritual books. Straightforward, Christian in essence though broad-minded in its approach. It was all about what the author called "centering prayer," which seemed to me indistinguishable from what I called "meditation." "Our spiritual journey may be blocked," Keating wrote, "if we carry negative attitudes toward God from early childhood." And, a bit later, "God has to lead us into a place that involves a complete reversal of our prepackaged values, a complete undoing of all our carefully laid plans, and a lot of letting go of our preconceived ideas." And, last: "There is really no such thing as private prayer. We cannot pray at this deep level without including everyone in the human family, especially those in great need."

Keating, it appeared from the book jacket, was still alive. His tone was so good-hearted, so forgiving, so determined to give mouth-to-mouth resuscitation to the idea that it was possible to be spiritual in this world without being a Pollyanna or a simpleton—that I found myself wanting to meet the man, to see such a Catholic in the flesh. I wondered, too, if he and Rinpoche knew each other, if they read each other's books, sneaked out of tiresome ecumenical conferences in St. Louis or L.A. for a quick round of miniature golf and a Coke.

The meditation I had then was the quietest of the retreat. For forty-five minutes I sat in a calm, warm pool. There were thoughts, but they were set against a larger, thought-free background. For long periods of time I watched them arrive and depart without being tugged along in their wake. It wasn't that the true cares of the world had ceased to exist, that I was no longer missing Jeannie or worrying about Natasha. But I could somehow let those things go without abandoning them, or feeling guilty about standing outside them in an unworried place.

With that, one hour of yoga, and my usual circumambulation of the cabin, the time before lunch passed quickly. Shelsa's quiet knock came as a welcome surprise. I watched her unload the basket: the usual assortment of fruit, seeds, greens, and today's entrée—one large acorn squash, baked and sliced in half with fresh strawberries in the center. This time, though, Shelsa took a folded note from the bottom of the basket and handed it over.

My Darling Brother,
I know this must have been hard for you, but I
can feel that you have turned a corner today.
Trust me, I can feel it. And please trust
Rinpoche. Let him guide you.
It is such a pure joy for me to have you here. I
really, really wish you would consider making
this your home.
Love,
Your sister Cecelia

Ravenous as I was, I enjoyed sharing the modest lunch with my niece. I watched her as we ate, looking for I don't know exactly what, some sign that she wasn't an ordinary six-year-old girl, some confirmation of the things I'd been hearing—and doubting—since before she was born. There was, I have to say, a certain shimmer about her, a glow. But isn't it true that all children, if they're surrounded by a normal amount of warmth and if they live without abuse or craziness, have a certain glow about them? I remembered it so well from Natasha and Anthony's early years. I remembered seeing it in my neighbor, Levi, on the flight west. It could be simply a lack of suspicion or worry, an absence of guilt, a full embrace of the present, the sense that one is lovable and loved. Or it could be something more profound than that—an as-yet-unforgotten link to another world.

The odd thing was, as Jeannie drew closer to death, there was something of that glow to her, as well. She became not more childish or childlike, but more open and vulnerable. The phrase I want to use is *less veiled*, but that would seem to assert that she'd been a woman of false personality, of armor, and that wasn't the case. Even as her body weakened, there remained some force there, some essence, and I remembered puzzling over that, feeling as if she were becoming *larger* in the room. I am miles past romanticizing her suffering. I'm not saying that. I'm saying there was this mysterious *her-ness* that swelled up around my wife even as her body and personality grew frail. I am saying I saw it very clearly, beyond her suffering, and I'm wondering if she saw it—or felt it—too.

In our last lunch at the retreat cabin I felt that same thing with Shelsa. What words can one put to it? There is the body, the personality, and then there is this *something else*. In her, in every childlike gesture and look, this something else was enormous, enveloping; it filled the room like oxygen. She looked into my eyes and smiled a small Buddha smile and for some reason then I found myself comparing her to Gilligan Neufaren. A brilliant, personable, enviable man, he nevertheless seemed to be someone in whom this essence was tiny, covered over, a seed in the center of a huge, pulpy piece of fruit with sugary skin. He had a hunger about him, and wanted to endlessly eat and take and ask and harvest. Shelsa gave.

"Did you have a *weewization?*" she inquired, fixing me with the bottomless brown eyes.

"I'm having it," I said.

And she smiled more widely then, in a way that could almost be described as ecstatic, and said she was going back to tell Papi and Mami and Tash.

"Tell Jasper, too," I said, and that made her laugh and clap her hands.

When she was gone, I went to the meditation cushion. The

reading for the day came from the very last passage of *Leaves of Grass:*

Dear friend, whoever you are, take this kiss,
I give it especially to you—Do not forget me,
I feel like one who has done his work—I progress on,
The unknown sphere, more real than I dreamed, more direct,
darts awakening rays about me—So Long!
Remember my words—I love you—I depart from materials,
I am as one disembodied, triumphant, dead.

I sat on the tattered couch and closed my eyes. I felt that I was sitting there not as a Protestant or a Buddhist, not as anyone's disciple or student, not even—and this is strange—as father, husband, uncle, or friend. I was a presence in the world, unnamed.

I sat very still and quiet, untroubled for once. My thoughts and concerns existed, but they were like threads on a beach, that small. After a few moments of this quietness I began to sense some gathering expectation, some huge new truth filling the room as though lightly scented air were being pumped in beneath the door. A little farther into the meditation—ten minutes, half an hour, who could say?—and in this you will simply have to trust that I am not a liar or a flake, that I was not drugged by denial of food or the long weight of mourning—some time into the meditation, as clearly as if she were sitting across from me in that room, I had the absolute sense of my wife's presence. It was as though I could feel her breathing, as if we were in bed together again, one of us asleep, bare skin touching. I fixed my mind on this sense of her. I went completely quiet inside; nothing on the beach now, sand, two dozen stones. A stretch of interior silence, vast and perfect, and then, I tell you, I heard Jeannie say this: "Otto, I'm okay."

Three words, the stillness otherwise undisturbed. I felt a quickening pulse of excitement but forced myself not to follow it. For that moment I sensed her in a thousand ways that seemed to combine into one, as if all those years and all those memories—her voice, her body, her face, her touch, her way of being in the world—all of it had been distilled into one drop of pure essence. The name "Jeannie" could no longer wrap itself around that essence, but it was uniquely her all the same. I knew that. I knew her.

And then, as if she were a satellite passing out of the gravitational pull of my own essence, I felt her moving away. I reached and reached then, tried to speak to her in the same wordless language, tried to hold on to her, but in another little while I was alone.

It was not the terrible aloneness I'd been living with for the past seven months, not that cold carcass of feeling, but simply a solitariness. I took a breath. It seemed that some new, unexpected comfort had been granted me. I opened my eyes and the first thing I did—and I did this by reflex, without analysis—was to send a prayer of thanks out to my sister and Rinpoche. Surely now it was obvious that they knew something I didn't know. They had access to a precinct of reality that could not be properly spoken about. There was a feeling then—too rare, in my case—of the utmost humility.

What did I do with that feeling? Odd man that I am, I walked over to the refrigerator, took out my last Mounds bar, poured myself a glass of cold water and stood at the sink, chewing and drinking and staring out the window at the golden fields of that property. Cottony clouds went on a slow march across a pale blue background. A meadowlark perched on a wooden post there—monument to an abandoned fence—and through the screen I could hear it singing as happily as if it had just been released from a cage. To say the sound seemed miraculous to me in that moment would be to diminish it, to cast it into the realm of magic. It seemed new, only that. Just made. Just invented. Without precedent.

Somewhere in the background of all this I heard a low grumbling, then a heavy *clunk* like a transmission makes when the clutch is let out too fast. And then two toots of a horn. I went and opened the door and saw Uma there on the dirt road, a small cloud of dust settling around her. In the driver's seat, one elbow out through the open window, sat a friend of mine. He studied me for a moment and then a pleased expression bloomed on his square, rough face, and I saw a satisfied smile there, as if he were on the welcoming committee of a club, and I'd just been admitted as a junior member. The gold trim of his robe was especially striking in the last light of that day, almost shining. He said, "How was it been, man?"

⟋ɶ 42

To celebrate my accomplishment—if that's what it was (survival might be a better word)—and to mark our last night together, we decided to go into Dickinson for dinner, all five of us. I drove the old Subaru, and Celia chose a family-owned place called The Country Kitchen that had a framed photo of the pope in the entranceway and that offered, among other options, a roast turkey dinner I very much enjoyed.

It goes without saying that I missed my son and missed Jeannie, but there was a delicious feeling of togetherness around our table on that night. Shelsa said a made-up grace ("The land gave us pwezents. Thank you, land!") and nuzzled up against her cousin in a way that made Natasha's face light up. Celia and Rinpoche sat close, like lovers on a date. And I was basking in a kind of afterglow, holding the moment of Jeannie's presence like a cherished secret. My flight left the following afternoon—that was the only stain on those hours.

Instead of having dessert there, we decided to drive down to the Dairy Barn and sample their soft-serve ice cream. Not the healthiest of treats, probably, but Shelsa loved the sundaes, and I have to say it brought back some nice old memories to stand in the parking lot sipping a root beer float on a summer night and watching the traffic on Villard Street.

I'd grown so untethered from the digital universe—what a fine feeling—that it was actually a surprise when Rinpoche reached into his robe, took out my sleek new telephone, and handed it over. Another minute and I was hooked all over again, thumbing through a list of e-mails and ignoring the real world against my skin. There were twenty-seven new messages. Besides a quick "I'm okay" from Anthony, one in particular caught my eye. It was from my boss, Frank Denig, and it had been sent on Friday morning, not long after I started my retreat. It was titled "DIFFICULT DECISION," and the first part of it went like this:

> Dear Otto: You'll forgive me using this format, but this is such a difficult message to deliver. You've been a good and loyal friend all these years, and an important cog in the machinery of Stanley and Byrnes. But, as I surely don't need to tell you, the publishing business has undergone a sea change of late. In order to survive, we've decided to make some strategic adjustments. We've brought in a whiz-kid just out of Columbia to bring us up to speed in the digital marketplace. And, in an effort to keep Gilligan in our stable, we've offered him his own imprint: Neufaren Books. First title will appear on the winter list, 2014.
>
> I'm sorry to say, however, that at this point in time we really need to remain lean and mean and stay competitive, and so we've had to make some other moves, too, and these were more challenging. And that, it pains me to say, is where you come in—

Just then, just as I was feeling a most bitter tsunami of anger about to overtake me, Natasha stepped away from her uncle and aunt and cousin. She was licking the last of the ice cream from her spoon—strawberry, as always—and she came and stood in front of me, a creature of light. Looking at her wide-set eyes and the spray of freckles across the middle of her nose, I suddenly had the strange sense that I could see all of her there—Tasha the slick-haired infant, just born, lying on Jeannie's belly and having her first meal; Tasha the toddler, the schoolgirl, the teenager gasping in pain after a fall on the soccer field. Natasha, just awakened from sleep at 3:00 a.m., coming downstairs to wrap herself around her mother's body, hot skin against cool, soaking Jeannie's face with tears. I felt I could see beyond that, too, into her middle and old age. Husband, home, children, bodily struggles, her eventual passing on. What was it all about, this passage in a breathing, pulsing bundle of flesh from womb to ashes? What was the point? And how could it possibly be true that a bond like ours would simply disappear at death, that it would turn out to have been merely the dip of an eyelid in the vast stretch of time? Could a benevolent Creator really have gone to all this trouble, fashioning such complex souls and letting them find and love each other, only to snuff them out for all eternity?

She saw that I'd been checking my phone, and she said, in a hopeful way, "Good news, Dad?"

I ducked under the big wave. I tried to keep myself in Rinpoche's blessed *now* and not worry overly much about what lay ahead for my daughter, my niece, and me. We had our destinies to work out—decision by decision and hour by hour—traumas to live through and joys to embrace. It did not matter, as the master in the maroon robe had taught me, what our theories might be about the universe and its Creator. What mattered was that we tried and kept trying, picking up one smooth stone after the next, row by row, until we'd shed all pretense and protection, peeled away every label, and come to inhabit our truest self.

And so, wondering what else I might learn from her, I looked into my daughter's expectant face, hesitated one beat, and said, "Yes."

THE END

Seattle, Washington, July 17, 2012
Danbury, Connecticut, October 10, 2012

Gratitude

As far as I know, I don't have any Jewish blood. But I do have a lot of Jewish friends and I do have a particular affection for the Yiddish expressions I hear from them. *Oy!* is one of my favorites because, to my ear at least, it expresses the heavy cargo life sometimes places on our shoulders, but it does so with the wry humor for which the Jewish culture is famous. Shining the light of humor into the dark places is something I've tried to do for Otto in this novel, and try to do—with varying amounts of success—in my own life. There's nothing dark or heavy about my feeling of gratitude for all the people who've helped with this book; it's just that the task of adequately thanking all of you is an impossible one. So I have to begin by saying *Oy!*

As some of you know, *Lunch with Buddha* has had an unusual publishing history: I turned down a healthy offer from a large, established house in order to bring out the novel with a small publisher, PFP/AJAR, owned by a good friend. That decision has meant both a deep satisfaction and a huge amount of work. Without the help of the people mentioned here it never could have happened, so I'm determined to thank every one of you by name and express my gratitude in this public way.

First, as ever, my thanks to Amanda for enduring the travails of the writing life—long stretches with no money coming in, long conversations about difficult moments with agents and editors, periods of my complete distraction while I'm buried in my made-up world. She is a steady light in the dark hours. I'm eternally grateful to our magnificent daughters, Alexandra and Juliana, who are perfect travel companions, active participants in discussions about plot and design, and whose presence on this earth is more precious to me than anything. All of us made the Seattle-to-Dickinson road trip together this past summer and that was pure joy.

My gratitude to Peter Sarno, my publisher, editor, and friend, for a superhuman amount of work, excellent advice, his business and literary acumen, and for bringing my backlist into print and caring about my books during a period when no one else in the publishing universe seemed to. Thanks also to Nanette Sarno for her efforts on behalf of my books and for being a loving force to buoy Peter in the rough waters. Being the spouse of a publisher is as challenging as being the spouse of a writer and both she and Amanda meet that challenge with great dignity.

A special thanks to those friends who took the time to read the manuscript and offer invaluable suggestions. It's a huge favor to ask someone to do this, and they all agreed without hesitation and on short notice. Amanda is my first reader, and her advice is indispensable to me. Dr. Peter Grudin's suggestions were particularly helpful, and our phone conversation about a couple of problem areas in the book saved me from trouble. Our twenty-five-year friendship has been a wonderful part of my life. Matthew Quick, of *The Silver Linings Playbook* fame, a fine writer and fine man, agreed to read the manuscript and conduct the interview you see here, and he did this with such grace, generosity, and skill that I'll be long in his debt. Jessica Lipnack, another superb writer and good friend, went through the pages with a fine-tooth comb and found things I would have completely missed.

I'd be remiss if I didn't extend a special hand of thanks to my wife's family: Bob and Martha Patrick for their great generosity and unflagging support; Anne and Gary Pardun for giving our Kickstarter program its biggest push; Sarah Stearns and Jackie Hudak for Kickstarter help and longstanding enthusiasm; and Tom and Jen Mottur for their help both with Kickstarter and introductions to other fine folk. Amanda's cousin Winky Stearns Hussey was gracious enough to have all of us to her home on Whidbey Island and offer suggestions about things we might see in that area.

In order to publish this book in a fully professional way, Peter Sarno and I came up with the idea of making a sort of Initial Public Offering as a way of raising funds for publicity and printing. This was an area where, as a small house, PFP could have been at a real disadvantage. But the response to our IPO surprised both of us. Thirteen people invested substantial amounts, and their generosity enabled us to do design, printing, and promotional work of the highest quality. Thank you to the following friends for believing in the book and for taking this chance; I can't wait to pay you back with interest: Bob and Martha Patrick, Rob Phipps, Randy and Bonnie DiTrinis, Mary Remmel Wohlleb, Kathy Sherbrooke, Peggy Moss, Wendy Barlow, John DiNatale, Jen Chiappella, Dan and Erin Davies, Russ Aborn, Lisa Wenner, and Carl Carlsen.

Those funds helped us hire a world-class designer, Hans Teensma, and a world-class copyeditor, Chris Jerome. Their contributions put a wonderful shine to this project. I should note here that any errors in the manuscript are my own responsibility, not Chris's or any of the others who provided information or advice.

My longtime friend Dr. Arlo Kahn gave expert advice on medical issues, as he has done for many of my novels, and also offered travel suggestions including, but not limited to, our visit to Yellowstone's Boiling River. He is Arlo the Arkansan and he and his wife, Theresa, have supported my career from the 1990s.

Joel Thomas Adams and his brother Dwight Thomas were most helpful in guiding us through the wilds of Montana. Both of them know the state well, and they led us to, among other gems, Bernice's Bakery in Missoula—a place I wished was closer by.

Anita and Dan Schoen kindly put up an entire family on the basis of one brief meeting and an old Revere connection, and Dan generously took time out of his work schedule to act as our personal river guide on the Little Bighorn.

My friend, confidant, and fellow novelist, Craig Nova, has given me so much good advice, empathy, and encouragement over the years that his name should be on the cover of this novel. His expertise, wisdom, and friendship are greatly appreciated, as were his Montana recommendations.

I'd like to thank Bonnie and all the folks at The Wagon Wheel in Gill, MA, my unofficial "office" in the cold months, and a place, unlike our home here in Conway, that actually has high-speed internet service. Both my home and the Wheel have good food.

Tony Pelusi was an early and avid supporter of this project, and is a man of deep wisdom. My thanks to him for his friendship.

For helping me with information about the great state of North Dakota, my thanks to Tammy Weiler, Terri Thiel and Debb Weninger. And for setting me straight about the elk and geysers in Yellowstone, thank you to a fellow former Bostonian, Jim Sweeney.

Some people help in intangible ways, with a word or a kind of friendship that makes the writing of books feel like a worthwhile endeavor. My mother Eileen Merullo taught me to read and love books and has always supported and encouraged my love of writing. I'd like to acknowledge also my brothers, Steve and Ken Merullo, cousins Joe and Susan Merullo, Linda and Joey Merullo, John Aucella, Bob and Ann Mulligan, Lois Holbrook, my aunt Cynthia Goodyear, my mentor Michael Miller, friend and fellow author Sterling Watson, Bill McGee, Dean Crawford, Cecelia Galante, Art and Pat Spencer, Margie Dunphy, John Recco, Bonnie Smith, Vivian Leskes and Frank Ward, Lee Hope Betcher, Bill Betcher, Tom Alden, Russ Hammer, Bob Baker, Renee Gold, Peter Howe, Wick Sloane, Suzanne Strempek Shea and Tommy Shea, and my friend and editor at *Golf World*, Tim Murphy, Nadya Shokhen and Vladimir Tokarev, Betsy Woods, Diana Miladin, Deborah Schifter, Dana Wilson, Chiemi Karasawa, Konrad Czynski, Shaye Areheart, Rob Phipps and Lou Certuse—all these people offered good words at key moments and I'm grateful for their friendship and support.

Someone, some angelic soul who must wish to remain nameless, sent me a large check in the mail one June day—no note, no return address. This money came at a time of real difficulty for us and we used it to fund the *Lunch with Buddha* road trip, the start of everything you see here. Whoever you are: a very large and heartfelt thank you.

Finally, to the fine people who contributed to the Kickstarter program, essentially giving me money so I could do what I love do to, and so Peter and I could publish and publicize this novel, my humble gratitude:

Anne and Gary Pardun, Rick Mahoney, Tony Pelusi, Bobbin Young, Mo Hanley, Agnes Sarno, Alice Sarno, Lisa Wenner, David Anthony, Joe Dimino, Anne Gilbert,

Jessica Lipnack, Tamsen Merrill, Lianne Moccia, Doreen Lloyd Quick, Bonnie Smith,

Ellen Stathis, Sarah Stearns, Mel and Peg Williams, Annie Chappell, Marjie Devlin, Charlotte Dietz, Richard DiPerna, Jennifer Eremeeva, Jeff Foltz, Peter Grudin, Joan Cusack, Handler, Beth Harrington, Daniel Harrop, Peter Howe, Tom Mellor, Askold Melnyczuk, Linda Merullo, Tom Mottur, Mary DeMarco OKeefe, Matthew Quick,

Linda Sarno, Kate Barber Schultz, Elizabeth Searle, Suzanne Strempek Shea, Michael Slaff and Ruth Urell, Susan Smith, Frank Ward and Vivian Leskes, Wendy Wetzel,

Julia Zagachin, Laura Proctor, Paul Sarno, Kate Barvainis, Kathy Bahamonde, Sue and Rich Calrendon, Harris Berman and Ruth Nemzoff, Jane Carlson, Sarah Christiansen, Henry Ben Clarendon, Jeremy Deason, John Dimino, Scott Evans, Brigitte Kahnert, Margaret Knight, Lois Holbrook, Radha Marcum, Tom Nickel, Bette Nockles, Matthew Phillion, Shawna

Rand, Nanette Sarno, Don Tingle, Ken Williams, John Zussman, Roberta Kuonen, Susie Mosher, Mary Anne Antonellis, Neal and Sara Anderson, Jana Black, Duke Corliss, Renee Gold, Alex Gonzalez-Mir, Priscilla Herrington, Bobby Keniston, Jen Laskey, Douglas Smith, Ellen Doyle, Helen Graves, Russ Hammer, Deb Penta, Bob Baker.

ABOUT THE AUTHOR

Roland Merullo is an awarding-winning author of 14 books including 10 works of fiction. *Breakfast with Buddha*, a nominee for the International IMPAC Dublin Literary Award, is now in its 14th printing. *The Talk-Funny Girl* was a 2012 ALEX Award Winner and named a "Must Read for 2012" by the Massachusetts Library Association and the Massachusetts Center for the Book; *Revere Beach Boulevard* was named one of the "Top 100 Essential Books of New England" by *The Boston Globe*, *A Little Love Story* was named one of "Ten Wonderful Romance Novels" by *Good Housekeeping* and *Revere Beach Elegy* won the Massachusetts Book Award for non fiction.

A former writer in residence at North Shore Community College and Miami Dade Colleges, and professor of Creative Writing at Bennington and Amherst Colleges, Merullo has been a guest speaker at many literary events and venues and a faculty member at MFA programs and several writers' conferences. His essays have appeared in numerous publications including *The New York Times, Outside Magazine, Yankee Magazine, Newsweek, Boston Globe, Philadelphia Inquirer, Boston Magazine, Reader's Digest, Good Housekeeping,* and *The Chronicle of Higher Education*. His books have been translated into German, Spanish, Portuguese, Korean and Croatian.

Roland Merullo lives in western Massachusetts with his wife and two daughters.

For additional information, please visit:
www.rolandmerullo.com or www.lunchwithbuddha.com

Lunch with Buddha
Reading Group and Discussion Question Guide

1. The main idea of this novel is a very somber one. How does the author use humor to soften it? Do you feel it's appropriate to mix such a sad subject with humorous moments? Does it dilute or sharpen the reader's empathy with Otto and his family?

2. How important is family in this story? At the end of the novel there is a shift where Rinpoche appears a bit less and other family members more. What did the author have in mind by doing this?

3. How does the author approach the sensitive subject of religious faith? Did you feel the book was ever "preachy"? If you have read *Breakfast with Buddha*, did you see any progression in Otto's spiritual search? If so, how would you describe it?

4. What role does food play and does that role change at all as the book goes on?

5. What kinds of images and objects does Rinpoche use as spiritual lessons and do these work for you? Did you connect this with Emerson's quote in the epigraph?

6. Is Rinpoche likeable and, if so, how is he made likeable? What don't you like about him? About Otto?

7. This story is fiction, but it's based on an actual road trip. In what way does that "factual skeleton" strengthen or weaken the novel? There are photos of the trip on the website. Did you choose to look at them? Did they correspond to the written descriptions in the book?

8. What are your thoughts about Shelsa? Landrea? Gilligan Neufaren? Rundy? Jarvis Barton-Phillips? What role or roles do these minor characters play in the novel?

9. It's a risk to end a book with a solitary retreat. Was it effective for you? Did it fit the rest of the novel?

10. What role does Cecelia play in Otto's spiritual education? Does his opinion of her change as the novel progresses?

11. What roles do Otto's children play? How are they different?

12. What do you think of Rinpoche's talk in Spokane? Did your opinion of it change as the book went on?

13. Is there an effort here to make a distinction between Otto's spiritual search and the "powers" that someone like Landrea has? Is there a difference between her contact with Jeannie and Otto's contact with Jeannie?

14. What role does the Spokane transgendered person play? When she speaks of troubles, and when Rinpoche mentions his worrisome dreams—where do you think that could lead in the future?

15. Why does the author mention roadside signs and radio programs so often?

16. If you read *Breakfast with Buddha*, how is *Lunch with Buddha* the same, and how is it different? Would you be interested in having *Dinner* with these characters?

A CONVERSATION BETWEEN TWO WRITERS
Roland Merullo & Matthew Quick

Matthew Quick: *We've known each other for five or so years, during which we've discussed—at length—writing, publishing, spirituality, and life in general. Your fiction often explores the questions and concerns that are most important to you. What led you to write Lunch with Buddha?*

Roland Merullo: From my earliest years, when I was a devout Catholic boy living in a world where the rules and traditions of Catholicism were the air we all breathed, I've been puzzling over what I'll call, for lack of a better term, "the meaning of life". Why do people suffer? Why is the suffering spread around so unevenly? What are we doing here in the first place? What happens to a person's spirit after he or she dies? In my twenties my eyes were opened to answers that came from places other than the Christian tradition. Rather than seeming like a challenge to that tradition, the wisdom of the East has always seemed to me like an expansion of it. Buddhism, especially, but also Sufism, Hinduism, and Taoism made the story of Jesus more understandable and believable to me, not less. I tend to write about what I'm most focused on, in my interior life. I've had a daily meditation practice for 30-some years and still do a lot of reading across the spiritual spectrum. I love to drive and see new places, love to eat different kinds of food, love to see the humor in life and make people laugh. So it was natural that all these things would find their way into a novel. And it was surprisingly easy for me, after a seven-year hiatus, to get right back into the mindsets of these characters.

And, it's funny, I feel like I've known you much longer than that. Those conversations have been a rich part of my life.

MQ: *Our talks have greatly enriched my life too. I understand that your family took a research road trip in preparation for the writing of this book. Can you tell us a little about that trip and how it inspired your writing? Did you visit all of the places mentioned in the novel? How did your wife and daughters color the research and writing?*

RM: The plain fact is that we did not have the money to make the trip . . . at first. Then one day I went to the mailbox—this is the unadorned truth—and found a letter there, addressed to me, no return address. Inside was a sheet of pale blue stationery folded in three, and inside that was a check. I saw the back of the check first, and assumed it was repayment of expenses from a recent reading on Cape Cod. Then I turned it over. It was a cashier's check for $10,000, made out to me. No note, no explanation, nothing. It was Saturday. On Monday I took it to the bank and the bank manager in our little country town looked at it for 30 minutes, pressed his fingers into it, held it up to the light, called the bank it was drawn on, called his own security people. At last, he looked up at me and said, "I think it's legit." And it was.

I suspected a couple of well off friends but I asked and no, they laughed, they liked me well enough, sure, but they hadn't just sent me a check for ten grand. I decided—and this, despite our bills, was an easy decision—that there was only one thing to do with this money: take the trip that would be the basis for *Lunch with Buddha*. So all four of us drove to NYC and caught a flight to Seattle, rented a car in just the way Otto does in the novel (same car, same foolish decision by Dad), and drove exactly the same route, across Idaho and Montana and into North Dakota.

The girls and Amanda love the open road as much as I do, and they were perfect travel companions, remarking on things they thought might be in the book, making suggestions. Amanda took 1,000 photos, and 30 pages of handwritten notes as I drove. We did everything that Otto and Rinpoche do—from the water slide to Old Faithful to Yellowstone's Boiling River, from the hike at the Cave B Inn, to the Coulee Dam visit, to the pitchfork fondue at Medora. We ate at all the same places, usually, in my case, the very same meal that Otto eats in the book. We heard what they hear on the radio, saw the same road signs. The only parts that are truly made up are the conversations and some of the characters they meet along the road (Rundy, for instance, is imaginary; I didn't pick up any hitchhikers with the girls in the car).

Someday I hope to be able to thank the angel who sent that kind of money to me, but obviously that person wishes to remain unknown. So here it is: THANK YOU!

MQ: *I've loved every Roland Merullo book I've read, and Lunch with Buddha may be my favorite yet. Why do you think that is?*

RM: I don't know. I'm too close to the book right now to have any kind of perspective on it at all. But I know from your fine writing, and from our talks, that you have the same great curiosity about life that I have. You wonder why people behave the way they do. You try to bring some light into the world when you can. And you make up stories that contain both the puzzlement and curiosity, and your idea of an answer to the big questions. We are mining that same vein, or maybe similar veins in the same mine. I really believe that every soul is put on earth with a certain set of skills and interests, and a certain purpose or purposes. I think we've both found what we're supposed to be doing here, and our job is simply to do it as well as we can, deal with whatever obstacles we face, and let the chips fall.

MQ: *Early in the novel you write: "Rinpoche seemed to live on the far side of some line that marked the boundary of ordinary American reality." Is that where you want to live?*

RM: I'm a very down-to-earth kind of person. I like realistic fiction and films. I like people who can cook, or hammer a nail, or fix a bleeding wound, or comfort a crying child. But I'm also not completely convinced that our assumptions are always 100% accurate. A few centuries ago people tormented Galileo for daring to say that the earth moved around the sun. For how many centuries before that was the assumption incorrect? Einstein's theories similarly challenged the prevailing "wisdom" of the day. So I think it's wise to be a little skeptical about our laws and truths. Maybe, for instance, at least some of the psychics who claim to be in contact with the dead are actually in contact with the dead. I don't know. I have very sensible friends whose late spouses "spoke" to them. Surely there are a lot of phonies and scammers out there, a lot of people who "see" the end of the world, or speak in tongues, or have visions, but are simply fooling themselves or someone who is paying them. Still, I leave the door open just a bit to the idea that there's more to life than the things we can measure and explain. In *Breakfast with Buddha*, Otto starts out totally skeptical of Rinpoche's interest in meditation and the interior life. By the end of the novel he's been moved off that position a short ways. In *Lunch with Buddha*, though he doesn't really want it to be so, he suspects that death is final, and he'll never have any communication with his beloved wife again. By the end of the novel that assumption, too, has been shaken just a bit. It's a tightrope walk. I'm a realist. I don't want to write flaky books. But I am all about pushing the boundaries of the interior life—which is the heart and soul of Rinpoche's talk in Spokane.

<u>MQ</u>: *"Destiny, I confess, was a word that had always given me trouble,"* Otto says. *Do you feel as though you were destined to be a fiction writer? Destined to write this book?*

<u>RM</u>: I had a great and memorable dream about thirty years ago, near the start of my writing life. My father—with whom I was very close, and who had recently died was arriving by train, coming from the East, from someplace closed and secret like the former USSR. I was waiting for him at a train station that might have been in Belarus or Poland or East or West Germany.

When he stepped off the train, I went up and hugged him and I said, proudly, "Pa, I have come to claim my birthright and my destiny." A VERY weird thing to say in a dream, but there it is. I think he'd be proud of my books now, but for a long time he wanted a more practical career for me—like most fathers and mothers would. In our time and place there was no such thing as making a living writing. It was not on the radar screen. He wanted me to be a doctor or a diplomat or a professor. My mother had similar ideas. So for a long time, because I wanted to please them and to "repay" them for all they'd done for me, I was blind to what I really wanted to do with my working life. It wasn't until I'd done other things—worked in the USSR for the US Government, served in the Peace Corps, collected tolls, loaded trucks, built swimming pools, finished and hated gradu-ate school—that I was able to admit to myself that I wanted to write.

I still have a little trouble with the word destiny. It seems pompous, like I think I'm meant for great things. I don't think that. Or, rather, I think we are all meant for great things, every one of us. I was a carpenter for a long time while writing my first novel, seven years, and I take a very workmanlike approach to writing now. I love it, but I don't think it's more special than carpentry or cab driving or nursing or teaching. It's just the right thing for me. I'm in my place in the world. I've claimed my birthright, yeah, but that birthright is my freedom, in this great land, to figure out where I want to put my energies.

MQ: *"Why didn't good prevail?" your character asks. It's a question you and I have talked about many times. In most of your books, good usually does prevail, if only in some small way. Would you say that your fiction is a vehicle of hope? Is that why you write?"*

RM: Yes, a vehicle of hope. I think we both work that way, no? And, yes, that does reflect my view of life. I'm fascinated—and I think this shows itself in every single one of my books, even the golf books—with the way people deal with difficulty, hardship, pain, disappointment, tragedy and life's seeming inequities. In *Leaving Losapas* the difficulty is a certain kind of post-war traumatic stress. In *A Russian Requiem* it's divorce and career dissatisfaction. In *Revere Beach Boulevard* it's a gambling addiction. In *A Little Love Story* it's cystic fibrosis. And in the last few books it's been: how do people deal with the spiritual search, in the face of life's hardships? My battles with my own demons and troubles, with illness and (a long time ago, pre-meditation) some periods of depression and despair, with my failures and flaws—that's really the center of my existence. In *The Talk-Funny Girl* I deal with that directly: how does Marjorie overcome her horrible childhood and be a decent mother? My childhood was far from horrible, but we all have our pains and challenges, and I'm—well, obsessed wouldn't be too strong a word—with how we deal with that. And I want to pass on to my children as little of that as I can. Some people indulge their pain and pass it on. Some fight it to a draw. And some people transcend. My goal—reflected in many of my characters—is to transcend. Not there yet.

MQ: *Your novels have a tendency to make me hungry. Your characters eat many wonderful meals, usually described in mouthwatering detail. Is this an Italian American writing thing?*

RM: (*Smiling here*). Partly. I had the great good fortune to live upstairs from and next door to a tremendously spiritual, wonderfully warm and loving grandmother who also happened to be a world-class cook. It wasn't fancy. It was what I think of as "southern Italian peasant food", but, man, every meal, no matter how simple, was a delight. It's a hard way to begin, because the world is always going to disappoint you—and not just at the table. So now I'm very much like Otto. It's not that I need fancy gourmet food; it's just that, like most of the Italians we've met in our travels there, I feel like what you put into your mouth matters. They use fresh food and prepare it carefully and usually eat it slowly. Like Otto's kids, my kids sometimes joke with me about the pasta being overcooked in a restaurant—a particular sore spot. Luckily, Amanda is a great cook and I like to do the dishes, so it works out.

MQ: *Please talk a little more about the "egotism of the intellect."*

RM: I like the Biblical idea of false gods. And I think it's easy, in our society, to make a false god of the intellect. It's better to be smart than stupid, yes, and it's particularly important to have the country run by intelligent, thoughtful people. But, as friends down the road said to me recently—and they've raised two marvelous children—"we care more about raising our kids to be kind than raising them to be geniuses."

There's so much societal emphasis on education and achievement (both good things) and on status and possessions (maybe not so good) because those things are measurable. Thanks to my parents, I had a very good education. I want my children to be well educated. But, first, I want them to be happy, and I want them to be kind and compassionate. I spent ten years in academia, and some of my closest friends are academics. They are fine people. But among some academics there is this "egotism of the intellect", as if the most important thing in life is to be smart, or smart-er. They don't care how badly they treat other people; what they care about is who's smarter. It's a false god. When I was a kid in Revere, the most important thing for a boy was to be tough, a good fighter. Another false god. They're everywhere, the little bastards.

MQ: *Otto says, "Whole libraries of subjects were off limits now, at least in my circles." Many of the ideas in Lunch with Buddha are "off limits" to so many people here in America, and yet, your work seems to provide a much needed bridge. Why does America need Buddha and Eastern thought?*

RM: As to the first part: he's speaking to the way conversations about certain subjects have become stultified in this society. The national discussion has turned into two camps ridiculing each other. Bigotry on the one hand, political correctness on the other. Thank God we still have comedians.

To make a bad generalization, I think Eastern thought is

primarily inner-focused. The pejorative term is "navel gazing." Well, I think we could use a bit more navel gazing in our society. We do so many wonderful things in the external world—photos from Mars, medicines for AIDS and other illnesses, remarkable surgeries, incredible technological gizmos. But when Steve Jobs (I may be wrong, but I believe he had a Buddhist practice) was dying he is reputed to have said, "Oh, wow!" As if he saw something. I somehow doubt that what he saw was the next generation of the iPad. I think it was some interior experience, some wider understanding of the miracle of life. Except in its mystical tradition—which is vast and of long standing but largely ignored in this society—Christianity is outer-focused. It's too often all about behavior and sin and loud prayer. Okay. But what Rinpoche does for Otto is to take that foundation of good behavior and show him that it is a starting point, not an end point. "The Kingdom of Heaven is within you." Jesus said that, not Buddha. But it's the Easterners who pursue it more avidly, and I think we would benefit from that pursuit.

MQ: *Please tell me there will be a Dinner with Buddha and that I will be able to read it relatively soon.*

RM: Well, first, thank you for these superb questions, and for your friendship and your books. As for *Dinner*, well, I have laid the groundwork for that at the end of *Lunch*. Just need to come up with another route, a part of the country we haven't covered. I've been to 49 states, which leaves only Alaska, but I somehow don't see an Alaskan road trip in our future. Maybe I'll take the whole cast of characters overseas. I'm open to suggestion.

Matthew Quick *(aka Q)* is the author of *The Silver Linings Playbook* (Sarah Crichton Books / Farrar, Straus & Giroux) and three young adult novels, *Sorta Like A Rock Star*, *Boy21*, and *Forgive Me, Leonard Peacock* (Little, Brown & Co). His work has received many honors—including a PEN/Hemingway Award Honorable Mention—been translated into several languages, and called "beautiful . . . first-rate" by *The New York Times Book Review*. The Weinstein Company and David O. Russell have adapted *The Silver Linings Playbook* into film, starring Robert De Niro, Bradley Cooper, and Jennifer Lawrence. Matthew lives in Massachusetts with his wife, novelist Alicia Bessette. For additional information visit:

www.matthewquickwriter.com

Sample Manuscript Pages *Lunch with Buddha*

(progressively edited/revised manuscript pages)

Thirteen

[handwritten margin note: That would be a summer morning in N.Y.]

I awoke, next morning, to a pristine silence. No road noise, no hotel fan, not even the

chirping birds. The view through the bedroom's glass door somehow was a twin to

that silence: still and striated gray/brown cliffs on the far side of the Columbia, and

behind and beyond and above them an expanse of dry land slanting up and away in

low, irregular mounds. On the ridgeline there, north of the hundred still windmills,

was a strip of green forest with an empty pale-blue morning sky above.

It was early for me, in the sixes. I washed quietly, so as not to wake Rinpoche

behind his closed bedroom door, then went out and walked the path to the pool,

grapevines brushing my shoulders, and found the dry trail that led down toward the

gorge. Other hikers had left a selection of walking sticks there on the ground. I

chose one that seemed to fit me and started off. It was cool in the shade but you

could feel that, once the sun moved around all this would be an oven. Dry heat, yes,

so it would be a dry oven but an oven all the same. The girl at the desk had said the

summer temperatures sometimes reached 110.

At first the path was steeply downhill and rocky, tough on the knees. But

then it flattened out and ran through a prairie landscape of sagebrush and tufts of

grass, and low-to-the-ground flowers I could not name. Not so different, in some

[handwritten at bottom: ...retraced the previous day's steps. There, near the pool enclosure, was the start of a trail that led to the river. Other hikers had left walking sticks. I found one that suited me & started off.]

Thirteen

I awoke, next morning, to an absolutely pristine silence. No road noise, no hotel AC, not even the chirping birds that pulled us out of sleep on a summer morning in New York. The view through the bedroom's glass door felt like a twin to that silence: still and striated gray/brown cliffs on the far side of the Columbia, and behind and beyond and above them an expanse of dry land slanting up and away in low, folded mounds. On the ridgeline there, north of the hundred windmills, ran a strip of green forest beneath an empty morning sky.

It was early for me, in the sixes. I washed quietly, so as not to wake Rinpoche behind his closed bedroom door, then went out and retraced the previous day's steps. Near the pool enclosure was the head of a trail that led to the river. Other hikers had left walking sticks there on the ground. I found one that suited me and started off. It was cool in the shade but you could feel that, once the sun climbed higher and swung around overhead, all this low area would turn into an oven. It would be dry heat, yes, so it would be a dry oven. But an oven all the same. The girl at the desk had said the summer temperatures sometimes reached 110.

At first the path was steeply downhill and rocky, tough on the knees. But then, flattening out, it ran through a prairie landscape of sagebrush, tufts of grass,

It was early for me, in the sixes. I washed quietly, so as not to wake Rinpoche

behind his closed bedroom door, then went out and retraced the previous day's

steps. Near the pool enclosure was the start of a trail that led down to the river.

Other hikers had left walking sticks there on the ground. I found one that suited me

and started off. It was cool in the shade but you could feel that, once the sun

climbed higher and swung around overhead, all this low area would turn into an

oven. It would be dry heat, yes, so it would be a dry oven. But an oven all the same.

The girl at the desk had said the summer temperatures sometimes reached 110. ~in~ ~most~ ~parts~

young woman

At first the path went steeply downhill, rocky, tough on the knees. But then,

flattening out, it twisted through a prairie landscape of sagebrush, small tufts of

grass, and low-to-the-ground flowers I couldn't name. Just below and ahead of me

the river surface was absolutely unruffled, a metal-blue sheet. I imagined that, had

Rinpoche been there, he would have made a lesson out of that stillness, likened it to

the perfected mind in meditation. That was a sticking point for me. During the

years I'd been under his tutelage, if that is the word, I'd had moments of stillness.

Just moments—he said that was the "beginning part. Good, Otto, good!" And there

was certainly an ease and pleasure to be found there. Sometimes that pleasure

echoed later In the day in unexpected periods of calm, or. . .*reassurance* would be a

better word. It felt like I'd touched the frontier of a world beyond this world.

Made in the USA
Middletown, DE
06 September 2017